Becoming Finola

Also by Suzanne Strempek Shea

Around Again

Lily of the Valley

Hoopi Shoopi Donna

Selling the Lite of Heaven

NONFICTION

Shell Life:
Romance, Mystery, Drama, and Other Page-Turning
Adventures from a Year in a Bookstore

Songs from a Lead-Lined Room:
Notes—High and Low—From My Journey Through
Breast Cancer and Radiation

Elyse!

Becoming Finola

the first reader for whom I'm signing this — YAAAY!!!!. love & best wishes —

A Novel

Suzanne Strempek Shea

[signature] 05·20·04 xo

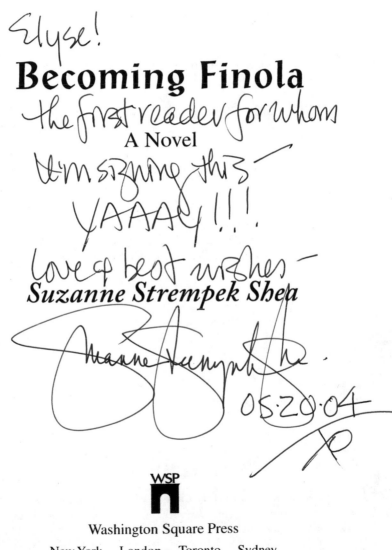

WSP

Washington Square Press

New York   London   Toronto   Sydney

WSP Washington Square Press
1230 Avenue of the Americas
New York, NY 10020

This book is a work of fiction. Names, characters, places and incidents are products of the author's imagination or are used fictitiously. Any resemblance to actual events or locales or persons, living or dead, is entirely coincidental.

Copyright © 2004 by Suzanne Strempek Shea

ISBN: 0-7434-0377-0

First Washington Square Press trade paperback edition June 2004

10 9 8 7 6 5 4 3 2 1

WASHINGTON SQUARE PRESS and colophon are registered trademarks of Simon & Schuster, Inc.

Designed by Melissa Isriprashad

Manufactured in the United States of America

For information regarding special discounts for bulk purchases, please contact Simon & Schuster Special Sales at 1-800-456-6798 or business@simonandschuster.com

For Mary Ellen Lowney O'Shea:
Soul sister, right wagon

Acknowledgments

Anna Lundell and Sara Persson once welcomed me to a faraway village, where, as I absentmindedly rearranged the travel books on one of his shelves, Jamie Storer asked if I was available to work in his craft shop. Padraig Stevens once brought me on a birthday trip to a holy well where damp wishes encased in Ziploc bags hung from strands of purple yarn tied to nearby branches. For no other reason than he always sends me books, Dan Shea once coincidentally mailed me a book on holy wells in general. Tanya Barrientos once suggested I write something in a different setting, and when I tried that, Suzanne O'Neill more than a few times edited into finer shape. Add additional help and support from Tommy Shea, Elinor Lipman, John Talbot, Elsie Osterman, and Fran Ryan, and this story is the result.

Becoming Finola

Cloud:

꩜

Dream, Refuge

(State Your Wish Three Times)

First time she saw it, the place was all in her head.

Made up. Dreamed up. Conjured up. Invented from necessity, much in the way a convict or a hostage or an inpatient imagines for sanity's sake a longed-for land of peaceful existence.

She wasn't in jail, or bound in a madman's cave, or bedridden in some cheerfully named long-term health care facility. She was simply in crisis. Though I guess I shouldn't use the word *simply*, because that squashes her situations and emotions down to pocket size. And what she had endured and how all of it left her feeling had the dimensions of one of those supertankers so mammoth that it can never come directly into port because no port anywhere in the world is huge enough. That's how enormously bad you can feel when the hand of fate suddenly decides your existence is a carnival game, and pays a buck to pitch a trio of baseballs at a pyramid of milk bottles representing your world. One. Two. Three in a row. Right on target and with speed worthy of a multimillion-dollar contract in the majors, there goes life as you know it.

Due to circumstances beyond your employer's control, you lose your job.

Due to circumstances beyond his SUV's controls, your husband loses his life.

Due to circumstances beyond anybody's control—because who was ever able to control her?—your daughter announces that the only parent who ever truly loved her is now gone, therefore she has become an orphan, good-bye, and she is lost as well.

Then comes far too much time and solitude in which to shuffle around a silent home trying to figure out the following: If I am not their employee anymore, if I am not his wife any longer, if I am not her mother, who am I?

A year and six months ago, in a very pointy sliver-span of two weeks, as the final leftover slice of her forty-third birthday cake sat still fresh in a triangular Tupperware vacuum, that trio of tragedies blindsided my friend Gina Stebbins. Hounded by reality each moment she was awake, she found rest only through a combination of five milligrams of Ambien from her GP and a trip to a place deep inside her imagination. A simple, peaceful, chiaroscuro-Thomas Kinkade-ish cottage by the sea was her destination. And if this smacked of the type of place to which every falling-apart woman ever featured on the Lifetime Channel has crawled for renewal, Gina couldn't have cared less. She'd felt a connection to the ocean and to cottages since childhood, when the first two weeks of every July found her and her parents up in New Hampshire, tucked into a rented green and white efficiency on K Street, a plastic sand pail's throw from the Coleman-cooler-paved sands of Hampton Beach.

So the ocean was where Gina imagined herself living when things in her head got to be too much. This particular ocean she thought of as being somewhere far away, at the edge of an unnamed hilly countryside washed the green of steamed asparagus. In the remote village sprouting from all that chlorophyll, a few cozy pastel-colored buildings standing shoulder to shoulder formed the uncomplicated heart. The soul of Gina's dream place was located just up the road, where waves the shade of iris petals unrolled like bolts of trader ship silk onto a smooth-stone beach, their unbroken rhythm matching the blessedly slowed-down breath of her newly recreated life. In her imaginings, Gina always began with a walk through the village, past the cottage, then down to the beach, believing that once she got to the sea, everything would begin to change for the better.

The second time she saw it was on newsprint. A few pages into the Sunday paper's fat travel section. In a full-page ad that, via anti-quated pen-and-ink font, extended to her and all other prospective visitors a total of "One Hundred Thousand Welcomes!" Below that big tally was a color photo—of the very same village Gina had made up for herself when the fast and bruising tumble of her tragedies had begun. Amazingly, the picture bore all the correct details: single road, wide stream to one side, seven pastel buildings on the other, with hardly a gap between. There were three small, boxy cars parked along the curb, and crossing the bridge that spanned the foreground stream, a group of fit and backpacked walkers headed in the direc-tion of the Mecca horizon, toward the green, the green—all that green painted across a sloping meadow that led to the hard amethyst line of the ocean.

This was the place in her head.

Gina's place.

Imagine seeing a photo of something after knowing it only in your dreams. OK—not once had Gina given even a thought about its existence—that she might have lifted the location from some-body's travel album or the setting of a movie she'd long forgotten. So deeply familiar was the picture that at first it was a bit frighten-ing for her to believe that this very village, this ocean could be out there in reality. If she were some kind of psychic, she might have handled this in stride. But Gina was like most of us mortals, and could not see into the future much beyond knowing there would be someone at the front door when the bell rang. So the photograph was a huge shock that had her setting down the travel section and slowly walking backward across the kitchen to stand at the counter and nervously jiggle the lever of her once busy four-slot toaster while she worked up the courage to return to the table to check if the image were still on the page. And when she did, it was. Was there, in front of her eyes, and, according to the ad copy, a mere three thousand miles from her home. "A World Away" is how that was put by the Tourist Board, which had recorded her dream place on film, had printed the picture where she could find it, and was inviting her there—at a preseason discount, yet, if she reserved a ticket within the next thirty days.

The third time she saw it, she stood on a hill three thousand miles from her home the midafternoon of the first day of the wildest thing she had ever done in her life. An action put into motion that Sunday two months before, when Gina had precisely pressed the digits for the 800 number and told the Tourist Board reservations specialist that she gladly would accept all those advertised welcomes—on the condition that the location of the village in the photograph be revealed. The reservations specialist said she would do her best, and then actually did, because the same day Gina received her plane ticket, she found in the mail a separate envelope bearing a map compliments of the Tourist Board, some member of which had taken the time to highlight in red marker the route from the airport to the coast and to the place in her head, the place in the photograph, a place bearing the house-pet name of Booley.

So Booley is what Gina stood above that May afternoon as the bus that had delivered her from the airport to an unmarked intersection of two lonely dirt roads fumed away, and after the full hour of pop music that had rained unabated from the ceiling speakers, she reveled in the silence. Now all was quiet as Gina looked down at the tiniest and most beauteous corner of the world, the one she believed held the great promise of being all she ever would need.

Others were of the mind-set that Gina needed something totally different. When she'd met with them to announce her plans to spend an undetermined amount of time in a village she'd spotted in the newspaper, Gina's puzzled circle of women friends had offered less drastic alternatives to what they saw as running away: A new hobby. A new religion. A new career. A support group. Prozac. Paxil. Elavil. Atavan. Alcohol. Pot. Ecstacy, just once. A man, more than once. Maybe a few men a whole bunch of times. How about volunteering to teach her many business skills to new immigrants? How about raising funds for a charity that assisted women who had it so bad in their marriages that if their husbands died they'd be throwing ten parties? How about buying a stack of fashion magazines and bringing them to the teen shelter in Springfield as an icebreaker that might lead to conversations helpful to the wayward residents, who might never have known a mother's true love? Gina listened to all of this. But her mind was made up. She knew what she needed. And now she knew where to find it.

In her head, she'd located this village easily, having traveled there more and more often since her life had become a foreign thing, mentally heading for the door just as the sharp-clawed bearers of deep despair began crawling across her idle mind. Bedside light snapped off, she'd flip to her right side, pull the covers over her head, create the essential breathing tunnel, and soon she'd be walking the beach, purchasing her breakfast bread, waving to the neighbors, drinking her morning tea, then closing behind her the rose-entwined gate to her rose-entwined cottage and walking to the ocean, where she'd soak in the peace that comes from finally knowing you are where you are meant to be, and through that, your true identity.

Right now, somewhere down this hill, Gina felt, that knowledge awaited. And the only thing left between her and it was the single street that ran through Booley, which on this gray but dry spring Wednesday showed no signs of life. From the hilltop, it appeared almost as it had in the travel section, as it had in her head. Quiet, still, muted ochre and pink and blue, even more silent minus the life spark of the hikers and only one car in view, rather than three, a squarish dull orange thing parked halfway down the cluster of buildings. A tan dot of a dog lolled in the road. Smoke levitated sleepily above a couple of chimneys. Gina's eye followed the pavement up as it threaded through an Astroturf-colored meadow and then to the massive span of sea, the hugeness of which actually gave her a start. She'd been studying the village so intensely, but just beyond that lay an entire ocean—bigger than the world, it seemed, and certainly more than large enough to bear all she was seeking. Anticipating her arrival, it had dressed for the occasion, dark midnight-sapphiry-purplish and tinsels of disco ball sparkles as it pitched forward a serious succession of surf-movie-size breakers. She watched one crash, then the next, and the next, holding her breath as if the waves were at her feet on this dirt intersection rather than on a beach a mile away. Then Gina did what she was there to do: Wanting to stand still not a second longer, and despite already feeling she'd gone under for the last time, she dove deeper, into the unknown.

And how do I know all this?

Well, the whole time, I was right behind her.

Knot:

Bond, Pact, Friendship

(State Your Wish Three Times)

I was there with Gina, ready to descend into Booley. But for none of the same reasons.

I had no husband to veer helplessly off the interstate and into the Dave's Soda and Pet Food City–sponsored "spay and neuter" billboard at the same moment I was in our bedroom turning his fabric-softened briefs right side out so he wouldn't have to bother with that pesky detail in the morning rush of dressing. I had no freaky eighteen-year-old to hurl her poisonous verbal spears through my already aching soul before declaring me totally unnecessary and moving away. What I did have was the same boss as Gina, the man who only days before she was to suffer her other two losses returned from a most unpleasant downsizing meeting with his own bosses to instantly lay off both our hardworking asses. I know the economy stinks, but I feel I'll eventually find a job in my field. At least I don't have to also deal with the loss of my spouse, my child, and my sanity. I retain a car dealer's handshake of a grip on the last thing on that list. So every day for the year and a half since Gina's world began cracking apart I've been there to remind her that, well, I am, here for her.

I'm no mental health professional. I'm only her best friend—if I may use that schoolgirl term for a bond between two grown women. And all I could do was generously spray the Bactine of my most sincere intentions onto the compound fractures she'd suffered from the ending of her dozen-year career as efficient manager of the outlet store at the Trim-True Sewing Notions mill, her twenty-two years as devoted wife of Norm Stebbins, and her eighteen as caring mother of Montessori-schooled trilingual World Economic Summit protester Gennifer, who for some reason during tenth grade replaced the *J* in her name with a *G*. I'm not bragging, just stating plain fact, when I tell you it was I who got Gina to her feet, to the kitchen table, to the lines on the forms for all the legalities awaiting those who find themselves in the left-behind boots of the bereaved. To the unemployment office I drove her. To the insurance company. To the lawyer's and the investment counselor's. To the plant-funded career coach, to the insurance-approved psychotherapist, to the free Thursday night relaxation and meditation course the hospital was offering to those already enrolled in the free Tuesday night widows/widowers' Open Arms Grief Circle. So it was only natural that I sprang into action again after she spotted the travel ad, locating a house sitter, informing the various service companies and utilities, packing her bags, and reserving a limo-van ride to the international airport.

The first Monday in March, when I'd stopped by her house to present a pair of the hopeful two-for-one spring bouquets the Grand Z had been offering those who carried its shopping club card, I found Gina at Norm's desk, studying maps and brochures and making many notes on red-lined STEBBINS, LPC scratch paper. I stood crinkling the floral wrap in an effort to get her attention, and she finally looked up, but only to ask me to wait a second, and after standing there for more than a few seconds, I went off to locate vases, arrange the two bouquets, place one in the kitchen and the other in her bedroom so when Gina awoke hopeful new blossoms would be her first sight. I went on to the regular tasks that since trim-true and all had become my new job. I'd become an assistant of sorts, paid with gratitude, and with regular envelopes of cash Gina said was for mileage but that would have been true only if the going rate were five dollars per. I retrieved the mail, checked the due dates of the bills and stacked them in sequence, started a load of darks, inventoried the pantry to determine her shopping list, and then returned to the den, and to the desk, to Gina, still engaged. It was heartening to see her involved in writing something other than condolence acknowledgments, so before leaving I made my usual offer: "Remember—if there's anything I can do . . . ," and instead of her usual hollow-eyed nod, Gina spoke: "Sophie, I'm going away. For a long, long time. Come with me." Then came the kicker: "I'll pay for everything."

I said yes without even asking the first letter of our destination. A teenhood of travel had installed in me a jones for new places. My favorite aunt had married into a family that towed a caravan of fried dough trailers to festivals and fairs. So I'd spent summers twelve through nineteen lowering baskets of flaccid dough into a roiling, seldom-changed grease bath, undoubtedly contributing to countless heart conditions eventually to be suffered by customers living along the thousands of miles we'd travel between New England and the banks of the slow Mississippi, up to the woodsy Canadian border and as far down into the very warm South as you could get before you started spotting those creepy billboards announcing "You Are Entering Klan Country." The circuit also gave me my first big romance. I spent the final two summers sleeping next to Al Turcotte in the cab bunk of the metallic red 18-wheeler with which he hauled around the country "The Largest Rat Known to Mankind, Ever." Exactly as Betsy the Psychic had predicted one week before that final Labor Day on the road (and on her dime because she thought it was very important that I know), Al would prove reluctant to commit to the year-round relationship I had been counting on enjoying now that I'd graduated high school. Because Betsy was some form of the real deal, spookily on target about fetus gender, biopsy results, and the last two digits of the nightly number whenever we were in the state of Illinois, I'd staggered from her tent to fall into a nest of clown laundry and sob out all the plans I'd dared to make for a life in the navigator's seat of a rat truck.

So from that I had a fraction of a sense of how shattering it could be to lose a man. But I had no experience that would qualify me to say to Gina, as so many others had the nerve to tell her in the wake line, "I know how you feel." Though it had been a long time since any contact with Al Turcotte, I had no reason not to believe he was still up and around on this God's earth, chauffeuring a new generation of *Guinness Book* rodents. The only portions of Norm Stebbins still above ground are Gennifer's DNA and a couple of corneas on a formerly legally blind stranger whose letter of thanks Gina had yet to bring herself to read. So four months after the day she signed the documents permitting what the doctor called the harvest of said corneas, Gina was wearing a genuine smile as she told me about a very weird coincidence—her nightly mind walk to the ocean and the appearance of a travel ad on her kitchen table— and how maybe if she visited this place, how maybe if she were in totally different surroundings, she might start to figure things out, and I said, "Go. I don't care where this place is. If you think it's going to help you, go."

I'd honestly felt that some trip like this just might be good for her. Plus, hey, it couldn't hurt me, either. It had been a while since I'd gone anywhere—more than nine since I'd visited any place that required a passport, map, guidebook, foreign currency or research on-line, where, the day Gina invited me, I consulted Google only to find these brief sentences: "Booley is in a remote area of great natural beauty. A walking trail along the edge of the sea. A holy well of minor note. Budget-minded visitors welcome at Diamond's Hostel."

I then entered *Booley* into Dogpile. Into Yahoo! Into Excite and Netscape and Whaddayawant. There wasn't much else to be learned. Another brief mention of the walking trail. And then: "There will be little in Booley to hold your interest. Continue on."

I believed the opposite. That in Booley, every single thing would hold fascination. To Gina, at least. I ended up pleased that reviews were sparse and not overly enthusiastic. The fewer who knew about Booley, the better. After all, it was my best friend's Mecca, and, as her loyal supporter, I was guarding it already.

The suggestion to continue on must have been taken by most travelers. Not a single Samsonite-stacked rental rolled past, and none of the sweaty walkers from the Tourist Board ad strode by. Except for being trailed for a short while by a swiftly trotting coffee-colored terrier that appeared overscheduled for the afternoon, we had the road to ourselves as we made our way down, the only sound being the ground slap of the boots the L.L.Bean sales associate had made us promise to break in on a series of lengthy hikes prior to starting our journey. We drove home to wear them once to the mailbox and a couple times to Costco. And again that day. Which was maybe the longest distance Gina and I had walked in any type of footwear since a few years back, when we attended the grand opening of the addition to the Holyoke Mall at Ingleside, a project that made the already mammoth consumer destination so much more gargantuan that a DisneyWorld–like monorail had been built to shuttle exhausted shoppers from one end of the complex to the other.

But the walk down to Booley was no Muzaked mall stroll. There was no Abercrombie & Fitch, no Victoria's Secret. Fresh manure rather than fresh-from-the-oven Cinnabons thickened the air. There was, in a word, nothing—if you were looking for the man-made, that is. I'm only guessing this, though, because I couldn't really see too far. On either side of the road, thick hedges rose seven or eight feet, pink with tight buds of what looked like the fuchsia I buy each summer to hang from the hook on my garage. Here the plants were free, and taller than your adolescent paperboy. Overrunning, unchecked. Tough woody bushes—trees, almost— rather than the frost-fearing succulent variety I knew. I touched a bud that eventually would transform into the same sweet bell shape I was used to seeing.

"Aren't these beautiful?"

Ahead of me, Gina had her head tossed back, arms flung out, and was spinning in the middle of the road. The weight of her backpack threw her off center and I ran to catch her.

"Steady, Julie Andrews."

Intoxicated by the moment, she shook me off and continued, wobbling, downhill. "Things are going to happen here," she called back. I didn't get what she was talking about, but I didn't care. All I knew was that Gina was the happiest I'd seen her in eighteen months. "I just know it!" she was calling from farther down now. "I cannot wait for this! Change!"

"What?"

"Change! I'm just so sick and tired of being who I am. Aren't you?"

I didn't answer. Because on that day I really couldn't think of anybody else I'd prefer to be. Sure, I was unemployed, and I technically had no home. But that first thing then now seemed like a positive, and that second thing had been my happy choice. Upon Gina's invitation to Booley, I'd emptied my apartment and placed all my stuff in storage, in preparation for a late-summer move-in with my boyfriend, Charlie St. Jean, who was at my door the once a month his actuarial-ing brings him from his office in the Midwest to the company headquarters in Hartford, one state below mine. In a few months, he would be at my door daily—and after turning his own key, he'll be inside my door. Our door. Because except when away on his frequent business trips, my home would be his. The next time I unlock unit number 26 at College Road Storage, Charlie St. Jean will be next to me, ready to load my earthly belongings into a $19.99-a-day U-Haul and drive it to a larger, newly selected and shared threshold. So I had a great man, a great friend, great health, and really, what more could I ask for? Rather than getting cut off at the knees by the fact I'd hit the traditionally dreaded age of thirty, I was looking forward to a bright new start with a guy whose cornball monologues about Kismet I scarfed down the way a starving turnpike driver might devour an overpriced box of gas station Crunch 'n Munch. At a time in my life when nearly everyone I knew was on antidepressants and in therapy and off to rehab after securing a restraining order, I was gliding along the smooth rail of psychology textbook normalcy. Actually content. Lucky. Just look at me that day. Most people, when asked a favor by a grieving friend, must do something totally dreadful—identify a mangled body or select a casket or yank the plug on the life support while the nurse is off checking his soul patch in the lavatory mirror. Me? I got a free summer in a cool foreign country.

I did wish change for Gina, though. Had done that since her troubles began. After every found penny, every streetlight suddenly gone black, every happy bluebird that swooped through my yard in heartening post-DDT resurgence, I used the allotted wishes for her. And maybe this, here, Booley, would be the start of them being answered. A break for Gina. Some peace. Maybe an adventure. A new view of life. I did a shin-splintering downhill jog to catch up just as she reached the bottom of the road. And there it was in front of us, glowing like a miniature Oz:

Booley.

She'd arrived.

The gateway, the stone bridge, turned out to span a mere and clear trickle. But the river's wide muddy bed and its banks of down-stream-leaning vegetation testified that it could kick up to a good depth when it felt like it. At the end of the bridge, a neatly painted blue-on-white sign nailed to a utility pole pointed across the street to announce the LAST RESTAURANT BEFORE AMERICA. Gina set her right foot onto the bridge and I expected to hear the tearing of newspaper as we entered the photo. But there was only the sound of almost virgin Vibram meeting pavement.

"I'm here," Gina said, only a little louder than if she were merely thinking the fact.

"You are," I said. "And without a single plan except to just be."

"And without a single problem." Gina said, staring down the road. She touched my arm to make sure she had my attention and said, "See? This is what I dreamed. Being somewhere totally unconnected to home. You come to a place you've never been, and it's like you're being born. This town has no record of me, except for my footprints as I stand here. I don't know my way around, I haven't said a word to anyone, haven't placed any of my belongings down—everything is new. There are no memories, nothing bad. . . ."

I could see she was deflating a little, so I got out my ever-ready pom-poms. "Nothing good, either," I told her, "if we don't cross this bridge and actually get to the ocean. We get there, good will start to happen."

"Change," Gina said, nodding, repeating. "Change."

She began walking again, determinedly, and, like a Geo Metro caught in the pulling wake of a tandem tractor trailer, I followed. We moved down the main road. Past the unnamed little stone restaurant with its vined entryway abutting that of what the sign announced was Attracta's, a little golden cottage with a roof of thick golden thatch sloped low over the windows like Jane Fonda's *Klute*-era bangs. I guessed it to be a weaver's studio, since its front window gave a view of a nearly room-sized wooden loom. Next was a thin alley and then a white cement house, the front of which bore a long blue sign on which E. DOLAN had been lettered. A separate green metal one announced AN POST. The cottage's windows and glass door were heavily decaled: LOTTO, Club Orange, HB Cornetto, *eircom* callcard, the *Independent* on Sunday, ESB Pay HERE! Flo Gas, and a cartoon of a winged monster energized by a drop of Lucozade. Many signs, but few of life. As if on cue, a woman maybe my own age stepped from the grocery store with a broom to sweep the three or four already clean cement steps. She wore a jail-ish black-and-white-striped T-shirt, red sweatpants, and ankle-high red Reeboks, and her thick black hair was a severe buzz cut that swirled at the crown into a golden tipped rooster comb projection. She smiled and nodded, and Gina and I smiled and nodded. Our first Booley resident. I gave an enthusiastic "Hello!" and she returned a cheery "Howya," and then turned and popped back inside like one of those little figures in a fancy ancient town square clock announcing another hour has begun.

E. Dolan gave way to Quinn's, a long and low building, also white, with a line of green and yellow churchy stained-glass windows and a jutting entryway with a big heavy door, an iron chain its handle. I had no idea what part Quinn's played in this village, because its one sign bore only the name. Then I spotted a row of metal kegs stacked three high at the far corner of the building. Quinn's . . . Bar. Bar/rental agent. Mrs. Quinn the rental agent to whom the Tourist Board had directed Gina for long-term accommodations in Booley.

"Hey!" This got her to turn around. "Here's where we pick up the key!"

Gina halted, looked at the door and its hardware. Nodded.

"C'mon. Let's toast our arrival!"

"After we get to the ocean," Gina said, starting up again. "We see the ocean first."

There were only two more businesses before the center of commerce ended. The one standing just before the final building was big and yellow and two stories, a relative skyscraper with a door at the center over which a long rectangle of wood was painted with the words FINOLA O'FLYNN. A sandwich board with uneven lettering and many words was propped on the sidewalk. A smooth-coated terrier the shade of the lighter of Kraft's caramel squares— possibly the same dog that had passed Gina and me earlier— snoozed on its side beneath the inverted V made by the boards that explained Finola O'Flynn was where you could purchase "Locally handcrafted jewelry and other handcrafts crafted locally." I peered through the first window to find a curly-haired man hunched and assembling jewelry. The table before him was covered with small boxes and dishes and cups of beads separated by size, color, shape, three-dimensional paint he worked from as he reached nearly without looking to take two or three and add them to what he was stringing. To his right was a wood stove, and the wall beyond was porcupined with nails bearing dozens of beaded bracelets and earrings and necklaces. The rest of the space was a storeroom jumble of books and T-shirts and CDs and big cardboard boxes. "What a mess," I whispered, but there was no Gina to hear me. As if motorized, she was already far down the road, well past downtown Booley's final building, a small and squarish pink thing, its front yard bearing picnic table, trash can, and phone booth.

I let her stay in the lead. She nearly loped, a woman on a mission, heading along the center of pavement that was breaking away to gravel, then to dirt, which was when she stepped to the left of the Mohawk of grass springing from the center and pressed on. Up a muddy little hill, right, left, then down toward the great throat-grabbing expanse of water. Twenty minutes or so and we passed a cottage on the left, then a few fields, another lone cottage, more fields, a few more, and that is when we saw it. I blinked, and wondered if a mirage could happen in a place that is the opposite of a desert. Because there was the cottage from

Gina's brain. Just as she'd described, right up to the approach.

As she'd told me over and again, it was set on a small rise that arced sharply like the highest crest of a wave the second before it breaks. Small and white and boxy, wearing a black slate roof, the place was surrounded by a stubborn-looking waist-high white cement wall that looked serious about keeping it from straying. Tall vertical rectangular windows flanked each side of the red front door like widely opened cartoon eyes. An iron gate was closed across the graveled driveway entrance, and several feet from the front door, a smaller one interrupted the cement wall to allow you onto the front walk. A heart shape had been worked into the center of the bars. I wanted to call out to Gina, but she didn't need any extra amazement. She was standing at the gate, reaching out a hand. As if the cottage were only a soap bubble, she stopped within inches of touching the iron. Next to her then, I said an unnecessary and slow "I cannot believe this." Her reply was a much shorter and much slower "Holy shit!" Then there were several minutes spent treading a soup of awe and puzzlement. I expected the occupants to swing open the tall red door and ask who the hell we were. But there was no door opening, no human in sight, no sound but a thin wind, and waves making landfall. And Gina, again, wondering why she hadn't gone into specifics when talking to the rental agent. "If I'd asked for a cottage, we could have had a place like this. Can you imagine living here?"

"Well, I know that you can. Want me to knock?"

Gina's answer was to step back a few feet and get a gaspy look from the possibility of entering a building she'd made up. As if here in an entire village she'd invented there weren't already enough reasons to be hyperventilating.

"Ocean," I whispered, taking her shoulders and nudging her in that direction. She lingered for a few more moments and then, without turning, said again, "Things are going to happen here. This will be a place of deep and profound change. You'll see."

I placed a hand on her shoulder. Despite not believing a whit of any of that, I told her, "That's my wish."

I stayed there, leaning against the front wall, allowing her the experience of walking alone the remainder of the road, up the little rise and down the other side, where, as she disappeared from my sight, the ocean first spotted Gina, and rushed to her feet to whisper whatever the thing was she needed to know.

Ringed Heart:

Kismet, Love of Your Life

(State Your Wish Three Times)

"Where ya off ta?"

The jewelry guy. In his store doorway, now offering me a cigarette before he lit up.

He was tall, maybe close to six feet, but did not fill the doorway in width, and I was guessing that he was the kind of thin that is more lucky genetics than careful living. His hair was the color of the plastic terra-cotta pots some people prefer to the costly real thing and was kinky-curly and short and profuse, considering the head on which it grew was maybe a little over forty. Sprouting from his face was either the beginnings of a beard or he was still making a decision about shaving that day, and on the rest of him was a gray turtleneck, knee-ripped jeans, and gray suede Tevas. The tops of his feet were so white that at first I thought he was wearing athletic socks. I jumped from them way up to his eyes, which were the holographic blue-green of a rainbow trout's side, and were smiley, and were focused on me with the help of little boxy glasses that, had they been round of lens, would have made him somewhat resemble Eric Clapton as Eric Clapton had looked around the time he won all those many Grammys for that very sad song about his poor dead son. I'd always had a bit of a thing for Eric Clapton, so if this had been a regular day and this man had appeared from his doorway to ask where I was going, I would have halted so fast that cartoon brake noises and sparks would have flown from the bottom of my boots. But this was not a regular day. The plane trip across the Atlantic and the bus ride to Booley and the walk to the ocean and the shepherding of Gina through her emotions and then, finally, to the sea, where I had left her to commune, saying I'd meet her at Quinn's whenever she was done doing whatever it was she was going to do at the water's edge. All that had my responses off. I only managed, "Huh?"

He repeated, "Where ya off ta?"

"Nowhere."

"No destination?"

Reality was I didn't have one any longer. I was in Booley. This was it. This was the point of the trip. To get Gina there, and to remain there for as long as she needed. A fast revelation, but it must have taken me longer to experience, because the jewelry guy was saying something else to me and I didn't catch it.

"I'm sorry," I said. "I'm just spacing out."

"*Lost in Space*," he said. With an electronic wave of his arms stiffly in front of him, he mimicked a robotic monotone: "Danger, Will Robinson!"

"Huh?"

"The television program. *Lost in Space*." He raised his hands, apologetically this time. I shook my head at the silliness and he nodded and smiled and I nodded and smiled and then I felt a strange pull to go inside his store—more a push, really—as if someone behind me were guiding me forward. Which is where I went. Forward. Into Finola O'Flynn. Because, really, where else did I have to go?

Merchandise was everywhere. Heaps. Piles. Retail with the feeling of a teenager's Superfund-site bedroom just before the exasperated mother barges in with a lawn-and-leaf-sized trash bag. Inventory mixed haphazardly, no rhyme, reason, or apparent concern about display, or even simply about making things visible to potential customers. Table linens and wrought-iron candleholders and wood-framed mirrors and plastic-sheathed note card packs, dozens of tiny bottles of some kind of field-themed perfumes, logs of soap you could slice into the desired size, books, semifolded parchment-colored T-shirts, woven caps, hand-knitted socks, lacy scarves, ceramic tiles, everything bulldozed into small mountains on tables that lined the walls of the room. Despite the presentation, I said, "Very nice," because the inventory, once your eye took the time to sort it, was that. No cheap dollar store crap, only decent-quality items that were the result of work and time and thought and soul. This was the kind of place I would return to when I again was able to focus and browse correctly.

"It's about time you came in to see me," the jewelry guy said appreciatively. He made it sound as if he'd been waiting for me all his life. His had the kind of flirty Irishman charm that the flight-mate to my left in row 12 had felt it was necessary to warn Gina and me about shortly after we'd had clinked plastic glasses of Merlot served from doll-size screwcapped bottles.

"They can be gas," the woman had said of her countrymen, and the animation in her voice tipped us off that she was describing a positive attribute. "But," she cautioned, "mind yerselves."

There seemed no reason to worry about this native. He was now safely back behind his worktable, squinting as he squished a length of wire with a pliers. He touched a button on a stereo and some bouncy fiddle music that went "deedly-deedly-deedly-deedly" began to dance from the speakers nearby sticking from a toppled stack of reading material, was a small folded Complete and Total Map of Booley and I had to buy it. Maps have direction. Gina needed direction. This would be her first souvenir. I slid out a copy and caused a miniature avalanche of inventory. Instinctively, I straightened. Cookbook, legend book, first-person account of life there a century back, coloring book of historical figures, guide to native flora, guide to native fauna, more copies of The Complete and Total Map of Booley. I spotted a pair of bookends meant for sale and put them to work.

"You've a talent for that."

The jewelry guy noticed what I was doing—what I hadn't meant to be doing. I'd just noticed it myself.

"Well, I'm sort of naturally neat—not that this isn't neat, not that you're not . . ."

"You're not sayin' anythin' untrue. This place is a kip. But I haven't the time . . ."

"I'm sure you're busy, tourists and all."

"Not quite."

"You're not busy?"

"No one's busy at this stage. And this year, who knows? New state of the world and all."

Like anybody who lived in my part of it, I knew well that new state. Had seen it dim on my living room TV the previous fall while I was doing the yoga routine Gina had shown me, telling me it was too bad that I couldn't join her in class, then taking that back due to the membership prerequisite. I did my practice, as Gina called it, every morning, daylight drenching my aptly named sunroom, the TV playing and my concentration sometimes more on reaching for the clicker during commercials than attaining some degree of calm and enlightenment. The hour the state of the world started to decline a mere two states away, the *Today* show played. I was on the floor, on all fours, a section of hair that had come loose from my braid pissing me off by falling across my face each time I did the cow half of the lumbar-hydrating cat/cow. As I curled into the head-to-the-chest arch-backed gut-sucking-in cat half, Katie Couric began interviewing the eternally good-looking Harry Belafonte and the talk turned to race relations and Harry was asking a rhetorical "When are all going to learn to live together?" or something along that line. By the time I extended my neck back up for the slack-backed, a wounded office tower filled the screen.

"Eight months later, and they're still afraid to board an airplane," the jewelry guy continued. "But who can blame them?"

I was looking at a row of ceramic bowls right then. Shallow concaves glazed in a mottled royal blue. I made a stack next to a knot of chenille throws. I hadn't been reluctant to board a plane. If anything, the terrorism had given me a strong boot in the ass. You want to do anything? Do it now. You could be gone tomorrow. Just like Norm Stebbins in his SUV. Just like all those people in NYC. And DC. And PA.

"Tourists will start traveling again soon," I assured the jewelry guy, echoing what I had read in hopeful media reports back home, even though those reports had predicted that the destinations would be domestic. "Everybody was afraid to travel at first. But memories are short, however unfeeling that sounds. And flights right now are very cheap. Kind of a sick benefit."

"That why ye're here?"

I folded a big length of some cushy but fuzzless fabric that could make you want to curl up on it for about a thousand years of sleep. I read the tag: ATTRACTA. I knew that to be the weaver at the start of the street. Rather than the jeweler's question, my mind chose to concentrate on how I already possessed that much of my bearings. In order to learn more, I needed to pay for the map. I was moving toward the bead table when my peripheral vision caught sight of CDs and tapes strewn on the final table like fat plastic playing cards. For some reason I was helpless as I stopped and watched my hands doing what they had done for the seven years since I started my job putting things where they belonged.

"Tanks," the jewelry guy said.

"For what?"

"Tidyin'."

I looked down at the recordings, all at right angles, and alpha-betized, even. "I should apologize. I don't normally—"

"—Not at all. It's in a desperate state, but I'm alone here, so I've been puttin' such tasks on the long finger."

"But that's what I do, for a living. What I did. I lost the job. But that was my job when I had one: displays."

"And what do ye—did ye—display?"

"Seam binding."

"Sorry?"

"Rickrack?"

Not getting it, he shook his head.

"Ball fringe?"

"And just where was this, this ball fringe?" He smiled. People will do that if they're new to nations.

"In a store. An outlet store. It's right inside the factory where they make the products. It's called True-Trim. Do you have outlet stores here? This one was in Massachusetts. In the U.S.A." I wondered if it sounded dumb to have said the U.S.A. part.

"Ah, Massachusetts! Boston! Been there!" He looked happy. And he said "bean" for "been." "I've a cousin in Dorchester. Traveled there as a kid. Viewed *Lost in Space* there. *Mister Ed,* too. Wilburrrr. . . . D'ya still have *Mister Ed?*"

I nodded. "On cable—TV Land."

"Sorry?"

"An entire channel devoted to the old shows. Twenty-four hours a day."

"Ah, they were mad for the television in Dorchester. And we went for a day to the sea, at Gloucester." He pronounced the second place like it is spelled, Glou-ces-ter.

"I'm at the other end of the state. In the hills. Past Worcester." I said "Wusster," as does everyone, including people from there.

"And you've come all the way here for your holidays."

"Right," I said, efficient and uncomplicated.

"One of them six days, seven nights? Or is it six nights, seven days?"

"Actually, I'll be here indefinitely."

I stole that from Gina, the word *indefinitely*. She liked how it sounded. Told people we would be staying "indefinitely," even though our passports had been stamped PERMITTED TO LAND IN IRELAND FOR THREE MONTHS. *Indefinitely* sounded like she—like we—had all the time in the world. Which, Gina not having anything else that mattered to her, and I having nothing but Gina's state of mind to concern me, I guess was sort of true.

"Indefinitely. That's a very long while. Indefinitely in Booley?"

"Yes."

"No!"

"Yes."

"Doin' what?"

"Well, the idea is to do nothing, actually. A rest. Time to think."

"A fascinatin' life can drain ya." He leaned and the back of his chair came to what was probably a familiar stop.

"I'm not the one who needs the rest. I'm with a friend. She's had a trying year and a half." I'd never before used the word trying when talking about Gina's situation, but just then I realized it fit. "She's up at the beach right now. We're meeting here in town after six."

"And stayin' indefinitely. Tell me—there'll be no one missin'ye for that long while?"

"Nobody for my friend. That's a big part of her problem. She . . . her husband died."

"Sorry for her troubles. And ye?"

"There's someone, but I don't have a husband."

"Wise."

"That's really more due to geography," I started, giving my usual list of reasons, even though one was not owed to a stranger. "Right now my boyfriend lives halfway across the country. I see him about once a month."

"As ye would the landlord."

"Only it's more enjoyable."

He grinned. "Fair play to ye."

I dug out my Ziploc-ed starter kit of euros to finally made my purchase. "I'm sure we'll run into you while we're here."

The jewelry guy held out my change and grasped my hand with a "Please God."

I made it to the door, but not through it. Because suddenly it was teatime. Because six bells had rung on the mantelpiece clock and from a church tower some way mutedly far away and that is what you do here in Booley at this time of day, said the jewelry guy after he asked and at the same time answered, "But sure you'll stay for tea?" He disappeared somewhere out back and made a lot of kitchen-type noises, and in the time it took me to try on a pullover and a cardigan and then brush the hair I mussed in the process, he returned with a big green teapot and a couple of mismatched mugs. Went back to return with ham sandwiches. Thick meat on coarse grain-studded health-type bread. This was all he had to offer, the jewelry guy explained, and he said he could run to Una's if there was something else fancied. Though I didn't know who Una was, or what she might have that I'd fancy, I told him everything was fine, and that was the truth. I realized I fancied everything about that moment, of which I was noticing every detail, unintendedly practicing what Gina's yoga instructor calls mindfulness meditation. Not that you have to exactly fancy what's going on in a moment, but that you are present for it. Noticing every second, every thought, every sensation. The idea is that you should be as present for your pelvic exam as you are for the acceptance of your Oscar. You're not supposed to be looking to the end of a task or day and the next thing on the list, you're not supposed to be rushing life. Happily, a sandwich and a cup of tea tea was a no-brainer, mindfulnessly speaking. I wasn't there then, present, rather than looking ahead to the night or to five months from then. There was some-thing I was totally enjoying about sitting in that messy little store, the fire snapping, rain beginning, tea being poured for me by the friendly and instantly comfortable jewelry guy whose lulling music-box accent was familiar to me only from my years of ingesting *Ryan's Hope*, Lucky Charms commercials, and QVC's annual St. Patrick's Day Shopping Marathon. To enjoy. Wasn't that some facet of why Gina wanted us to get away? If so, then by my simply sitting there, at least one of us already had found some success.

I told him my name, which he repeated in full and without the usual space: "SophieWhite". He gave me his: Liam Keegan. Told me he was originally from someplace with a name nine miles long and on the opposite coast and he had lived in Booley for an even dozen years. The shop was his, the building was his, but up to two years ago he hadn't been there on a daily basis. His part in the busi-ness was traveling to sell its trademark handmade beaded jewelry to stores nationwide and in the U.K., which was a nice benefit because it allowed him the opportunity see his son, his only child—the only one he's aware of, he added with a wink after I asked if he had oth-ers. The only child he was aware of was now an adult and a printer of "in memoriam" cards for the funeral trade in Scotland and Wales. No, he answered, the person who made the jewelry in this shop was not his wife, not the son's mother. That woman and Liam had not been together for what he termed "donkey's years." She was in America, finally got married to her woman in Hawaii, where such unions were now legally permitted, and she had remained there, working in the courts as a mediator. He hadn't visited the son for at least two years. "I can be specific about that number," he said, "because it's two years ago now this place fell to me. Before that, I always had enough to do without having hair work as well."

Was there a salon in the back room? I easily could picture the females of Booley eagerly lining up at 6 a.m. to get a blow-out from this guy. But I noticed that when he said the word hair, Liam had motioned with his mug to the a wooden nameplate on the wall behind him, was a small replica of the sign above the front door.

"Your boss?"

He laughed, but only three brief ha-ha-ha's, because what he was about to tell me wasn't funny. "You could say that. Once was, I should say. Was my 'boss.' My landlord. My girl. The one true love a my life. Now she's all that to someone else."

That bundle of information landed like a stack of junk mail shoved through a slot. Hard onto the floor, where it slid into a fan shape and awaited acknowledgment. So I said oh and that I was sorry.

"Be sorry for him, not me. The poor bastard." He said "par" for poor. Done with his sandwich, he put down his tea and went back to his table and returned to his stringing, flat black stones that had something sparkly in them.

I watched the process. I asked, "Is she still in town?"

"I've really no idea where she is. Cept that it's in Germany. Cause he's German, from there. Here on his holidays two summers ago. Booked a room at Woodbrooke House. Came in the shop of an afternoon, for a souvenir. Found one, I'd say. When he left at the end of his three weeks, Finola left as well. Left her business, her home, her possessions. Said she didn't need any of it, didn't want it, all this no longer suited her, no longer was who she was. Nothin' here held any meanin', she said. Includin' me, after nine years a love. The reasons' she was unable to put into words. But I couldn't have repelled her too greatly, for she soon after gave me most everything she owned. All right and proper. Papers delivered by her solicitor several months later. Whether I like it or not, what was hers is now mine."

He picked up a red oval bead that looked like something from a Christmas ivy bush. Put it down, searched for something that was a more fitting match for what he'd already strung.

Nobody had ever run out on me like that. Nor had I ever done that to anyone. I wondered the impetus that would bring about such a drastic move. Had life with the guy at the bead table been that insufferable? Or had the prospect of life with the guy from Germany been so irresistible? All I could think to say, the response ball being in my court, was another wake-line comment. I ventured that the sudden loss of his girlfriend must have been a great shock.

Liam exhaled. "I've a great talent for inspirin' women to make massive life changes," he said brightly, and without looking up from his work. "The pity's I can't make a livin' at it. This is my livin', here, makin' these things, and I've always enjoyed it. But ever since she left I've been up to my eyes with work and I'm totally knackered. Have had no luck findin' help that stays longer than a week, or that won't help themselves to. Another summer comin' and though I don't know how many tourists we'll see, I know I can't do this alone again." He stopped there to slide a gold bead on the wire. And to ask, "Perhaps you're available?"

I gave my own ha-ha-ha's. Even though I had no idea what I would be doing for the next three months, I was in Booley to help Gina. Plus, wasn't hiring foreigners illegal? I answered, "On holiday and all, you know."

"Holidays can cost ye," Liam noted, because it was true, and also because he didn't know about Gina's generosity, about the hefty out-of-court settlement with the automaker responsible for the faulty steering system that had sent Norm off the road. And he and Gina had been doing OK long before that. Norm had been a CPA whose hard-earned income meant huge annual contributions to the IRA that was to have funded retirement in Fla on a golf course sanctioned by the PGA. After Gennifer began grade school, Gina had wanted to pull her own weight, and had made a dozen years of progress from shipping clerk to inventory chief to manager of the outlet store at Trim-True (a plus because she sewed and was generally creative like that) and one of our area's largest employers. We met when she advertised for a display artist/store clerk, and I showed up with photographs of the work I'd done during the Filene's internship that had been a requirement for my marketing degree from UMass. She was particularly taken by the picture of the five-foot-long nose I had built from chicken wire and papier-mâché and suspended over a glued-together trail of perfume bottles that disappeared into the cavernous, inhaling nostrils. The merchandise at the outlet was somewhat less glamorous, but I was delighted to be offered a full-time job doing the work I'd studied—and for such a likeable boss as I sensed Gina would be.

"I'm serious," Liam continued. "If you want to work here, you're more than welcome. You seem well suited. You're experienced, and, well, you're female."

"That's a requirement?"

He put up a hand to caution me. "Don't take this the wrong way, but I'm desperate for a woman."

Instantly, someone did come through the shop door. But it was a male. And a dog. The terrier from the road.

"Pepsi," Liam said, "we've a new employee." Probably knowing that wasn't true, Pepsi continued through the room to the back kitchen, where he disappeared.

I wondered whether Liam had been lonely for the two years since Finola O'Flynn up and left, but I found it hard to imagine him lacking for company. Even if you did not go for a certain-era Eric Clapton—or even for Eric Clapton in general—Liam probably would have held a good degree of appeal. I'd only had maybe two hours in his presence, but I'd noticed that he did and was many of the things many woman are always complaining that most men can't, or won't, or aren't. He listened. He was smart. He was funny. He was employed. He apparently knew how to put together a basic meal. And when he handed me my change for the map, and we had those few seconds of palm-to-palm contact, well, it could have been brain addle on my part, but I felt like I'd become one of the straight pins I'd regularly dropped to the carpet when pinning samples of lace to the wall of the outlet. It was how they must have felt when I came after them with the big magnet. They had no choice but to stick. I found that even though he wasn't even holding my hand, it was strangely difficult to pull away.

"And ye're a woman . . ."

"And you're talking about needing a salesperson, right?"

"Sales, and what you were doin' just now. Organizin'. Why?"

"Well, why does it have to be a woman?"

"I dunno. Maybe it's mad, but it's almost like I need somebody to be, I dunno—hair."

Another motion to the name behind him. "People see the sign, they enter, and where there usta be a woman, where there usta be hair, there's just ugly aul' me. Not hair. It loses a little somethin', I think. They see the sign, they walk through the door, and they want a charmin' lovely Finola sittin' here. God help 'em, but they do. Right off, big laugh comin' in and sayin', 'Ye must be Finola O'Flynn.' Now you—I could see you sittin' here . . ."

Was he comparing me to someone charmin' and lovely? At this point in my short strange trip to Booley, I was not feeling much of the first compliment, though with enough acclimation to the time zone, I could prove cordial and welcoming. I certainly didn't feel lovely, either. I needed a bath and a shampoo and some sleep, and after all that I would be a little more visually appealing. I resemble my mother, but since you probably didn't know her, I'll say that the only other person I seem to bring to people's minds is Mama Walton. Not the Grandma Walton who had those stomach-turning bedroom scenes with saggy-assed union-suited Grandpa and who valiantly remained on the show despite suffering a stroke and it just could make you cry to watch her croak out the name E-liz-a-beth. I look somewhat like the younger mother, Daddy's wife, "Mama" to John Boy and all the many, many rest of them. In real life, Michael Learned is her name, despite that she's a woman. Many times I've been told I look like Mama Olivia of the very fitting olive-shaped face, the little pursed bird lips, the bunned-back blondish hair, the one who, when she decided to leave the show, was written off to a sanatorium with something awful like tuberculosis or polio. It's her face I possess. Nice. But lovely? Considering the country we were in, I took the compliment as, well, blarney. But I was embarrassed nonetheless, and looked away. I spotted yet more boxes of merchandise shoved beneath tables—tables I decided needed tablecloths, if only as a means for hiding the extra inventory not too well concealed right then.

"Why don't you just change the name of the store? Change it to yours—it's yours now. You could avoid the confusion, avoid the subject. Make a new start."

He shook his head. " 'Finola O'Flynn' is printed on everythin'—signs, brochures, vouchers and the like. And Finola actually made a fair good reputation across the country. Business-wise, at least. I don't need a new name. I just need a new woman. I'm serious. Finola's old home above is vacant. You could have it. For nothin'. Consider it part of your wages. A grand place for your friend to rest, and ye'd enjoy it as well. The work here? I could teach you in an instant. You'd have to be an eejit to not be able to string beads. I'm serious. Tink about it. Try it. Give it three days. Then he added with the grin you could have seen coming even if you were back at the bus stop on the top of the hill: "Ya never know. It could be a life-changin' experience."

Bow:

༤

Gift, Surprise

(State Your Wish Three Times)

$\mathbb{B}$y the time I got to Quinn's, Gina had filled seven and a half pages of the Mary Engelbreit journal in which she was planning to record her evolution in Booley. The cover bore a drawing of a little girl standing fierce with hands on hips and shouting "SNAP OUT OF IT," which I thought was a rather severe and unfeeling message, but all Gina had said when she found it among the going-away good-wishes gifts wrapped and presented by her friends from Trim-True was "She meant well," even though the giver, perennially frowning Sunny Blatz from Human Resources, definitely had not.

If Gina had been of her mother's vintage, she would have been the recipient of religious medals and prayer books and beautifully calligraphied Mass cards certifying that the nuns locked up by choice behind bars in that monastery on the hill behind the Route 5 Abdow's Big Boy would be remembering her in their incessantly chanted prayers. Instead, Gina's gang purchased more New Agey necessities: scented votives heavy on the citrus family, which was said to bring about clarity of mind; a tube of minty cream meant to be applied to the sternum during times of stress; a matchbook-sized collection of positive quotations to carry around in coat pocket; a tiny copper-colored brick etched with the word HEALING; a T-shirt that announced in hard-to-miss fluorescent orange I AM THE LIGHT; a small paint box and pad of watercolor paper to capture those emotions that could not be put into words; and a deck of cards depicting forty yoga poses, a dozen mantras to repeat while meditating, and five sets of directions for five different ways to breathe in order to achieve a state of bliss.

Without the aid of cards—they were still deep in our back-packs—Gina seemed to have managed some of that last goal already. I sat down at her small round table to find her so serene she was unaware that I was an hour late.

"I knew when it was six," I said. "I just didn't connect that I was supposed to be anywhere at that time . . ."

"No problem!"

"So how's the ocean?"

She grasped my wrist in the fashion of someone taking a pulse. But I think she meant the gesture to be dramatic, because she followed it with a definite "We're never leaving."

"Then let's celebrate. What are you drinking?"

"Would you mind if we checked in first? I'm nervous that it's getting late and the man won't be there."

"What man?"

"The one who has the key. Mrs. Quinn was here earlier, said we need to see the owner of where we'll be staying."

"And where's he?"

"Do you remember a craft place?"

The door to Finola O'Flynn was closed, the sandwich board and its etceteras leaning lazily against the front of the building, folded for the day. Pepsi absent Gina knocked. Called the kind of hello that is followed by a question mark. No answer. "He was here half an hour ago," I said as I tried the latch, which was unlocked. The shop was dark and silent but the top of the brown carpeted stairs, directly in front of us a light shone, and radio broadcaster with a British accent loudly was reporting that a ferry had capsized.

"We're home," Gina whispered giddily. "Mrs. Quinn said this man regularly rents his place above." So we climbed the stairs.

There was no door at the top, but there was a man. Liam Keegan. In the kitchen. In the nude. Without clothing, he was of course even thinner than he'd been downstairs. But still, muscles were able to fit between bone and skin, cultivated by the rowing that, over the sandwiches he'd told me he liked to do now and again on fine early mornings, setting out from the pier and rounding a place called Goat Island. I'd seen naked men, including naked men who used the rowing machine at the Y, and I made a note to recommend the real thing, all that fresh air and real water obviously making a big and positive difference in physical results. I couldn't take in the sculpted Liam for too long, though, for fear of hurting my eyes. His Cloroxed flanks, as blinding as a CIA interrogation lamp, shone on us full force as he bent to pull on a pair of jeans.

Our hellos got unplugged just after the H.

"Hallo yerselves!" he answered, cheerfully, as if being walked in on were an everyday occurrence. I should note the absence of places for him, or us, to hide, the second floor being one big room, a cluttered combination of the minikitchen and not much larger living room. I turned and focused on the pile of clothing in the basket down on the worn brown and gold linoleum. The radio man described the panic that had flared when the passengers realized that half the lifeboats needed didn't exist. "Some returned home"— pause—"some never did," was his stab at an artful conclusion to the story.

"I'm decent," Liam announced from behind our backs. "Well, as much as I'm ever going to be . . ."

I turned my head, Gina turned hers, and he was. Covered once again and viewable again by two strangers who'd already seen more than their share.

"I didn't know you were comin' back." He buttoned a wrinkled black shirt, began on the wrong button, started anew. "Hold on— Motheragod! Yer interested?" He bugged out his eyes and grabbed his chest. He appeared breathless, like someone had just spared him from certain death. Had located a lifeboat when it appeared there were none to be had. As if on cue, Liam said genuinely, "You've just saved my life!" He walked over and caught me in a lumpy hug that reminded me I still wore my backpack.

I slipped it off, onto a kitchen chair holding a sports section, most of the first page taken up by a huge color photo of a racing greyhound pursuing a live rabbit. Gina elbowed me and I made a quick and apologetic introduction.

"She's savin' me life!" Liam told her as he took both her hands in his and Gina told him I was good at that, at saving people. And at working. Said she conveniently could vouch for me, once having been my boss.

Gina liked this idea, that I have something to do. That a pasttime had been handed to me my first hour in Booley. This she told me over the drink we did have after I told her I certainly knew of a craft shop, which was where I'd been the past few hours. Hearing a man's story, and having him offer me work. Gina saw it as perfect. I saw it as unfair. I'd come along to be company. And what sort of company would I be a mile away from nine to five?

"But I'm not working here" I told them. "I'm not here to take the job. I'm here for the key. This—Gina—this is Gina Stebbins. We're renting from you."

He smiled and offered his hand slowly, as at the same mph he said, "Yer jokin'."

"Nope."

He checked his watch. "Today? Did Jimmy Quinn not tell me Friday?"

"I don't know," said Gina apologetically as she set down her backpack and leaned against the wall, choosing to skip the nearby dingy armchair. Her eyes were sweeping the room that in its confusion resembled the store downstairs, except that these heaps of clothing and paperwork and kitchenware weren't for sale. She had to be hiding her discouragement about our new, extremely lived-in quarters, because I couldn't detect a trace.

"We apologize for barging in," I said. "We heard the radio, figured you were up here getting ready for us. You know, for us to check in."

"No harm. T' me, that is!" He Velcroed himself back into his sandals. "Especially the two if it's ye! of Sophie White. You'll recall that a position in the shop entitles ye to accommodations above-gratis."

"Sorry, you're kind, but I really won't be able to help you. Honestly. This is supposed to be vacation. With Gina."

"She's brilliant, I know that already," he said in an aside to Gina, who replied "You won't hear an argument from me."

Then no one said anything. The radio assured us we'd love it at Londis, where Sunlight soap, Mikado biscuits, and Batchelor's beans were the specials this week.

"Perhaps a change of mind after a night out," Liam told me. "Would you ever come along? Music, crack."

Gina and I swapped appropriately wary looks.

"Thanks, but my drug days are long over" is what I came out with. Even though this was true, I felt embarrassed verbalizing it, like the buttoned-down goody-two-shoes in a public service announcement promoting the Reagan era "Just Say No" campaign.

"What?" Liam regarded me as if I were an aberration. Did my being American automatically label me as some variety of an addict?

"No thanks," I said.

"No thanks," Gina echoed.

"I'm talking about harmless crack here!"

"We know what it is." Gina pitched this in. She had her stern mother voice turned on, the one I'd heard over the years in enough conversations with Gennifer. But Gina and Liam were probably the same age.

"Crack," he Berlitzed. "*C-R-A-I-C.* Here, it's an enjoyable time. Fer some, that's smokin', and who'm I to judge? But all I meant was *craic:* harmless music, a coupla pints."

"Who knew?" Gina rhetoricalized. I smiled and said nothing, too busy wondering what else we'd already misunderstood without anyone going to the trouble of explaining.

Rabbit in Hat:

~~~

Memorable Magical Acts

(State Your Wish Three Times)

The *craic* was incredibly convenient. Located one door away. At Quinn's, which Liam called his "local," and where he was to join in a "session," which is pronounced as such but was spelled on the chalkboard as *seisun* and was explained to us as being a sort of musical jam. Anyone who wanted could join with instrument or voice, skilled or un-, though what we would go on to hear was really nothing that could be called amateur.

Liam led us to a table at which a pointily coiffed woman sat whispering to a big, wide, and—there's no better or polite word for it—ugly man. Why did she look familiar? The grocery steps flashed.

"I'm Una Dolan," she said, greeting us warmly. "This is Noel Heaney." The Noel guy rose and shook our hands. "Welcome to Booley," he said.

"E. Dolan is mine," Una told us. "Noel's shop is two down: Attracta's."

Gina and I nodded as we attempted to file the info that this was Attracta.

Noel must have been accustomed to a missed beat at this point in an introduction. "Me granny was named for the saint Attracta," he said, ending that mystery before adding, "and me granny taught me to weave."

I wondered if both the saint and the granny had been such lookers that the name was a natural. If so, Noel definitely had missed the departure of that particular DNA boat. I'm being reportorial rather than cruel here when I ask you to picture one of those vegetables entered in your state fair's freak produce contest. Should have grown this direction, but turned and went that way instead. Ballooned out where it should have curved in. Wore a big bump here, where things should have been flat, and was flat where a feature should have been sticking out. Tucked in a basket with the Hubbard that resembles Nixon and the white eggplant that is a dead ringer for Liza Minnelli's new ex-husband, Noel easily could have been a brother of some starchy tuber dug from the ground at harvest time. And at the same time was someone who, in the right light, closely resembled a very unattractive forty-something-year-old man.

Gina said to Una, "We saw you—when was it . . . ?"

"This afternoon," I answered. "Can you believe this is the same day? I have no idea of the time."

"Half ten," volunteered Noel. "The night's but a pup."

"Where you booked?" Una asked as she helped Liam unload a tray of murky-looking glasses of beer he'd carried from the bar.

"They're stayin' above," he answered for us. "The lovely Sophie and the lovely Gina are absolutely and totally on holliers."

"Quite the accommodations," Una said, sounding convincingly envious.

Gina, good sport that she was, nodded that she agreed. Once we were alone, I'd assure her that we'd spend just the one night in the apartment above the store and relocate in the morning to someplace a little less unkempt.

"To your new home," Noel said, lifting his glass. "May it suit ye."

Then the three Booleyans together said some word we didn't understand but that appeared to be a signal to drink, and we joined them.

The *seisun* music was along the lines of what had been playing on Liam's store CD, and earlier, on the in-flight stereo channel titled "Celtic Calling." It was pleasant and head-bob-inducing, though I have to say that for me, at whatever was this hour, one tune blended into the next with little differentiation. Liam and his guitar sat between a peppy teenage girl who pumped a concertina type of thing, and a ruby-faced senior citizen who appeared to be in a trance as he tapped on a flat drum the size of a personal pizza. Arriving late was a scraggly haired wild-looking old woman bearing a fabric-rolled arsenal of metal flutes, and a very jovial ponytailed man bearing the second guitar and challenging Liam to a deedly-deedly version of those center-stage rock show ax duels.

Gina and I sat contentedly, drinking beer that turned out to be warm on purpose (we asked) and that also was fragrant and thick with all the basic beer components we were accustomed to having extracted in the process of brewing our American flip-topped six-packed lites. The pub was half full, and included a pack of children that occasionally dashed past. It was more parish hall than smelly neighborhood bar into which only fathers and veterans and bikers dared venture. The sound level of the makeshift band was low enough for a decent conversation, and Noel and Una quizzed us on our places of origin and why of all the choices we had selected Booley. I explained how it had been Gina's idea, and she quickly informed them, "I dreamed it," though she left out why the dream had been necessary. "I saw this place in my head for months, and then I spotted a photo of it in the newspaper travel section. I just had to come here. I don't know if that sounds weird to you. Nothing like this has ever happened to me. Maybe you'll laugh, but I have the feeling this is a place of great change."

"I'm not surprised," Noel offered, and he truly didn't seem it. "There's some who say places in Booley are holy. Magical. Whichever you prefer, or believe. That it could call to ye, I would totally believe."

Una nodded. "Not unlike the manner in which Finola found this town."

I perked up. "You and Finola were friends?"

Una said yes and smiled at Noel, and that was how I came to hear my first story about how Finola O'Flynn, during her years in Booley, to borrow another public service announcement phrase, made a difference.

That's what she had done right next door, for Una and for her boys. Single-mother Una said her pair, twelve-year-old Derek and fourteen-year-old Ralpho, so far had escaped drugs and other modern-day horrors because of the advice Finola liberally had dispensed during their earliest years.

"They are who they are in great part because of her, so they are," Una told us solemnly.

As far as who Una had been in her own teens, we next were told. Adolescence and hormones and such being universal, she said, she felt Gina and I could relate to how at age fifteen she took off to the city—Limerick, sixty or so miles away—in hot pursuit of the boy she'd met there while on a school outing to view a traveling show of holy relics belonging to saints no one ever had heard of, but when you weren't given the opportunity to see holy relics every day of the week, sure you took what you could get.

"We were in queue for ages," Una started, "and when I got my turn, I knelt to peer into the glass box, at the bones arranged in a cross shape, all holy like, on a fine silk pillow, but they were bones, really, nothing any more special in size or form than you'd see Pepsi carrying up the road. Something made me look past them, through the box, to a face. Looking back at me was a teenage version of Robbie Williams." She regarded Gina's and my blank reactions.

Asked, "From Take That? The pop group? Nevertheless . . . bold thing, he winked at me there, winked with Robbie's eyes, and with saint relics a breath away. He's kitted up as an altar boy, and he's kneeling with hands folded all proper in front of the remains of a genuine saint, and he's winking at a girl. He found me later at the souvenir stand and leaned close to whisper that he'd something to show me."

Under a spell, Una followed the boy past classmates rooting through a selection of holy cards and looking up to gasp, "Una! We're leavin'!" Through some old door she expected would creak, but did not, he reached for her hand and Una gave it. His starched gown swished as they descended marble stairs so old they'd been worn into a series of little dishes, and you had to mind yourself so's not to slip and kill yourself. He shoved open a door at the bottom and led Una into darkness and silence, and into the stupidest and most thrilling ten minutes of her brief yawn of a life. Those minutes were happening to her, to Una, in a city, in a church, with a boy who looked like Robbie Williams. If nothing of even minor note ever took place in her life, Una would have knowledge of this moment, of all she saw and felt and tasted and smelled and touched and touched and touched in the cool dark suddenly turned golden because Robbie Williams had struck a match and lit a fat candle on a tall brass stand, then another candle on another stand, and another, and a fourth, and as Una's eyes adjusted, she saw they weren't alone after all. "Jesus," is what she said aloud, because wasn't it he? The Son of God, hands reaching out in a welcome: Jesus frozen there in painted plaster or whatever it is they make statues from.

Statues. The room was loaded with them, each as big as, or larger than, life size. Una recognized the gentle Theresa with her armful of roses, hope-giving Jude with the club no one ever was able to explain to her the need for, bearded Peter with the sword because he'd been that sort before starting up the One True Church, and yer man Custus or whatever the name, the black fella from the Three Kings, there next to Patrick, bishop-hatted, shamrock-clutching, and curiously here in storage. They lined the walls three and four deep, Christmas lambs at their feet, staring forward to the center of the circle.

"We've interrupted their meeting" is the first of maybe eight things that Una ever said to this boy. And his response was, "Pray they don't interrupt ours," as he eased her slowly against the camel of Custus there in the cellar of a church, directly beneath the glass coffin of holy relics. So, according to the Una, you know the direct road to hell she'll be taking one day. But the Una she was then had no such concern in her brain as the earth below dropped away and the sky was ripped open like the top of a Corn Flakes box and the gathered heavenly witness were left absolutely speechless.

Sort of like our table had become. Noel appeared a bit uncomfortable, rubbing the shar-pei skin folds at the back of his neck, then shooting to his feet at the realization that several of our glasses were just a little less than half full. As he headed quickly in the direction of the bar, I remembered how the airline magazine had encouraged tourists to take the time to sit in a pub to listen to one of the country's many unparalleled storytellers. We certainly were doing that already, though I would have expected the subject to be, say, the sorrow of starving émigrés sailing for America rather than the passion of oversexed teens headed for trouble. We'd met Una maybe half an hour before, but there she was describing how she missed the coach home, and her next period.

"Following month," she added, leaning in, "still no sign. But my state was sign enough. An in-utero ticket out of Booley. Finally. A reason to leave this feckin' place, and a future that would be something other than running a shop like Mam and her mam before and God only knows how many other mams before her, catering to people all the day long and never to themselves. I wanted something different. So I ran off to the city to find him."

Noel and a tray of full glasses returned to the table just as Una was describing her return to Booley three years later. Options exhausted, psyche spent, a child on her lap and, make no mistake, another swimming inside her. Whatever experiences had filled the years away, they were bad enough to drive Una back to the place she'd shaken from the soles of her bubble-toe Doc Martens, and toward whatever mercy her mother could offer. That unseasonably cold morning in June of 1993, she sat at the kitchen table, listening for her man shuffling down the hall to begin her day, then finally saw her stopping in the doorway to tie the belt of her dressing gown, pull the belt tighter, slowly, then drop the ends of the ties, and her hands to her sides.

"She'd not heard from me for three years. She coulda started shouting, she coulda thrown something, coulda thrown us out." Una listed these possibilities then consulted the screen of the cell phone next to her glass, pressing it on, then off, before continuing. "She moved toward us slow and I held my breath. She'd hit me as a kid, as all kids are hit, I haveta say, though I've yet to strike my own. Would she do it again, now? And with the small boy here? In an instant she was past us, though, filling the kettle, and as she did, I saw it tremble. She brought mugs to the table. Cutlery. A piece of bread got placed in front of Derek. That was a gesture, and it was all she could manage. She didn't touch him like you might reach out to a dote in a pram. She didn't come near me. She said nothing. She made the eggs. The toast. The kettle boiled. She warmed the pot, poured out the water, tossed in the leaves, filled it again. Covered it with the blue towel like always, brought it to the table. As she the Delph and cutlery.

"She sat down in her chair there nearest the door. And we had a meal. Because that's what Finola had once told her she should do when I came back home. Finola knew I'd come back. Just knew. And whenever she'd say that to Mam, Mam would ask, 'And just what am I to do if I come to the table one mornin' and she's sittin' there?' Finola would answers, 'What do you do when someone's at your table? Do you not feed 'em?' She told Mam not to kill me, not to start giving out to me about where I'd been and how I'd made a right bags of my life and how she'd been out of her mind with worry. Finola told her to do nothin' but make the eggs and the tea, and she said that the rest, in time and with the help a God, would sort itself out."

Una and her mam and Ralpho and, after his arrival, Derek had nearly three more years of eggs and tea together before the mild April afternoon that Frances Dolan died of a massive coronary as she was coming in from admiring the progress of her rhubarb. Una found her when she stuck her head in from the shop to ask were there any more Cadbury's Roses because the woman from New York was back for the second box she'd decided against earlier in the day because she feared she'd end up eating the lot.

"Without Mam, I was lost," Una said, and just then the music tempo slowed appropriately. "But like she'd done for her, Finola helped me. Called over and sat in Mam's chair. Not so much with grand plans, just to offer simple things. She just did, dyaknow? Knew what we needed, did it for us when she had the time. Minding the boys, minding the shop when I just could not, making sense of what was running through my head when I just could not."

Gina said, "I have a friend like that. You were lucky."

"I was, yeah—both fer havin' Mam and fer havin' Finola." Una traced the B of the word Bulmer's printed on a cardboard coaster. "Then Finola left as well." The words hovered. "Now, I don't begrudge her"—here she moved the finger from the coaster and into the air, where it was to emphasize that lack of begrudgement— "I just wish she'd explained. But it's her life, I suppose."

"'Tis." Noel was agreeing. Nodding.

"Is," Gina said, and I agreed, nodding with him, with her.

The tune evaporated, and the man with the drum wasted no

time in starting a new one, taking a little bone-shaped stick and banging out a version of a one, two, three, four, after which the rest of the musicians joined in. I saw Liam start, get mixed up, fall into laughter, and as he tried again to join the melody, he looked from the accordionist to our table, to me. He was sweaty and joyous, and he was smiling, and I smiled back because, well, it was only polite. I turned to Noel and Una to ask them what I also wanted to ask Liam:

"You didn't see it coming? Before she left, Finola didn't hint that she wanted to up and run—or that she liked this guy—"

"Udo," Noel said, and I said, "Excuse me?"

"Udo's his name. Odd to us, but perhaps in Germany they've as many Udos as we've Seans. Though one Udo seems to have been enough for Finola. And no. There was no hint—at least none given to me."

"Nor to me," Una said. "I was completely flabbergasted when Liam told me she'd left."

"How did that make you feel?"

I noticed that I'd started asking people this question shortly after, at Gina's nervous request, I'd sat in on the first couple of her sessions with a psychologist. As each of the next few inches of her life story were revealed, the counselor asked how that particular time, place, experience, comment made her feel, and the dialogue was bounced back to the person who was paying for the swift fifty minutes.

Una shrugged. Noel looked uncomfortable, as if his clothing suddenly didn't fit, and then he said, "Not a day passes that I don't think of her."

"'Twould be hard for you not to," Una admitted, and then to us explained, "Finola loved the process of a weaving. Just watching a length of fabric come t'life. She'd call up the house and sit for hours and talk and watch Noel at the loom. Two summers before her German fella, she got the idea how he should become serious about both the weaving and the selling."

Noel picked up the story: " 'You must open a shop, you must be visible,' says she. I wove at home then. She asks 'How many Yanks have you walkin' through yer mam's front room?' 'None,' says I. 'Go up the town,' says she, and she adds, "less you want t'be shovelin' shit your whole life.' That's what I was doing then—not all the day, but a good portion of it had something to do with shit. Shovelin' it, spreadin' it, shovelin'. But that's farm life, and it was a good portion of my day. The other thing I did was the weavin'. Other lads were out in the field throwin' the football. I was inside throwin' the shuttle. It's the only thing I've ever felt I could do well, and I had it somewhere in my mind that it might be what I'm supposed to be doin', if you believe in things like that—which you seem to, Gina. I said those words to Finola once and she asked did I hear myself. Nothing's worse, she said, than wakin' from a dream to find yer real life a great disappointment. 'Yer a long time dead'—that's how she ended that conversation, and the words have followed me."

"Three years ago now," Una said. "We were in the Last Restaurant, just up the road. Birthday of Noel."

"Finola presented me with a package wrapped in silver paper. Silver paper and a red ribbon. Inside, a square of cloth, nothin' but simple twill, of natural linen."

"For a tea tray, like," Una explained.

"Tells me the antiques shop in Dublin placed it at maybe half a century old." Noel continued. " 'Where'll ya be in half a century?' Finola asks me. 'Course I tell her I dunno. I never had thoughts like that. Not before I met her. I just assumed my life would go along as me dad's had. Born on the farm, work there, live there, die there. Finola, the way she always was thinkin'—it was as if she was floatin' above the world, seein' it from a level occupied by the very wise, havin' all opinions, and sharin' with those who cared to listen."

"This was not the kind of person I was accustomed to," Una threw in. "Talking with her sometimes made my head ache. But I enjoyed the talking, despite that."

"So next she asks me, 'Where'll ya be in a year?' Again, I say I dunno. She says 'I do. You'll be above, in Willie Lynch's.' I ask her where'll Willie Lynch be then? And she says, 'He'll be counting the pounds you'll have given him for the purchase of his shop.' I laughed, and we left for Quinn's, and as we did, we passed Willie Lynch's, and Willie sittin' there working into the night, repairin' shoes, and dentures, as he had for the fifty years previous, in the very same great window where my loom stands."

And just short of one year later—even a little sooner than Finola had predicted—Willie Lynch was counting Noel Heaney's meager deposit on the little building between the Last Restaurant and Quinn's. The money was the granny's, given with pride and fore-sight to old friend Willie so grandson Noel could do his weaving in a place where tourists could at least watch him weave and buy his wares.

"I took the advice," Noel said. "And I am making a livin'. Now my brother shovels the shit. Thanks to Finola and the good kick she gave. If she could see me at this stage . . ."

Next to him, solemn Una nodded.

You easily could think we were discussing a dead person. But because we weren't, Gina asked Noel and Una how often Una and Noel were in touch with Finola. "We aren't," each said, almost at the same moment.

"We'd ring her, but she's ex-directory," Noel explained. "Can't find her on the internet. Nor can we Udo. So if we feel the need, we write to the address Liam has for her solicitor—I do, I should say. Not once has she responded."

"Not once," Una said sadly. Then, as if she were trying to con-vince us of something, Una added, "But sure she's getting what she wanted: new life. Those of us in Booley—I reckon in her eyes we're back here in the old one. Even so, as understanding as I'd like to be, it would help to know the reason: Why does a person feel the need to do that? Up and leave?"

rd5

Gina, who actually could answer this question with authority, gave the answer: "The need for change?"

Nobody spoke for a while. It's tough enough to come up with philosophical probabilities when you're rested and sober, never mind when you're a handful of time zones from your own and you've had maybe three consecutive beers—no, pints—no, now they were calling them jars. And another round has found its way onto the table, and the music sadly has turned sad, and it has words to match that Una began to sing in a not half-bad voice, and even though they were foreign to me, I felt I could interpret. At least I pretended I could. I knew the song was that of a woman who needed to do what she needed to do. And then went and just did it.

The notes were rising, climbing to something the way a piece of it can, but this style was so loose and wild in form, the melodies so unfamiliar, that I couldn't predict when the end would occur. The tempo quickened—strings and buttons, fingers and hands, entire bodies went into overtime.

"I like to think that she found herself a new Booley, and that it suits her," Noel said, speaking louder in order to be heard. "Maybe she dreamed her own dream. As did you, Gina, maybe she conjured a new place to be, and it just happened to be the same place Udo came from."

"Conjured," I repeated, because I wanted to say the word.

"Is that what I did?" Gina turned to me and asked. "Conjured?"

I nodded. Then I shouted, because that had become the required volume, "You're a powerful woman, Gina. You have to know you can do anything you want."

Wheat Sheaf:

❦

Abundance

(State Your Wish Three Times)

In what felt like four hours later, but was only a little more than two, Gina and I were back at the top of the brown carpeted stairs, alternately complimenting Liam on his guitar playing and thanking him for the enjoyable night in general.

"I'm available for weddings and wakes," he told us as he reached into an old leather glove hanging near the door and fished out a key on a ring. "Now. We're off!"

"That's OK, really," Gina said, and she took a seat on the chair she'd avoided resting on earlier, to underline that she was staying put. "You've been more than kind."

"You don't want to go?"

"I think we'd prefer to stay here," I said.

"Here?"

Nods from both of us.

"You want to stay here. With me."

Nods again. Then head shakes.

"Not with you . . ." I began. "Here."

"Well, then, just where am I to sleep?"

Gina suggested: "Home?"

"This is my home."

I rubbed my head. "We're renting. Your place above."

"Emm, and ye will. But not if I don't deliver ye there."

"Where?"

"Above. To the cottage." He said this as if it made sense.

"Whose cottage?"

"Finola's."

Silence, while we interpreted. "I thought she lived here," I said. "I mean, when she lived here."

"No. I live here. Her place is above."

"Isn't this above?" I pointed down, toward the store, which was below. When you were standing in that store and talking about a place that was above, wouldn't it be natural to think you were talking about the second floor?

He let my question sink in, then got it. "Right. Now . . . this is above the shop." He pointed to our surroundings and slowly explained: "Finola lived above. As in over there." He pointed out the window, in the direction of the ocean. "We used to live there. Finola and I. When she left, I moved to town. Closer to things, and farther from her things. I rent it out, her cottage up the road."

"And that road, that's 'above'?"

"That's above."

"Right."

"Right."

"Right so."

So Liam and Gina and I went above, to the cottage above, took the right after what he called the chip shop, which was the final place of business in downtown Booley, a grease joint, all french fries and onion rings and breaded hunks of fish and lumps of meat on skewers and something called red sauce administered from a squeeze bottle. Samples of most of the above were given to us by the owner, Emilio, whom we met when Liam dragged us inside and ordered each of us a big bag of chips and a burger to go, and then put all that and our belongings and us into his car and drove the road Gina and I had followed to the sea earlier in the now-previous day. We headed up the muddy little hill, veering right and then left and then descending toward the great throat-grabbing expanse of water. We passed a cottage, then a few fields, and another lone and dark cottage, also dark, and then a few more fields, a couple more, and then we were there. At the cottage just before the sea. Where, it turns out, Finola O'Flynn had once made her home. Where, the previous afternoon, Gina had stopped and stared. Now, just past midnight on a new day, we pulled alongside the heart on the gate that, earlier, Gina hadn't had the nerve to touch.

"When she called Mrs. Quinn, Gina asked for a place with two bedrooms and a kitchen. She was thinking an apartment. How'd she end up with a house?"

"There are no apartments in Booley," Liam said. "This will have to do."

I looked out the car window. "I think it will."

Gina already had exited and was standing at that gate much as she had hours before. Her conjuring Booley and then finding it— that was astounding enough. But a house, too? Should I say anything to Liam? Tell him this is not only Finola's place, but Gina's? I decided on nothing more than "Is there anything you need to show us?"

And he said, "Sure, with your accents, there's nothin' you haven't seen."

When I didn't laugh, mainly because I knew he was waiting for that, Liam said, "Now," and handed me the key, which dangled from a short length of rawhide looped through a plastic tag, the paper inside it reading O'FLYNN in even, thin penciled lettering that made all those vertical lines look like an evenly planted stand of pines. "There's another key beneath the gas can out back," he added, pulling up the emergency brake but leaving the engine idling. "I've been usin' the cottage as a guest house these few years, so there is a list of instructions for the heat and water and so on. It's posted on the notice board in the kitchen if you've any questions."

I got out and held the key high to Gina, like a first prize. In the glow of the torch Liam had dug for beneath the front seat, only to come out with a regular old flashlight, she gave me a look packed with all the unbelieving that was washing over me just then, and took it. She inserted the key in its high little hole at the right-hand side of the door, turned it left, then right, then left—

"Give it a kick." That from inside the car.

"Can you, uh—" Gina struggled. The door behind us slammed. Liam was next to her now, coaching, "Anticlockwise—yeh, yeh . . . yer in!"

As the door was pushed open, a wall of staleness advanced, along with a serious chill, and also the hint of a smell that was earthy in a good way. Liam found a flat switch on the wall and pressed it. The short skinny hall in front of us became illuminated. A Monty Hall house with a choice of three doors. To begin, Gina picked the one to the left, the ocean side.

"Light," Liam announced, pointing to another switch once we were inside a living room with the large front window to the left, a kitchen table to the right and a fireplace straight ahead. Three chairs were arranged in front of the stove that jutted from the hearth. One aluminum and kitchen table-ish, another red cloth and fat, and the last a sharp dark-stained Danishy thing that was sports-car-ish and low to the ground. A chrome floor lamp goose-necked over the top of the red chair, and a tall stack of books next to it made a table.

A skinny slatted door to the right of the fireplace led to a small square kitchen, where Liam pointed out a sink to the right and an adjacent counter bearing a row of lidded ceramic jars in a silvery raku glaze. Gas stove and dorm-size cube refrigerator to the left. Past the counter, a door to a bathroom. A cantaloupe-colored tub ringed on three sides by a collection of bath and body products that could lure you in to spend hours. Scrubbing gels, masks, shampoos, conditioners, bath oils. Next to the tub, the toilet loomed as enormous as all the others I'd encountered in this country, its giant flush handle looking more suited for use on a slot machine. Across from that, a white sink with peach-checked skirt below and an oval mirror above. Just by being a part of the cottage, the bathroom was a relief. "Toilet's through there, love" is how Jimmy Quinn had answered my question a few hours before, pointing to a hall that led to a door that led to a grassy little backyard. Was I supposed to go right there, a dog on the lawn? In a dark corner to the right, serious-sounding things were being whispered by a woman and then I heard a male voice urge her, "Shed your man." Next, a door opened on a little utility building about twenty feet in front of me. Two tipsy women emerged and gigglingly guided one another back to the bar, arguing, "Ah, ya didn't, ya wagon!" "I did!" "Dint!" "Did!" "Dint!" Through the open door from which they'd stumbled, I found a small room with all the basic plumbing necessities. Bathrooms don't need to be connected to buildings, I guess, but the one in Finola's cottage was, and I was grateful.

"It's a regular Taj Mahal" was Liam's introduction as we entered the first door across the hall from the living room, a pair of single beds stood waiting, small oldish-looking color prints of a mountain-edged lake above them, and between, a night table holding a stack of fashion magazines that, though probably dated, definitely were foreign and therefore would be good *craic*-y reading for a stormy night. Across from the beds, at the house's front wall, was another large window, this one covered by iron-thick curtains in a sixties-ish rust color.

"A room for each of ye," Liam said as he led us back out into the hallway and to the final door, which bore a small four-pointed straw wreath and opened to a double bed, and a built-in table and closet to the left of it. On the back wall, another window. I looked into the dark, past the very deep sill that held books, assorted small shells, a little rubber fish, coins, and a pocket-size photo album.

This would be Gina's room. Unless I had my bearings wrong, when she woke from this night's dreaming, her view would be of the ocean. In the black of the window's reflection, I saw her looking out from behind me. I turned. "Unpack," I told her. "This is yours."

"Room, cottage, the whole of Booley," Liam told her. "Yours."

He extended his hand again and we shook for the fiftieth time or so, then walked him to the gate.

"Another day for the memory book," he said as he started the car, then easily made use of the extra space offered by the beginning of the gated driveway, something he'd once done often, deftly turning the Volkswagen around and giving us the national wave, a little upward movement of the fingers with hand still attached to the wheel. Then he drove off, leaving us alone at what literally was the end of the earth.

We now saw nothing but black, heard only waves. As Liam's taillights disappeared to the left, I realized that what I'd always known as dark was but a runner-up. This here was pitch, anthracite, eyes closed behind a blindfold in a cellar closet. This here was dark.

"What do you think, Gina?"

"What do you think?"

"I think it's a little bit freaky. But it's also a wonderful sign. You're getting what you wanted. What you need."

She didn't answer. I repeated the mantra that I'd said daily in the world we'd left: "Just remember to let me know what I can do for you, OK?"

"I will."

Straight Line:

꧆

Path, Destiny, Choices

(State Your Wish Three Times)

On our first morning in Booley, I found myself in an unfamiliar and vault-quiet room, fully clothed, and immobilized by a couple of fifty-pound quilts. Then snapped the slide show of details: our arrival, the sea, Quinn's, the cottage. The jewelry guy. The reality that was this moment—my being here, our being here, in what once was known only as an imagined place. Past the foot of the bed, through a space where the two drapes should have met but did not. I saw a sky that had been stirred into a neutral gray. Raindrops the size of Good n Plentys blopped noisily against the glass. Beyond, the visible slit of sea was wearing countless lines of cro- cheted end-table doilies that paraded to the shore and disappeared into foam. This was far from travel ad weather, but the scene was still so wondrous that I actually gasped, shooting to my lungs a rush of sub-zeroish air. The bedroom, I quickly realized, was as chilly as had been the entire home of my childhood playmate Sandra, a perennially sniffling kid whose cheapo parents believed that requiring heat in the winter equaled weakness of character, so they kept their thermostat just high enough to prevent pipes from freezing. I burrowed beneath the covers, and there in the warm dark pressed the Indiglo feature on my new-for-the-trip blueberry-plastic waterproof Timex, of which Gina had a tangerine version. It was 11:03:14. She had to be up by now.

We'd bought a new wardrobe just for this trip. I should say that Gina had. For the two of us. Identicals of everything, if not in size or style, then in color or print. I'd worn matching clothes voluntarily only once before, and I was eleven at the time, and so in love for the summer with a girl first cousin who was the coolest, smartest, prettiest creature. So infatuated was I that my daily dress was a version of her ragged-edged denim cutoffs, halter top made from three red calico kerchiefs, huaraches, and hair in single braid that fell across her left shoulder. I loved Gina, too, but I was also long past the age at which matching fashions are considered cute by the outside world. However, few things were exciting my friend at the time we'd gone shopping, and if getting us identical wardrobes was going to put a smile on her face, I wasn't going to put up a fuss. At that point in the planning, after a pair of airline tickets and a place to stay for the entire summer, I guess a few hundred more bucks spent half on my behalf wasn't worth arguing over.

At the outlets up in Kittery and Freeport, Gina and I stocked up on garb befitting the most up-to-date hill walkers. See, that's what Gina thought we'd be doing a lot of the time: walking. When Google told me Booley was a walking place, and I told that to Gina, she said that would be perfect for another daily practice, and wanted to outfit us properly. We would be doing our walking in the new items we chose from the Patagonia outlet and L.L.Bean's warehouse store, the majority made of Polar-this and Therma-that, microfibered and spandexed, every inch magic in some special warming, cooling, stretching, water-repelling, perspiration-wicking way. And none of it cheap. The socks guaranteed not to smell no matter how many days in a row you kept them on had cost Gina a whopping $17. The long underwear boasting the same claim were $50 more. Per piece, yet. From there it was up, up, up, the top price award going to the $267 Women's Mountaintamer Strato-packs. It was important to Gina that we have backpacks rather than suit-cases. She wanted us to be able to pick up and leave instantly if the place or a situation was not to our liking—which is what she half-joked should be the rule for all of life—and said she couldn't imag-ine taking off down the road dragging the sky-blue hard-sided Samsonite she'd received as a high school graduation gift. The backpacks we ended up with were lightweight, rugged, and ready to rock, to quote the salesperson who pointed with giddy excitement to the fully adjustable suspension system and something called a hydration sleeve. The Stratopack weighed less than four pounds, provided 3,900 cubic inches of space, was designed to the unique proportions of a woman's back and waist—in short, just what we needed, the salesperson noted, for a journey of any importance.

From this real pack on this real first morning in Gina's real made-up cottage in her real made-up town, I pulled a real fleece turtleneck and real jeans, both with their real tags still on, and I released a real coffee-colored pair of nonpollutable socks from their real protective cardboard sleeve printed with a unisex ice climber hacking its way up the side of some ALP. I dressed quickly more due to the temperature than because of excitement, though I was thrilled in a way for nothing more than being where I was. I could have gotten up this morning to squint out my bedside window at the same-old blurry sight of the Pernells' swing set just past the bor-der of our neighboring properties, little hors d'oeuvrely-named Brie Pernell out there sometimes as early as 7:00 A.M. like she was punching a time clock and being paid to swing back and forth on her pressure-treated play structure, singing a nonstop peculiar hybrid from both her born-again Christian day school and contra-band Britney Spears music videos, first-grade falsettoing how Jesus loved her, and, then—oops—she did it again. Here I heard only the surf. It was nothing short of heaven.

I opened my bedroom door and looked down the hall to see that

Gina's still was closed. I didn't want to wake her, so I slowly turned the handle to the living room, slowly pushed it open, and, just as slowly, registered the scene: Gina. In full dress, coat and boots, pack at her side, standing and waiting for me. So she could say good-bye.

"But you just got here. I don't think we've been in this country an entire twenty-four hours. OK, well maybe twenty-four. But still. Could you at least give it forty-eight?"

"I know you're not going to understand this," Gina began correctly, "but I don't need to give it forty-eight more minutes. I need to go home. Today."

"Are you OK? Are you sick?"

"No, no—I just need to go home."

"You're tired. Did you sleep at all? Maybe that's what you need."

"What I need is to leave. I made a mistake. In coming here."

"How could it be a mistake?" I heard my voice rising, which it did because of the following truths, which I stated: "You needed something pleasant to think of, you made up a little town, you made up the road that goes through it and the river that runs next to it and the buildings along the one side of the road, you placed the town on the ocean, and just before the ocean you invented a beautiful little cottage. There's the town"—I pointed in the general direction of Booley—"there's the road"—same direction—"and the buildings and the river. There's the ocean"—opposite direction—"And here"—I waved toward the red door—"here is your cottage. Above. Here. How could this be a mistake? Everything you want—it's right here."

I told her to sit. She had been standing and waiting for who knew how long. But Gina refused. She folded her arms defensively as she corrected me rather sternly, considering all this had been her idea: "Everything I want is not here." The "not" was a sledgehammer on steel. "Norm is not here. Gennifer is not here." The first names got banged out for me as well. "The life I want back is not here."

I wanted to remind her of that desire for change, but I stayed silent and let the noise echo and settle until only the sea could be heard. I counted the waves. Picked a number. When fifteen in a row had crashed without Gina speaking, I decided to provide additional reasons for staying. But I stopped the process in mid first breath, run over by her. "You've been so wonderful to me. A straight year and a half you've been totally devoted. Who else would have done that?"

"Anybody else who was unemployed at the very same time."

"That's not true—you know it."

"I wanted to help you. I still do."

"I know that, but I think I have to start helping myself." She poked the rug with the still-pristine toe of her hiking boot. "I hardly slept last night once I gave into the truth that I'd made a mistake by coming here. Want to know what I dreamed of to calm myself last night? Not this place. I dreamed of home."

"But you need to get away from it all." I sounded like another travel ad.

Gina wasn't very loud as she said, "I realize I don't want to. I want to be back there, with it all. In my home. With my stuff. With Norm's stuff. With Gennifer's things. This isn't the right time for me to be doing this. Not when I still feel that pull. Being some- where else, so far away—I can't right now. I just can't."

He'd been talking about a job, but even so, Liam's suggestion came to me. "Three days," I asked of her. "Try it for three days."

"No," said Gina. "I'm leaving now."

When I was of pajama party age, I got invited to lots of them, but made it through the night at very few. Connie's house had an in-ground pool with slide, Emily-Amy's room contained a crate of her Avon-selling aunt's outdated samples, DeDe owned what seemed like a herd of ponies but in retrospect added up to only three. But that was three more than I owned, so I went to her sleep- over, and to Emily-Amy's so I could put on rouge, to Connie's so I could experience over and over those few seconds of free fall just before cannonballing into the deep end. But there came a point in all that fun when I'd seize up and get so homesick that I'd grab my hostess's bedside Princess phone and dial my mother so quickly that the lit dial would loosen. There was nowhere else I suddenly wanted to be, and I was frantic until safely behind the quickly slammed the door of the family car.

Gina had to be feeling somewhat the same way. Only she had nobody to retrieve her. She had only me, only me to accompany her back home.

"OK," I said because there was nothing else to say. Except a slightly less than enthusiastic "I'll get my stuff together. You have the schedule for the bus?"

"Yes. But no," Gina said. "I have the schedule, but your stuff's staying here. You're staying here."

"Oh yeah, while you go home."

"You're staying." She moved toward me, the various metal fastenings on her jacket and bags clinking with each of the few steps. "What you've done for me since, since everything—I can't imagine how I would have coped without you. I'll never be able to thank you properly." She got teary at this part, which affected me the same way, but in my case it was because what she said was exactly heartfelt and how many times does somebody tell you that your absence would be unimaginable? Nobody—not even Charlie St. Jean, to whom I have staple-gunned every one of my hopes for a lifelong love—has ever said such a thing to me.

"Whatever I did, I did because I wanted to be of help. Not to get some free trip." I was trying to make a point, but got muffled by the GORE-TEX of her shoulder, where my head had landed when she grabbed me for one of those awkward hug-then-push-back embraces.

"Especially not for a lousy free one-day trip. Which is why you're staying. Right here. For the summer. You've made all the arrangements to be away, there's nothing to worry about back at home. And I'll be fine. Think I might redecorate. Norm's sister—you've met, Shirl. The nice one? She says that's how she coped when she lost her husband. A home makeover. Maybe I'll paint every room a new color."

"I can paint . . ." I sounded pathetic.

Gina took from her pocket the navy bandana meant for hike sweat, and she wiped at her nose before saying, "I know you can paint. I know you can do anything. Don't take this the wrong way, but maybe, maybe I need to try to cope without you. You know, without your help. I'm not an invalid. I'm grieving, just like Dr. Hooten says I should be. But while I've been doing that, I've been relying on you too much."

"That's OK, I . . ."

"It's not."

"But I . . ."

"No."

"I could . . ."

"No, Sophie." I almost heard the mother voice again. Which told me she meant business. As she did when she said, "I have to do this alone now."

Silence. Then more waves.

She said, "The thought came to me when I first walked down to the ocean. I was alone there, and I realized alone is OK. That I should try that for a change. If I was to have come here for an answer, maybe that was it. Got transmitted a whole lot sooner than I thought it might, but I received it. And I think it's the truth. That I need to live my life alone for a change."

"I could leave—you could stay. This is your place."

"I'm going home, that's what I need to do," Gina said quickly, and she straightened the backpack straps grasping her shoulders. "Alone. I won't be pestering you with phone calls or letters or email. I really think I need to be incommunicado."

"You could do that here. Be incommunicado and all."

She reached for my right hand. Said softly, "Nothing personal, but I need to be out of touch with you."

That hurt. I winced. She had both my hands now and was saying, "I've come to rely on you too much."

"So I'll leave. You stay."

I heard a new sound. Closer now. Gina identified it: "My ride."

"You have a ride already?" I checked the Timex. It was not even noon. Seems like Gina already could cope fine solo. Without a telephone, and in a town without a taxi service, she had managed to arrange for someone to pick her up in the middle of nowhere.

"From Noel."

"You've been down to Noel's already?"

"He found me. Do you know he walks to the strand some mornings? Do you know they call it a strand? The beach? It's called 'the strand.'" She tried to make this sound fascinating and motioned to the water.

How would I know where Noel walked, what they called it? I'd only gotten here yesterday. Gina explained that very early in the morning she had been standing, saying her good-bye to that beach, that strand, thanking it for the instant wizardlike wisdom in this Oz-like place where the stuff of classic cinema had been made clear to her: There's no place like home. Walking past at that moment, Noel had greeted her, then lent her his huged ear, into which she had poured out the jagged details of her circumstances, and her sudden longing to hightail it. He'd protested a polite amount, was the first who suggested she give Booley a few more days, but her mind was made up so Noel offered to return with his car if she needed transportation to the airport. At noon he'd be here. "I assumed you'd be up by noon," Gina told me. "I would have woken you if you weren't."

"Thanks." I wasn't certain I believed her.

"You're upset with me."

"No," I lied. Then I asked, "What'd I do?"

She picked up her bag. "You did nothing. Nothing wrong. You just did too much. And every single day you've told me to let you know what you can do for me. Right now, all I want you to do for me is to wish me well."

"Well," I repeated, and "Hallo," Noel said at the door, and "OK," Gina was telling the pack as she slung it over her shoulder, and "You have a good time" is what she said to me, closely now, into my ear, as she hugged me again fast and tight and walked through the door and closed the gate, then crossed over to the wrong side of the front seat, which over here is the correct side if you are a passenger, and I stood in the doorway and Noel nodded while looking just off center at me because it was, he knew, an uncomfortable situation. He executed the same practiced turnaround that Liam had made maybe ten hours before, and in the time it takes you to put a hand to your mouth in an acting-class gesture of disbelief, they were gone. Gone from Gina's made-up cottage at the edge of Gina's made-up ocean down the road toward Gina's made-up town. But none of it was made up. It was all real. Including what had just happened, what was happening now. Gina. In Noel's truck. Going home. Me. Here. In Booley. Suddenly alone. Change definitely having arrived.

Compass:

Direction, All Possibility

(State Your Wish Three Times)

I'd had no plans when I'd arrived, and suddenly, if it's possible to have a list that goes into negative numbers, I now had fewer.

Or maybe I just couldn't count them correctly because I was so stunned by Gina's decision, which dropped to the ground in the dead silence that returned once Noel's truck rolled away. Rain fell as I sat on the wall to feel my feelings, as Dr. Hooten, would be suggesting were she there making a therapy house call. The main feeling I identified: obsolescence.

Since Trim-True, since Norm, since Gennifer, I'd become quite skilled at daily saving the day for Gina. I had grown up with only my dopey brother for a sibling, and though I'd had lots of close female friends over the years, upon meeting Gina, I felt I'd found the sister I'd always longed for. And only-child Gina had bonded to me with strength rivaling that of an infomercial glue. At holiday parties, Norm would get sappy from J&B and take me aside and thank me for filling a void in his wife's life. "Zosia," he'd start, using my Polish name, the extent of his bilingualism, which he never failed to haul out during occasions of high emotion. "Zosia, Zosia, Zosia. . . ." As for Gennifer, she would introduce her friends to me in this way: "She's like my mom's friend, but she's more like, like an aunt." I was nobody's real aunt, so such a comment, said with honesty, lobbed a couple of steel cables around a good portion of my heart and won Gennifer an extravagant height-of-fashion gift at each birthday and Christmas.

And when the friend with whom I exchanged corny "For you, Sister" greeting cards got her heart broken by life, I felt a sympathetic crack in my own. I had wanted to do whatever I could to help her. Now, here, a world away, my function had ceased. Ground to a halt. The plug yanked with the awarding of a lovely parting gift: a round-trip ticket to and an indefinite stay in a faraway land. A land I'd never had a particular desire to visit. A land where I'd been left.

I had a phone call to make. And a door to close behind me as I stepped back into the wet morning air, a mix of incensy turf smoke from Joe's chimney and a faint bacony smell from the little cluster of newish-looking B and Bs just ahead: A Star of the Sea, St. Botolph's, Woodbrooke Court, the curiously spelled Tír na nÓg. Exiting St. Botolph's were two pairs of obviously out-of-town men and women dressed in immaculate hooded windbreakers, pleated trousers, and untested sneakers, and heading toward the ocean. I wondered how I appeared to them. Were my new clothes and boots also screaming my identity as someone else just passing through? I couldn't tell what they were thinking, because "Looovely day!" was all the first man, with a pronunciation that gave him away as something like Scottish, called out as I approached. The second couple of people smiled, said nothing that could pinpoint for me their nationalities. After passing, they began chattering in something guttural that I only guessed to be German. The language of the man Finola O'Flynn had followed out of town. I wondered then how much German she had known to begin with—and how much English had he? Had she easily picked up just the basics of "Hi" and "How are you?" and "Where's the bathroom?" then purchased a dictionary or enrolled in a night class? How conversant were she and Udo at this point, two years later? Or was that even important in the grand

picture of what they shared? Were they living some dialogue-free
foreign movie in which overemoted looks and touches were all that
was needed to communicate? And if so, how long would that sort of
exchange be practical? If the rent is due, how many eyebrow
twitches does it take to say it's time for you to fork over your half?

I'd never had a foreigner for a boyfriend. A few guys from another
planet, maybe, but even them I basically could understand. For a
while, anyhow. Al Turcotte had only been from Pennsylvania, which
you could get to from my state by car in roughly six hours, not counting any rest area stops. In my early twenties, I lived in Cambridge, a
hundred minutes east of my hometown, spent a penniless fall and
winter there with this Brian guy from Martha's Vineyard who
couldn't shut up about being from an island, how island culture had
shaped him and formed him, and had in no way prepared him for life
on the mainland. He made it sound like he was from Bora-Bora
rather than some little lump of rock a sandwich-long ferry trip away.
Charlie St. Jean is from plain old Wisconsin, which is an easy three
hours away by plane if you don't mind riding in one of those twin-
propeller things for the quick leg from O'Hare to Milwaukee.
Charlie's claim to fame is hailing from West Allis, the same town as
two-time Olympic gold medal-winning speed skater Dan Jansen.
Charlie has an autographed hardcover copy of Dan's autobiography,
but it is not personalized in any way other than a sincere "Go for the
gold!" because the two had never met before the day Charlie spent an
hour and a quarter in line at a bookstore in a Milwaukee suburb. I
don't know what Dan sounds like, because I couldn't pick that up
from the book, and I can't remember his voice even though I must
have heard his speed-skating commentary at some point in all my
rabid Olympic broadcast viewing. But I've heard Charlie's voice, and
I've noted that his *A*'s are all drawn out flat like they've been run
through a pasta machine. All in all, though, it is still American
English, and I certainly know what he's saying when speaks.

Like how I understood "Don't worry—I'll visit you," which is exactly what he'd assured me just before I left with Gina. "We have an office in London. I can arrange to do some work there and get a flight over to you after that."

The previous afternoon, I had imagined walking with Charlie down this very road between the cottage and Booley. Hand in hand. Lovingly. Like an ad for a vacation website or erectile dysfunction pill. Already I had a collection of things I wanted to show him—the panorama from the bus stop, the little main drag and its handful of shops, Finola's fantastic cottage, and the view of the sea as admired from her bed. But there were no firm plans as to when we'd be together in any of those places. There never have been plans in the year and a half since we met. If he were explaining this, Charlie would have said "in the seventeen months" we'd been together. Because from the start, he's described the length of our relationship in the perplexing way some people give double digits to the age of toddlers.

"Junior's twenty-eight months," they say.

"We're seventeen months," Charlie says.

It probably comes from working with all those numbers, spending his days estimating life spans and concluding things like how one in seven thousand something people will miss those red WRONG WAY signs as they tragically head up the highway ramp that everybody else in the world is correctly, and quickly, driving down.

Charlie and I met when he was wandering through the new indoor farmer's market in downtown Springfield two winters ago. He was killing time before a lunch meeting that was part of his schedule on a business trip to the Northeast, and I was building a display in which would hop dozens of indigent bunnies being cared for by my friend Vernon's homeless bunny society. I was assembling an easel when Charlie stopped to read the sign it held. Because he had nothing else to do, but more because I was crouching and, according to him, he became mesmerized by the small slit of lower back flesh that was visible between the bottom of my shirt and the top of my jeans. He took in my nebulous tan stain of a birthmark that floated across my pre-political-correctness Crayola box flesh-tone skin, saw it as a scar, wondered what its story was, what my story was, and felt that I had endured some pain that he in the good fortune of his tragedy-free life could only wonder about. When our relationship progressed to the point where he was taking a lengthy tour of me one morning while Brie Pernell sang a syncopated "Kum ba ya" from her swing, he stopped at the mark and asked tenuously, "What happened here?" I don't know what came over me, but my expression changed to forlorn and I answered, "I don't like to talk about it," when the cause was only the process of being created, something that happens to everyone, really, and something I can't recall at all. I guess I didn't want to appear as white-bread next-door regular as I was, and in Charlie's question I saw an opportunity to create some mystery. "Suh-uhm-one's cr-ry-ing, Lah-ord," sang Brie that morning as I lay with and lied to Charlie St. Jean, who held me protectively and tenderly and said nothing, but the day after FTD'd a huge bouquet of dizzyingly fragrant ruby lilies, their Charlie-dictated card reading, "I will see to it that you never experience pain again."

I'd felt a side stitch of guilt while pouring into their water that little accompanying packet of life-lengthening crystals, but, really, I'd only told the man that I didn't want to talk about it. He had drawn his own conclusions, which I came to see was his habit in many less-pleasant experiences—taking lots of things for granted, including that he could visit all various sections of me, both birth-marked and flawless whenever in town. Once a month. The rare twice. I never knew when—there was only the call out of the blue and perky: "Whatcha doin'?" He assumed I'd say, "Nothing." Which, total truth be told, I did say, even if I was busy. But when he proposed coming to see my flesh while it was in Booley, I had answered, "Let me see how Gina's doing first," because, after all, she was the point of the whole thing, and Charlie agreed that time with her would be crucial, then added, "I'll get there sooner or later. How could I spend an entire three months without seeing you?"

"Fuck if I know."

That was Liam Keegan saying the last thing. Not to Charlie, but to somebody at the other end of the cell phone conversation he was holding in his front doorway. "I'll ring yiz when I do." Then he beeped the off button and stopped to take me in from head to toe before smiling widely, and asking, "Where ya off ta?"

"Una's. Unless you sell phone cards."

"Sorry no. How was the night?"

"I had a very good sleep." That much was true.

"Gina?"

I nodded, knowing only than that I didn't want to discuss her. The whole morning was still being processed. I answered, "Wonderful rest." I got ready to add, "Here's the key, I'm going home," but Liam was already talking.

"Yanks."

He raised his eyes the sky, which was maybe one shade brighter than when I woke.

"Yanks and rain. . . . Simultaneously. That's all a shop should ever pray for. It may become too wet for the cliffs, for the strand, for sittin' out with a point, for golfin' unless yer in a boat, like. It's never too wet for shoppin'. Yanks and rain—and a favorable rate of exchange. Best money's made when the Yanks have nothin' to do but spend, and are carryin' a strong dollar. And better yet, a rate of exchange that isn't difficult to figure. They'd prefer two to one, in their favor, but for us the opposite would be best. That said, one to one is best for them—they don't have to enter everythin' into a calculator, they don't get confused about the maths involved and walk out. They just see a pound (sorry, a euro—half a year with the new currency and still forgettin') as a dollar. So, ye'd want Yanks, ye'd want rain, ye'd want a fairly simple exchange rate—ye'd want it easy, like, for their brains. Fag?"

Liam held out a pack of Marlboros.

"No, thanks." It was jarring to hear a pejorative when being offered a cigarette. But as I'd learned in the pub the night before, everyone here seemed to use the word, just as everyone seemed to smoke, big gray clouds following most people like the puffs of dirt always tagging along after that filthy kid in the Peanuts cartoon. "I just want . . ."

"What ye'd want is the whatchacallem—usta be the Orientals, now they're the Asians—the Asians. Ye'd love to have the Asians now. Rare's the empty pocket on them. But not too many of those in Booley—and more's the pity. But it's only fact they've no connection to anythin' Irish—real or imagined. Yanks, now—so many of them actually do. Or imagine they do. And there's yer reason for the proliferation. Normal year, they're here in droves, plastic Paddies in search a the 'real' 'Oirland.' So many coaches pullin' in, we've actual traffic problems."

There was no handy segue. I interrupted with "I need a phone card." As I turned to leave for E. Dolan's, Liam touched my shoulder so notice him searching for something in his wallet. Fag firm between his lips, he checked the cards in his wallet as he continued, "Each of the Yanks has to stand for their picture at the ancestral home, at the church where their great-great-great-great-great granddad was baptized. They'll queue for ages at the Blarney Stone, or at a purpose-built castle for a meal served by a genuine wench. They must have a few pints, a few more pints by which time they've stopped complainin' that they're served warm. Then a chance t'sing 'Danny Boy' in front of a turf fire, buy a fuck-ugly jumper or a badge with their family crest, or t'spend their life savin's on a piece of Belleek or Waterford they'll foreverafter be too nervous to use. They're only here maybe two days and three nights—or is it three days and two nights?—yet without fail they go home weepin', can't bear t' leave the 'aul' sod.' It's like everybody in the states is Irish, and eventually, every one of ye discovers some long-lost 'roots.'

D'ya know even Muhammad Ali's people were from Cork?"

I shrugged. I didn't know that. As I didn't know why he was telling me. Or why I was standing there looking into the wallet of a stranger as he flipped through folded papers, currency, credit cards, guitar picks, and what was either a condom or one of those little sealed Wet-Naps served with your lobster bib. I spared him what I'd been told as a child, how at the beginning of the last century, the very second they amassed the fare, my grandparents had steamed straight from some long-forgotten poverty-stricken fold in the geography of southeastern Europe. Tore off for the U.S.A., figured out what their surname of Bia???y translated to in English, began going by that, and never once looked back. Not surprisingly, neither had any of the subsequent generations. There were no fond memories—real or imagined—passed down. Just scrap hints that the old country was no freedom, no food, no funds, no fun. Therefore, you'll find no rabid genealogists on any branch in my family tree, no one saving for study trips to the genealogy vaults in Salt Lake City, nobody burning the midnight computer screen tracing possible leads for long-lost relatives.

Liam was now deep into his lecture, telling me how since time began, there had always been some struggle on this soil. "Invasions, famine, emigration, poverty, drink. Fear a God put inta yer brain generations before yer brain's formed. Now drugs, racism, and acourse don't forget the age-old fine treatment a women. Divorce here's nearly as new as the euro. And if yer in need of an abortion, first you'll be needin' a ferry or a plane. This country never was perfect, and certainly isn't now. But to listen to the Yanks, this is heaven and where's the queue for a holiday home?"

His answer was a thunderclap.

"Ah, and the perfect climate!" Liam noted. Overhead, a flat smoky rain cloud the size of Australia was heading inland. In front of me, the man had found in his wallet what the print on it told me was a Swiftcall card. "Not a second's been used."

I was startled to hear myself ask "Who do you call?" and "My girl," he'd answered. And after wondering why so many men here referred to women as girls, I next wondered who his girl was. On that day, my best friend had just disconnected our friendship indefinitely, yet poking from the brambles of my anger and sadness was the need for the identity of the total stranger-girlfriend of this almost-a-total-stranger man.

Liam seemed unfazed by my nosiness. Probably due to being on a track—He had an impromptu lecture to conclude. "I hope ya don't think I'm complainin'. Without the Yanks, I doubt I'd be in business. Simple as that. It's just a bit daft to me—with them, everythin' here's so brilliant that the leavin' fairly crucifies 'em. Are they so unhappy t'be born in the U.S.A.?"

He sang the last part in a low Brucean tone.

"Thanks. For the card. As for the speech—"

"Not a speech, it's the requisite background necessary for anyone workin' in a tourist town."

"God, you're a pain. I don't work in a tourist town."

"'Cos you spend the day standin' in the road. In with ye."

"I can't go in. I have to make a phone call."

"Make it on the shop phone. No card necessary."

It was cordless, so I dialed Charlie's number as I walked across the street from the shop to the stone wall. From there I watched the river as the satellites and fiber optics and all those other things about which I am clueless combined to transmit my call only for a generic female voice to inform me that the party whom I was calling had a mailbox filled to overflowing.

I returned to the shop, returned the phone to its cradle, where it beeped its thanks and I spoke my thanks to Liam, who pointed to a chair near the fireplace and a mug of tea he'd poured. It wrote in steam that I needed to sit. Or at least that's what I thought happened, because there I was sitting, as I had been the evening before,

Liam again at his bead table, picking up a bowl half-filled with tropical-fish blue orbs and asking, "Sophie White, tell me. Why do the Irish Americans want to be here so badly, rather than in their America. Especially if there they have TV Land?"

I didn't know the answer, because I'd never known many Irish Americans. My own hometown was mostly fellow Poles, and French Canadians, evidenced by its two churches, which rarely are called by their proper names so much as they are "the Polish church" and "the French church," and their corresponding boneyards "the Polish cemetery" and "the French cemetery." One town over, there were enough Irish in the population to have long ago felt the need to build St. Mary's A.K.A. "the Irish church." Kids from that parish belonged to an Operation Friendship chapter that each summer swapped its teens for some from Ireland. The weekly paper ran photos of the visitors getting dragged on a tour of the Friendly Ice Cream plant, posing around the stone in the scruffy grass at the edge of the Kmart parking lot that marks the site of the long-gone inn where George Washington actually once was a lodger. I never met any of those kids. The few Irish Americans I knew personally were like anybody else, except maybe paler and sometimes with the expected red hair and freckles and apostrophes in their surnames, and several wore green clothing in the middle of March and that same month drank beer on the chilly front porches of relatives so fortunate as to own houses thirty minutes away, along the route of the Holyoke St. Patrick's Day Parade, second-largest such to-do in the country. I knew that Irish Americans took vacations, or figured they had to, because the rest of us Americans did at some point in the year. But I never really paid attention to where they went. Maybe the destination indeed had been Ireland. And maybe they did, for whatever reason, feel crucified when it was time to come home. But if they were unhappy in America, none of them had ever shared that with me. The only American I ever knew who craved this particular country was Italian. And she hadn't even lasted twenty-four hours here.

"Maybe Ali will come to Booley," Liam ventured. And spend all his pounds here and we can retire to Malta." He clapped. "Add to that initial list: Yanks, rain, exchange—easy exchange—and Ali, or any celebrity. Any such very wealthy sort."

"Liam, I don't want a job. I only wanted to use the phone."

"Right so. Now ye're familiar with the phone. Fer starters."

In the next hour, I was shown how to lock and unlock the shop door and unfold the sandwich board and where to place it at the edge of the road for maximum tourist luring. Liam reviewed how to switch on the lights, where to find the money box upstairs in the oven he never lit, how to register the credit card sales, accept traveler's checks, figure something called the value-added tax, fill out receipts, and wrap breakables for safe carrying or for mailing. He led me also the lidded metal bin where Pepsi's food supply was kept, and the exact measurement he was to receive twice daily along with the morning treat of a bone-shaped snack from a box printed with a picture of a flying dog. I watched it in a blur, hearing him but not hearing him interrupting the lesson every fifteen minutes or so to stand in the doorway and dial Charlie St. Jean again. Rain began and was starting to shoot sideways as I got disconnected for the fourth time. When I returned with jacket sopping, Liam said/asked, "Would you ever phone from in here."

I said quietly. "It's private."

"Go above, then." He pointed for a joke, but I didn't feel like laughing.

Upstairs, I shoved aside a cardboard box and sat on the arm of the chair by the door. Thought of Gina, dialed Charlie, got disconnected again. Walked downstairs. Liam was bagging a guide to Irish wildflowers for two Canadian women in anoraks who whined that six of their eight days in the country had been partially or totally wet.

"Sure you didn't come here for the weather," Liam remarked

with the right amount of bewilderment, and the pair twittered as you knew they would, all the way out the door.

"Important call," he determined when I sat down again.

"I need advice."

"I've plenty."

"No offense—I need the advice of my boyfriend."

"None taken. But you'll oblige me one bit?" He walked to my chair, took my arm and ushered me behind the bead table. "When I'm vexed, I find it's best to do some work." He pulled another chair over, effectively blocking me between himself and the window through which I'd seen him and his mess that first time, all of maybe twenty-four hours ago. "Like I said, a plonker could do it. Here you have yer stones, yer glass beads, yer wooden, yer metal, and yer . . . whatchacall 'em?"

"What are those?"

"Yer wee . . . yer wee symbols. See? Heart, peace sign, bird, that."

"Charms . . ."

Liam poured them into my hand. Tiny sculptures, microscopic details. "Finola loved 'em. So she overbought four years ago. And I've underused in the last two. Do what you like with 'em. Toss 'em, even. I've loads more in storage."

I touched the little fish, the little hat, the little world. "What wouldn't you love about these?"

"They don't sell. They sit in the shop because no one wants to be wearing a bicycle."

I poured the charms back into their bowl. Ran my fingers through their neighbors, aqua discs that were frosted. I almost expected them to feel chilly. "Sea glass . . ."

"Plastic," Liam corrected, before noting with pride, "but plastic from Italy."

He pushed back his work chair and pointed out the horizontal metal bar below the table, from which hung spools of cord and elastic and wire. "Everything you'll need for the stringin'. And here, against the wall, in this cabinet—findin's. That's what they call the little books and all. Clasps, like. Clip the wire after measurin' it along this." He unrotted a length along the yardstick nailed to the edge of the table and threaded a hook through one end, performing some expert twisting and crimping of the wire, then started stringing.

Back in my unsuccessful sleepover era, my 4-H club took a tour of the town newspaper. This was eons before computers and laser printers, and we watched the typesetters picking out the metal letters that would construct each word of each story. They moved deftly and almost without looking, reaching for the alphabet spread throughout a large and confusing grid of small boxes. Liam craft reminded me of those men, spelling out in beads the design he was aiming for, no planning, no use of the nearby template on which you could line beads on first to see how they looked together. He already knew to pick this one here in blue, then this with the lines across it, then two of these clear squares—one of them shaped like faint smiles—plus silver for the accent in between, and in no time at all, he was threading an eye to fit through the first hook he'd twisted on to begin, and he had created a necklace I definitely would grab were I a tourist coming through Booley and wanting a little something to remember this place by.

"I'll take it." I said instinctively, but Liam pulled it away from me and harmlessly sneered, "Make yer own."

So that's what I did for the remainder of the afternoon. Art therapy, Liam called it, for those awaiting the phone. Also training, he added considering I'd be working in Booley indefinitely.

I consented only after one attempt to make another call. And then asked to use the computer for a quick email. Liam said I'd have to go elsewhere. Turns out he was a rare bird in his technology-mad country: computerless and disinterested. After talking with Una and Noel I had the impression that even the most ancient stone fort here was wired and online. Surely the Finola O'Flynn shop had a website complete with online catalog and credit card ordering capabilities. The night before, Noel had mentioned that the screen of his Dell Dimension 2300 blinked with frequent emails bearing custom requests, and Una said she'd been thinking of getting a similar model for the back of the store, where she wanted to open Booley's first internet café.

But that wasn't in operation yet, and I happened to know that Noel was en route to the airport, so I stayed put, Liam seated to my right, staying close in case I had any questions about the work. I had plenty, a fact that had me occasionally apologizing, and Liam told me that was unnecessary, said he'd had the same ones himself when Finola first instructed him in all this.

"I don't know why," I said, "but I had the impression you had an art background."

He sniffed. "Right." And he explained that the now-abhorred technology had been his schooling, how he had come to Booley those dozen years ago as a refugee from all that. When so much of the youth of Ireland were leaving village and town for the country's cities and freshly constructed technology centers, Liam was headed in the other direction. He'd actually been a programmer in Dublin, and had made the most of the skills so sought after as the Celtic Tiger got its claws on track toward some semblance of a respected position in the world economy. For nine years he worked the kind of hours that have you guessing what day it is—if you have the energy left to make such an effort. Once in a while, the challenge was guessing the month. There was no major crisis that led Liam to Booley, no failure of project or relationship. All that happened was that he got exhausted. Sometimes that's enough. He emptied his flat, filled his gas tank, and headed into the west.

"As I saw it, I was livin' too far t' the east. Any farther, I'd be in England. That's nearly the same as bein' out in the rest of the world—and what good's that? I wanted t' slow down. I wanted t' drive as far as possible before running into the sea. I got on the Naas dual carriageway, kept going. Buildings grew scarce, roads quieter. Late that day here I was, over the bridge and into Booley. Finola was the first person I saw. She was standin' in the center of the road. The sign with her name had just been painted. She was gazin' at it, perfectly content. There was no one else about. I stopped the car at Una's and was watched by Una from her window for as long as I watched Finola, which is for as long as she stood there. Maybe yer expectin' me to recall Finola's clothin' or for me t' say that her hair was tied in the manner that a piece of it was blowin' back and catchin' gold from the sunset, that it was like a scene from the start of a film, all magical like, and would have me realizin' she would come to be important. But I wasn't noticin' details. It was more like how the woman was feelin' right then— you could fairly see it around her like rays in a holy picture. Her enthusiasm, her havin' somethin' she cared about in her future. I was envious, jealous, whatever, like—I wanted t' know that contentment. Finola walked back inside her shop, and that's when I noticed the sea beyond where she'd been standin'. Knew I was at the end of my journey."

I was attempting to construct a bracelet of yellow, green, yellow, green beads. Sea glass with a centerpiece of a charm in the shape of a suitcase. Yellow, green, yellow, green. Same time, I was wishing that Booley had been such a place for Gina.

"I've bored you."

I said no just as the bells began.

Following my second 6:00 P.M. ham sandwich in two days, Liam offered to drive me back to the cottage. But the rain had all but stopped so I wanted to walk.

If only to experience extra hours of daylight this particular latitude affordee a May night. "You can do me the favor of driving out if I get my phone call," I told him, and Liam answered that would be his pleasure. I thanked him as I zipped my coat and snapped the patented MoistureGuard TM placket. "Liam?"

"Yep."

"You can sleep tonight knowing you helped somebody today."

"While on the subject . . ."

"Of sleeping?"

"Of help. With . . . one more thing Finola left me."

"Cat? Dog? African violet?"

"Aul' fella." He motioned in the direction of the sea. "Up the road."

I'd been prepared to be Gina's caregiver, but she was a dear friend, and a woman, and not some stranger, who also was an old man. Would I be expected to scrub the hide of some frisky ninety-year-old?

"So what about him?"

"He needs stuff done."

"What stuff" I tensed for the list.

"Errands, like. He can get around the house and garden, but not as far as town. Shoppin', the post, both at Una's so nothin' too difficult. Finola began this when we were the only other bodies above and she felt yer man needed some help when he was recovering from a fall."

"That was awful nice of Finola."

Liam sniffed. "She was the mother a Mother Teresa around that guy. Even took him t' the cliffs on a regular basis—he's not fit t' go up there by himself, mind you. She'd walk with him there once a week or so, like a private guide. She said a man needs t' see his land. Without her, he wouldn't have seen much more than his back garden. I do it when there's no one out there t' pin this on. But with you at the cottage, it'll save me some time. You pass his farm on yer way. Call over. If he needs anythin', he'll have a list. I'll ring, let him know ye'll be by. It's clearin'. He might want a walk."

I took a step forward. I wanted to tell Liam he was the height of presumption. But his was the house that held my belongings and his was the number Charlie would be calling back. And I needed to talk with Charlie. So I only said, "A walk. OK."

When the Chicopee Falls Uniroyal tire plant closed in the early eighties and my father found himself unemployed after thirty-seven years, he got a job cutting the grass and painting vacant apartments and doing other needed tasks as the maintenance man at our town's housing-for-the-elderly complex. More than a few major holiday dinners were interrupted by the phone ringing, one of the tenants calling to say, "I hate to bother you on a day like today, but I'm having an electrical emergency." My father would push his chair from the table of turkey and all those greatly anticipated fixings and he would drive the thirty-five minutes to find that the crisis was nothing more than a closet light bulb that had been partially unscrewed so as to appear burnt out. "I'm so sorry to have disturbed you on a holiday," the tenant, usually an woman, would continue, "but while you're here, would you like something to eat?"

My father was a nice guy. He would sit, he'd eat a little of the holiday meal that had been prepared for one and hopefully two. He'd listen. He wouldn't talk because he knew well he was not there for that. He was there to be there. These people needed somebody. It was a holiday and they were alone, and if it took a bit of harmless deceit to snag some company, that was no sin. It was a basic soul need. And my father was filling it. As had Finola, as I now would. For one time. One short time. Because I am not my generous and selfless father. Today, I was truly concerned about nobody but my own deserted self.

"I'll see ye in the mornin' so," Liam said as I was closing the door behind me.

"One way or another," I answered. Because there was every chance that his next glimpse of me would be as I zipped past in Noel's truck, airport bound.

Lightning Bolt:

~~&~~

Ideas, Inspiration, Revelations

(State Your Wish Three Times)

Joe Cronin's house was hard to miss, being the only other structure that far out from town. Maybe half a mile before Finola's, two stories, rectangular and made of the cement like the cottage and with the same tiled roof, but with the exterior painted a dirty white. A chimney at the left end of the roof puffed smoke through the rain that now was more of an almost invisible mist, the type that in beauty magazines pumps from the Alpine water dispenser you are supposed to spray onto your face as part of the makeup process. I lifted my face to this free application as I made the left to Joe's.

A low cement wall edged his property, too, with access provided by a gate containing the centerpiece of a spiral shape somebody had recently painted a shiny black. I raised the latch and pushed the hinges screeched an ancient sort of alarm. I continued up the patchy cement walk that led through a very short front yard sprinkled with short delicate daisylike flowers and up to a small boxy addition at front and center that served as a sort of mudroom and vestibule. The door was open. Inside, a raggy tweed coat hung on the wall hook. A dirty cap over that. On the floor below these was a pair of high rubber boots of the type that Lady Diana looked so fashionable in back when she was taking those first shy country walks with Charles that you wished she had never said yes to. A couple of lumpy white bags of what the printing told me was Polish coal rested in the far corner. A shovel. A coil of rope. I tapped on the inside door. Waited. Did so again. Used that little seven-beat cliché of a definite knock, and it worked. The latch lifted, and then there was a slim opening, and then a little pink face squinting through it, at me.

He wasn't ninety, as I'd imagined. Eighty-eight at the most. And if he was frisky, he wasn't displaying that tendency just at this moment. He was a few inches shorter than I am, maybe five-five. Thick white hair that started at a Dracula-like widow's peak was swept back to meet his shirt collar, and kept in place with some stiff-looking yellowy goo. He used thumb and pointer to hold on to the chicken sag of skin just under his chin as he regarded me through the crack in the door, which was widening just a bit.

I said, "Hi. I'm Sophie. White. Sophie White. Liam's new friend. Liam from the store. He was supposed to tell you I would be stopping by . . ."

A light went on somewhere in the closet of Joe's brain. You could see the illumination glowing right through the mottled skin of his skull.

"Ah. Liam!" Joe nodded pleasantly at the recognition.

"I'm here because I'm staying at Finola's cottage."

"Ah. Finola!" More nods, these with a brightness. "Finola!" Same dipping of the head, same motion, like the drinking bird statue that bobbed when I dipped the beak into a glass of water on my mother's kitchen windowsill so long ago.

"I wanted to know, do you, um, do you need anything?"

"Anything. . . ." He said it "Annythin'." Wrinkled his face in thought. Continued to pull at his neck. Looked down for the answer. I looked there, too. For what, I don't know. The floor of his house was cement like the one at the cottage and was covered along its center with a trail of old rugs in no particular color scheme that led to the faintly glowing open fireplace.

I prompted: "Food or something?"

Joe made his decision. "Today? Ah, no. No food."

"OK. Well, then . . ."

"Have ye seen the cliffs?"

"No, I sort of just got here."

"You're here to study?"

"Uh, no. Vacation. But, really, I'm leaving tomorrow. I think."

"Tomorrow?"

I nodded, standing there where I'd just made up my mind. Joe widened the opening further, leaned close, the cataract clouds suddenly parting from his Pyrex mixing bowl eyes as he whispered: "Ye cannot leave without having seen the cliffs. And the holy well."

"Holy well."

"Holy well," he said through his grin.

I said, "Wow, thanks, how nice of you, ah, OK, great." Because I wasn't sure if he was kidding. But if I pushed aside my suspicion that a joke was about to be played on a clueless foreigner, I could nearly quite almost buy that Joe was serious. Nearly could feel that he was giving me a gift by imparting the location of a hole in the ground. And he probably did feel that way.

"I think I read about this online. The well . . ."

He nodded, reached for his coat, and we were off. Through his back garden, where socks of gray wool and one pair of long underwear gray due to age were draped across a bush on an impromptu laundry day. Joe walked ahead of me with hands linked behind his back as if cuffed by police. I followed, except when he was opening the gates for me and closing them behind us as the metal signs wired to them requested. He was dressed in shabby chic, suitable for one of those second-page gatefold Sunday *New York Times Magazine* ads for unfathomably expensive clothing that looks like it was found in the back of your dead uncle's closet: worn tweed cap, tweed jacket over thick holey sweater, some kind of baggy canvassy pants, wellingtons. The few old people I'd so far seen in Booley reminded me of the ones back home, those you'd never ever catch wearing jeans or sweat suits, sneakers or shorts because they had no such things in their wardrobes. And as did some of those old people I knew back home, Joe moved more quickly than I was expecting, but his lopsided gait did turn the trip into some measure of an effort. Our walk was not merely a pleasant process that got us from point A to point B. Rather it took on the feel of a procession. Somehow holy and meaningful beyond what you noticed at the time. Quiet and slow up one field, through a wide gate that creaked a low greeting as you pushed it open, then up to another field, and another gate, another field, at this point the sea nowhere in sight, just the rising hump of another span of green, green of Key lime, though you didn't concentrate on the exact shades on the vista as much as you did on the ground at your feet, where rain-flattened hubcap-sized deposits of manure added an agility challenge to the aerobic workout. Joe carried a cane, which he called a stick and which he used only in places of unsure footing, and turned it into a sort of schoolroom pointer for the facts he once in a while chose to note. Like the oval stones that so long ago had been set into a her-ringbone pattern in the sides of the earthen walls separating this field from that one, they were the work of his youth. He and his father had gathered them from the beach when harvesting seaweed they'd used as fertilizer and that he dried to chew in the same man-ner you would enjoy a stick of Juicy Fruit.

"Dulse," he said, naming it, and pointing the cane in the direc-tion of its oceany origin, and then waved out toward the mountain, where a great fire would be lit when the summer solstice rolled around. He directed my eye to the birds that soared past, and named for me the razorbills, kittiwakes, the guillemots and the storm petrels. Plants, too—the yellow bird's-foot trefoil, pink sea bindweed, the kidney vetch woven between. He pointed the stick downhill to the school he attended as a child, when his route was a winding boreen that since has been incorporated into that popular coastal walking trail. And, at the end of the fifth or so field, he swept his cane along the drastic drop to the sea, these were his cliffs, and there he ended the lessons.

Joe set the stick on the top of the final stone-studded earthen wall alive with tufts of grass and more of those tiny daisyish things. He folded his arms across his chest and leaned to gaze at the sea throwing itself against iceberg-shaped black rocks a dizzying six hundred feet below. To the north, a trio of islands rose gently like arcing whale backs, and the necklace of the coast disappeared into mist. Joe set his focus in that direction. He soaked in the metronome bash of surf against rock wall, the gift of the warm air, and (I am guessing here, because who knows if Joe indeed does such things) psychically joining the birds as they spread wings to hitch-hike on the strongest wind currents. He was savoring his favorite place on the earth of which he estimated he'd only seen about ten square miles. As he noted quickly, that was more than enough to suit him.

I walked far enough away to give him his privacy, to the left— the south—where a ledge grew from the drop below and birds that appeared to be penguiny puffin sort of creatures complained and fought for space on the scant horizontal surface. I leaned, too, and watched, too. The water, the wave crests. The sea foam, the cliff sides. All those things that in a tacky resort town would be used as names for motels. Then Joe was beside me, telling me how Finola had given this place back to him.

On a similarly post-rain evening six years before, as he left for his cliffs, Joe slipped and fell just beyond the gate that led from his back garden. He lay there in the rain and the muck for a day and a half before Finola found him in her morning hike. She began making morning check-ins after Joe returned from the hospital, a first-ever experience with modern health care that found nothing to be broken only because they have yet to invent a machine for gauging the condition of the spirit. Joe long had known that he was very old, but he'd always been fit, healthy, moving along on the gear teeth of an unbroken routine that never left him wondering what to do next as he progressed from breakfast to cliffs to garden to lunch to walk to town to tea to nap to walk to the pub to walk home. The fall's impact on his spirit would have been no greater had he tumbled off the end of his land and into the sea. For the first time, he truly felt helpless. And because of that, doomed.

After being released from the hospital and deposited back at home by the Quinns, Joe rested by the fire, awaiting the certain arrival of Death. He knew it would, its knock sounded later that morning. He swallowed nothing and blessed himself and kissed the crucifix on his mother's rosary, the one he soon would hold between folded hands in his coffin, then bravely called out, "Enter." Because Joe was only so brave, he shut his eyes tightly at the sound of the slow footsteps that stopped somewhere near the table. Death is lightfooted, was Joe's thought. And smells of tangerines.

"Time t' go," said a voice.

Death was also soft-spoken. And—who would have guessed?—female.

Another step closer, and the sound of his name: "Joe."

It knew him. Of course it did.

"What?" Eyes still shut.

"Up, now."

Joe didn't want to go. There was no feeling of the preached-about blessed surrender in the last moments of life are said to hold. He heard no voices of those who'd gone before him. Saw on the inside of his eyelids no saints and angels flying toward him, no blessed long-awaited sight of his mammy and daddy, no long-awaited reunion with the stillborn brother he'd never gotten the opportunity to chase around the pitch. Joe saw none of what he'd always thought he'd be seeing at this moment. Heard only the voice of Death, who was asking, "Will I put the kettle on?"

Death fancied tea. Maybe the afterlife wouldn't be so bad after all. Joe opened his eyes to a loose squint. Saw a form standing at his cooker. It turned. Smiled. "You're looking grand. Much better than when I last saw ya."

It was the girl.

From down the road.

The one he'd been told had found him. Now here to make the tea, and, she explained, to take him for the daily stretch of the legs that were doctor's orders.

He reached up. Pulled at his neck for a few moments. The birds continued making their racket, pecking at food grasped between claws, painting the rocks with their droppings. An entire bird universe teeming.

"I'm not dyin'." He said this quietly, to me, now, in his recounting. "I said to meself: 'I'm not dyin'.' I saw herself there and I knew that. Gohl Finola, she did that. Got me up, out-of-doors. Without her, I might be sittin' below yet. Waitin'."

I let the story sink in. Said, "Wow," which was my true reaction. Joe said, "Now." Then; "To the well."

He waved the stick in the direction of one of the few trees shooting up from the otherwise grass landscape maybe a quarter mile away, and that's where we went.

I wanted to tell Joe that back home, wells are cutesy little old-fashioned things topped by a small decorative house of sort. The guy in the lipstick-red Colonial down the street has one in his front yard and a few Christmases ago stationed a life-size illuminated plastic Santa inside. The wells I know are that, or they're nothing more than modern pipes sticking in the ground in the front yards of new construction, the tip of the iceberg of several hundred more feet of pipe descending to an underground river, the visible few feet to be topped sometime in the future by a rounded cover of molded plastic rocks just the perfect size to disguise them. A well from my world was not what Joe brought me to. His was merely a circle of water the size of a manhole cover, naturally edged with a few flagstones of the type you'd find on a backyard patio.

There was that plain fact, and then there was all the decoration. On one flat-topped stone was a now-collectible five-pence coin with its profile of the ready-to-charge bull, a few inches of a gold chain, a fangish tooth that maybe was human or maybe was not, and a few smooth pebbles. The tree maybe three yards away, more a tough shrubby thing than a tall shade giver, also wore all sorts of dross. Rosaries, small crosses, holy medals, more coins, a picture of a uniformed male athlete, a knotted shoelace, and a pacifier hung from branches. Some of the items had been stuck into bark, put there so long ago that the tree had grown around them, encompassed hungrily the key, the metal picture frame, the horseshoe, the bone. Plastic bags sealed with tape and hanging by lengths of yarn or string contained folded papers with ink blurring despite the protection. Through the transparent wall of a misted Baggie, I could read the faded words *please* and *trouble* and *son* and *anything* and *please* again and *please* again bleeding in purple ink.

"What's all this stuff?" I asked myself in a whisper, in case the site of a well called for churchy behavior.

"Petitions. For blessins. Answers. Bit a luck. But mostly for the blessin' of a return."

Joe had startled me again. For a feeble type, he had the great ability to pop from nowhere.

"From God, or what?"

"This is the well of Saint Faicneam. He's a great one for the lost."

"Like Saint—I forgot his name. . . . My grandmother had a saint she prayed to when she couldn't find her purse or keys or lottery tickets . . ."

"Antny."

"Right. Saint Anthony."

"Well, Faicneam here, he'd be more of an Antny for tings that aren't purses."

"Wallets then?"

"No. I mean things not physical. The invisible. Health. Love. Hope. All that. If you ever had any of that, and lost it, you'd come up here."

So that explained all the signs of visitors having been there, the pilgrimages evidenced by the glove, the towel, the pen, the yarn skein, the nails, the pale gray Nokia 3330 nestled in its soft leather case complete with handy pocket/belt clip and carrying strap. A phone! I pressed the on switch and the screen announced IRL DIGI-FONE. The mobile worked. Who would leave a phone in a field? Maybe somebody to whom a granted wish meant more than the price of a piece of electronics. If you don't count all those happy Buddhist types like the ones who last summer came to the art museum in Springfield and made such a beautiful painting using only colored dust and then after a week's displaying went and dumped it into the river to show how impermanent things are so smoke 'em while you got 'em, who in this world is not searching for something? In need of something? All these signs of somebody's presence, somebody's longing. And how many more had come here to leave behind only invisible pleas?

I a plastic Pokemon key chain that dangled from a branch next to a faded bow made of oval pink buttons sewn to a once-pinker strip of cloth.

"So if I wanted to regain something—say, my health, or somebody I wanted to see again—I'd come here?"

"Yes. And you might bring somethin' of yours and leave it. When I was a lad, there was nothing but religious items, statues of saints and the like, and, acourse, the clooties."

I nodded, like I knew what clooties were.

"Them." Joe knew I didn't and motioned to the pieces of cloth tied to the branches. Some as new as last week's run to the mall, others so old they were little more than rotted threads. "Touch the cloth to the location of your pain, your sickness, your sin, your sadness, tie it to the tree, the tree takes it on. Some say as the cloth decays, your problem does as well."

"And you've done this."

"I have, yeah."

"With success?"

He raised his right hand. "He's yet to fail."

"Gina would love this." I hadn't meant to say this aloud.

"Who's that now?"

"A friend. Who's lost things. People."

"Ah, yes."

I looked at the possessions before me. So many people desperate for something, somebody. Coming to this place because, as had been done for me, somebody had shown them the way.

I thought about Gina's losses. How she could stand to have some hope for a better day. How Booley had represented that for her. And as bright as the enormous finally setting sun was the huge cartoon light bulb shining above my head that moment at the Holy Well of St. Faicneam. Now maybe the sight of all those trinkets and keepsakes left by the believers would have touched you in some way that renewed your faith or strengthened the faith you already possessed or maybe made you think outside yourself for the very first time in your existence. While I did think the well and the tree were fascinating, what really hit me was that, until proven the power, this place was basically a myth, and that lots of people had bought the myth, and if they would buy this myth, why wouldn't they buy others? Why wouldn't they buy Liam's?

So as it was because of Liam Keegan that in one day I'd become a maker of beaded jewelry, it was because of Joe Cronin that in on that very night I'd become something else. Some might call it a liar. But some, especially some here in this story-appreciating part of the world, would see it as a good thing. As for what I think, well, I'm just good at marketing. I've spent thousands of hours working in retail. I know what attracts people to merchandise, what gets them to put their hand to their money clips or to those little oval rubber purses that you squeeze from the sides until they open like a mouth containing your spare change. I know a lot about the psychology of consumerism and have a very good idea of what sells and what doesn't. I looked at the water-filled little hole in the ground and something clicked. I didn't need to be hit over the head to see a moneymaker as clearly as I could see the soggy half-empty pack of Silk Cut cigarettes placed straight against the tree root like it was a priceless offering, rather than litter. And after I escorted Joe back home, I took the right back to town.

The door to the shop was unlocked. Up the stairs, Liam's apartment was lit, and the radio played some sort of sporting match, loud pokes of commentary against rolling cheers. I switched on the light and sat at the bead table and, using nothing more ancient than a black Biro and my best penmanship, I created mythology. On the little tags bearing the Finola O'Flynn name, I added free interpretations of the meanings of the spiral, the Arrow, the concentric circles, the flower, the yin, the yang, the suitcase, whatever symbol charms hanging from the bracelets. I'd made that afternoon. Faith, Hope, Love, Luck, Respect, Dignity, Peace, Rest, Energy, Friendship—all the gifts it would help to have—I doled liberally.

When you're simply inventing, you can be extremely generous. And I was giving a gift of sorts. To Liam, A little marketing device that might move some of this product a bit more swiftly, and were it successful, a thank-you gift for his kindness. Same time, the wearer might gain, too. Might feel that a longed-for quality or emotion or experience was that much closer now that a symbol for it was elasticized to the wrist. "State Your Wish Three Times" was the final line it just came to me to add. Maybe it was from Liam's suggestion to try the shop for three days, or from Joe's pointing out the shamrock carpet in his back garden, bending slowly down and slowly back up to present me a stem and a trio of perfect leaves. I didn't dwell on the inspiration. Only the fact that the number seemed to bear an extra sprinkling of magical possibility.

Rain I hadn't seen coming arrived in great waves that flew against the window glass next to the bead table as I made up my words, lightning flashed as if I were a sorceress summoning my powers. Were this a film, the tags would be glowing. The end of the Biro would shoot little electric zigzags of energy. In turn, soft rays of silver and gold would hum radiation-like from the bracelets I'd titled. And the next day, a constant line of shoppers would be drawn to the those bearing the yin and yang, the fish, the knot, the moon, and they would read the tags and enthuse to companions how this sounds just like what your mother needs, or, God, this would be perfect for Clodagh, for Ma, for Aunty Liz, for me, because did you know this stands for Hope, I didn't know this here meant Peace, Help, Healing, I'll have to get this one, get another, would you have another, would you take traveler's checks, debit cards, pounds leftover from our last trip, when we didn't find a souvenir that was anything close to this unique?

This wasn't a film. So there were none of the above-mentioned special effects, and I could only imagine the reactions. Right now there was just me, waiting for a call, waiting out the rain, waiting.

Eye:

Awake, Aware

(State Your Wish Three Times)

"**S**tay."

That was the advice I got from Charlie St. Jean.

It wasn't as dog-obedience-school-command as it looks there. The word was more like sung, as if it were the most natural answer and why had it even crossed my mind that I might need to consult with him on this? The *s* and the *t* were high and the *a* and the *y* were lower. "ST-ay!"

It was noon for me, seven in the morning for Charlie, when Liam's mobile rang in the middle of my gift-wrapping a scarf for a customer and, as I did, learning a new word—*cellotape*—for what stuck the paper together. I was beat. I'd spent too much of the previous night listening for Liam's phone-bearing car, but any noise was wind or some other natural seaside sound that wasn't a vehicle delivering a telephone so I could return the phone call and hear what I hoped Charlie would say: that if I had no obligations here any longer, I should get on the next plane and he would free himself up so we could start our real estate hunt. There'd been no car, though, no phone, no Tony the Tiger "Grrrreat!" in response to the news that I was now free and, unfettered, could meet him anywhere he'd like.

"Stay!" is what Charlie St. Jean told me at noon on the day after Gina had left. Said that not once but a bunch of times—however many you could fit in the maybe ten seconds it took me to carry Liam's mobile over to the wall across the street from the shop I'd returned to first thing this morning like I didn't have anywhere else to go. Charlie had gotten the gist of my situation from the messages, and he'd cooed appropriately when I told him I was confused, didn't know what to do, felt stunned, dropped into this place by the woman who'd dreamed it, by the woman who wanted to be out of touch, who was now back home selecting paint swatches.

I told Charlie St. Jean about the town. "Perfect!" he raved, and gave a very loud "Outstanding!" when I described the cottage. Then he said, "Certainly I'd love to see you sooner than later, babe, but even if you were in the same country I don't know if that would happen. So if ever there was going to be a time for you to be away in a cool place, this would be it. I'll finish up this project, I'll get over there in a month or so, and then maybe you can fly back with me. Then we'll find ourselves a home."

As always, I cringed at the "babe," but that got overridden by Charlie St. Jean's use of the word *home* rather than *house*. Not that we'd end up with a house—we'd most likely buy a condominium, he said, because with his demanding travel schedule he wouldn't be around often enough for the maintenance a house required and all that shouldn't fall to me. A condo would be fine with me. A Wheaties box can be a home, if it's where you feel loved and content.

"Stay!" Charlie St. Jean broadcast again. "Enjoy a vacation! Gina's had it tough, but it hasn't been easy for you, either. Everything you've done for her. I wouldn't take it personally. She needs her space. So do you. Everybody does."

To him, it was that simple. If space is needed, give the space. Problem solved. Charlie St. Jean excused himself to put his hand over the phone and there was a moment of muffled conversation before he returned to tell me he had to run. Then he downshifted to an affectionate whisper, and from thick in some crowded office setting he dared to growl, "Remember that I love you. From the bottom of my . . ." before the line chopped off Charlie St. Jean, and whichever part of his anatomy from which his passion for me sprang.

"Success?"

Liam asked this when I returned to the shop.

"Success."

"Advice received?"

"I guess . . ." I now had Charlie's input. That I'd be crazy to leave right now, to run back for what?

"Pull yer socks up, now."

I looked down at my boots.

"Expression: Get busy." He motioned to my empty chair. I placed the phone back in the charger and returned to the seat I'd occupied for the second day, behind the bead table, trapped in the corner by Liam, who'd kept the second chair there so he could get his work done and also to be able to instruct should I experience any jewelry construction emergencies. During my morning of waiting for the phone call, in the store where I did not work, I'd figured out that my favorite pieces to make we are the easiest—stringing beads on elastic, for a bracelet that needs no hook-and-eye closure. Because there wasn't much room behind the table, Liam sat very close to me, Pepsi often tucked beneath us, legs twitching as he dreamed of his next tour through town. I could smell the dog's canine-ness, and the man's tangerine shower gel. I could hear the ticking of the man's watch, and the little Morse code taps he made with his tongue when he was deep in a decision about color or what to do next in his day or would it be time for another fag. I could see way into the depths of his left ear, the lobe of which bore a small shiny white-silver ring and a plot of fine white down. If the angle was right, I could nearly see his wiseass brain. The brain that I was finding thought a little like mine.

I say that because first thing after my arrival this morning, after giving me a solemn "No message, sorry," he pointed to the dish of bracelets with the embellished tags I'd worked on during the storm and he said, "The fairies were through during the night."

"Were they?"

"Mighty stuff." Liam looked pleased. "The work and the 'information.'"

"You don't mind? That I was playing around with—I don't know—your history? Culture?"

"Goin' to all this effort on somethin' no one wants—that, I would find offensive. D'ya know I've sold three already?"

I found that hard to believe, but only because I'd seen not a soul as I'd walked into town.

"I'd say yer yer a retail genius." Liam scanned a tag on which I'd written that the wavy lines on this bracelet's charm translate to energy, the ability to maintain a course, or to start one that you might think is beyond your ability. He picked up another, a circle of grayish green beads interrupted by the silver disc on which mountains had been etched, and he read my translation: " 'A symbol of abundance that lies ahead, keep your eyes on the horizon for better days.' You're a genius and an optimist."

"I doubt they'd sell if they tell you it's time to buy a tombstone."

"Yer right there. But when did you do this?"

"After walking with Joe. He brought me up to a well."

"Faicneam's. He's mad for that well."

"And he's not alone. All that junk up there . . ."

Liam whispered, "Don't go callin' it junk." A cultural nerve now had been struck.

"You believe in it?"

"I'll believe in anything—if I've had the correct number of points."

"How about when you're sober?"

"When I'm sober, I hear enough stories. Una's man, Ger, was in Ardmore years back. There's a well there near this massive stone on which Saint Declan traveled to Ireland, if ye can imagine floatin' anywhere on a stone. Nevertheless, on Saint Declan's Day, you're to crawl beneath the stone and it'll heal your back. Ger, you can't get him to believe in gravity. So it was on a lark that he crawled beneath—and was cured. Now he's whatchacallit—sold—on the concept of the holy well."

From the bookshelves, Liam zeroed in on a fat paperback. Flipped to a portion toward the back of the *West of Ireland Myths and Legends*. A chapter dealt with the idea of the holy well, which dates back to pre-Celtic Ireland, when the country was seen as a place where power literally welled up from the earth. He read the names of some still visited: Father Moore's Well. Tooth Well. Well of the Wethers. St. Fechin's, St. Molua's, St. Erc's, St. Molaisse's.

Liam told me that devotees visited the well on specific days of the year or whenever the site's touted power was most in need. The faithful—or maybe simply the hopeful—left the coins, rosaries, nails, the general flotsam I'd seen on my visit to St. Faicneam's. Many touched strips of cloth to an afflicted part of the body, then tied the cloth to the branch of a sacred tree or bush that the book said is part of the rock, tree, and water combination found at many wells.

"There's that combination where Joe brought ye," Liam noted, and pointed to pages of other examples, ameteurish black-and-white snapshots that smacked of a parody. Some of the wells were no more than a puddle. Others were fancier, starring life-size saint statues protected from the elements—and perhaps from pilgrims—by glass cases resembling telephone booths. Never alone, the wells kept company with abandoned orthopedic devices, stuffed toys, photographs, and Sacred Heart statue after Sacred Heart statue.

"Wells can be holes in the ground with no sign that Christianity ever existed," Liam said. "Then there's the likes of the Mam's favorite, St. Brigid's in Liscannor. The water flows from another well on a hillock, down through a hole inside the hill, into a stone cistern. To get to the cistern there's a hall, like, a passageway in a cave, the walls absolutely plastered with all manner of religious medals, rosaries, sticks and crutches left behind by the cured, and holy cards and photographs of the dead who weren't so lucky as t' be cured. A ledge along the hall that I suppose was meant for sittin' when they carved it out, it's crowded with Brigid crosses, scores of crucifixes, statues choked by layers of rosaries. Fore she got Christianized into St. Brigid, ya know, yer wan got her start as the mother goddess Brigid, which is why the women love her. A woman goddess for women. Also, Brigid is connected t' the dairy— ye'll see a paintin' of her in that hall, Brigid and her cows. Cows everywhere. She's the one to call upon fer dairy-related concerns."

Whatever the well, the advertised power or saint, what it represented was faith, which filtered down to hope. I was in a country in which belief was nearly visible fuel, sustenance, a wall to lean against when nothing else was left standing. I got a heart jab that made me wish Gina had stayed.

"Attracta, Noel's granny, Godresther," Liam was continuing, "she came into the world only after her mam left a stone at St. Fechin's, on Omey Island. It's one a them wells to which women bring egg-shaped stones with the hope a becomin' pregnant. The island is said to be ages old, some of the earliest women from the first invasion of this country populated it. They were related to Noah, but weren't allowed on t' the ark for whatever reason. They found their way to Omey, along with three men, who soon were killed from too much sex. So remember t' make a bracelet that guards against death by sex."

"Is that a custom order?"

"Acourse," he said. "Who wouldn't hope to need one a them? Ye've already covered the other major subjects: friendship, success, faith, and love,—that'll go quickly. The world's mad fer love."

He was right, and that went without saying, so I said nothing. Only listened, as Liam went on to tell me that storytelling time was over and that he was leaving the shop in my hands. "But my you know I really don't work here, I was just . . ." got steamrollered by Liam's monologue about how there hadn't been much foot traffic— much traffic of any kind—it'll be for only the final two hours of the workday, and Una can run from next door to help if needed. Liam was leaving early because of a gig. He told me he fills in for a three-piece pub band called The Chancers, the regular members of which, he explained woefully, wear waistcoats, and specialize in the bad American "country" music that has infested Ireland like audio kudzu. Liam abhors waistcoats, which I had to ask the definition of, and he pantomimed the invisible edges of a vest, but when I said vest, he said no, no, vests were worn beneath everything else, were underlayers, so I just let it go. Anyhow, he abhors waistcoats, so he refuses to wear the uniform. He also hates American country music, but not the additional income and *craic* that can be had by a last-minute Chancer, so he plays it. He makes a series of trips from the apartment to the car, and then he is gone. Leaving his store with an employee who is not one.

The Chancers had launched their first CD over the previous Christmas season. A self-produced thing, it bears a cover photo shot by Max, a Chancer by night and a farrier by day who'd purchased a digital camera the summer before and who, according to Liam was unable to walk two steps without putting it up to his eye. Max enjoyed making drive-by photos, sticking the camera out the car window, and the CD cover was one of those, the pointy peak of a black slate roof backgrounded by a flotilla of threatening clouds. Suddenly alone I snapped the disc into the player, The Chancers began a cheerfully twangy thing, and I got to work.

Pepsi out patrolling, the shop is still. Following Liam's directions to use up the beads that were in abundance, I surveyed the table. The abundant charms fell into that category, and I gravitated toward them again, the tiny people, flowers, birds, letters, numbers. Out the window, a couple of tourists leaned over the wall across the road, studying the river, videoing it with one of those cameras that plays the image on a little screen at the very moment you're recording it. The morning had been wet, then dry, then wet interrupted by sharp snatches of sunlight. You couldn't predict just what the next hour would bring—but wasn't that the case with every twenty-four, and not just weatherwise? Liam had lit a good fire before he left. The shop was warm. I'd made tea that sat on the shelf behind me in the green pot that wore an old cozy that was knitted and could have doubled as, or originally could have been, a hat. Not too annoyingly, The Chancers sang that they were fools to be such fools as to fall for the same old fool again. It was a good moment. I was in a foreign country, playing at making jewelry, playing foreign country music. And then someone was asking, "Are you Finola O'Flynn?"

I looked up from the knot I'd been trying to tie. The questioner was an older woman wearing the kind of flimsy foldable see-through plastic rain bonnet they used to give away at the openings of banks and supermarkets. She carried a green and white vinyl tote imprinted with the name ERINTOURS, and around her neck, over her bright blue raincoat, was a backstage pass type of laminated ID hanging from a green cord. This told me she was "ERIN-TOURS Guest #32 Vivian Teague—Wently, Michigan, U.S.A.," and it was proof positive that the first tourist coach of the season had arrived.

"Oh, no, I'm just a helper" is what I answered Vivian Teague, at the same time half awaiting the trumpet herald I expected might accompany this anticipated moment of Yank-tourist landing.

"Well, tell her that her jewelry is very pretty," Vivian said cordially as she poked a forefinger into the dish of bracelets. I watched her slip on the one with the small bird that I'd written represented, or wished you, a light spirit. "Hmmmm," she said, and stared at the tag forever, like there were fifteen paragraphs to read rather than just two lines. "Hmmmm."

Then entered another woman, "ERINTOURS Guest #16 Mrs. James DeLuca—San Francisco, California, U.S.A." She stage-whispered a churchy "Excuse me, excuse me" as she nudged past Vivian and began serious browsing. Mrs. James DeLuca came to my side and watched me work, which of course made me start dropping things and otherwise fumbling, and then she took out a notebook and flipped to a page headed with the underlined words Souvenirs For said Finola? I'd like to know what you'd suggest for my granddaughters. Both of them are in their early twenties . . ."

Vivian called out, "She's not the owner—she just works here" She yells this from over at the basket of scented goat's milk soap balls made by a couple of women who raised the required animals on a small farm out past the new graveyard. The soap was said to be aromatherapeutic, not unlike some of the creams and goop that Gina had received. Right now, the shop inventory contained milky white peppermint soap, for consciousness; yellow-speckled lemon-grass/oatmeal, for clear thinking; and an orangy-golden ylang-ylang, which, according to Liam, who takes delight in sharing the occasional titillating fact, was an aphrodisiac (wink-wink) Vivian Teague picked up a small globe of ylang-ylang and inhaled deeply. Her eyelids dropped slowly, the curtain at the end of a stage performance. She invited Mrs. James DeLuca. Check it out!"

Four or five more ladies flowed in, and a lone man. Three or four of the ladies wore green plastic rain capes, the backs of which announced: ERINTOURS HAS GOT YOU COVERED!" Two or three of the caped ones approached me. One or two of them produced a camera from under their capes and photographed me dropping more beads on the floor. I'd been in the country not even three days, but already it was odd to hear the steamrollered American accent.

"I love to watch native craftsmen in action," enthused one photographer, ignoring my gender. "I took some wonderful shots of a small boy at some kind of pottery wheel when we were in India. He powered it with his feet . . ."

"An American," said Mrs. DeLuca, who'd joined the group to pass a ylang-ylang ball beneath the collected nostrils.

"No, he was definitely Indian. And I'm certain about that because he was in India."

"Her—I mean she—here—she's an American."

"You're right," I said brightly and invitingly and as happy-to-have-you-here as you would hope any store employee would be. We were Americans, all of us, here, having dared to venture abroad despite the state of the world, getting back to the plans of our lives and spending our money to benefit the economy, just as our president had come on TV and encouraged us to. Yank solidarity, I hoped, might fuel the ladies to drop a ton of money. But the lady who'd photographed the Indian in India pressed the button on the back of her digital camera, deleting the image from her cache as she said aloud, "No use saving that one."

"You're not Finola? Finola . . ." The other one scanned the room, saw the sign behind me and motioned to it. " . . . Finola O'Flynn?"

"Nope."

"You're not from here?"

"Nope. I'm from Massachusetts."

"Oh." The word was cold, served on a bed of soggy disappointment. Then the woman examined the dish of bracelets, walked her fingers over Serenity, Energy, Shelter, and Health before throwing me enough paper money to cover the four of them and left. The group noticed her leaving, and like the sheep of Booley that I see following one another simply because one of them has decided to turn left rather than keep on straight, the shop suddenly was as empty as if they'd never been there.

Next up, another mishmash of older men and women opened and closed their wet umbrellas at the doorway as if pumping bellows at the fireplace. Their ERINTOURS tags announced their points of faraway origin: Pennsylvania. Florida. New Mexico. Vermont. And their conversations told of their being at the prime point Liam had described to me, but that I already knew well from being a pretty practiced consumer: that time in a journey when a tourist—typically a female tourist and he was not being sexist here, only truthful—has viewed enough art and scenery and local color and wants nothing more than to shop. The whole carrot-at-the-end-of-the-stick idea that is the reason for those long lines at museum shop cash registers. You've done your time gazing at art or culture or whatever, now you can have some real fun.

"A store! Thank God!"

Relief audible to life on Mars came from "ERINTOURS Guest #13 Aurora Nolan—New York City, NY, U.S.A.," who gazed upon the heaps of merchandise as if it were gallons of refrigerated Poland Spring stacked at the end of a desert marathon. She beelined over to the packs of photo note cards next to a box containing shrink-wrapped enlargements of the best-selling images. The photos were made a few years back by a group of kids in the Booley National School, after each had been given a disposable camera as part of a college student's project on how contemporary Irish children view their everyday world. Each of Una's boys had the honor of one of their prints being turned into a note card. Derek's was a rear view of Pepsi trotting down the main road of winter-deserted Booley, and Ralpho's was Una's TV screen tuned to the Irish-speaking channel, the English subtitle "There are no goats here" floating on an otherwise black screen. The backs of the note cards told that they were being sold to raise money for the school, and this benevolent Paul Newman salad dressing-ish fact increased their chances for being among the more popular souvenirs.

Aurora Nolan had two packs of the cards in her hands when "ERINTOURS Guest #10 Pip Larkin—New York City, NY, U.S.A." joined her in pawing through the box of enlargements.

"Couldn't you just see these in the gallery?" Aurora placed every word in the air with exactly two feet of space between to stress what an incredible idea had just been formulated by her very own brain. Pip, meanwhile, removed rectangular fire-engine-red glasses from a rhinestoned case so she could bifocal the info about the project.

"And . . ." breathed Pip, jamming herself into high gear, "we fly the young artists over for the opening. A sort of cultural exchange type of thing . . ."

"For the season of St. Patrick's Day!"

Pip slapped a hand to the side of her astounded face: "You read my mind!"

In my own mind, Derek and Ralpho were in New York City, which, from their name tags, was where I figured Aurora and Pip's gallery had to be, and where I of course would have to travel to meet the boys for a few days of touring. Derek and Ralpho wore Jeter jerseys fresh from some sports superstore in Times Square as they leaned against the railing of a Circle Line tour boat set to make its way around the circumference of Manhattan. Once we docked, I would take them and their mother to Monte's for Italian, to the Strand for books, and to the Empire State Building for a good scare.

"Do you have this in double X?"

"ERINTOURS Guest #40 Rocky Warner—Jenkintown, PA, U.S.A." held up the only T-shirt design Liam carried: parchment colored with black hand-lettered quillish printing of the word Buaille. No logo, no decoration, no tiny shamrock or harp to provide the slightest hint at the nation in which you'd found this. Only the word, which is enough, according to Liam, who'd designed them in response to customers' requests for T-shirts. If shoppers wanted something that screamed souvenir, they had Una's gift shelf, which included shirts that announced that Guinness was "Not Just For Breakfast Anymore." Buaille, the only wearable message they'd get at Finola O'Flynn, was the spelling of Booley until a couple hundred years ago, when the British Anglicized each place name for Ireland's first-ever ordnance survey. That's how Gaillimh became Galway, Corcaigh became Cork, and Buaille became Booley. I don't know that the other words mean, but I know that *buaille* were huts at higher grazing lands to which flocks and herds traditionally were brought each summer, sort of a vacation that was instinctive for sheep anyhow, and with the addition of cattle and cows, kept critters from traipsing through newly planted crops and also made use of land unsuitable for farming. I know all this only because it was printed on the tags that hang from each right sleeve of the shirts that are available only in small, medium, and large, which on that first visit—was that only two days ago?—I told Liam was losing him sales to the great numbers of Yanks who are very often extra-large and larger in size. As was the Mr. T-sized Mrs. W who eyed me suspiciously before asking, "Where you from?"

"Massachusetts."

"She's from America!" Rocky Warner broadcast this fact to the room, the occupants of which turned and gave me looks that varied from that's nice to so what.

Rocky Warner returned the T-shirt to the basket where she'd found it. Just in case Pip and Aurora and the few others wearing name tags hadn't been part of the same tour, she listed in an exasperated tone: "We had a Swedish girl serve us breakfast, a girl from The Netherlands bring us our lunch, that kid from Latvia took our tickets at the famine museum, now an American is selling us T-shirts to take back to America. What is this country coming to?"

Nobody answered. Then a woman whose name I couldn't see right then because she was carrying a turkey-sized serving platter pressed out in a leaf shape by whoever is Mudpie Potters cautioned, "Well, we must remember," and launched into a speech about Ireland recently becoming a new land of immigrants, and how we had to be as accepting of the ones here as we were of those in our own country because, after all, if you aren't a Native American, you were an immigrant, too. There was more silence, during which shoppers become overly interested in the fine-print laundering directions for the dressy lace scarves tatted by the old ladies in the convalescent home where Mr. Quinn's mother lives. I saw Rocky Warner glare at the speechmaker in a way that told me had she been living in my town last fall, she would have been among the idiotic paranoids stoking the rumor that the Middle Eastern guys who'd recently purchased Convenience Corner had been seen laughing and otherwise in great spirits on the morning of September 11. A few quiet moments later, Rocky Warner exited the shop. All but one of them trickled out. Remaining was the woman with the platter and the newcomer's defense. She told me she had to apologize, and put the plate on the bead table so she could extend her hand to me, which is when I saw the Ph.D. typed after her name Christina Giliberti and above her hometown of Boston.

"I'm a cultural consultant for ERINTOURS," she said in a low voice, hooking her fingers into quotes around her title. "I get trips free of charge in exchange for being on hand to answer questions about the people, the history, the geography, the politics. It's a great job, but some days . . ." Here she made a *sheesh* kind of noise. "Too many of these people think they're going to be walking onto the set of *The Quiet Man.* They don't like to see the kids in the lounge of their B and B hooked up to Playstations. They bitch and moan that their great-great-grandparents' village has electric wires and how will that look in the photos they want to show the people back home. They want the country that's in the brochure. In the few years since immigrants and asylum seekers started coming over in numbers, I have heard so many stupid comments. One woman in a group I was with pointed from the bus window to a black man on the street in Dublin and actually asked me 'What's he doing here?'"

"I'm proud to be an American." I sappily Lee Greenwooded, hand over heart.

The cultural consultant rolled her eyes as she picked out her Amex from a weathered ERINTOURS fanny pack.

"They don't want anything here to have changed," she said, looking toward the empty door to make sure there were no guests to offend. "Well, baby, sooner or later, everything changes."

While I wrapped her platter for travel, the dish of bracelets caught her attention. As did the one Liam predicted would sell fast. She paid fast, then just as quickly asked for scissors and clipped the tag from the bracelet that bore the heart that is self-explanatory, though that didn't keep me from writing the four-letter word on the tag.

I extended my hand. "I'm Sophie White," I told her. "From Massachusetts, too. Just here for the summer."

"Well, Sophie White from Massachusetts, too, all I can say is don't go around with a banner advertising yourself to your fellow Americans. If you want to make your plane fare home, you'll tell 'em what they want to hear. You'll say you're . . ." She stopped and read at the sign behind me. . . . "That you're, I don't know . . . that you're Finola O'Flynn."

The cultural consultant, of course, had no idea what she was suggesting. To be Finola O'Flynn I'd almost have to have descended from the gods. After the stories I'd been told in cinematic detail, I imagined Finola had to have emerged into being from the depths of the sea, riding along on a scallop shell like Botticelli's Venus in the print that hangs across from my bed back home, the seasons and the winds heralding her emergence from the deep, and she just born yet completely formed and with all that wonderful blond hair instantly long enough to modestly drape across her crotch. Finola was not the goddess of love, but she could have qualified for the one of potent good works. Coaching Una. Kicking Noel in what he called his arse. Getting Joe to consider that the end was maybe not as near as he'd feared. And accomplishing the other feats Gina and I had learned in asides and overhearings and additional recited testimonials that night at the pub. After two days of searching by professionals and volunteers, Finola alone located and returned to his frantic family a tourist boy who'd wandered into a seaside field and slipped into one of the sudden openings created by the tide washing away the earth below. She founded a much-needed monthly collection of recyclable bottles and tins at the side of the chip shop, where she loaded them into a borrowed van and delivered them to a depot near the airport. After a series of complaints to the owner and to officials went ignored, she outright stole from a farm near the fizzy water plant the starving dog kept night and day on a three-foot length of baling twine, and Pepsi will be forever grateful. Finola is the one who wrote to the Western Health Board suggesting they hold a forum on spousal abuse in the area, and even though only three women attended and only two of them remained for the entire program, it still was considered a success. And she was, after all, the one who first spoke aloud the idea that a regular ferry to the islands would be a help in drawing additional tourist dollars, and even though it's just an inflatable with an outboard and seats for no more than eight, starting each May don't the walkers line up early to catch the first boat for a day away?

Sure, yeah, first thing you might think when you list the things Finola did in Booley is how she injured the heart and soul of nice Liam Keegan, and who could ever imagine wanting to do anything bad to him? He might be all carefree to a point, full of double entendres and winks and grins, but one thin waxed paper layer deeper is someone who is real and human and who didn't deserve what happened—certainly deserved, at the least, an explanation. But when you stop and think about it, you realize that we all trample somebody at some point—whether or not it's intentional. And despite how Finola and Liam's story ended, look how it began—a fried, aimless man rolls his car to a stop at the end of the earth and merely the sight of Finola's contentment over a new sign hanging outside a new business reaches down into his confusion and leaves the calling card of hope. Finola did that and without even trying.

To fib to customers that I was Finola O'Flynn would be impossible. The only imitation I could do right then was verbal, a version of Liam's affirmative, which was a simple and easy-to-master "Yep." Three letters, a short word that takes no time at all to sound out, a fast thing, a small breath, a quick clearing of the throat, a tap on the shoulder, the snap of a twig, the start of a lie I didn't see as wrong.

So for the next hour, that would be my reply.

"Finola O'Flynn?"

This time, an actual Irish person was asking. It would be easy to forget that they vacation in their own country, the bulk of holiday-makers having traveled from other places. But as well as going to the Canary Islands and Belize, Irish people also go to Booley. I know that because some others had been in this morning. Four in total, a woman and a man and their pair of mothers-in-law, titles they told me without being asked. Liam was there at the time, so there had been no need for me to speak, I was alone now, with a genuine citizen standing before me, asking my identity, and waiting so patiently as I gathered my courage (because what else might she want to know?) and said "Yep."

I followed that by fibbing to a real Finola. Finola Kasparian, an American of Irish descent who shared how she'd married an American of Greek descent and who rarely sees her first name anywhere back home, never finds it on those racks of plastic license plates and note pads imprinted with first names, but here, she's tripping over Finolas. "Do you find that?" she asked. "Large numbers of people bearing our name?" And I'd answered, "Yep."

It's ironic that I lied to the next woman. Because what I got from her was a huge dose of the truth.

"This must be Finola O'Flynn."

The woman, another Yank, was at the doorway when she announced this to her Yank daughters, who were maybe no more than eleven and twelve but already had her height, which was no great accomplishment as she had the petite stature Olympic gold-medal-winning gymnast Cathy Rigby still did last time I saw her anywhere, which was toward the back of a magazine, in a linoleum floor ad that proudly called her "Our Spokeswoman". Like Our Spokeswoman, the mother and daughters in front of me were true blondes, and they had nearly identical haircuts, the brief choppy style Mia Farrow wore in *Rosemary's Baby* after she ditched her pageboy, returning home to stand in the doorway and announce to her creepy husband, "I've been to Vidal Sassoon!" The cut gave the mother and daughters a look that was at once out-of-date and tee-tering on the edge of cool, like some old styles surprisingly can be.

"Yep. Finola."

"Look, girls! Isn't this wonderful? This is the very woman who makes all this jewelry! See? It has her name on it."

"Uh-huh," is what they uh-huh-ed, more distracted than rude, and then they branched off in opposite sections of the store. The mother stepped forward to watched me work.

"Did you learn that as a child? Do children in Ireland learn crafts as a rule?"

I didn't know the answer. When did Finola actually get into all this? I'd yet to hear that part of her story. But knowing Finola as I already knew her so after not yet short days, she probably had been born with an eye for color, balance, style—some of which you can't learn. As for what kids did here, I so far just knew what I'd seen in my walks to and from town: They rode their bikes, listened to Walkmans, wore sports team jerseys and when helping on the farm, the big tall rubber boots like Joe's. They played soccer that they called football, and football that they called Gaelic football, and, for whatever was the sport of hurling, they chased a small ball with a small curved stick. Una had said that some of the kids—boys and girls both—got driven several nights a week to a cultural center an hour away, where they danced and sang their way through a thou-

sand years of Irish history that they found boring. The kids in
Booley saved for bus fare to Limerick and a day in an actual city
with a JCPenney and a multiscreen cinema and a range of electronics stores. Did the woman want to hear truths like that? I knew
from Una that Derek and Ralpho were mad for the television. They
right now wanted a DVD player more than their next breath. They
loved Gaelic football and of course were going to play in the All-
Ireland final one September half a dozen years or down the line. My
answers for this woman were "Yep" and "Yep."

She said, "I tried to teach my girls, you know—knitting, sewing,
cooking—what my mother taught me when I was their age. But
now, at that same age, they're more interested in sitting in front of
MTV. Do you what MTV is?"

Pause. Then: "Yep."

The woman stood silent as I strung onto either side of an arrow-
head shape a row of orange glass beads shaped like little rigatonis.
One or the other girl would call, "Mom, look at this," and then the
mother would look and say, "How very nice," would ask them how
much the thing cost, would ask them did they have that much in
their souvenir budget, and if they did, was it something they really
needed or simply wanted, and that they should remember there is a
difference. And then she would concentrate on me again.

She touched the bead containers and, like many, stirred the one
containing the charms. I'd slyly placed them next to the dish of my
supposedly magical bracelets. It worked.

"Oooh . . ."

As she arranged five or six bracelets along the edge of the table,
the woman read the titles. She'd gravitated toward titles of the type
that could fill a political speech: Peace, Prosperity, Safety, Home,
Family.

"You made these?"

I nodded.

"I've always wanted to do something like this," she told me, and

I nodded as I reached to change the CD. Earlier, I'd curiously popped in a disc of bird songs from the midlands. Now the birds had fallen silent and I replaced them with another recording from the same series, this one of shorebirds whose calls scared over the constant surf, something I could have recorded up at his cliffs.

"I'd like to run a shop that would carry handmade things," the woman went on. She answered two requests in a row to look at something a daughter was waving, then added, "I don't know if I could make much to contribute myself. My strength would be that I am good with numbers, running things. I could be in charge that way, be the business manager. I've only done so in the home, but that's sort like a business, wouldn't you agree?"

"Yep."

"I think it would be fun. Do you enjoy it, running a store?"

"Yep."

"I bet it's wonderful."

"Yep."

"Well . . ." she said, then ventured, " . . . you're not married?"

"No." A new word for me, but another easy one.

"I am, of course." She nodded toward the girls, as if in this day and age there had to be a connection between them and her marital state. "So a business outside the home would be out of the question."

I went to say the yep, but stopped myself when I realized I did not agree. "Why?" is the response I chose.

"My husband." She gave a few seconds here, maybe waiting for me to nod. But I still didn't get it, so I didn't move. "He prefers me to remain at home," she explained. "Raising the family."

"He doesn't!" I tried, but didn't quite succeed, at delivering both a level of indignation and an accent.

"He does."

"He doesn't."

"He does."

"Neanderthal" is what I thought, but kept my mouth shut. I wanted to if the husband needed his wife's permission for his life choices, but decided not to waste my breath. Poor thing, I thought, zombie woman shuffling down somebody else's track. Then it came to me that this had to be one of the points at which Finola O'Flynn, seated at her bead table, would have dispensed her trademark wisdom. Giving that a try would be the least I could do for this oppressee. So I stepped beyond my former limited vocabulary.

"And you're to have no interests outside the home?" I sounded more Bostonian than Booleyan, and would have laughed at myself had I not been in a serious conversation.

"Someday maybe I can. When the girls are in college, maybe then."

I made an elaborate search for my next bead, and my next comment. I knew what I wanted to say, and tried to imagine it coming from Finola: "How d'ya know you'll even see that day?"

"Pardon me?" The woman looked slightly alarmed like I knew something she didn't. Which was sort of the case, actually. I knew what had happened to Norm Stebbins. The swiftness, the absence of warning, the fact that he'd been instantly gone from a planet on which he rightfully still should be loving Gina and floating another loan to Gennifer and estimating people's quarterly tax payments. This woman couldn't have known Norm, but hadn't September 11 sunk in at some minuscule level? So many souls vaporized as they shook packets of NutraSweet into their morning coffees?

"We've no guarantees of making it t' the evening," I told her. I knew that. I believed that. "If there's something you'd like t' be doing, let no one stop ya. I mean 'ye'."

Because of the accent, maybe, the woman made a tight little face. Looked out the window at a clutch of ERINTOURists drinking their pints on the river wall. Glanced over at her girls giggling about something amusing found on the bookshelves. Then she tried on the bracelet bearing the clasped hands that I'd decided represented Promise, and she offered a line of defense for her husband.

"He's very supportive, but right now his life is our focus, you see. It's all in the marriage vows, I don't know if you use the same ones here—*love* and *honor,* those words, I said them and that's what I'm doing. He's the one who makes the living, supports us. Sent us on this trip, actually. We were flying to London but the plane experienced some sort of engine problem the captain didn't announce until we began to descend for the emergency stop in Shannon. We were given the option of a commuter plane to continue on, or a free overnight and a larger jet tomorrow. I prefer a larger plane, so we have a day to drive around, see the countryside. My husband doesn't even know we're in Ireland! Wait until he gets our message, girls . . ."

I wondered if these people were Mormons, or belonged to one of those other religions big on men, giving them the last word, or the only word. Since September, Americans had been given a crash course on the Middle East, including the often shocking plight of women a male-dominated culture. The woman in front of me wore no burqua, but I felt as sorry for her as I did for my sisters who get beaten for reading a magazine or even leaving the house unaccompanied by a male. I checked this woman for jewelry that might give away her religion. No symbol on a chain at the neck because I couldn't see the neck through her fleece turtle. The sleeves were long so I couldn't check her wrists. Her ring finger bore a wide gold band and a blinding diamond the size of a garbanzo bean, but you couldn't tell anything from that, aside from that she was either wealthy or that she collected Diamonique off home shopping networks. Whatever the case, she obviously was not one who followed the suggestion to leave your fancy-looking jewelry at home when you went on vacation. When she caught me looking, I said, "Lovely ring," even though it was quite ghastly.

"We're sixteen years," she said, and I said, "Brilliant," and she said, "He is! Really—honestly—I know you might be used to something different in your country, relationshipwise, but you'd love my husband."

I said another new word: "Right."

The daughters were at the woman's side now before the expression she'd just used for the length of her marriage could settle in my head. The girls were handing their mother the soap balls they'd each chosen—one lemongrass and one that is actually a ball of mint shampoo.

"Look!" said their mother. "These bracelets have stories! They mean something!"

"Lemme see!"

"Gimme!"

As the girls shoved each other and fought and transformed into an ad for birth control, the mother whispered "jet lag" in my direction, and she reached for her money. Fittingly as old-fashioned as her outlook and lifestyle, the woman's wallet included a photo section that came unfastened and waterfalled onto the table, a big linked lineup of school photos, and grandparents, and baby snaps, and candids, and the face of Charlie St. Jean.

The details of the small family picture came at me like I was being given a list. The stone bench, the brown Dockers, the white polo, the sharp too-short haircut he'd gotten the August before, the shiny white gold ring on the finger I only knew to be bare. Behind him and just enough to the side so she could rest a knee on the bench was this very woman, in one of those odd little khaki skort things with the front flap of fabric concealing the fact of shorts. Her blouse was too pink, and its rounded collar hung heavy with eyelet lace. She'd placed her ring hand on one of Charlie's shoulders, and the other one came around and touched the side of his face. Seated sideways on the left end of the bench, but looking into the camera lens, the older girl leaned against her mother's arm, smiling like this was actually enjoyable, a little taste of the modeling life she maybe secretly dreamed for herself when alone in the bathroom and able to strike poses and try out expressions with nobody else looking. She wore a sleeveless soft yellow summer dress and was barefoot. Her toes were pointed into the grass like a ballerina's. To the right of Charlie, dressed in the silver and blue full uniform of the West Allis United soccer team, the younger daughter sat in what once was called Indian style, fists to chin, elbows on knees, and smiling to reveal an almost over-the-top detail of a missing front bottom tooth. To her left, her best friend chocolate Lab sat obedience school perfect, West Allis United bandana around his neck. With Charlie as the sun, and the four others as his revolving planets, there was the St. Jean universe. Captured bright and perfect and focused as ever, disappearing into white at the artistically blurred edges.

A Discover Card that at the end of the year would return this family a check for up to 10 percent of its annual purchases was handed to me and the surname came up sharp and unmistakably legible on the credit card slip I clipped to her receipt and placed in the bag. And in case I needed another sledgehammer to my skull, a Wisconsin driver's license was held out to me. Belonging to Jane St. Jean, 42 Watson St., West Allis, WI 53227. I took the license in my hand because I needed to touch it, needed to know that this was truly happening. I examined it a lot more closely than a retailer usually would, from the helium-filled letters of the signature down, the holographic images of the state seal, the orange disc that notified the world that, if you ever needed them, Jane St. Jean was ready to hand over the organs of your choice. After all, what's the big deal with a lung or heart handed to a stranger, when she's already sharing her husband with one?

The guest book Liam kept CD player was signed by all three and the girls were instructed to say good-bye, as they did, the older one smiling, the younger one looking tired but managing to wave at me before she leaned against her mother's shoulder. "I homeschool," said the woman. The mother. The wife. "Do you know what that is?" I didn't, couldn't, even get out a yep. Jane St. Jean said that as their teacher, in the fall she would be assigning the girls a paper on Irish handcrafts, and that this visit certainly would be a highlight! Meeting the actual craftswoman! "I have your card. We'll send copies!"

She waved, wrist sparkling with some bracelet I didn't catch the meaning of, then three of them were gone.

It took them maybe a year to clear the threshold, they moved that slowly, it seemed, until the room was empty again and I could direct my hand toward the guest book, which roosted on a flat panel at the corner of the bead table. I spun it slowly toward me, but even so, the writing still appeared to be upside down. I read the columns from right to left, starting with the Comment line first, where Jane St. Jean in perfect Palmer Method hand, had written "Thank you, Finola!" Then the Address section, in which she'd written "West Allis, Wisconsin, U.S.A." and had drawn a fat heart protectively around the U.S.A.

Finally, I read the Name line: "The St. Jeans: Joan and Jeanne and Mrs. Charlie (Jane) St. Jean

You of course say it can't be.

The world is huge.

Bigger than huge.

Maybe not the largest planet around, but still enormous if you are merely the size of a human and have no other frame of reference. And on this bigger-than-huge planet, there have to be more than a few people bearing the same name as a lot of other people. Even if the name is a bit unusual. Anything can happen, anything can be. Lots of people have identical surnames and come from the same towns as do those others with the same last names. A wallet's family picture can include someone's identically named twin. Anything can happen.

It just did.

I waded through this line of thinking in the five-mile walk to the shop door. Stepped into the road to look inside the chip shop. It was empty but for my new friend Emilio, wiping down his counter as he recited to a customer the litany of burgers—regular, king-size, double-decker, Emilio special, bacon, chicken, Hawaiian, Mexican, spicy, curry—before concluding "I myself would choose the doner kebab." He said it "Kebaaab."

Out front sat the Irish couple who were touring with the mothers-in-law, all of them now studying a big unfolded road map while eating fries from greasy paper sacks. "There," one of the mothers was saying, thumping a finger to a definite point on the map. "Leisureland!"

I looked down the road. A small group of loud adults was exiting Quinn's and stopping one door down to decide if they needed a trip into Dolan's, supplies for the road, a round loaf of brown bread and a block of Kerry Gold for a cheap lunch, and a *News of the World* just for yucks. Past them was the wife from West Allis. And the daughters from West Allis. At Attracta's now, planted in front of the big window. They already had were carrying something of his in a bag, already had been in, were just enjoying watching Noel do his work like he was part of some exhibit in one of those living museums in which personnel pretend its 1620 and dress in the style of the day and make like they know nothing of modern-day life— What kind of machine is your camera and your mobile phone and why do you allow your wife to bare her arms in public? The woman from West Allis pointed to the window and narrated something, looking at each of the smaller faces occasionally to see if they noticed this about what Noel was doing, did they see? They might want to write their second back-to-school compositions on this cute small town and the fascinating people who lived there. This Irish man who spends his day at that huge loom, the Italian but probably also Irish couple who make the french fries, the Irish woman whose jewelry lines the walls of her shop and who, though she wouldn't point this out to the kids, by using just a few short words said things that stuck in your mind.

Now that I'd located the three, I didn't know what I wanted to do with them, or about them. Or to them. I stood on the sidewalk holding the corner of Quinn's to steady myself as I considered—well, I don't know what I considered. I know I watched. I watched Mrs. Charlie St. Jean place a hand on the shoulder of whoever was Joan St. Jean and whoever was the unfortunately named Jeanne St. Jean, and then I watched them walk to the door of the Last Restaurant, where they read the menu posted each day inside a frame surrounded by climbing roses. Pepsi trotted from the leafy space between the restaurant and the riverbank, and sniffed the shoes of the girls whose loving responses of "Aaaawwww!" I could hear all the way from my end of the road. I watched the three of them cross the bridge. Then I watched them, along with a lot of other things, disappear.

Rope:

⌣⍩⌣

Perseverance, Connection

(State Your Wish Three Times)

Jane St. Jean and I have a couple other things in common. I, too, am good with numbers, running things. So for the remaining twenty minutes of my obligation in the shop, I was able to make sales, answer questions, perform those tasks—all that despite deafening distraction of my heart dropping to the cement floor. The dull thud-splat it made upon contact echoed continuously, a skipping record playing behind the too-short documentary of my romance with Charlie and all the hope it had held. The meeting at the bunny display. Feeling his eyes on me as I adjusted the adoption information sign. Turning to locate those eyes, which were the same shiny dark blue of the recycling bin I set on my curb the first Monday of each month, and which were looking at me from the face that Gina always thought was, with its flat planes and blond bangs, beach-movie surferish. Charlie's and my first limping chitchat, about pets in general, and his recalling a childhood dog, no fool, who on the hottest of summer afternoons sat for hours in a water-filled galvanized washtub. That childhood, that dog, that washtub all had been in Wisconsin. Where he had been raised and where he still lived, but obviously not in the no-kids townhouse complex he said does not allow pets of any sort, a rule he does not mind because he is always on the road for work and there would be no one left behind to care for an animal.

No one.

I'd heard those two words clearly. I would swear this on an Amazon.com warehouseful of New Testaments. Because when you are in your late twenties and you hear a man say he has no one to care for any pets while he's away, bells go off. Not cliché-ish wedding ones—not for me, at least—just bells of the type that signal the opening of a door, that say here is one of the few possibly interesting males who have made it to this point in life and are floating around untethered. There is a different sound, a cabinet door closing softly, when you hear that there indeed is someone available to tend the pets. Then the specific word: girlfriend, fiancée, wife. Some guys use the word *lover*, like it's the sixties. Some say it's the boyfriend who's back in Wichita changing Budgie's cuttlebone. All these people, they're all taken in some way. Claimed. Some level of connections already promised. No bells means there's an invisible stamp on the hand marking them as unavailable, and there were bells going off all around Charlie St. Jean, who had no stamp. Had no one, he'd said, erasing the total existences of three entire people—maybe additional ones, for all I knew. There could be a troubled unreachable older son who slept all day and was out all night, went nowhere with any member of his family, never mind all the way across the Atlantic. Or how about an additional daughter, one gifted and prematurely mature, who excelled at the viola and had won an invitation to an exclusive music summer camp held this same month at Big Sur. But the three St. Jeans I knew about for certain were three too many for me. One person—even one connection—merited mention. But there had been no mention, off the bat, or at any time in our eighteen months. There was no one, Charlie had said that first day. No one. So I saw for me and Charlie St. Jean a future that would be unmarred by the unpleasant routes many at similar ages and stages of life were having to navigate in order to proceed to a new future. I'd been grateful for the blessed absence of any landmined divorce proceedings, complicated custody issues. Because there is no pain to be inflicted when there is no one to hurt.

The film of our story ended right there, the tail of it flying around tick-tick-tick-tick-tick-ticking before the projector snapped itself off and everything in the movie house of my head fell silent. Walking into town on Wednesday, I'd almost been boasting that I had nothing from which to recover or heal. Now I did. Isn't that life for you? Laugh on Saturday, cry on Sunday, morose Mrs. Jeden down the street had told me throughout my laughing youth. It was only Friday. I was way ahead of schedule.

I found my way back into the shop. I found my place behind the bead table, and back into my consciousness floated the sound of the sea birds still cawing and screeching from the CD player, the same creatures that had been soaring carefree around the room when the three people from West Allis were an arm's length away. I was feeling the same chilled panic that coated me the time I was driving to the post office at nine in the morning and a deer that rightfully at that time should have been back home in his deer house enjoying his second cup of decaf shot across the road and I hit him smack full-on with the front of my old blue Honda. He sailed to the side of the road, and though alone in the car I began to repeat aloud and very loud, "What do I do? What do I do?" You don't hit a deer every day, you don't kill something every day (I was certain—and, it turned out, correct—that I had killed it). What do you do if you do? I didn't know. I just kept asking myself. And then I asked the two people who had been nice enough to stop after I'd pulled over, I asked them, "What do I do?"—and they told me to do nothing, that it wasn't my fault, the deer had come out of nowhere. What had leapt from nowhere into my path this afternoon here in Booley were multiple creatures of reality. And the shock was just as great. What do I do? What do I do? What do I do? My first idea: Call Charlie St. Jean, he being the place I'd brought my troubles for the past seventeen months.

Then I heard another name.

"Finola O'Flynn?"

In the doorway, Asians. Asians saying, "Finola O'Flynn." "Finora O'Frynn," rather, and that is no easy joke, just their pronunciation. Another first of the season. Seven Asians in all, smiling and cliché-ishly bowing their heads as they entered, and then speaking excitedly as they went straight for the CDs. Liam would be elbowing me now, if he were here rather than two and a half hours north, launching into "A Boy Named Sue." If he were next to me, he would be concentrating on a knot or some paperwork, smile barely perceptible, but inside he would be leaping. Asians. Here. Pockets full. There were eight now in the shop, then another, nine. Safety in numbers, I picked up the phone and poked out the numerals that got me a voice in Wisconsin. The voice that a year and a half ago told me that he would have no one at home if there were a need to throw a few flakes to a guppy or to milk a Holstein. The voice that two months ago had agreed it was time to begin sharing a home. The voice that in the same conversation had made the case for living somewhere in my town rather than in his town, making it clear that he'd still have to travel often and would spend a good part of the month at the Wisconsin headquarters, but our home would become his real one. Now that voices was saying his full name, using the Charles even, and giving his "You know what to do," which I once had excused as his only true fault. The beep sounded and my heart loosened itself from all the muscles and fibers and whatever else holds it into place down in the chest and it popped up in my throat like one of those red and white fishing bobbers, then began jackhammering with a fury as I struggled to force out words I imagined wrapped in razor wire: "I have met your wife, and your daughters. I don't want to meet you again. Ever."

Advances in technology have prevented any dramatic effect from the action of hanging up a call made on a portable phone. You must first press the off button, which, no matter how hard you hit it, makes only a happy *eeeep*. I squished that button, then shoved the receiver into its cradle. But did all that only after I looked over at the Asians, who'd shown not one sign of knowing English other than the ability to read the sign over the door, so I growled into the mouthpiece a final "How dare you do this to me?" It was more of a statement than a question. A final statement. The end. I put down the phone and the little red light illuminated again to tell me the unit was recharging.

A small line at my table, waiting for me to wait on them. I took their euros for the four Buaille T-shirts and the entire carton of ylang-ylang soaps, three boxes of kids' photo cards, the last of Max's candle chandeliers, his salmon wine rack I'd never got the chance to put aside, as Charlie St. Jean's welcome gift, half a dozen trad CDs, eight of Liam's necklaces, eight of his bracelets that more or less matched them, eight sets of earrings that went with any of the above, two of my charmed bracelets (the Christmasy-sounding pair "Comfort" and "Joy"), and three dozen of the handblown goblets Liam stocked as his answer to Waterford crystal, a staple in gift shops nationwide, high-end cut-glass displayed alongside Belleek porcelain in huge cabinets that required unlocking by salesgirls. The glass Liam chose to carry in his shop was created by a family who ran a summertime craft school for adults one hour inland. Free of form, no two alike, and as far from the precise etched Waterford as a kindergartener's drop cookie is from a wedding cake, each piece was packed with a booklet showing a sweaty T-shirted man twirling a bulbous glob of molten glass, a fire-filled kiln doorway just behind him. I accepted the paper on which the Asians had written their mailing addresses in beautifully printed English as I promised to wrap the purchases for proper shipment by air, which the woman who seemed to be their spokesperson requested. Though I would do so only once my hands felt less like strangling somebody. I was putting their money into the till and listening to their excitedly bubbled mentions of pub-pub-pub-pub-pub as they passed the window en route to Quinn's when I felt a touch on my shoulder. The smallest of the small men who had just been in the shop, who even if he didn't understand the language, had to have picked up something from the tone of voice I'd used in the call to Charlie St. Jean, came back to stand before me and put a hand over his heart and make an expression on his face that in any language would be accepted as his sorrow for me in this hour. Then he exited for the pub and my strongest wish right then was that I could be him. Could be a little Japanese man. A little Japanese man headed for a pint and a piss and another pint and a chance to sit and change the Flash Memory card in my Fugi Finepix because my biggest problem today was having taken too many shots, was rather than finding out that the man I was hoping was my future had kept from me the facts of wife and kids. If possible, would pay all I had to be able to become that little Japanese man. When a bad patch hit, wasn't it natural to want to be the one who was smarter, better connected, or simply without a problem in the world? In my shoes, wouldn't you want to? Need to? Need to be him, or one of his fellow tourists, or one of the Quinns next door, or Una past them, or Noel past her, any of the crew at the Last Restaurant, or, as you almost run out of options, and Booley itself, wouldn't you want to be anybody other than who I was that moment? Whatever their personal burdens and struggles, I certainly would have. But all that would be impossible.

At least I thought so right then.

Maze:

⌣⋏⋏

Difficult Path, Challenge

(State Your Wish Three Times)

"Monkfish!"

Earlier in the day, the Last Restaurant had been the only business in Booley with fives to spare. The loan would have gone totally forgotten on this day had Liam not Sellotaped a note—FIVERS—to the front of my jacket. I had enough problems without being arrested for theft, so I slammed the shop door for the night and walked up the road.

The Last Restaurant was owned by a couple whose names resembled a draw from a consonant-depleted Scrabble bag. Aoife and Eoin had spelled them for Gina and me at Quinn's, a mere two nights ago. Joining our party after their last diner had left, the couple I would have spelled Efa and Owen told us how their staff spanned the globe, how most of them had stumbled upon Booley during a wandering holiday or aimless period of life, and then found the seven-euro-a-night Diamond's Hostel tucked up a dead-end over looking the stone bridge, and then spotted the HELP WANTED stuck inside the menu frame just across that bridge. Right now, the staff was Dirk the cook, a retired Belgian forester; Terry from New Zealand, who would do the washing up until he entered

University College Dublin in a few months; and waitpersons Sara and Anna, musicians, recent college grads and best friends from Sweden who'd come to Ireland for the summer to perfect their talents on the whistle. The lineup at the Last Restaurant could change daily as heip frequently was lured away by a spectacular airfare deal to Iceland, or the overnight birth of a romance with someone leaving for the Giant's Causeway, or a reason as bland as the end of allotted vacation time and the commitment to reinsert back into a nine-to-five existence. But on the night of the day of the St. Jean women, the staff were Dirk and Terry and Sara and Anna, and they were idle and waiting for customers and watching as Aoife beelined over to me with notepad in hand.

"Monkfish!" she announced, and led me to a table. Tried to, at least, as she continued, "Or . . . cod, or trout or salmon. Mussels in wine as a starter?"

Aoife moved on to list choices of vegetables and styles of spud before she realized I had my hand out, the pile of owed fives a fat clump. She stuck them in her apron pocket and said, "Thanks for remembering, Sophie. While you're here, a little tandoori mackerel with aubergine?"

"Can't."

"Mind you," she whispered, "sounds wojus, but it's grand. And for afters, lavender mousse?"

"Another time."

"Right. Perhaps when yer man's here on his holidays."

I was in the process of finding the door. I stopped. The "yer man" thing was as constant in Booley as precipitation—used for everyone from the husband on your arm to Kofi Annan on television. In this case, I knew that Aoife meant the boyfriend who Gina had volunteered would be here to visit me one day. I stopped, hand on knob, said "He's not my man."

"Yer man. Yer boyfriend, like."

"I know what you mean, but that's not what he is. He's got a wife. Kids. He's got kids. Wife. Kids. I just found out today. They were here. Today."

Past her, the staff was big-eyed.

"Never a word to me about them," I said to the group.

"Stop!" this was Aoife.

"Total surprise."

"Stop!"

"It's true."

"Ye're jokin.'" She smiled, really seemed to think I was. And I responded, "I wish."

Somehow I next was walking through the kitchen of the Last Restaurant. Through that and to the garden door, where Aoife sat me in a chair, told me to breathe, a reminder I appreciated. There was a release in the being cared for, and I accepted it. I leaned back and watched the plunks of rain drop from the roof edge and onto the knotted fleet bikes resting against the back wall. Joan and Jeanne had to have such bikes. Probably stored them next to the minivan in the attached garage of a neat two-story ivy-clung brick home out there in Dan Jansenland. The smaller girl was still young enough to be keeping a basket on hers—maybe white woven plastic strands and a Hello Kitty face staring from the front. All pink and handlebar streamered like the rows of bicycles displayed at the front of Kmart come Easter. The tea Aoife brought me had an unfamiliar kick, and I was silent until half finished, when Aoife pulled a crate to the door and joined me.

"We're all fucking stupid when it comes to love." She said the word as "steeupid," and that made it sound even more true. Despite her being maybe only a year older than I, she pushed back a bit of my hair the way a mother would in a calming gesture. "And we're especially fucking stupid," she added, "scangers, bloody Fecky the Ninths when in love with a sneaky git."

I should have asked for a dictionary. But all I could manage was,

"What should I do?" Aoife was there. Somebody was there. I needed to ask.

"D'ya not want to speak to him?"

I half did, and although it is mathematically impossible, I more than half did not. "No."

"But would ya not, in the least, like to hear his explanation?"

"What's to explain? It makes me sick to think of him. How I had no clue. . . ."

I wouldn't want anybody saying anything this trite to me, but these things happen. I'd once seen an old movie in which a sailor woke when his ship's bells signaled the halfway point between Africa and Europe, and he used the wake-up to switch his wedding ring to another ring, and to flip over the photograph of his wife to display a picture of a second wife, the one who lived in the country to which his ship was headed. More recently, I'd read the stories you couldn't make up, the true double lives that had been led by some of those killed September. Hidden girlfriends, wives, mothers of a second crop of secret children coming out of the woodwork to stake their claim in the compensation being doled to survivors. I couldn't imagine knocking on Jane St. Jean's door to tell her that I, too, loved Charlie. Though I could picture her answering the door, probably wearing one of those aprons with the ruffles at the edges, or a more modern one screenprinted with some sappy legend: I LOVE MY FAMILY, FOOD FROM THE ♥. The door she'd open would lead to a living room, and behind her you could see the thick blue rug with its fresh vacuum-wheel tracks, a long floral camelback couch, above it a family photo the size of a refrigerator door, shot outdoors by a skilled photographer whose name was embossed, angled and in gold, at the right-hand corner. The same picture that had been wallet-size in her wallet.

Jane St. Jean stand in her doorway asking, "May I help you?" as had Mary Jo Buttafuoco when Amy Fisher rang her bell, in real life, and in all three of the television movies. Unlike Amy, I would not be there to shoot Jane so I could have her husband for my own—though what I would have to tell her might on some level kill her but good. Unlike Alyssa Milano's Amy, I would not tell my friends, "I hate huh," because I do not have a Long Island accent and because I have no reason to hate Jane St. Jean. Like Amy, I might make up a story about being at her door to sell candy bars. Then I would move on, really having no business at all being there.

Aoife was putting a drinking glass in my hand now. Had it filled a third of the way up like it was orange juice rather than the whiskey it contained.

I waved it away and stood.

"Sure, you're welcome to stay—no bother."

"But you're being so kind. And I don't really know you . . ."

She stomped right on that word. "You know where ya are this evening. And I know the road."

"You walk past the cottage?"

"I have, yeah, but I'm saying I've felt the same feelings. Before Eoin. Two men prior. I believed my match had been made, happy ending, full stop. He was charming and intelligent and spoke to me in Italian, *bellissima, bellissima,* knew how to say things like that because even though he was from here he traveled frequently to Italy, imported religious goods from there to all the major shrines—Lourdes, Fatima, and also Knock up in Mayo. Went to Knock to take orders for more things relating to Our Lady, Our Lady being the one who appeared in Knock, and therefore Our Lady souvenirs are the best selling of any found in the shops there. He imported thousands of statues of her, some life-size nearly and fit for churches and hospitals. Statues of her small enough to fit in the pocket, to slip in there with the coins and the keys and when you rummage about, there's Our Lady, reminding you she's there. He imported statues the size you'd place on a corner table and honor with a vase of flowers and a candle to be lit at the hour of the

Angelus, or when saying the rosary. Some marble, some plastic, some glass, some plaster, and the ones he asked me to keep crates of in the shed because he had plans for them, they were hollow. Sorry—had been hollow, before he'd filled them with cannabis from Lebanon and heroin from God knows where."

Now I was the one offering a hair stroke.

"Snared rapid, he got prison," Aoife said after a swig from her own glass. "I was a hairsbreadth away from the same. For having one of them Virgins on a bedroom table when the guards descended. My world vanished, for it had come to be filled with only this man. And everything connected to him. I've a now-useless set of sixteen audiocassettes that had been teaching me the Italian I'd need for when we moved there, as was our plan—one of the million plans we made and sure Italy would have been heaven but I'd have gone to the Siberia fit meant I'd be in his constant presence. I was one of them, believing that a man is the necessary piece to a life."

"So they sell that story here, too?"

"Think the Americans invented that as well? It's ages older than Coca-Cola. Eve was formed from a man. No Adam, no way for Eve to have a life. Shite's what it is, and I tell my girls that even now—I remind 'em they are complete as they stand, even this day, at only eight and nine years. Men can be a fine piece of yer life. But just a piece. Not the crucial thing. Not even close."

I took a swallow of the whiskey. The ends of my hair throbbed. When I could speak again, I asked Aoife, "How'd you get so smart?" And Aoife, in something I should have seen coming from the start of her story, answered, "Finola O'Flynn."

The night she would impart wisdom to Aoife, Finola was on the strand, at a white-orange fire she'd built from driftwood collected earlier in the day. Aoife was still reeling from the new reality that her life was not going to be as bel as she'd believed. She was legally a free woman, but psychically a damaged one, a future with no prison time, but with no dream man, either. She'd walked to the ocean, past a fire, heard her name called.

"Finola was new here, didn't know the extent of my problems. I should say she didn't let on that she did—the way things are in Booley, she likely could have them chapter and verse the moment she crossed the bridge. I found myself reciting my story. In return, Finola said very little, though her words were wise. I'll give you the bit that has stuck with me to this very day. She told me I was all I needed. And I'll say the same to you. Sophie, cop on! You can't be relying on someone else for happiness or fulfillment, you can't let their actions or moods dictate yours, or think that when you claim them all will be eternally well. Finola telling me that, and my realizing that, helped me. Sure, I have Eoin now—it's not like you can't fall in love with a man. But use caution—don't fall in such a manner that you damage your brain and lose all common sense."

Busted. That was me, to a T. More subconsciously than blatantly—still, I'd gotten all turned around by the prospect of Charlie St. Jean as a constant. Despite living a life I enjoyed, liking myself enough, somewhere in the storage room of my mind a masking-tape-bound carton held the age-old idea that two people together were better than one alone. I certainly was familiar with the Adam and Eve thing. I'd long ago owned a Ken for my Barbie, and had been raised by and beneath the roof of a man and a woman, and when my mother died the first words from my father were that his life was over. He used those very words: "My life is over." Wept, even, and he never wept. Choked out, "I am nothing. Alone, I am nothing." It sickened me to see him so devastated because who wants to see a parent in such distress? It made me sad to a depth that you would think the three little letters of that word would be unable to sink you down to. His reaction—and I have never really recognized this but I have now—also gave me a few prickles of jealousy. That my father had somebody who'd meant so much that when she was gone his very existence held no meaning. What would it be like to be loved in that manner? What would it be like to be the person who was everything?

In time I came to realize that the bulk of his grief was because my father for the first time ever in his long seventy-eight years would have to do some actual work. Cooking, cleaning, paying bills, shopping, getting himself to and from the club and the park and Mass without the taxi service that was my mother, her Chevy Nova idling faithful at the curbs of the haunts and obligations that made up his week. What I wanted was somebody who would value me that much, but for reasons on a level higher than the ability to operate a vacuum. But with every email inviting me to visit tietheknot.com for fast and easy perusal of another friend's bridal registry, I adjusted that goal. What I wanted was somebody who would value me. And when that didn't come through, I settled for settling. All I wanted, in the end, as politically incorrect as it might have been, was somebody.

Now, through Aoife, Finola was suggesting that I alone was enough. Maybe if this were a weekend self-esteem seminar featuring a morning show regular who'd authored a series of inspiring texts and accompanying workbooks and small assortment of bookmarks, bumper stickers and mouse pads all about believing that you were worth something, maybe then I would get caught up in the fervor and buy into the idea. But this was being presented to me in the back room of the tiny Last Restaurant Before America only a couple of hours after I had met the St. Jeans. And I was feeling far from complete and whole.

I took a different route back to the cottage that night. Just by feel, taking my chances under a rapidly graying 8 o'clock sky. I made a left from the Last Restaurant, and started on the road out of Booley, up past Diamond's and then angled back north, out to the cliffs. I hiked cautiously, picking my way along the rocks jutting from the puddingish mud that the path running parallel to the sea had become. For a time, the route swung inland, down a hedge-edged boreen that connected with dirt lanes on which each of three ramshackle farms stood far from the next like estranged relatives at a carefully seating-planned wedding reception. When I came upon the first, I spooked a child playing in the road past the time of night you'd think a child would be awake. She was a young thing, maybe eight, a small grimy girl charmingly entranced with poking a stick into a lake-size puddle in the center of the road. Noticing me just after I noticed her, she jumped with a start and ran through a gate and up to her farmhouse, all the while screaming, "People, Ma! People!" From somewhere inside, the ma flew to the door, interrupted in some chore that required a full apron over her dress, and she shoved the child protectively behind herself. The father emerged from around back brandishing the kind of pronged pitchfork I previously had seen only of red plastic and sold with Halloween costumes of the devil. A black and white dog, snout encased in an ancient leather muzzle, jetted across the front yard straight toward me, but slammed on the brakes when the man roared something unintelligible but apparently very clear to the dog. From inside, a baby, maybe two of them, wailed. I waved to the family, called out a hello, trying to show goodwill. But they only nodded.

Past a few more farms, then out again to the cliffs, the fog crawling now onto land. I cut onto a cart road, toward the sea, continued north, and there it was. The rock. The tree. The well. The well of St. Faicneam, who is a great one for the lost. For those seeking to regain the invisible. Health. Love. Hope. All that sort of thing. If you ever had any of that, and then you lost it, Faicneam's yer man.

Just as there supposedly are no atheists in foxholes, there probably are no heartbroken people who visit a holy well without taking half the chance that it might help. Even if the night before they'd seen it only as the inspiration for a scam. I searched my pockets for something to leave behind. Found the key to the cottage and my plastic bag of money. Unzipped my jacket a few inches and remembered the black silk scarf I'd found on the back of the door at the cottage. Drew it from around my neck, magicianlike into the increasing rain. Pressed it to the front of my confused skull. Then, lower, to the general location of my beat-up heart.

I tied the scarf to a branch. The high-fashion clootie hung just below the strip of hot yellow polyester knit that would never ever ever disintegrate, and next to a dirty time-battered knot of threads that once had been red-printed cotton. I didn't know if I was supposed to say anything—a prayer or an incantation. Or a thank-you. Because according to Joe, the bush was now supposed to take on my pain. Was the effect to be immediate, or would I have to wait? I kept silent. The rain quickened. My neck felt bare and cold. The legs of the scarf dampened and flapped weakly in the direction of the cottage, which is where, after a sufficient time of awaiting relief but feeling none, I walked, soggy, cold, now somebody other than the woman who'd left there that morning.

Dragonfly:

⌣⌣

Transformation

(State Your Wish Three Times)

𝒜mericans come to Booley because, a very long time ago, a whole lot of Booleyans went to America.

To stay. And without many other options.

According to the quick few sentences of Irish history slapped onto the back of The Complete and Total Map of Booley, between 1845 and 1849 an estimated one and a half million Irish left their famine-ravaged country for new lives in the States. The emigration devastated Booley as much as any community in the country. Out near the new fizzy water bottling plant, the celebrated coastal walking trail threads through the remains of stone houses and outbuildings, not a soul in sight save for the sheep that come and go through the gaping doorways. One hundred and fifty years later, descendants of the humans who left that place and countless other specks on the Irish map make their pilgrimages to the birthplace of long-dead ancestors they refer to as "their people."

Since the first waves of Yanks were sparked by JFK's 1963 Irish trip and that spring's cover feature in *National Geographic*, E. Dolan has stocked its small selection of souvenirs, most of it knitwear that fell from the needles of Frances and her friends and filled two shelves above the produce bin. After the death of Frances, and most of the other knitters, Una learned of a cheaper source and continued to sell Aran sweaters, but only after clipping from their necks the tags revealing their Taiwanese origin.

The woman who would kick Booleyan souvenirs up more than a few notches materialized at the bus stop on a Monday in late March of 1993, checked into Diamond's Hostel, moved into the far top bunk around the corner at the end of six-bed Room 5, ate peanut butter toast and drank tea and walked the cliffs for four days until an envelope bearing a check arrived for her in care of the post, and before the end of the day Finola O'Flynn had secured her the keys to the second-to-the-last building on the main road. Inside, the last of the Quinns' furniture awaited being moved up the hill to the couple's long-coveted modern home well away from their next-door pub, a newly constructed all-wood chalet that had been ordered through the mail and shipped from Norway in giant-size puzzle pieces. In the interim, Finola was at introducing herself around the town, saying she would be opening a craft shop, and if anyone knew any local artists, would they kindly pass along the word that she was in need of merchandise. For your trouble—even before you'd had time to consider whether you'd be going to any— she handed you a unisex-suitable key fob with a short length of sil-verish stony-looking beads knotted to it. To the chip shop she went, to Quinn's, to E. Dolan, to Willie Lynch's, to the Last Restaurant, and back to Diamond's, making her introductions, her requests, leaving her gifts, rhapsodizing about her goal of providing an incomparable selection of items for people to take back home and enjoy and cherish as reminders that they once had been amid the beauty that was Booley. Locals will tell you that, if the mood struck, she could speak of retail with the fervor of a tent revivalist, saying how fortunate she felt to be in a position where she could showcase the work of craftspeople to visitors from all over the world. Which she went on to do for a decade. And then the German. Her shop had no Finola, but it still had Liam. And now it also has me. Who, since that first Saturday in May, has been becoming her.

Didn't you ever want to become somebody else, somebody new? Didn't you ever need to?

When a bad patch hit, wasn't it natural to want to be the one who was smarter, better connected, without a problem in the world?

I know, I know. Not long ago, I was telling you that I didn't have anything to recover from, was walking behind Gina and into Booley almost boasting that. Carrying on about the level life I was enjoying. Well, I might not have had a problem when I got here, but this little speck on the map suddenly became the stage for a major one. The lights dimmed, the curtains drew back, and there was my own sad reality standing tall in the spotlight.

Gina had came here to discover who she was without the titles of wife, mother, employee. Major introspection had been the plan. When trouble landed on my borrowed doorstep, I wasn't interested in looking at even an inch of myself. Instead, I slipped into the persona of a person I'd jokingly been trying on shortly after arriving. Conveniently, the wrappings of a woman roughly my age and size and creative ability had been abandoned here, so close to the beach that it was like some sort of shell that had been outgrown. From what I would be told about the former occupant of this life, I knew her to be strong, wise, loving, possessing the answer for every situation. In short, everything you'd want to be. Especially if you were extremely confused.

Becoming someone new would not have been possible back home. There, even if I were enduring the worst tragedy, I'd have to go through my day being myself. Being Sophie in Sophie's bed, clothes, routine, world. In Booley, nobody really knew me. Certainly, I would become friendly to one extent or another with several who made their living on the same short street. But would they truly know who I was?

I began to use Finola O'Flynn like some people use Jesus. A savior was what I might have required, certainly, but I mean using him in the way that some of the most trendily faithful Christians did, with those WWJD bracelets. Reminding themselves in the instance of a moral quandary to ask What Would Jesus Do in their place. Would he take a hit or just say no? Would he throw a nutty or express himself calmly? Would he live a lie or be up front and spare his girlfriend a load of heartache? According to most everything I'd been told, Finola was wise as a prophet, patient as a saint, strong as any god, one to whom, once I emerged from my shocked haze, I converted.

I will admit, though, my first instinct was to run.

"Choi Luck. Sam Yin. Lee Yee."

Liam was fanning credit card receipts the morning after the St. Jeans. "Choi Luck! Asian luck! Brilliant! Ya did good, woman, I should mitch off every day."

And that's when he looked up and saw me and my backpack.

"Here are your keys." I set them on the bead table.

"Sophie. Were you not going to give it three days?"

"Two's more than plenty, thanks." I stepped back, checked my pocket for the bus schedule I'd found in Gina's room.

"Is it the cottage? Too remote?"

"It's nothing to do with anything here. Except that since I got here, everything's gone wrong. You have no idea."

Liam: "I do now."

Everybody here knew. Because, as Liam went on to inform me, around here, even if you don't give the first letter of the first word of the situation, everybody knows everything. Is wide, as they'd say. And is usually unable to keep silent. Therefore, news, both the good and the bad, regularly pinballs with fiber-optic speed from one end of Booley to the other. The less positive news, he noted, never ceases to move considerably swifter than the cheerier bits of information. As had been the case my first morning in Booley.

I didn't ask, but Liam went on to explain how on Thursday morning Una had come over from next door to tell him she'd got it from Siobhan Greene, who'd been in to mail a package, who'd gotten the information from Dicky Dunne when he'd dropped off the skateboard her boy had left at the youth center, who got it from Turner, who, as if she didn't already have more than her share of problems in this life, at half-noon was barreling down the Limerick Road, much too close to the last of Batty Slattery's bullocks progressing down the road, and that started the chain reaction of spooked animals, all big eyes and leaping forward and shoving and tumbling around the corner and almost into the front of Noel's van. One of the Yank's who was with Una and Noel at Quinn's last night—the quiet one—wasn't she there in the front seat, turning ghostly, stopped her car. Apologized. Inquired about any injuries. Noel said there weren't any, and that he had no time to chat. His explanation: "Catching a plane."

I let that sink in for a second, then remembered that's what I soon was going to be doing.

"The bus . . ." I pointed up the road, up the hill.

"If that's your decision"—Liam looked sadder than you'd expect—"I'll give you a lift."

The fire was cranking. The heat I'd never figured out how to work at the cottage melted something in me and I asked, "You know what else?" and I meant that as a rhetorical question, but he took it as an actual one. Because it turns out he knew about Charlie St. Jean, too.

"Sophie, my apologies."

"You didn't do anything. He didn't, either. That's the problem. He didn't tell me. That he—you know . . ."

"I know."

A big man with a big camera around his neck and a big camouflage vest fit for a big safari, his laminated photo ID clipped to one of the hundreds of vest pockets marking him as belonging to some official society, barreled over to one of Max's wine racks.

I moved to get my sad self out of the way of any spending.

"Price, please," he said to me in a surprisingly squeaky little accent. He was holding yet another of the racks with fish silhouttes worked into the sides. A copy of the exact thing I was going to present to Charlie St. Jean. My extremely shallow myth-related research had told me that here, the salmon is connected to knowledge. In America, the salmon is connected to efforts to lower cholesterol, and to leave your pain-in-the-ass family for a drunken guys' weekend on the river. Here, it represents wisdom. And I was going to give it to a man about whom I thought I knew everything.

"Price? Please?"

"Fifty quid," said Liam, "emm, euro, fifty euro."

"I would like."

"Brilliant. Tanks a million."

I watched wisdom swim out the door, and make the left, and head up the road, the same as Charlie's family had done.

"'Twasn't Aoife who told about yer man, she's a right vault when it comes to confidences. Someone in the kitchen, it was—"

"That's where I told her most of, in the kitchen . . . —well a door at the other end of it . . .

"The kitchen's where this party over heard. And took the news to Quinn's."

Others compared notes there, Una told Liam first thing this morning. Due to the religious-sounding surname being applied to credit card slips up and down the road, the trio was memorable to Booley's shopkeepers and restaurateurs. The mother and daughters had their dinner at the Last Restaurant, where the mother wanted the waitress, from Sweden, mind you, to correctly pronounce the Irish dishes on the menu. They went to Noel's and photographed him at the loom, then purchased table linens in the shade "natural."

They each had a Fanta outside Emilio's, and then they were in here, no news to me, then to Una's for stamps and four of the Taiwanese Irish knits, they also wandered into the hostel, where Diamond filled out the paperwork for his new moneymaking scheme: selling "a piece of Ireland" complete with certificate of ownership for the square inch. Theirs was made out to Charles St. Jean A.K.A. Daddy.

"What's 'acca'?" Liam asked.

"Oh—A.K.A. 'Also known as.'" I laughed then despite none of it being particularly funny to me. "Another name for somebody. When they're known to be more than one person."

New shoppers. More people going over to the dish of bracelets and snooping at the tags, connecting my made-up titles to the little metal charm of house, giraffe, book, generic squiggle. In the quiet spaces, I told Liam about Gina. What we shared as friends, and then what I'd tried to share when her life changed so drastically. A few times Liam reached over and touched my arm in a way that was nothing but sympathetic. I had hoped to disappear as a wave of shoppers receded, but had been delayed by one of the last, a gnome-like mushroom-shaped woman with a pair of canes and one knee that didn't bend who took me aside and asked was there a money-back guarantee on this bracelet labeled Romance and the women who were with her went riotous with laughter—Ha-ha-ha, oh, Mary Ellen, you're killing us already, knock it off, oh, please—and they told me that this one here, she was the true comedian of the group and that those with bladder control problems had learned to sit out of earshot.

The weather was turning, brighter by the hour, like somebody had found the knob labeled Contrast. I drifted farther towards the door, from where I watched Emilio in the chip shop's front garden, kicking a soccer ball to his grandsons, who were twins from Italy and who, at little more than the age at which you get the hang of walking, already had figured out perfect relationship of foot to ball. Their mother, one of those simply chic chopstick-thin cosmetic-free black-clad European types who could would never be mistaken for anyone from any other continent, clicked photos from the side-lines and cheered in the language that almost had been Aoife's. "Good on ya, Emilio," cheered Ralpho as he cycled past the scrim-mage. I wanted to hop on the back of his bike. I had explained my share to Liam. It was time to leave. I ducked behind a customer checking the window on his phone. Collected my coat and pack from the stairs. Heard the word, "Stop." Liam was at the door.

"Wish I could," I told him "Wish I could have stopped the whole thing. Wish I'd never told Vernon I'd set up his display of rabbits. But I did. Fast-forward nearly a year and a half, from set-ting up a rabbit display to having a display of St. Jeans in front of me. Three of them. Not just one—that would be bad enough—but three. Three. Two kids. Nice little girls. At least they seemed sort of nice."

"Christ."

"Yeah, he's got something to do with this, too. I suspect the wife's a heavy religious type. That they both are. Not that I ever saw Charlie attending any kind of church or synagogue or pagoda or bonfire or anything. He always had an excuse for being extra busy around Christmas, Easter, so I don't know what kind of worshiping he chose then, if any. But I guess now I do. Maybe half an hour before I saw her name written out, his wife was describing him for me. He's in charge, she made him sound like from biblical times. Man has the last word. Of course I gave a little opinion about that, and she said that despite whatever I thought along those lines, I still would love him. I would love him. She said that! Didn't know I already did. But only for about twenty minutes more, up to the point where the sale was made and I saw her name on her card, and a photo of the entire family hanging from her wallet."

"Sophie."

"I don't want to make a big deal of it. It's over and, well, it's over."

"But yer plans with him." He moved back to allow a trio of shoppers to enter.

I made a "What can you do?" kind of face. And said, "I feel saved in a way. Spared. Like Aoife, kind of. She told me her story last night. What if she'd gotten farther in with her druggy boyfriend? What if I'd gotten farther in with Charlie? There's maybe a dozen pieces of his belongings in my house right now. I'm at least spared having to toss a hundred bits of his shit. I can be glad for that much."

"Sophie."

I wasn't looking at Liam during all this. I was looking at the twins and Emilio, and remembering how I'd once thought Charlie and I could somehow turn my father into one of those men I saw Emilio being on this morning: all regular business out there in the world doing his work, but melting into useless gush at the sight of a grandchild.

"So I'm saved," I said. "That's a good thing. Truly no one to rush back to now."

Liam did the arm-touching thing again, then straightened in his chair. "If you'll forgive me for being bold, it seems to me that what's bothering you most—about Gina, at least, and perhaps with Charlie—is the fact you've been made redundant."

"Huh?"

"Emm, as you were made by the rickrack mill. Your services weren't needed any longer: You were made redundant."

I knew the word to mean that something was being repeated. And as far as Charlie St. Jean went, I was not so much replaced as I was a duplicate. Another woman in another town. Liam decided from the silence, "I've hurt ya."

I hurt, but not from anything he'd done. Other than being right on target, that is.

"No," I said. "No."

"Friends?"

"Friends."

"Then you'll help me one more day," he decided. "First day was only a half. You still have one more to the work the promised three."

"I promised nothing. And I'm afraid to stay and see what might happen today. But, really, what's left to lose? I don't have a job, I don't have a home, my friend doesn't want me, and my boyfriend wants me—but he also wants his wife and children."

"Correction. You've work here. You've a home here. There's those who'll become friends if you need, and certainly, Sophie, once word of your single status spreads, we'll have to bar the windows and door."

"I need to leave. I'll get one of those cheap flights to, I don't know—Wales? To somewhere else." "Haven't you ever been really confused?"

"Confusion's what drove me here, if you'll recall."

"Well, it's driving me out."

From somewhere up the hill, bells sounded. The ones inside the clock on the mantel responded. After their combined twelve rings, Liam spoke.

"But not without a cup a tea first."

And as a group of priests at the bookcase boldly copied notes from a travel guide they did not want to have to buy, I was suddenly hugged with all the empathy I rightfully deserved, right there in the doorway of the craft shop called Finola O'Flynn, which this moment brightened ever so slightly with the sparks of the first real fire to burn there since the last one had gone out.

Coin:

ᗑ

Gain, Profit, Reward

(State Your Wish Three Times)

Thing is, I don't usually drink this much tea.

But I took the offered cup.

And another.

And—"G'wan, g'wan"—"No, I'm fine"—"G'wan, g'wan"—another.

You'd think all that caffeine would have me further charged to leave. But the only place I went whenever I stood up was to the bathroom—sorry—toilet. Then back into the shop. Where, needing to have some function in this life, needing, honestly, to be needed, and seeing an opportunity for that here, I decided to do what I did best. I did what I wished someone would do for me right then: I saw a mess and I made order.

That day, I said yep to Booley. And in between inventorying everything in the books and music section, I replied the same to every shopper who entered and wondered if I were her, or, sometimes, "hair."

"Yep."

The question had been posed by ERINTOURS Guests #6 and #7, Shannon Ferriter-Garvey and Tim-Pat Garvey, both of

Schaumberg, Illinois, U.S.A. The pair was half the average age of the other tour members who'd come through in my few days, and despite the drizzle, they hadn't swathed themselves in plastic. I knew ERINTOURS tourists came around in the coaches Liam had said were so vital, and when I saw their name tags I wished he were in the shop rather than upstairs trying to reach his girl on her mobile.

Tim-Pat wore a shiny silky green Notre Dame jacket, the back embroidered with an angry swollen-headed leprechaun poised with fists ready to coldcock his opponent, the left front telling everybody this garment belonged to "Tim-Pat," in quotes like that, from the class of '87. Shannon was more tastefully attired, wrapped in the calf-length ruby and jade tweed cape I recognized from Attracta's window and knew to be sold for close to $450. Pinning it closed was one of the first-sized hammered brass brooches Noel stocked for that purpose, and for the equivalent of $65 a pop. Shannon's fingers bore the contents of a small mine of gold and gems, including a large ring with a pair of hands cradling a heart, the Claddagh design that I learned from a tea-towel hang tag originated three hundred years ago up in Galway and that, according to Noel, no self-respecting Irish American, genuine or wannabe, can leave the country without wearing on neck, wrist, finger, or earlobe.

Shannon moved around the shop with an eye trained for the unusual. It was all "Honey, look at this," and when she asked that, her honey did, with a hand on his wife's arm, admiring the this, and the her. She studied a pair of iron wall sconces forged by Max, but ultimately picked out his large eight-legged candle chandelier. She stood back and regarded and in the end liked, but didn't love, an oval mirror with a frame painted in waves of green and blue by the ex-nun who runs a therapeutic bodywork business at her place out by the castle ruins. Shannon preferred sister Tobia's larger square mirror with the carving of a small boat at the top, a piece I was delighted to see claimed because Liam had referred to it as a relic, having had it in the shop so long. It had been housed in a dented cardboard box, and wrapped inside that by few protective yards of cloth. Technically, it had been in the shop, but you would have needed X-ray vision to find it before I'd hung it above the soaps the previous. Tim-Pat carried his wife's selections to the side of my table and set them on the floor next to the CD player, which, as the little display sign I'd made up pointed to, was now occupied by a disc of a group of old ladies who'd been recorded as part of the Irish radio station's effort to capture the region's ancient music before it died along with the few left who knew it. The words were in Irish, and were chanted rather than sung, echoing miles deep from a secretly located cave of memory.

Shannon found her way over to the bead table. Considering the double-digit karat count on one of her fingers alone, I didn't take her for even a semiprecious stone gal. Even so, she showed interest, and I got this question: "Did you happen to make this?"

She was holding up an elastic bracelet that consisted of a lineup of green stones, some glass, some ceramic, along with a few pieces of peridot and agate that had been tumbled to a smooth and shiny finish. The centerpiece was a silver disc with a raised knotted triangle. I had finished making the bracelet maybe ten minutes before. The Krazy Glue that hopefully cemented my questionable knot hidden inside one of the larger bead's holes probably had dried only seconds ago. Now Shannon was twirling it, and rolling it in a way that made me worry that all the components were about to go flying around the shop. In a slow-motion tragedy, Tim-Pat Garvey would step his snow-white Nikes on one, go flying, whack his Hair Club for Men toupe on the edge of Max's iron-framed tea table and Liam would return to not only a death but a huge lawsuit.

But Shannon completed the toying without incident.

And I said, "Yep."

"This here." She pointed to another piece, specifically to the little silver yin–yang Liam had strung between two green ovals of the prized Italian plastic. "The tag says this is a symbol for Light and Dark."

Nod.

"As in for good and bad, right?"

Another nod.

"Like how life is, right?"

A nod again. And again. And the thought that Shannon was insightful. And the wondering, because I am basically nosey, what were the bad things had ever happened to her, with all her poise and beauty? Because no matter how together you might appear, bad things must have crossed your path. As they do everyone's.

Shannon placed the piece back on the table. Thought for a moment. Glanced over at her honey, who had thumbed to the G section of the *Complete and Total Book of Irish Surnames* and was deep in concentration. Shannon turned to me. Said, "I'll take four."

"This swirly thing. What does it mean?"

I jumped in my chair. I'd been getting into the process, trying to be present to the clacking of the beads when I put my hand in a cup, the cool weight they comprised when a piece was done, the little circles of art they could be if you gave some thought to color scheme or theme. Right then I was concentrating on making a pattern of beads that ran gray to blue to gray, and the centerpiece a stone in the shape of a bird. Looking up, I saw a pair of college students from America—or at least two young women who wore maroon sweatshirts that read, in white capital letters, HARVARD. From that I figured they were brains. Or, at the very least, once had visited a gift shop back in Cambridge.

"This," the girl on the left repeated, holding out one of my bracelets, on which a silver metal swirly thing glinted. "This, like, swirly thing. What's it mean?"

"Read the tag." Her friend was impatient.

"Oh . . ."

I thought how Liam might put the reply. Which probably had been the same way Finola had pronounced it. So "Life," I answered, steamrolling the *f* between my top teeth and lower lip.

The girls grinned. "Liiiffe," one repeated, and the other laughed. "Liiiffe!" And I don't know if they were getting the kick out of me, or the word, or the concept, but each of them ended up buying a bracelet with a little swirly thing on it. They left repeating the word. *Life. Life.* And I'd made two more sales, and that was the point, after all.

"Woman, ye're fuckin' *deadly*." Liam was in the shap, a box I figured had something to do with one of his calculated million long-overdue chores.

He was smiling as he said the words, so I was confused. I also was embarrassed, caught in my yepping and nodding and liiffes. I hesitated, then: "And that's a good thing?"

"Yep." He stopped. "But brilliant's more like it."

"Toilet?" From the doorway, a rotund man carrying a huge golf-course-appropriate umbrella asked this in the common vernacular that cut through all the skirt-the-issue words *bathroom* and *ladies' room* and *restroom*. He stood in back of Liam, was looking at me.

"Sorry," I said, complete with an all-apologies-for-disappointin'-ya wince.

Liam winked. The man pushed past, leading a string of senior citizens who *oooohed* as they entered. However urgent the group's need for a toilet, it was not as great as the pull of the armful of elasticized bracelets—rough-cut green moss agate from which dangled silver discs bearing raised knotted designs. I'd just replenished the dish, taking another dozen bracelets from the wall and coming up with a few lines about their meaning. The leaf was Growth, the mountains were Challenge. I swiped the alleged qualities from the creams and soaps and candles Gina had been given, and slapped Healing, Patience, and New Life onto whatever seemed appropriate. The bracelets filled the dish like a sparkling dessert. Properly lured, the front line of tourists moved forward in unison.

"Beau-tee-ful," said the first woman, trying out the English that I could tell was a far reach from whatever she was used to speaking. I gave a "Tanks" as I took her money and she took the five bracelets I'd just granted powers. "Tanks a million!"

"Look—a little fish!"

Yanks this time.

Three of them.

This woman admiring the bracelet featuring a weighty silver salmon was older than the collegians had been. She wore a spanking-new white sweatshirt printed with an American flag and a fire truck. In his T-shirt reading SACRILEGE, and sporting so many piercings that his ears resembled spiral-bound notebooks, her lanky son hunched over the CD shelves, flipping the offerings noisily, probably looking for something loud and mainstream and alternative radio station that wasn't sold anywhere for at least fifty miles. The first album by Jimmy Donnelly, recently re-released on compact disc, was coming from the speakers right then. "Harses, harses, everywhere harses," sang Jimmy, Booley's version of local boy makes good. That good was quite dusty, said Liam, now at the table paying bills while enjoying the opportunity to teach Booleyan Culture 101. Jimmy's hit had been back in 1973, when piles of fan mail, some of it addressed only to "Jimmy of Booley," regularly awaited him at the *An Post* window at E. Dolan. But despite the passing of years, his appearance on Ireland's version of the *Tonight* show remained legendary. And the reason he'd been a guest—the surprise national hit single "Horses, Horses," which told of his visiting the horse fair held each August on Booley's main road but spoke thematically larger of a fine Irish day in an era long gone by—was now taught to every class of Booleyan schoolchildren and sung at wakes of the old people who would have been young when that kind of Ireland actually existed. Unable to find a follow-up hit, Jimmy took early retirement in the hills above Booley, collecting royalties sent regularly by the Irish Music Rights Organization and making most of his living through busy summertime workshops in songwriting and the art of the pennywhistle. And, of course, a standing appearance at the still-annual horse fair.

"Harses!" sang Jimmy.

"Harses!" sang Liam as he, climbed the stairs with a box of correspondence he would finally tackle.

"This is painful," moaned the kid clacking through the CDs. His mother ignored him and said, "I like this whole fish thing," to no one in particular.

"Fish are an ancient Celtic symbol, you know," the man to the her right informed her in the tone of an annoyed public radio host who'd been given a call-in topic that could not have interested him less. He pronounced Celtic with the soft *C*, like we do at home for the basketball team, an error I'd realized my first day here.

"Oh! Carol at the office loves shit like that, ancient symbols, mystical mumbo jumbo, all that," the woman told him excitedly before asking me, "Got any more?"

"It's not shit," the man corrected in a loud whisper. "It has meaning to these people." He lifted his chin toward me, wordlessly reminding her that I was one of these people and therefore might be insulted. I gave a no-offense-taken smile and continued my stringing.

"I apologize," the woman said, tilting her head apologetically. "But do you? Have any more of this stuff?"

I said yep to that, then went back and said nope to the man who asked if Mudpie Potters used glazes containing lead because in some Third World countries, which he'd read somewhere that Ireland was, the practice still continues. I said tanks to the three high school girls who each selected a bracelet. I said grand to the man and woman who decided upon matching Buaille shirts. I said bye to them all then I closed the door to end this very long day. Behind it stood the backpack. And the man who, hours before, had removed that burden from my shoulders. Now asking, "D'ya need a lift—to the cottage?"

"The coach is yer only man," Noel said once I joined his table at Quinn's after ten because there is no point in getting there before ten, don't ask me why because the only answer I've been given when I've asked is that's when you get there.

It had been a good day of sales for all along the road, but Noel had done the best. Grand, brilliant, fantastic, unbelievable, truth be told.

He'd sold another cape. A stack of scarves. Three brooches plus the one to woman from Chicago—let's not forget her cape—and two shawls for two granddaughters of a woman who had a list of names under the heading Souvenirs For.

A table runner in linen, another in cotton, and two sets of place mats to coordinate with each. The first four sales from the new line of floppy hats that Noel's cousin in the Bullwinklish-sounding village of Borris had sewn up over the winter from cloth Noel had woven up over the winter.

"Didn't think they were coming," Noel admitted as he raised his glass toward me. "Did not. But sure there's hope yet."

"For Yanks."

"Right. Yanks. Yanks are crucial. Ye'll learn."

"She's already learnt," Liam said, "It's my shop, but I'm a total *amadáin* when compared to Sophie."

"When compared to anybody," Una shot.

"But especially when compared to Sophie," Noel said.

All were being kind. Knowing what they knew about me—which was just about everything—they were doing their best to cheer me. Liam had driven me to the cottage, after ducking into Una's for a canvas bag of groceries. Bread, milk, tea, eggs, basic Joe necessities, meant for me, who, as someone who'd be living here, would need food at some point. He parked in front of the cottage and went for a walk on the strand, an hour later knocking to see if I wanted to go back to town for the evening.

I said yes. Mainly because it beat being alone. And I wasn't, there at the table with Una and Noel and Liam, whom I was informing. "Main thing, I know-now at least is to keep my mouth shut. Americans don't seem to like the idea that they're buying from another American."

"Understand," said Noel, and he leaned in to give a lesson. Raised his hands to emote. They were at once stubby and enormous and strangely elegant in a way that made me want to reach for them. He folded his hands and I wondered what it was that this man prayed for, the seed of that being Liam's telling me earlier in the day about Noel's recently having gone back to Mass after decades, and I imagined the hands meeting in the long-ago-taught steeple fashion a child would use. "They want everythin' authentic," Noel was saying to me, and I had to come back to the present and to the Yanks and to what a pain some of them can be. "Mary at Tír na nÓg? Last summer, had no help atall. Then some Spanish girls on holiday mentioned they'd like to stay in Booley and work. She had them hooverin' within minutes. They were brilliant. But the Yanks whinged. I can't do the Yank accent, like, but what they said was"—and here he made himself sound all indignant, and I have to say that he was right in that he could sound nowhere close to a Yank but, as they say, fair play to him for the attempt—" 'Spanish people? I thought this was Oirland.'"

"Yanks are a funny bunch," I told him.

"No offense . . ."

"None taken. I'm learning."

"It does help to know the consumer," Noel said. I liked how he said "consumer," how he made the *u* a big *eoooh*. "Knowledge like that can be the difference between life 'n' death for shops like Liam's and mine. Una? She'd sell the bread and tea daily 'til the end of time, even if she had ten horns growin' from her arse."

"Might sell even more in that state," Una threw in.

"What I'm sayin' is the world requires bread and tea—the world 'round here, at least. They'll be going without if they don't patronize Una, or some such shop, though who'd go anywhere but Una's? What Liam and I carry, it's lovely—but it's total extravagance. Today, yer wan from Chicago. Her life wouldn't end if she'd left without that table runner. Food? It's another thing entirely." Noel stopped here, took a swallow of his milkshaky pint. I did the same with the one before me. As did Una with hers. Liam with his. "That being said, though, I like t' think we offer somethin' vital in a different way. From us, tourists can get some thing that reminds them of the peace, beauty, whatever it is they found here. It might remind them of a fine time with a beloved person, or with no one atall." He stopped here, you could see his concern that he'd said something that might have bothered me. I, who had no one atall with which to travel, gave him a smile. Noel he nodded and went on: Yer wan in Chicago, she passes by her table, she looks at my runner, maybe she recalls a memory. It's possible to look at something from Liam's shop or mine and remember somethin' good that happened in a life. That might be the most important thing we sell."

Una nodded, I nodded. Noel nodded.

"That is the science of the souvenir," Liam said, and he apologized that he didn't know French atall, but said he has been told the word souvenir means memory, or something close. I liked the image Noel had given. I could see "yer wan in Chicago." Was she Vivian Teague or Pip somebody? The names on their tags still floated before me.

"Finola, now, she Yanks," Una said without, I noticed, any sign of concern that she might have said something that might have bothered Liam. I glanced at Liam, who could have added the jab "and Germans," but he was focused on Una, listening as if just another listener. "Never was to the States in her life, mind, but could read their thoughts as if they were shouting them aloud. Knew what would sell to them, knew what they wanted to hear. Charmed 'em. Ab-so-lute-ly charmed 'em."

"She did, yeah." Noel was saying this and was nodding, and now looking somewhere through and beyond the walls of Quinn's, suddenly wilting and wistful when he should have been enjoying the initial happy stages of a beer-buzz conclusion to what he'd called a fuckin' unbelievable day. Quickly, the quiet at our table got filled up by the button accordionist who'd been unpacking his instrument at the next bench. He appeared to have stepped from another era, and, if put next to Joe Cronin, would have made him appear to be a young colt. A strawlike, careful woman of the same vintage, who had carried the case into the pub, placed the straps gently on the man's shoulders once he took a seat. But age was no issue when this man began to play, his fingers picking out tunes eagerly and fast, like they were rare coins thrown in a field of short grass. Noel still appeared pensive. Lonely, even, despite the joyous sounds coming from two seats away, and despite that I was right next to him in a room jampacked with people. He was thinking, I was certain, of Finola. Who had charmed 'em. And then had left this place where, nearly two and a half years later, another woman had decided to remain.

Wheel:

ᘛᘚ

Travel, Moving On

(State Your Wish Three Times)

Finola could have charmed them with her wardrobe alone.

Take a look in her closet.

I've done more than that with it.

Beige and white herringbone-weave housecoat, full from the waist and down to the floor, worthy of a forties starlet. A pink shirt-waist dress with wild palm leaves waving over the whole of it. Broomstick skirt in a rainbow gauze. Chinese-restaurant-hostess black satin jacket with dragonish embroidery. Silvery button-down shirt of Space Age see-through net that screams for the use of an undergarment, or, maybe, against.

Nubby raw silks, lightest shimmery polyesters, all lengths of sleeves, hems reaching to thigh and to toe hung above five pairs of footwear lined up in two short rows: sandals with a complicated series of suede laces, navy Chuck Taylors, reptilian pumps, lug-soled hiking boots, slippers of midnight blue terry cloth sprinkled with white embroidered stars. Next to the closet, and below the night table, were a pair of shelves puffy with the kind of fisher-men's knit sweaters the girls from Trim-True had given Gina and me money to bring them as souvenirs. Thick with gargantuan cables of wool dyed ecru, gray, orangy brown, and the sodalite blue that colors everyone's eyes at the start of life. The various skins Finola had shed and left behind, not unlike the transparent diamond-puckered snakeskins I've found in summer at my driveway's edge.

I know I had no business looking at her clothes, and less business eventually putting them on, but eventually, honestly, I couldn't resist. Though Gina had been exceedingly kind in purchasing our entire trip wardrobe, she'd stocked us up with stuff that was trail-ready. I quickly tired of wearing clothing that made brushing noises with every movement and that, should the need arise, could double as either a personal flotation device or a high-calorie snack. Heeding the siren call of Finola's various left-behinds, I opened one of the baskets in the corner of the front bedroom, found a stack of neatly foldeds. Closed the lid. Opened it again.

So that was me there. Me in Booley, in Finola O'Flynn's cottage, in Finola O'Flynn's shop, in Finola O'Flynn's chair. And now, starting my third week here, in Finola O'Flynn's clothes. Leaving a post window at E. Dolan, wearing Finola O'Flynn's clothes and opening her mail.

The envelope was addressed to Finola O'Flynn, so I expected to find something about the shop in general—a special order, maybe, or a bill, or an ad, or a thank-you like those Liam keeps displayed on a shelf behind the bead table, very nice notes from people who say they are grateful for his special care in packing a glass piece or who appreciated the recommendation of those stables beyond the new cemetery, if only for the opportunity to photograph a husband wearing a World War II-style helmet and being led along a path atop a nag. This letter, I quickly figured out, because I went on and read it while in line to make a deposit, was actually for me.

On stationery from the Limerick Inn, with the silver business address crossed out and replaced with one from Maryland, was:

Dear Miss O'Flynn,

I was in your store last week as part of a tour group that was through Erin Tours tour groups. I bought a T-shirt for my son (least I could do, he paid for my trip, it was a gift, for my 70th b.d., he thinks I need to travel now that I am retired, and I did like the trip, nothing personal against your country, but I don't think I am cut out to be a world traveler. I am much happier back home, and not roaming around with a bunch of strangers who all they want to do is drink) and after I paid for my purchases I saw a container of bracelets and I then read the word gratitude on the label of one of them and I didn't care what it looked like (though it was very pretty, peach-colored beads and a silver thing of some sort hanging from it). I wanted to buy it for my daughter-in-law. I figured it would be an easy way to thank her for the trip without having to write a letter of thanks for the trip because we are not really buddy-buddy in-laws who write letters to each other and this would get me off the hook and that duty over with. Well, I gave the bracelet to her when they picked me up at O'Hare and she couldn't stop admiring it and saying nice things about it and I thought that would be the end but do you know that ever since then she has been at my door just about as often as the mailman and before my trip and me giving her your bracelet she never came over unless it was a holiday. Now she's always checking in to see if I need anything when she's on her way to the store or to make sure if I heard about the possibility of a tornado, and I want to say to her don't you have a telephone but—and this is why I'm writing this letter, sorry to take so long—there is something sort of nice about getting to know her finally (she's been married to my son for nine years, so maybe it's about time. My problem, I guess, was that I liked the first wife better). I probably could have gone another nine years still having not much to do with her. The bottom line is: She's kind of a good

*kid, which is what my son was trying to tell me all this time
but I never saw it because I never gave her a chance and she
never gave me a chance, and maybe I wouldn't know she's kind
of a good kid if she didn't like your bracelet so much and if she
didn't think, as she seems to, that the word on the label was
written by me rather than by you.*

I read it again, then slid Mrs. James Mooney's letter in the
pocket of Finola's gauzy lavender pull-on pants to show it to Liam
when I got back to the shop after the banking. I didn't buy the connection between a metal charm and a change in a relationship, but I
felt pleased about this weird happy incident in Mrs. James Mooney.
I didn't remember the bracelet, or waiting on the customer, but I did
know that something I'd made, or made up, was appreciated. And
that was cool enough.

"Finola O'Flynn?"

"What?"

I really should be asking, "Whattt?"

I've noticed you have to let the *t*'s go on like that. Not stuttered,
as it might look here, rather, breathed, ending in air. Any word that
ends in a *t* gets that treatment, final letter hanging dainty and fragile off the end of the word like icicles from a roof edge on a sunny
day. I love their words that end in *t*. Let get set bet met. "Pet" is
what Una calls her kids when she's being sweet to them. "Yes,
Petttttt" is what she'll say.

I didn't ask, "Whattt?" of this woman who's asking for Finola
O'Flynn. I only ask, "What?" Because she's a bank official.

"No, no, I'm not Finola."

"Don't I know you're not Finola," stated the teller emphatically.
"I was assigned to this route the same year she opened her shop.
Saw her weekly those many years. I'm Kathleen O'Donnell." She
gave me a smile as she pointed to the name engraved on the golden
plate pinned to her white blouse.

I had no nameplate, so I just said, "And I'm Sophie White. Here to make a deposit for Finola O'Flynn. The store. Finola O'Flynn the shop, I mean." Then I handed the zipper bag of coins, bills, traveler's checks, and credit card slips up to Kathleen O'Donnell, through the window cut into the side of the big green boxy Bank of Ireland van that, when it pulled up for a two-hour duration every Thursday afternoon, became Booley's center of finance. The town had no bank. Not even a hole in the wall, or a drink link, or whatever is the current slang for the ATM Booleyan business types were lobbying for.

"I was saying Finola O'Flynn to speak the name, is all," Kathleen told me, though her explanation really hadn't clarified anything.

While she emptied the deposit bag of its contents and keyed numbers onto a computer screen, I thought ahead. To one night, maybe in the frigid dark of next February, to being back in my old living room, reading some book while sleet shot into the glass of my picture window. I would be deeply deposited back in my regular life then, once again living in the same old world, routine, home, clothes, room, the very same center cushion I occupied so many nights that the couch was beginning to take on the look of a faint smile. Looking up from my page, I might out of nowhere whisper: "Booley." Then the slide show would begin.

"Almost like you're conjuring her," I said.

"And wouldn't it be grand if we actually could?" Kathleen O'Donnell asked as she handed me my receipts.

Liam Keegan felt I already had some kind of power.

"You're only magical," he'd say often, the first time being exactly a week after the exit of Charlie St. Jean and Gina Stebbins from my world. Most waking hours of those seven straight days, I occupied myself getting the shop in order, some close version of the picture I'd imagined the day I first walked in. I painted walls, shelves, tables, anything that wasn't for sale or that wasn't a person or a dog. Using a passable version of the crouched ancient lettering on the signs that read FINOLA O'FLYNN, I made signs for the mini-departments of music, clothing, home design, books. While those dried, I wrote out smaller cards to inform shoppers that all merchandise is made right here in Ireland, most of it in Greater Booley, that special orders can be requested from any artist represented, that all purchases can be shipped to any point on the globe, and that we honor most credit cards, debit cards, and traveler's checks. I sorted the merchandise, organized it by size, color, title, then gave each item its own home, fresh and visible. Pyramids, stacks, rows, everything with the necessary merchandising textbook focal point. I nailed a row of hooks into ceiling beams from which to hang Max's wrought-iron candle chandeliers, previously stored beneath one of the tables like heavy and threatening spiders. I stood back to admire. And to realize that soon after parachute-landing into Finola O'Flynn, where I supposed I now was employed, I had changed it for the better.

"How's the form?" Una would ask me, or Noel would ask me, or Aoife would ask me, or Emilio, in his odd mix of Italian accent using Irish parlance, would ask me. To all, I answered, "Fine." Which physically I was, so it was not really a lie. But much of that response was fiction. I felt a loss in my life. A hole. Plural losses and voids, actually, but who was counting? I tired myself with work, with walks, with errands for Joe and trips to the cliffs and nights in town, but I kept my sleeping hours to a minimum because I was not very successful at rest. Fiction was the world in which I spent many of my waking hours. Making up meanings to go with each of the bracelets bearing a charm or two or four. Flipping through an Irish coat-of-arms book to learn that fruit represents Freedom and Peace, that oak leaves mean Strength. Or looking at, say, a boot, and thinking of all it might symbolize Walking, Moving, Making a journey, Slogging through a field of shit. Whatever meaning I came up with, the bracelets with bore explanatory tags were the ones that were selling. Nationwide, businesspeople whose livelihoods depended on tourists already knew well what the papers were reporting: We're only just into the beginning of the season and already there's been a 30 percent drop in income from tourists. The state of the world started the slide, and the summer's persistent rain looked to be another spike in the coffin. For most of the past month, rain had not only been falling, it nearly had been the air itself, annoying the visitors, but absolutely killing farmers, who had little to do aside from plowing under their rotting crops. Not since the mid-sixties had a summer's weather been so poor, and with this kind of start, who was to say it wouldn't surpass that record? The radio gave the grim news in the daily weather reports for Malin to Carnsore Point, Valentia Island to Hook Head. But in any season, Una told me, "Blue sky is always a temporary bonus." So the general idea was you smoked 'em while you got 'em.

Anything that was selling well despite the weather, Liam wanted stocked and ready. So I'd been matching charms to a widened rainbow of goals for which customers could hope: Success, Swiftness, Protection, Friendship, Luck, Alertness, Peace, Wisdom, Peace, Sustenance, Travel, Happiness, Abundance, Strength. You name the emotion or desire or potential problem, I had it covered. Just that morning a postcard of Sir Bob Geldof as on display in Madame Toussaud's London wax museum had arrived sent by someone named Loop, who wrote to tell Finola that "Last Monday while in Booley I bought two bracelets—'Serenity' and 'Joy'—and, since, have felt increased amounts of both. One question: Must I remove them while in the bath? Please advise. Yours sincerely."

Enough people were joining Loop in finding the dish of bracelets and reading the tags and connecting the charms and their nonexistent powers to their own deficiencies or wishes, or to someone right then in need of whatever was written on the tag. And by bankday the last week in May, four more coaches filled with tourists had made the stop in Booley and I had amassed a pretty decent wad of pounds and euros, plus a stack of credit card receipts and traveler's checks, to hand up to the window. A chilly breeze was lifting that afternoon, but my zippered pouch containing seven days of the shop's income was enough to keep me warm for the ten minutes I had to stand in line behind Mrs. Quinn, who was waiting behind four young hikers busy removing stashes of traveler's checks from somewhere deep within the recesses of their overworked underclothes.

"Coaches?" asked Kathleen O'Donnell as she stacked the paper money into neat piles, pulling the bills taut, as if they were tiny bedsheets.

"Coaches rock," I answered, and Kathleen O'Donnell chuckled a line of coffee-percolatorish ha-ha-ha-ha-ha's as she made out my receipt.

It was banter, but it made me feel connected. Back when I lived in Cambridge, I remember the exact moment I first felt it was home. I was nowhere near my apartment. I'd just cut through the parking lot of the Broadway Market en route to the square and a passing car honked. Not for me to get out of the way, but in recognition. The driver was the Body Shop clerk who regularly sold me my favored banana-scented conditioner. And she recognized me. And wanted to wave. Silly, maybe, but it made me feel that somebody in my new town knew me. Even if it was only because I regularly gave her money. Someone knew me that can matter more than you'd think. Everybody seemed to know Joe, but in my three weeks in Booley, I'd seen no one else come to or leave his home, except on Sundays, when the Quinns drove out to take him to Mass up at the new church and then to their home for dinner and then to the pub for the remainder of the afternoon. It seemed that Finola's daily morning stop, inherited by Liam, and now asked of me, had been Joe's most regular contact with the world. A human face, proof of a world beyond the boundaries his disappointingly unreliable legs

represented. Though nowhere near a Finola, I was a becoming version for Joe. This I figured out after only four mornings. His
humanity thermometer had gauged my level, decided I was harmless, and that I could be some version of kind when I wanted to be,
and that with Finola gone, I was the only person for a good few
miles unable to say no to an old man living at the end of the earth
who just needed a few moments with another human heart beating
in the same room.

As for what he represented to me, the feeling was some sort of
mutual. I had been wary of this chore, but I was human, too. A
cloudy yearning for company had surprised me at a few points since
I'd decided to stay. But I saw the same in many solo travelers who
stopped in the shop and fell into conversation with Liam or another
browser. The topics were like so much of what they might have covered with a traveling companion—observations on cuisine, terrain,
culture—and unloaded sometimes in a torrent. I had a bit more on
my mind by that fourth morning in Booley, when Joe asked/told
me, "Sure you've time for a cup of tea," and that was when a morning cup of tea with Joe became a regular thing, too.

As had using the collection of growth-tweaking mind-healing
calm-inducing equipment Gina pointedly left in the back bedroom
that I since have claimed as my own. I used the gifts as directed,
shuffling the sunlight-colored yoga cards, rarely getting beyond the
restful position named "Corpse." Jotting a few short entries in the
spiral-bound LifeWords journal, though, never having kept any sort
of diary, I felt silly, an adult smushing a silver gel pen (came with it)
along the lines after the printed prompts of "Today I feel . . . Today
I think . . . Today I want . . ." I brewed the bags of organically grown
tea aimed at the goals of Revival, Energy, Perseverance. If the
weather were lousy, I'd sip it while standing at the kitchen window
that was the frame for an ever-changing Viewmaster disc. In better
conditions, I'd bring the cup outdoors, and I'd sit on the wall. I wore
around my neck Gina's left-behind still-in-the-box chain threaded

with the dagger-shaped healing crystal that sometimes poked my chest in the daytime and that rested at night on the deep windowsill to catch any rays of moonlight, which the accompanying brochure said would act as a battery recharger for its multitude of powers. I'd put a match to the wick of the votive labeled "Possibility." Having read the directions on the kitchen notice board, I knew to snap on the water heater the required two hours before running a few inches of hot water into the tub and adding grains of lemongrass something or other that were supposed to turn the room into a perfect universe of clarity. Sliding into my pair of what was to have been our nighttime uniform of blue flannel pajamas printed with dreamy blue clouds, I gave a touch to the supposedly healing stone I kept next all the rest of the flotsam on the bedroom windowsill. I pushed that window open a few inches to hear better the surf unfolding on the shore, climbed beneath the ton of bedding, applied a smear of the calming cream to my temples, snapped off the light, and did not care if no dreams came. I was living one. Somebody else's, certainly. And one including a few nightmarish scenes. But a dream nonetheless.

All this I wanted to tell Gina. She is a lover of conversation, chatting, interaction—especially the types containing great amounts of minutiae. She craves the kind of recounting you would give to the sightless, with intricate mentions of every sound, scent, nuance of color, and emotion. "No detail too small" is the line she always gives wholeheartedly after requesting a report what's new in my life. I wanted to give her the latest now, from here in Booley. Electron microscope views of everything she would have observed and overheard and felt and tasted here, each footstep she'd take in a day. For the sake of a truer experience I wished I could fill her in using the words that made up the language here, those that were unconsciously selected and lined up in an order that made them sound so much better than any ever were formed by our blasé American tongues. I'd never watched any of the home-and-garden shows on my TV, but once my cable service expanded to include BBC America, I adjusted my supper hour to 7:00 P.M. so I wouldn't miss the sixty minutes of British people digging fish ponds in their back gardens. They were doing the same work their American home-improvement show cousins were taking on, but their simplest chitchat made fascinating even the application of a coat of primer. There's no TV at Finola's cottage, but I live a foreign drama, it's dialog quarterback-sneak twists of words and meanings, roller-coaster cadence and unpredictable pronounciation that is Booleyan Irish-English. It fascinates ears, which are used to the heard-it-all-my-life-everyday speech of a Slavic-rooted New England community in which I should note, if I'm listing differences, the *F* word as nothing but angry profanity. It could be that here, too, but very often was sprinkled as regularly as dinner table pepper and salt. As they'd say that was "No harm, for fuck's sake." I had to realize that the term "fucking deadly" described nothing short of greatness. And to become acquainted with its little cousin, feck.

"Feckin' gee-eyed dosser," Una would snip after a time-wasting drunk finally left the shop, but while he was there, she'd bubbled, "Thanks a million," after he'd finally paid her the equivalent of a dollar for a copy of the newspaper. And in that newspaper purchased by both him and me, a gold mine of terms for me. A front-page story about the opening of the area's first creche, a word that I knew to be the sloppily built pine-board manger my brother long ago had hammered together in shop class for my mother, who wept proper maternal tears as she set her nativity scene statues inside it. This country's creche. I figured out from the accompanying photograph of tiny moon-faced children waving teary farewells to departing adults, was a day care. On the next page, the competition for this year's Tidy Town was announced, and residents were urged to do their best in presenting a unified clean appearance of home, business and roadside. The section titled "appointments" sought participants for a three-day course in which future telephonists/receptionists would learn helpful lines including "She is in the canteen, you will have to ring back," "She's tied up at present," and "He is gone out for a smoke." That vice, the Health section told me, was to be done in smoking gazebos being constructed on the grounds of the university hospital. Here, smoking was done in something as elaborate as a gazebo, a structure in which, back home, marriages took place.

An historic cottage featured for decades on postcards had burned down in the wake of an ownership dispute, a manufactured pop band had been unveiled, a bowler in cricket had suffered an "excruciating surfeit of wides" and the last to do so, the paper noted, had been sacked. Obits were jammed with Delaneys and Kennedys, the deceased were said to have expired "unexpectedly," "peacefully," "in the loving, compassionate care of the staff after a short illness borne with intelligence, wit, and courage."

The pages held more than a few familiar names and issues. A free information line had been set up by the health authority for those affected by clerical child sexual abuse. Permission to build an incinerator was being fought. A columnist wondered why the morning-after pill was not obtainable over a pharmacist's counter, People here were watching *Dawson's Creek* and *Becker* and *The Simpsons* over and over and, if they had satellite, cable, or digital capabilities on their sets, tuning into Jackass on MTV, and *Sex and the City* on C4. A new advertising campaign asked young males to drive with caution and stem the rise of auto-related fatalities. Drug trafficking plagued a housing estate, a setting that sounded ritzy but was what we would call a development or project. Two men were fined for possessing cannabis after a rave party. Videocassettes and computer equipment had been seized in Operation Amethyst, a nationwide effort against child pornography launched just this month and involving more than five hundred law officials, several of whom had netted a load of kiddie porn in the homes of a city councillor and a well-known solicitor. Asylum seekers and other immigrants, or simply people with skin of another color who were legal residents or legal visitors, were being beaten regularly in the city centre that was spelled that way. In my copy of *The Irish Times*, a reporter held the title of Social and Racial Affairs Correspondent, those issues being large enough here to require someone to be assigned just to them. For anyone in any trouble, the classifieds noted that the Samaritans would go through it with you, and could be rung at any time day or night, and also emailed.

All this I wanted to tell to Gina: the things she should be here learning firsthand. But she'd wanted space, and as much as that hurt, I'd given it to her. Didn't even send so much as a postcard until three weeks to the day after she left Booley, I rode the crest of a double wave of homesickness and heartsickness over to Diamond's, and the village's only public email machine.

The hostel was up a set of stone stairs, at the base of which a rock-muscled bicyclist performed a series of impressive hamstring stretches. He nodded, I nodded, then I entered the front hall of Diamond's and decided among its three choices: a vacant lounge through the door to the right, a set of stairs straight ahead, and door to the left, ajar. Through the opening I could see the counter and guest book and rack of keys and CASH ONLY sign that gave it away as the place to check in. I heard guitar strummings, the stop-and-start kind you know are being made right there rather than playing from a stereo. I knocked. Got no response. Called a hello. Repeated that. A door behind the counter swung back and next emerged a guy wearing a crabby frown and a red, white, and blue Tommy Hilfiger sweatshirt. He was thirty-something, sleepy-eyed in the permanent way that has nothing to do with rest. Had straight dark brown hair that touched Tommy's crew neck. In the room from which he'd come, an ugly couch of wine and green plaid cradled the shiny blond acoustic guitar this guy'd been playing. He spotted me doing the inventory, hooked the door behind him with a foot, and deftly slammed it.

"I'm sorry to bother you."

"Right," he said.

"I'd like to use the internet machine."

"Right."

"Runs on coins I've heard?"

"Right."

This was like a quiz.

"Yank," he said.

"Excuse me?"

"Yank. You're not from here, like."

"Right," I answered.

"Arrived with the one who stayed but a night."

"Right."

"And you're staying at Finola's."

"At Liam Keegan's. I'm staying there."

"At the cottage."

"At the cottage, but it's . . ."

"Was Finola's."

"OK."

I now was certain this was Diamond, about whom I'd been warned early on by Mrs. Quinn. "Be dog wide of that one" was her caution in a nutshell as she'd scrolled for me the list of Booley's merchants and businesspeople. Diamond, the only one to whom she'd given less than a passing grade, spoke with an accent clipped and heavy—German?—yet rolled in the jimmies of local color. I ventured, "You're not from here either, right?"

"Right." Then quickly and snidely added, "But sure I've been here long enough."

"Long enough for what?"

"To know I've been here far too long, to be vexed as to why any-one would want to come here for their holidays."

By anyone, I knew, he meant people like me, Yanks whose names and addresses had been written across many of the pages in his register. By holiday, he meant vacation, but used the word that gives a gift wrap and fireworks and potluck barbecue BYOB image. Holiday sounded too frivolous for what Gina had mapped out to do in Booley, for her effort at renewal and rethinking and re-whatever-elsing that needed to be done by her, for her, in her life, here in this place where she'd left me. I considered presenting this defense to Diamond, but his attitude grated on me and he did not deserve to know such private information as Gina's innermost challenges, and how they were the reason I was here for the summer. So I simply agreed with him and answered, "Holiday."

"Right." The word was basted with tremendous boredom. "And now you're booking in here? I require payment up front."

"I don't need a room. I'd like to use the internet machine?"

"Are you asking my opinion?"

"I want to use the internet machine." I tried to sound conclusive. "Where is it?"

He rubbed his eyes and stretched and yawned. "'Round the corner."

As if I were there to act as some Yank poster child and change Diamond's perception of an entire nation, I wasted a valuable portion of psychic energy to smile and say thank you, then located the machine, a ten-inch screen bolted to the wall inside what once had to have been a closet. "Welcome to IRENET," the shamrock-edged display greeted cheerfully, though its name sounded angry from the get-go. "Insert euro and select your internet provider."

Outside, Diamond, or whoever he was, passed the booth to click the TV to a broadcast of a pool game.

"No smoking in there," he called out. "Smoke in the lounge if you like. Make too much noise, you will be barred."

"I won't be noisy," I told him as the IRENET logo swirled in an attempt to connect.

"Yanks," he corrected, "are always noisy."

I wanted to argue. But really, how could he have known that at least partially, I really wasn't one of them?

Another identity and its trappings had been handed to me. And I'll tell you, 'tis grand to be Finola. When you're as amazing as she, every moment is a thing of wonder.

You wake to a universe holding not a single bit of dread, nothing but a world of promise. You storm the gate. The day is something to be celebrated, cherished, greeted eagerly as would a former insomniac in an Ambien commercial, with wide stretches and cranking open the window to shove out the face for the first good deep breath you've taken in, I don't know, ages. It's the kind of existence hinted at in the exclusive interviews of those by those plucked from disaster, cured from horrible ills—the world is seen through that long-awaited set of Norm Stebbins's corneas, and it never looked better.

When you are Finola, you enter your day gracefully. There is no typical stumbling, there are only effortless movements worthy of consideration by Broadway choreographers. You almost glide, floor untouched, over to that first check in the mirror, which brings no instant rush of criticism, no ticking off the list of how the past eight hours have sapped that much more of any decent looks you have managed to retain at this stage. If anything, you look better than you did twenty-four hours before, skin of a newborn, hair of some endangered species that ended up in that predicament because so many covet the feel of even an inch of its coat. You are unique and exotic, and though you are fully aware of these facts, you are further enhanced by the fact that these facts do not matter to you. If you were the twin of Noel you would stand just as erect, you would feel just as competent, equal, worthy as anyone else in creation.

Deliver that feeling and idea from your cottage down the road into town, to the shellacked wooden door that leads from Joe's mudroom to a low-ceilinged kitchen with the fireplace to the left, old wooden chair to either side of the hearth, where a rod above the glowing coals was hung with several once-white socks and, without an interruption of space, a couple of very flat white fish fillets. Joe welcomes you, he's just after making the tea, would you ever have a cup? Light glares from a bare bulb hanging by twisted wires in the middle of the ceiling, blinks from the red Christmas tree bulb flickering candlelike beneath the print of the Sacred Heart, pulses similarly from your edges as you enter the house.

If you are Finola, there is still another mile to walk before you spot the little cluster of buildings down the hill. They are sodden, drenched—any of the thesaurus's thick listing of words for wet would apply to them, but to you they glow warmly as the vibrant center of your world. This town is where you've built your life, made your friends, furthered your art, nurtured incalculable souls. And down there, between the chip shop and Quinn's, is your headquarters. The golden building that holds the bead table, and all the magic you've worked there.

If you are Finola, whenever you decide to take a break, you call in to E. Dolan. You might need to drop off Joe's two- or three-item grocery list. You'll probably find Una sitting behind the little An Post window, sorting mail and saying how she was dying to see ya, she suspects Ralpho's in love but she's not certain with whom. Have you heard anything? You always know everything because everyone—including mute teenagers—talks to you. There's Noel to visit as well, and if you are Finola, you have to check in on him, must accept the invitation of a tactile tour of the crates of silk yarn he drove to the airport yesterday to pick up. The carton you open contains neat spools of green. If you are Finola, green is your favorite of all colors, so Noel has to remind you that you'll be searched on the way out if anything from there goes missing.

As Finola, you will want to at some point in the day go over to the Last Restaurant for a read of the menu that includes a sampling of what's ready for harvesting in the vegetable garden that Eoin and Aoife dug behind the house that has yet to be completed but already has behind it a thriving, blooming anti-bunny-fenced plot. They're just opening for lunch when you get there. Marie and one of her sisters, whose name is spelled Caiomhe but is pronounced nothing like its spelled, are standing posture perfect in front of the restaurant's rose-covered front wall being photographed by five French-speaking people who have conveyed their wish to snap the girls simply by gesturing and cooing in their cool French way. The French-speaking people turn to you, scan your Finolawear with obvious head-to-toe once-overs and then, unless you are mistaken, unmistakably compliment your outfit and wave you into the photograph. You stand to the left of Marie and Caiomhe, destined for infamy in photo albums belonging to French-speaking people who took you for part of what they found Booley to be.

If you are Finola, even though you should be opening the shop right now, there's a lot of such socializing to do. Because you are loved. And because you don't have a lover, people are more than willing to volunteer candidates.

"He's mad for ye."

That's how Una, over the sale of a jar of lemon curd, which I was buying during a break simply to taste something with that name, broached the subject of Max's brother.

Three seconds before, she'd been describing Derek's summer job helping Una's Ger, he of the abrupt name and of the big powerful MAM brand truck, its windshield hung with stalactites of braided county-color yarn that swings happily as he rolls along on deliveries of construction supplies to the many, many, many rural building sites. Ralpho had opted to spend the summer splitting his time between training for a career as a sports star, helping his mam, and cycling to the pier to sell minerals and crisps and various other packets of universally recognized junk food to the ravenous and therefore gastronomically indiscriminating tourists.

"He instinctively knows the exact time of day at which to drop the hurley stick or slam the till and pedal fast to meet the boat just back from the islands," Una was boasting, and then she switched to "He's mad for ye," and her smile didn't fit with the idea of her adolescent's yearning for a thirty-year-old.

"Who's mad?"

"Max's brother."

I knew Max only as Liam's friend, fellow Chancer, regional farrier, and fashioner of wrought iron fixtures. A fair amount of Max's farrier business was traditional and hoof-related, but in the country's newly affluent age, he was turning his efforts to domestic hardware (hinges, latches, gates, grates, racks, hangers) and accessories (fireplace implements, hot plates, plate racks, candleholders), marketed to those responsible for the brash infections of holiday homes spreading across the countryside. Sold to domestic Yuppies, and foreign rich people—mainly the Germans, Dutch, English, and certainly a good few Yanks—many of the unimaginative mass-produced structures were occupied only for a few weeks a year their owners could get away on vacation. Holiday home complexes with names like Mervue and Riverside were the fate of so many of the fields whose gates wore plastic-covered white paper notices that began, "Notice to Planning Authority." There were plenty of these around Booley, typed out in legalspeak by some solicitor applying on behalf of a client seeking planning permission "for a serviced dwelling house at this location."

All this translated to the soon-to-be-concrete-and-glass fact that yet another probably hugely ugly building was being proposed. And that somebody else would, for only two summer weeks of each year, be in need of a six-hole wine rack hammered into shape by Max Kelly.

"The brother's the one does the designin'," Una said as rung up six bottles of water stands at the forge, poundin', whatever's done at the forge. The brother tells Max how a piece of iron should be shaped."

"And just how did the brother come to be mad for me?"

"Seen you about, I reckon. Told me, 'I'm mad about the girl who rearranged Liam's?'"

"Well, that explains it. It's as simple as that I brought his merchandise out from beneath the tablecloths. It's seeing the light of day, so shoppers can see it for once. So they're buying it. No wonder he's enthused."

"I'm certain he'll thank you when you meet. Over dinner. Friday. Here. Diamond'll be there as well."

"That's a plus? I thought it was smart to be dog wide of that one."

Una smirked at the lingo. "Who told you that . . . Sure I suppose it doesn't matter. Most would agree."

"He's very crabby, that's all I know."

"He's harmless. True, he'll eat the head off ya on his best day, but I feel sorry for him. He came to Booley on the offense, knowing how beloved was the original Diamond Godresthim. When he bought the hostel, he had Diamond's shoes to fill. But all he ever managed to duplicate was the name."

"You mean that's not his name?"

"Notatall. He's Dutch. Real name's Wouter—Walter. Neither of them's very Irish. So he took the name of his predecessor. Hasn't the sense to know it takes a bit more than simply pretending you're someone to become the person they were. Anyhow, yer man Fabian, Max's brother. He's the one you need to focus on. Lovely fella, that Fabian."

I was three weeks from meeting Jane St. Jean and saying goodbye to Charlie St. Jean. I wouldn't have said yes to a dinner party involving someone who was supposedly mad for me, but Una shared the fact that entertaining was a very rare thing for her, something she did maybe once a century. I knew Finola would have gone, though. Would meet Fabian, would strike out into new territory. Though I couldn't know the tone of her voice, I heard Finola saying that if you're going to restart your social life, you can't pass up the chance to forever have a story about a night with a guy named Fabian.

So I went to Una's dinner.

With Liam.

Walked over to it with him, that is. With him and Sinead. The woman with whom, since the spring, he'd been doin' a line, another illegal-sounding term that meant nothing more than dating.

Not having met Sinead or Fabian before, I had pictured that a ducktailed gee-whiz surf-movie icon would be seated on one side of the table and a bald angry Pope ripper on the other. But Fabian turned out to be the hairless one, on purpose—shaved. And Sinead had enough hair to cover the six of us at the table, and maybe a couple passersby, too. She wore it in braids wound crown like around her head a couple hundred times, a style she said she'd taken on in nursing school. These days, she was a nurse for the Southeastern Health Board, and she spent her days zipping about the countryside in a mammogram van.

"That's how we met," Ger said, and you could tell he enjoyed owning this story, which turned out to be nothing more than that a wheel on his truck had gone all wonky and stranded him in the middle of the road between Knocknagoshel and Ballymacelligott, effectively blocking traffic. First in line was Sinead's van.

That was a few months ago. And this was the woman Liam had meant when he'd offered me use of a calling card the day Gina left.

It was probably because I had few other friends here, and also because we spent a good part of the day together, that Liam's life quickly became something to think about. Also, I slept each night in the bed he'd once shared with Finola, which naturally had me giving a few thoughts to the passion that, just from the sparky aura of the man and the force of nature Finola sounds like, you get the idea there had to have been a nightly celebration there. Maybe morningly as well, middayly, afternoonly. How many times had their holidays been simply the locking of the front door? Nothing else needed, they could go everywhere they needed to within the cottage's four walls, the seven or eight or how many there are wonders of the world not even remotely comparing to the awesome beauty and power of what they were together. I'd been told by more than a few Booleyans Finola and Liam had been a pair so perfect and equal, and so in love, you could almost see a force field glow surrounding them as they walked up the road.

I could believe some of that, just from knowing the male side of the equation. Liam was charming, fascinating, smart, funny, and was more or less, to use the parlance of Gennifer, a hottie. And now he was a wounded hottie, which in some eyes gave him added appeal. The kind of guy you desperately wanted to help heal despite the fact that, at least according to the multiple-choice quiz in the most recent *O* magazine, doing so would label you codependent, a detrimental condition all too common in women and for which there was an entire 12-step program complete with workbooks, affirmation diaries, and certified counselors. But really, even if it made you disappear into the woodwork of the world, how could you not want to throw aside your own concerns to step forth and fix this guy's every woe? On the days when his joky front developed a crack, I could peek through it to his battered soul, a flat muddy misty field, a sepia Civil War–like daguerreotype of toppled cannons and massacred soldiers. The losses had been enormous, but Liam made it look as if he'd never been nicked. I'd wondered what it would take to make that battle field lush once again. How much effort would be involved in lugging away the ruins of the old weapons and the haunting skeletons, to rake out the smallest reminders of injury, to reseed, stand by, and watch new possibility grow?

I wondered that sometimes. And while wondering that, I again wondered why I wondered. Even though I knew the answer, and it was lots more than having Liam as a friend, spending so much time together, or any such previous excuse. I wondered because I craved what he and Finola had before it ran off to parts unknown. Wanted badly to know what it was like to feel you were somebody's universe. Wondered about it enough to drag out the Rolodex of my love history and mentally flip the cards in an effort to recall a man who had made me feel I was truly his constant first thought. But I'd never been that blessed. Seems I always stood in line behind other interests, and ultimately would feel like I'd been fit around yet another graduate program, efforts to please an unnoticing boss, inerasable memories of a one true love, management of a rotisserie football team, or visits to freeporn.com. The place I've held with the men I've clearheadedly chosen was best spelled out by the commercial fisherman I once actually thought I wanted to marry. Several months after removing his name sticker from my mailbox, he sent to it a flyer advertising the services of his newly christened fishing boat, First Choice Charters.

Long before meeting Jane St. Jean, I was very aware that Charlie St. Jean was married to his job, dreamed about numbers and percentages rather than me, doodled age/weight charts instead of my initials. I was certain Charlie was mad for his work. I was certain of that much. And I had believed that having more time together ultimately would improve my place in line. Once we began sharing a home, Charlie would have had to pay me lots more attention, and maybe a month or two of tripping over me daily would have left him helpless but to tumble irretrievably into the wondrous muck of total love. The kind I believed had been sparked and nurtured and made and made and made and made again in this very cottage, in this very bed, a piece of furniture that somehow was spared incineration by the heat, the fire, the passion it once held. This small mattress, hardly more than a twin size, belonged in a lover's hall of fame. But it was spending its retirement being letted out to visitors like me. Solo visitors like me. Whom someone felt might like to be paired with the likes of Fabian Kelly.

To his credit, Fabian richly praised me and the night-and-day difference he said I'd made in the shop. Said the new layout and look rivaled that some of the craft galleries in the city:

"Have you visited the city?"

"Which?" I asked.

"Dublin?"

"No."

"Galway, then?"

"No."

He smiled and offered a weak, "Limerick?"

"No. I should stop you . . ." I said, and Una broke in with "Good timing, 'cos he's nearly out of cities."

"I haven't really been anywhere here but Booley."

Diamond shook his head. "I'm stymied as to how a body can transport itself several thousand miles and be content to remain within a square kilometer."

"I've Sophie on a tight schedule," Liam said. "Little time for travelin' the world."

"Time for travel is one of the major benefits to doing a nickser. It's come and go as you please."

"What am I doing?" I needed to know.

"Nickser's work on the quiet. No tax paid on wages." Una whispered this, as if there were government agents lurking. "Common practice. Even in some of our most heralded hostelries." Diamond had no reaction.

"However the wages are made, they easily can be spent on an enjoyable day away," Fabian told me. "A tour is in order."

"Of what?" I asked.

"Dublin, Galway, and Limerick, of course."

Though I really didn't see the joke, everybody else laughed in that dinner party way that makes you feel happy to be included in the circle around the table rather than home, where you would have been had you declined the invitation, and you'd be there now thinking, as you often do, how the rest of the world is somewhere out there at this very minute, having a better time than you are. And you would have been right. I was glad to have come, to feel a comfortable reception from the group and not too great a push into Fabian, whom I found myself trying to imagine with a head of hair. I have nothing against the bald, but Fabian had a head shape that made him resemble a walking penis. "I'm far too busy at the shop to do any traveling" was ready to launch from my vocal cords but got run over by Ger's opinion that, but for a pint at Dolan's Warehouse as you're heading out the Dock Road, there's absolutely no reason to remove your foot from the gas pedal anywhere in Limerick.

"The Hunt Museum?" Fabian protested. "Picasso, O'Conor, Yeats, Renoir. And the Archer Butler Luck Stone."

"Seen it," Diamond sniffed, unimpressed.

"The stone?"

"The museum. See it every time I'm rocketing outta Limerick."

Fabian turned to me. "If you see nothing else in this entire county you must visit the Luck Stone."

"The lovely Sophie has a great belief in such things, luck stones, like," Liam said from his seat across from me.

"A perfect crystal ball—five or six centimeters in diameter and crossed with ornate circles of copper and bronze," Fabian said as if narrating a slide show. "From somewhere in Tipperary. Neighbors shared it to safeguard cattle from disease. They'd dip it into the water supply, which you can almost picture. But they'd also hang it from the animals' necks. Think of it."

"So it's right in there in the middle of the Picassos and all?"

"Oh, no. You have to go looking for it. I never would have found it had Finola not been with me. Years ago she brought me there. Took me by the hand and walked me to a secluded case, shared it with me like a secret."

"Jesus." That was Sinead, Liam's girl. And that was the first we'd heard from her all night.

"That was 1991," Fabian continued, unbothered. "I was doing the bead thing at the time—festivals, gift shows—it's how I met Finola. Her showing me that lucky stone inspired my first line of pendants, my first designs with metal." He slipped a hand down his shirt and hoisted up a small silver chain holding a tiny clear crystal hanging from a copper loop. I could see them selling fast Liam read my mind and waved a butter knife at me.

"They're no longer in production so no orders can be placed."

"That's due to Finola as well," Fabian said. "Sold 'em faster than I could ship 'em down here. That brought in pounds to fund larger creations. What I design now—the home design pieces Max hammers—you could never wear around your neck. Even if you indeed were some form of a farm animal."

"She also brought me to see that stone," Una told us. "Ages ago. I don't remember feeling inspired, but I do remember feeling, I dunno, lucky. Lucky stone and all, and me lucky to have a day away, looking at nothing but beauty, with my friend."

"Jesus."

Sinead again.

Napkin tucked at the neck to protect his gray jersey from Una's curious artichoke curry. Liam put his arm around Sinead's shoulders, which shrugged him off automatically.

Sensing the problem was not her cuisine, Una quickly asked, "More curry?"

Sinead did an eye rolling. "I am sick to death of her."

"Of Una?" Ger asked.

"Of Finola."

I was going to hear another Finola story! They fascinated me as much as if I were sitting at Quinn's hearth on a Sunday afternoon while Joe recited the intricate folktales that were this country's first Bible stories. For the price of a pint he'd tell of warriors, lovers, crazy people, talking animals, witches, banshees, the Celtic superheroes Cuchulainn and Fionn MacCumhaill. Joe often slipped into Irish, which was lost on me, and just as often spoke very softly, which made even some of his English a mystery, but when you caught the thread of a story and hung on tightly enough, you met the men and women and otherworldy creatures said to have once trod this very same land and existed beneath its waves. I got the same effect from the stories about Finola: what she had done for the people I stood in line with at the chip shop, or at E. Dolan, sat next to in Quinn's, met walking the strand. It was like starting high school and hearing about a girl who'd graduated the spring before—oh, if you'd only been here when she was, the things she did, said, got away with . . . What must it be like to be such a memorable person?

Joe had a photograph pinned above his table, a full-length unframed shot of a woman in a long black skirt, black blouse, and black shawl, her dark hair pinned back. She stood tall at an open doorway. The shadow of a small child peered from behind her. The kid was blurry, as were so many people in the photos taken back then, when exposures were long enough to record both the closing and opening of eyes, pupils spookily visible behind lids, or, as in this case, a small figure appearing and hiding at the same time. People come and go, just like that. Except some of them you can still see standing there even after they've been absent for years. I had no idea what she looked like, yet I was beginning to see Finola O'Flynn everywhere. She preceded me as I moved about the small world that was Booley. In Una's kitchen, she was seated at the back door open to the intoxicating late spring air, sending her smoky exhalations into the yard where the boys shouted would she watch this now, Fin—that's what they'd called her, Fin. watch this now. In Noel's studio, she leaned over his shoulder as he shot turquoise silk weft through the plum-dyed warp and as he wondered if his unvoiced psychically sent message of love was hitting anywhere near the mark of her heart. She was there in Joe's garden, checking the progress of the rhubarb flaring its leaves skyward. And when I sat down at the jewelry table, she took the place to my right. I could smell the tangerine soap she, and he still, used . I could hear the precise harmonies she added to whatever CD I'd have playing—and she of course knew all the words, including those foreign to me. She bumped me with her left arm because she was left-handed, and I think she actually enjoyed bothering me in that way. She followed Liam to the apartment each time he went upstairs, and she returned on his heels when he returned. He walked right past her as if she truly were invisible. Went about the routine he had created for himself since her abrupt leaving, the work and the travel and the music and the nights out alone and the occasional return accompanied. He went about his life as if Finola weren't still right there all the time, with him, as she was in some measure with us all. Including with Sinead. X-ray had an interest in settling down.

"I thought I could find a place for myself here," she said as she stood. "But from the first visit—the stories. Friends, neighbors, feckin' strangers, even. Not a night here passes without a mention of that woman." She was up and in the corner now, finding her leather blazer on a chair and digging her keys from a little pineapple-shaped purse then turning to Liam to say, "I told you. I told you I was reaching my limit. Each and every visit Finola O'Flynn is spoken about like she was some class of saint, martyr. But sure wasn't she more a sinner?"

So that was the end of this story. A small letdown for me. Still, it was something to watch how Finola could reach all the way from Germany and push a woman down the road and over the bridge and out of town for once and for all.

"Crikey," stated Una as the door slammed behind Sinead, and just barely behind Liam in pursuit.

I wanted to say I was sorry. Finola didn't. We both kept quiet.

"Never a dull moment," Ger said to Fabian. Diamond leaned back in his chair to peer out the window.

We heard a car door slam. An engine start. The upward arc of shifting gears and a vehicle moving in the direction of the road out of town.

"This sort of thing happens with his women," Una told me as she refilled my wine glass. "There haven't been many, but those who spend any amount of time in Booley usually soon have their fill of 'the other woman.' I'm sure you've noticed she's still, shall we say, around?"

"You certainly don't talk about her on purpose . . ."

"In most cases, no," Ger said. "Despite Liam being accustomed to the name not disappearing along with the person, it still doesn't seem right to me to bring her up."

"She was his girl, but she was my friend," Una protested. "Am I never to mention her?"

Ger shrugged.

"She just surfaces so easily," Fabian said. "If you'd known her . . ."

"I think I'm beginning to," I said. "As weird as that sounds."

"Sure you couldn't begin to imagine the woman she is," Diamond told me.

Fabian studied me. Said, "I think you two would get on."

"I'd like to think so," I told him, and I did feel that, as I looked toward the door through which Liam never returned on that night.

Dove:

⌣

Love and Affection

(State Your Wish Three Times)

Dublin had been named the Syphilis Capital of Europe.

Nigerians were now the biggest group among those seeking asylum in Ireland.

A gang of thieves had been targeting rural phone boxes, using battery-operated drills on the locks and taking as much as 200 euros a whack.

The Sam Maguire, the sacred and coveted trophy that is to Irish football what the World Series trophy is to baseball, was kicked down a street in County Galway shortly after that county's team lost its place in the All-Ireland championship. Initially Borrowed for the purpose of photographing by fans, it was grabbed by a member of a respected business family and subsequently violated.

Rain, ranging in intensity from light to dousing, was forecast for the northeast, the northwest, the southeast, the southwest, and the central midlands. Sorry was being promised. They didn't forecast here, they promised. As if there was no question.

Radio I gave all this information before wishing me a pleasant good morning and surrendering the airwaves to Marian Finucane and the current affairs she'd chosen to chew on that morning.

The program played loudly from the sitting room of the cottage. Radio here—this station, at least—had the effect NPR has on me back home. Just having the dial turned to it—even if the radio wasn't playing—made me feel more intelligent. I listened to everything here. The morning chat shows. *Sports International Europe Today*. The evening think pieces. *Book of the Week*. *The Shipping Forecast*, the Farming Forecast, *Prayer for the Day*. Music on *Late Junction:* Verity Sharp introduces a wide-ranging selection of artists and tracks, including Tonto's Expanding Headband, the Afro-European group Tama, Lotti's *Crucifixus,* and Rhoma Irana. A Liszt recital given in 1961 by Clifford Curzon. The *Mystery Train*. The Radio 2 *Funk Factory*. Lyric 24's *Music Through the Night*.

I tuned to Joe's all-Irish-language station even though, aside from milk and bread, I had no clue as to content. I listened nonetheless. To the Irish and the non-Irish talk, chat, news, music to the small local stations that broadcast even the holiday return of former residents, and the departure of those who'd been here all their lives: "The death has occurred of Micheal Dunn, better known as Mikey Boy, of Holywood. Removal will be this evening to the Church of Our Lady of Perpetual Succour. May he rest in peace."

I kept the radio on much of the time I was home. And I was home right now, down the hall, and the radio was turned up so I could hear it in the toilet, where I was applying to my face Finola's root vegetable and algae no-shine hydrating cream, which smelled and looked and felt a whole lot better than the name would lead you to believe. I checked my hair, which I had pulled back with the help of the wooden combs Finola had kept at her bedside. I picked from the basket in the bedroom a weirdly knit baggy tan skirt, which went with a weirdly knit baggy top and cardigan, and I laced up her armyish boots. I had my toast and tea outside. The cottage's backyard had a neat little lawn on which rested a slate bench and table. Off to the Booley side stood a clothes pole, one with the umbrella-like shape that rotates when the wind blows. That wind was picking up just then. The empty lines, some still wearing plastic pins, vibrated with a low whistle. Past that, along the far wall, lay a bowling-lane-shaped strip of garden showing off clusters of some spiky purple things that had chosen to sprout up there. Beyond the wall sprawled more flat and empty fields, then, past those, a series of more fields gently lumpy against the sky like a body under a blanket. Then hulked the high round-backed mountains that kept the rest of the world just a bad rumor. I hugged Finola's cardigan to my chest. I rested there, in peace. In Booley. Where, just as Gina had hoped, things were beginning to happen. They were. For me.

The first was that I was getting a steady stream of mail. Finola was, actually, but I opened it for her, I read it, I added it to the shelf where we displayed the kudos from the new crop of Finola O'Flynn bracelet fans. Just yesterday she received one with no return address, but there was an NJ in the smudged postmark, and an American stamp on the square white envelope that held the piece of square white paper.

Dear Mrs. Flynn:

My friend was in your town and bought a bracelet from you to give to me. I don't wear jewelry. I don't even wear my crucifix anymore, but that has nothing to do with this. The bracelet she bought me was labeled 'Self-esteem.' At first I got mad at her. I thought, Who brings somebody a present like that? Especially when I already heard she brought her other friend a beautiful linen runner and a box of individually wrapped chocolates.

But this is the same woman who bought me Dr. Phil's book on correcting your life. I got mad at her for that, too, at first. She's pushy, but her heart is in the right place most of the time. According to Dr. Phil, and his tests, I don't have any

self-esteem, and when I think about it, I know he's right.
Wearing your bracelet reminds me that I have no self-esteem.
And sometimes I get mad about that. But that is nothing
against you.

I am writing to say that the reminder is reminding me
about things I never really wanted to be reminded about before.
Thank you.

And then an email that got sent to Noel's machine by someone
in Wales whose name was a series of *L*'s and *Y*'s, and Noel, as he was
asked in the heading, delivered the print out to me by hand:

Greetings: Does Finola O'Flynn have a website? I would
like to reorder, specifically, the bracelets with the titles.
Specifically, "Hope?"

And laser printed onto paper bordered with a line of sunflowers,
and mailed all the way from Atlanta:

Dear Finola O'Flynn,
I apologize for intruding on your privacy, but I need to
relay to you a story. My husband and I were returning from the
dentist. In my car. As we approached a curve a service vehicle
was backing from a driveway. I slowed down and the young
man in the vehicle became highly agitated and gestured w/his
left hand over the roof of the cab. I thought his middle finger
was extended—the second time he repeated the gesture, I was
sure.

My husband told me to stop—he said he wanted to con-
front this meatball and introduce him to common courtesy & a
quick course in manners, but what did I care—I know people
make this gesture & even though I have not myself, I have been
in some situations where I have wanted to. So I ignored him,

& my husband, & drove on & then stopped for milk & then for mail. Then home.

My husband took the car, my car, returned to the driveway where the man with the finger had been, but he was gone by then so my husband went up & down the road looking for him, but had no luck in finding him. He wanted this young man to call me, to make an appointment to see us & apologize to us, in person. My husband was fuming upon returning. He said, "I don't care how bad his day was, there is no excuse for his behavior. He doesn't know me or you. Grown men would cut off their finger rather than offend you, or me!" Do you understand from this that I live with an idiotic hothead? It is no picnic, let me tell you. This sort of behavior goes on constantly. It is tiring and I'm sick of it, but it is my problem. However, let me tell you one thing that has helped. I was in your town last month as part of a trip I'd won through making a donation to my son's parochial school raffle. I only donated five bucks, but everybody who gave anything got their name put in, and they pulled mine and I won a trip! & in a few weeks I was in your town, and while my husband was back at the bed-and-breakfast trying to get a refund because the hot water in the shower wasn't as hot as he wanted it to be even though I thought it was fine. I took a walk & ended up in your store. I was thinking what a shame it was to be in such a beautiful town & to be preoccupied by yet another problem, again of his invention.

There was some jewelry on your table. With tags. I saw the word "Detach." I pulled out the tag. It was tied to a bracelet made of black beads generally the shape of Raisinettes. There was a charm in the center, a little boat pulling away from land. At least I think it was pulling away—maybe it was arriving at land—but I saw it as leaving. I didn't spend any other money at your place, sorry. I bought that bracelet, put it on & had a wonderful day walking along the cliffs, alone & content.

And back home, the incident with the young man & his finger,
which was only last week—it was the most recent opportunity
to just let my husband do his own fuming & not get all tied in
it. As time is passing, I am becoming a pro at this, & I don't
know why I'm telling this to a perfect stranger, but I'm enjoy-
ing the feeling so much I just might detach for good. Thank you
for giving me the idea.

"Dear Finola," began the one with the Illinois postmark and with
the elegant fine-line-pen script inside the Gustav Klimt note card
of a golden torso so large and right there.

I don't expect you to remember us. My husband and I
recently purchased four of your bracelets, the ones you made,
among those a green glass and stone one that includes a yin-
yang symbol. You verified for me that the symbol could remind
one of the two sides of life, and you were quite kind in doing so.
With the way things are in my country I find myself in need of
a reminder that even in dark times, light is just ahead.
Shannon Ferriter-Garvey

Shannon! Shannon Ferriter-Garvey! Somebody I actually
remembered. Shannon of the leisurely examination of every item in
the store and with the husband and his bad hairpiece and with the
pricy cape from Attracta's and the yin/yang bracelet and now writing an order for eight more—but added, "On second thought, why
don't you just make up a dozen and I won't have to bother you
again," then P.S.-ed hopefully, "Until next time!"

The idea I'd stolen from the well of St. Faicneam strangely
seemed to be going in a circle. I'd attached a card bearing a word or
two or three, and people were believing they could attain the benefits of the word just by wearing a doodad that I'd casually decided
to title. And now they were believing, and they believed things

were happening due to that believing, and some of them were asking for more.

Tourist traffic increased as the first week of June began. Liam and I worked to fill a modest amount of wholesale orders to fill the requests placed by regular customers, and to fill the dish that was regularly emptied by shoppers. I could smell Liam's tangerine soap. I could hear the precise harmonies he added to whatever CD was playing—and he of course knew all the words, including those foreign to me. He bumped me with his left arm because he was left-handed, and I bumped him with my right because I'm the opposite, but we didn't switch chairs because he wanted to be free to get up and tend to customers. Pepsi strolled in and stretched out at our feet. The music would end, the *deedly-deedly* stuff fading out, and there'd be only the dog's measured little snores and the clacking of the beads as we searched through the dishes, the whirr of cord unwinding from the reel, muffled voices from the mouths on the faces on the other side of the window and then the sound of these people entering the shop, and their question a few moments after they watched me work: "Are you Finola?"

Did they need assistance? Liam would ask as I continued with my work, and the customers would have more questions, about the bracelets in particular, to which they felt drawn, we heard time and again. Drawn. Like there were fishing monofilament pulling them to the table and toward the dish, and pulling out the change purses or the money clips or the wallets or the wads of strange currency that when you're a tourist, can seem like something from a Monopoly game so it's very easy to part with and it's very easy to say I'll take another one of these, why not, when am I going to be here again, when have I ever had the chance to buy an artist's creation directly from the artist who created it, what the hey it's only money.

A version of all that last stuff was said by a man who went on to explain that he had five nieces and that they would love these bracelets, as would have his fiancée, excuse me, his ex-fiancée, she adored handcrafts, as he called them, and she would have adored all this here but she was not here with this man to adore anything. Religion, he told us. They thought they had it all figured out, as it can need to be figured out when you come from two different schools of belief—the religious education that would be given to the children who did not yet exist and probably would not exist for several years but whose beliefs and studies had been worked out and would be ready for them. They'd come to an agreement—or so the future parents had thought—and then their future mother balked, saying she wanted no blending of the two faiths, no mix of that observance and this holiday, she wanted the children to stand on her side of the fence, that's how she put it, the fence, and this man told her he hadn't realized there even was a fence and she said yes there is and it's far too high for either of us to climb to the other side, announced that all dramatic like somebody had written her a script, and she said it was just not gonna work. So it didn't, because it can't if you've already made up your mind that it won't. And that goes for anything, really.

So all that was why the man was standing here recounting his sorrow for us. Another total stranger opening up in a retail setting, as people do when there's nobody else in the shop and you're just sitting there working, fair and immobile game for anyone who wants to stand there and start reciting the history of the world. Usually what you get are the histories of particular worlds—those belonging to the narrators. They're far from home, they find they speak your language, more or less, they're a bit lonely, perhaps, even though they wouldn't have believed that fact before they walked in and felt the good vibe of your welcome, and lots of these people, if they find themselves in Booley and are not from Booley, have come here to this place at the end of the land because they are on the run from some life occurrence. Like this man was. Had run all the way from South Africa. Alone but for his clubs.

"Golf will help," he told us, and he mimed a swing in case Liam and I were unfamiliar with the sport. "I could have golfed at home, but I just needed to be somewhere else, far away."

After the man finally traveled again, next door to Quinn's, Liam said, "Poor bastard." The *poor* was pronounced as *par,* which seemed fitting for a golfer. "Running away," I said, "the universal cure."

"It's the preferred method a copin'," was Liam's view. "Lookit yer Bible, yer fairy stories, yer films, yer myths and legends, yer ancient history. The ones in them are always on some journey. Rare's the star or legendary figure who spends his life rooted in front a the television eatin' a potato farl. They're always forced to leave home, or are sent on a quest, or feel the place they've always lived is suddenly all wrong. The important occurrences of life can happen when you're far from yer start."

It made sense to me, though it hadn't to some of the friends who, despite being friends, had frowned on Gina's decision to go away. One of them, Lila, who drives a Gremlin and who, if you don't mind cleaning off the shells yourself, will give you all the eggs you want from the Rhode Island Reds she keeps just so her yard will have a farmy feel—she said the trip was a geographical cure, and that Gina's problems would still be here when she came back. And because she'd delivered this opinion on a particularly fragile day for Gina, I had to take Lila aside and ask her to please shut up, and Lila argued that it was nothing but the truth, and I said she was maybe right but couldn't she cut Gina a break after all the shit she'd been through, and that's when Lila got all teary-eyed and trembly and shoved at me the carton of eggs she'd come to Gina's to deliver, and then she blubbered, "We all have shit. She's not the only one, ya know."

Standing at Gina's sink, I picked the shit off the eggs and I picked my brain for some idea of what Lila had to cope with. I didn't know her well so I had little material to sift through other than the poultry and the car and, excepting this encounter, her usual morning-show-host-happy happiness. Whatever Lila's sniffle-inducing garbage was, hadn't it ever made her want to run—even for a shred of an instant? Something poked my right arm. Liam's left elbow. Gina's sink disappeared and I was back at Finola O'Flynn's table, a line of orange ceramic scarabs alternating with tiny blue glass squares on the cord before me, and a big blue ocean and a couple of wild months between me and Lila and the eggs, which I'd used to make a frittata from the recipe I'd cut from the *Self* magazine page on which each month they translate a normally fat-laden item into something that won't gunk up your arteries as much as the original version. I'd been gone from the present so long that Liam had time to brew a pot of tea.

"The stories." He said. "I think it's the stories. They're always in a time long ago and a place far far away. So perhaps it's in us that when we want some other existence, we immediately head else-where. Hopin' we'll find that place where all that magic from those stories happened. We take ourselves somewhere new and see if that makes a difference. Anyhow, it got me to Booley. Considerin' all the side roads I coulda turned onta, and despite things not bein' picture perfect in recent years, I coulda done lots worse."

He touched the boom box button and there was music again. The singer, a kid who'd called earlier in to drop off a sample of his first recording on the hope we'd carry copies, sang dangerously close to off-key about being on the dole, which I'd always known to be a pineapple manufacturer before I learned that here it was the word for the public assistance that Noel's youngest sister chose to receive over holding down a job because she could get more money for doing nothing than she would for tying herself into a pink and white candy-striped apron and filling orders for smoky bacon burgers and Snack Boxes at the Limerick Supermacs, a fact she knew because she'd done both. Liam hit the button that moved us to the next track, thankfully an instrumental. I knocked into his arm as I reached for the scissors. Pepsi turned over and snuggled against my feet still laced securely inside Finola's combat boots. This place, this country, this village, this shop, this chair behind this table next to the other chair behind this table and next to the person seated in it—all of it was, on this day at least, the end of a journey I hadn't intended to make. And for having no plans at all, I, too, coulda done lots worse.

Four days later, Liam and I finished the largest order first, sealed the last dozen necklaces into their individual plastic bags. The order of two gross were for a store in England somewhere, and to ensure safe delivery—and save freight and insurance—the package would be delivered by Leslie, a friend of Liam's who would be flying there tomorrow. Leslie lived an hour and a half away, and Liam said that if I'd never had the opportunity to see the interior of a castle, which is what Leslie had renovated as her home, I should come along. I said I would, and that I even would drive. I figured Liam had enough time at the wheel during his weeks away, but more than that I wanted to try out my newly acquired skill for driving on what initially had seemed to me to be the incorrect side of the road.

"Want to give it a go?" That's what Noel had asked one evening when I was admiring his van, a dark red Toyota Hiace, the kind Una said often is favored by Irish Travellers, not tourists but native nomads of a sort with their own culture, history, and language, and some of whose caravans were parked at the halting site near the airport turnoff, a site that was under threat of being made illegal and, like so many other stretches of roadside that once accommodated them, soon probably would be dotted with boulders to prevent anything larger than a bicycle from stopping there. I'd balked at the offer, of a lesson and Noel said he was a fine instructor, had taught Finola everything she knew about driving, ah, them were the days, firin' down the road with Finola at the wheel. On my walks, I moved facing the traffic, and when looking at an approaching car, then at its driver, I often was startled to see a sleeping old woman, or an infant, or a dog in what I was used to considering the driver's seat. But a few weeks ago, only because Finola once had sat behind that very wheel for her first drive in this country, I settled in what

I'd always thought of as the passenger's side, and drove behind those old ladies and infants and dogs, and their drivers, maneuvering the Hiace along the roads above Booley, Noel seated to my left, invoking the help of all heaven though 99 percent of the time it was in fun. We started at the car park, stared at by this guy Tomeen, who, for the price of only five euro, will have his dog smoke a fag for your photographing pleasure. Only after I needed no reminding about pushing the shift down in order to move it into reverse, and only after I'd sellotaped to the dash three bright yellow pieces of paper on which I'd drawn fat black arrows pointing to the left and to the side of the road that was mine, Noel allowed me out into the world. Four outings later I had the hang of it and pretty much could keep the left wheels from the ditch and the left side of the van from the scratchy arms of roadside bushes. Liam's Golf was smaller than the HiAce—it would be a snap in comparison. That's what I told Liam, and he said he'd every faith in me, and would welcome the chance to be a passenger. So after closing on Thursday, we headed off.

Sinead hadn't been an option as a passenger for Liam. Because she no longer was an option as anything for Liam. She'd had three months of hearing about her boyfriend's ex-girlfriend, possibly more often than if Finola still were living in Booley, and as she'd said at Una's table, she'd reached her limit.

On the other hand, Fabian had enthusiasm for me. Wanted to bring me to the Hunt Museum posthaste. Perhaps this Sunday, he said on the phone, and "Perhaps this Sunday," Max reminded me with a wink when he arrived to fill in so Liam and I could leave a little early for our road trip.

The weather was a Booleyan first for me. Early June sun hanging perfectly and unobstructed in a cerulean sky, ocean showy but almost slow-motion gentle, breeze just enough to ruffle the taller grasses. The kind of front-edge-of-summer gift that back home would have all the teenage girls on my street setting up beach towels and radios on the front lawn, where they'd show off the season's latest swimwear, grease up with minimum SPF Coppertone and fry to the whoops from bass-thudding boy-filled cars. The version of this in Booley was the carrying of kitchen chairs into front gardens and rolling up sleeves and removing caps to reintroduce porcelain flesh to the wonders of Vitamin D without a thought given to the horrors of melanoma.

I'd never been far from Booley. The trip from the airport, and, since, a few jaunts to neighboring towns with Noel or Aoife or Una. I had no real interest in going farther. My time in this country had begun with more than enough excitement, and I was pleased to have settled in as well as I had, and felt only that I wanted to cocoon there more after dumping Charlie and slipping into Finola's view of the world. So I was surprised by the zingy anticipation as I piloted Liam's car up the main road and over the bridge and took the left and then the right up the hill down which Gina and I had descended that first day one long month ago. There was no one at the crossroads bus stop, where I took the right and asked Liam if he were enjoying the ride and he took the opportunity to point out something he said he'd been meaning to point out and now was as good a time as any, as we were on a drive, not a ride, and did I realize that when I asked some-body for a ride I was asking them for, well, you know (though I really didn't before he told me), sex. I glanced at Liam to my left, at Pepsi perched happily in the well between the two front seats, then shoved the car into third gear and concentrated on the road edged with the now familiar green of the light that says it is safe to go-go-go. The sun was washing the color as it drifted into the sea, and gold was starting to coat everything in sight, including the profile of Liam as he watched the road and pointed out the turns that took us farther up from Booley and over the protective hills and through a mountain pass with a James Bondish tunnel cut into one of the rocks and then into the busier world that I remembered was out there all along but for the most part had chosen to ignore.

The landscape became moonscape, barren plateaus from which grew lumpy white rocks and on which grazed the occasional space sheep and along which leapt the stray space goat. We flew close to the ground, zooming through what, for me, was the totally unfamiliar. But I was next to somebody who was becoming more familiar by the day, by the stories we'd swapped as we sat elbow to elbow, of times much earlier than the ones we'd already recounted—things that had happened in years prior to the most recent veerings off the smooth roads we'd been traveling. I heard about Liam's babyhood spent sleeping in a tea chest, how he learned to read, learnt, as he put it, by figuring out the words on the women's problem pages of his mother's magazines. His classmates entered primary school with no clue as to even the start of the alphabet, but Liam was already well educated about the intimate concerns and tribulations of what would become his favorite gender. His father ran an Esso petrol station. The pre–convenience store kind that catered only to the automobile. None of this modern-day landscaped forecourt and custom-order deli counter and tea machine and pop background music, the Keegan Esso was an old-fashioned full-service-for-autos-only animal, the dying breed being ushered to its extinction through the passage of laws that make illegal design realities like the manhole cover for the storage tank being located under a rug behind the counter. The only food for sale at Liam's father's station was a tray of packaged sweets, and Liam would nearly send himself into shock by overindulging in something called Fox's Glacier Fruits. His mother gave birth to a litterlike nine children but somehow also found time to play the church organ for all Masses, weddings, funerals, you name it. Liam, scrawniest and youngest, sat to her right on the organ bench and turned the pages of her sheet music. In his teens he formed The Revelations, playing the parish's newly incorporated folk Masses, with the newly assigned trendy priest adding his bass at the points of the Mass when he'd normally be just sitting in some big throne chair, head leaning on fist, meditating on his recurring dream of returning to the show band circuit that had been his first and true calling. After earning his leaving cert, which sounds like a breath mint but is actually just a kind of high school diploma, Liam moved from home to Dublin with two cousins, the younger one of whom got a stranger-girl pregnant the second night in town—actually good fortune because her father was a shipping magnate, and even though you hear that term, who's ever really met one? Well, this cousin did, eventually, and now he, too, is a magnate, more or less, his home a multi-million-pound palace in Enniskerry with breath-taking views of surrounding countryside, terraces and landscaped gardens over seven acres, cinema and gym/garage, so you never know. The other cousin talked Liam into joining him in attending technical college, and into concentrating on the computer. Liam, who'd quickly risen from waiter to manager of the smoke-free dining room in the at the Grafton Street Bewley's, agreed. The cousin who made the suggestion now teaches at the college, full-time, days, goes back to the family home in Bantry for the summer, when he lets to Trinity summer school faculty his semiattached house appropriately located in Bachelor's Walk.

Additional puzzle pieces of Liam's history fell into place in that order. Ending, as usual, with food. The actual thing, or the promise of it, or the memory of it. Now it was anticipation. Where shall we eat, and what do you have in mind, and I wonder will Leslie care to join us?

In order to find that out, we knocked at Leslie's big wooden door, using Leslie's tennis-racket-sized iron door knocker, which required the two of us to pull back so it could be let go to smack against an iron panel bolted to the wood. The castle had some very wonderful expected details like that, but the exterior was generally ugly and far from the perhaps expected children's book illustration. Basically three round stone stories protruding from the crest of a hill, it had been falling apart for four hundred or so years before Leslie came along on holiday from England in the mid nineties and bought it, patched up the exterior with concrete, and continued on to paint the concrete patches a purple that, whatever the weather, was supposed to have the ability to blend in with the surrounding sky. Even so, most of the time, the paint just looked purple. There were complaints put before the county council about inappropriate refurbishing of historical property, and the protests continue to this day. But deep inside the thick purple walls, Leslie Snell enjoys her frequent holidays, as she did this June night, on her roof, gazing out at the surrounding uninterrupted nature through the lenses of the world's tiniest rectangular sunglasses.

The sun was nearly at the horizon. Leslie invited me to the edge to admire the view. I wanted to tell her I couldn't move, that I was far too afraid of heights to go anywhere near the edge, and that even if my feet were interested in the view, my hands were locked on to one of the pair of metal poles from which hung a purple hammock. She and Liam had their backs to me, were discussing some guy Felix's increasingly frequent visits to clinics offering red vein removal, teeth whitening, and photorejuvenation, and whether such treatments, supposedly good for you, could be considered an addiction and, even if they were, wouldn't they be better than his last one he kept up? I stared at my hands, frozen to the pole. The nails were turning a pinkish yellow white from the grip. My only jewelry was the Indiglo Timex, and, just above it, the blue and green bracelet that had found its way onto my wrist every day since the first I started using up Finola's charms. Three glass beads with blue and green shapes swimming inside. Then a ceramic scarab in cerulean blue. Then three more of the others, the pattern repeated in a circle, interrupted only by a silver peace symbol, a yin/yang, and a white-gray stone disc etched with a spiral. Finola had picked out the charms for her inventory. Which had been her favorite? What would she have worn? I didn't know because I'd never seen any photos of Finola. There were none in what had been her house, none in what was his, Una didn't display any pictures other than those of the boys kitted up for football, and a black-and-white of her mam when she was eleven and holding the medal that was her second-place prize for dancing at a *feis*. Noel's shop had a wall covered by large photos of his woven wear as modeled by locals. It was gas *craic*, Una said, to pose on the strand for a photographer friend of Noel's. Next stop: *Vogue*. That was their joke, Una's and Aoife's and Mrs. Quinn's, who were wrapped in Noel's scarves and hoods and ruanas up there on the wall now, the three of them, and the fourth, who early on had been my guess for Finola. Perched on a rock wearing a togalike white dress was a spinning instructor's body and a face so head-snappingly gorgeous that God probably had to attend a special weekend seminar to learn how to build it. Mahogany hair in a braid thick as an economy-sized roll of gift wrap, fists planted on hips, ready for anything, she raised her closed eyes to the sun as a wave crashed at her bare feet.

"Fiona. Fiona from the fizzy water bottling plant," Noel corrected when I asked. "Not Finola. Close, but only in spelling. One letter short in spelling and a galaxy short in everything else." He'd left it at that, giving his woeful look yet again, so I'd left it, too. I didn't know what Finola looked like, but I knew what she acted like. She did what she wanted, and though I needed to stay rooted at the hammock on the roof of Leslie's castle, I also wanted to be brave and Finola-like and stand at least near the edge. So I loosened the fingers one by one and shuffled slowly over to Leslie and Liam, in time to hear him inquire about Richard and Conal and Fran and Keith, Niamh and Felix, and who had the plans for the coffee bar franchise? Right, Helena. I placed my left hand on Leslie's shoulder, and with my right hand I grabbed a handful of Liam's fleece pullover. And I stood there and joined them in watching the sun as Leslie gave updates. She no longer saw Richard. Saw far too much of Conal. Would absolutely love more of Fran's company but she was moving house and now totally absorbed with a musician called Bott. Keith had a baby and it was the stamp of him. Niamh and

Felix, well, it was well past the point where they should even be mentioned in the same sentence. "You know the road," she said to Liam, who didn't nod.

Leslie was maybe sixty, and she was fit if you judged only by her forearms and her face and neck, which were as fat-free as a peeled stick of celery and were all of her that was visible and not covered by the hippie-ish cornflower blue tunic and boot-cut pants. She had the kind of hairdo Suzanne Pleshette wore when she was married to Bob Newhart on TV. Her curls were black and short and poufy and she was pushing the part that was before her ears behind her ears as she said very suddenly and quickly that we should help ourselves. Now that she had our parcel, there was a plane she could get that night, we could stay as long as we liked you know where the key is, Liam. "I'm off," she said, and we followed her down the stone steps of the thin spiral staircase. Liam loaded her duffel and his carton into the back hatch of her hatchback. Leslie waved and threw kisses as she drove off, we only waved back, and Pepsi went running after the cloud of dust.

"Well." I said this because I didn't know what else to say. We'd driven maybe two hours and it looks like it's time to turn around.

"Well." Liam said that, then he asked me if I wanted a proper tour.

I did. Upon arrival, we'd gone straight to the roof, without exploring each floor because Leslie had called to us from there when we knocked. Had leaned over the side in one of the cutout spaces from which you probably would dump boiling oil on intruders. Had yelled "Halloo!" and made motions with her hands as if trying to levitate us.

The ground floor was basically a few wooden-backed white puffy-cushioned chairs for waiting on if you were expecting anybody and didn't want to stand out in the rain. There was a small round table between the two chairs and Leslie had picked wildflowers to put in the vase that was really a stone somebody had gone to the great trouble of drilling a hole in. The windows on the ground floor were small and round topped and their glass was stained and churchish but with no biblical figures that you could pick out—abstract shapes, really, but when I see stained glass I think church and I go searching through the design to see if I can spot Jesus or somebody. The top panel, at the round top of each of the five windows, was clear and you could see out easily if the sun weren't shooting through as it was right then. Beneath the stairs, in a room shaped like a slice of pie, was a small bathroom, tiny toilet and sink and wall-mounted heater and corner shower, Barbie's castle bathroom.

The second floor was, except for the stairwell bulge, a perfect circle with a counter separating kitchen from seating area. A picture window had been cut over the sink and already, from the second floor, you could catch a view of the sea, or some harbor or bay, what it was I can't tell you because I had no idea where I was except that I was in a four-hundred-year-old purple tower with a flat-screen TV on the stone wall above an entertainment center crowned by a DVD player. A black leather couch sat invitingly, kept company on the floor by a big black leather pillow that looked like a dog bed but was larger and probably for reclining humans. Other than the TV screen, the only thing on the wall was a framed lithograph of a fat scrawled sheep, a Dervla McHugh limited edition of twenty-five. We sold them exclusively, Dervla and her sheep subjects—all she drew were sheep—living just outside Booley.

There was nothing on the walls of the third floor, the center of which was occupied by a round Las Vegas Elvis Presley bed covered with a round duvet of flame orange velour or velvet, but I bet it was velvet. Windows rose floor to ceiling for two-thirds of the room, including in the direction of the setting sun that fell across the bed in a way that made the color and shape and placement all total sense and not just kitschy. Beneath the staircase, a thin closet—I opened it, so I know—was organized by color scheme and by length of the shapeless boldly screenprinted linen pieces of the type Leslie had been wearing this day. We sold some of these, too, and I say some because they were all one of a kind, and when you plaster that on a tag it raises the price considerably, even at wholesale, so the shop can only afford to carry a couple at a time. Plus these are from the Burren line that are printed with rocks from that area and all the proceeds go to a fund for needy artists, so that jacks up the price even more. Simply stated, they aren't cheap. Leslie had to be loaded.

"What does she do?" I asked loudly because Liam now was way ahead of me on the final stairs to the roof.

"Yanks have a great need to know what people 'do.'"

"Yeah, we do." He had said this to me before. But it didn't stop me from asking again. "So what does she do?"

"Dunno."

"You don't know?"

"Dunno exactly. Emmm, somethin' with films."

"Actress?"

"God, no—though you nearly could see it, couldn't ya? She's involved in the writin'. All I know is her Barclaycard Platinum has gone through each time she's phoned up to order somethin', or she makes the odd visit t' Booley. I don't ask for more than that."

We were on the roof again. I held the pole again.

"You've known her for a long time?"

"Maybe a year and a half. She's invited me out for a hooley or two."

"A what?"

"Hooley. Y'know—party. I delivered the sheep print—oh, that had to be August last. She goes to England as often as she goes to the toilet. So when I want to ensure a safe delivery of an order from a shop there, or I'm sendin' one out I ring her to see if we can connect."

I was lying in the hammock now, the sky swinging above me, and all feeling of height gone once I no longer was looking toward the ground. "It's a shame she had to leave."

"Doesn't mean we have to," Liam said. "Fancy a dander?"

I looked to him for a clue. He was nodding down the hill, so I understood, and so we walked, made our way down Leslie's meadow. Pepsi whipping around us in widening circles, a spiral in progress, provoking unseen creatures in the thicket, barking a warning to overhead birds. The humans gave their voices a rest. At the base of the hill, a stream. Pepsi flopped in, up to his neck. Liam and I sat on rocks and looked back up the quarter mile to Leslie's castle, definitely purple against the fading gray light. "Far out," I said, and Liam said, "Yeah."

You might want us to be using better English, or to be saying something bearing profundity and seriousness. We were, after all, in a magical setting, and we were, after all, getting to a place in our knowing one another where deeper thoughts are usually shared. Maybe so, but that's what we said because that's what we were thinking. Things don't always go as they might in one of Leslie's films. Sometimes one person says far out and the other says yeah and they eventually stand up and start the long walk back up the meadow and something like that takes time and energy and by the time the two people are back to their car and get in and get the dog in as well it could be too late for little else but driving home.

Or this is what happens sometimes, and I know because this is what happened this very time: Leslie had a castle. She had a refrigerator that might not have been full but that contained enough basic ingredients for a few omelets or a pasta dish. She had one shelf devoted to four-packs of those big tall cans of Guinness. She had a Max-crafted wine rack, every hole occupied. She had that big sofa in front of the flat-screen TV that was now all the rage. Because of her work and connections, there was a carton of DVDs that had yet to be seen by anyone but critics. There was all this and there were all those choices. Without a word proper or improper, somehow, at the same instant, the two people agreed to stay.

Flames:

Warmth, Heat, Passion

(State Your Wish Three Times)

Did I ever tell you about the hot press? I can't remember if I did. I've been meaning to, and sometimes I mean to do something so much that I get to thinking I already have done it. So, because I'm not sure, I'll tell you. It's a big closety cupboard that—in my cottage, at least—is just inside the living room. It houses the hot water tank. There is no basement here, so the tank has to live on the same floor as the people do. Swathed in yellow insulating material, it sits like a Buddha in the center of the cabinet, surrounded by stacks of linens and towels and whatever else you think would be nice to have at a cozy-toasty temperature the water heater emits once you flip it on to start heating the water. It speaks in gurgles when the temperature gets to where you want it. I don't talk back, though. Finola has linens and towels stored in there, and also some nighttime stuff: a few pairs of unisex flannel pajama bottoms, a couple sets of long silk underwear you'd think she would have taken with her to Germany, having Alps as they do there, and snow. Wouldn't you think you'd need long underwear there?

• • •

The machine went blank. The IRENET logo and its frame of happy shamrocks popped into view, inviting me to insert a euro and select an internet provider. Yet another thwarted attempt to reach Gina. I took the disconnection as a gift. I would have only continued to blather on to Gina about stuff that really wasn't that fascinating, because the big new best details weren't the type to give to a woman who, last thing I knew, was feeling very alone. So I left out how the above-mentioned underwear had been left behind at the castle, a detail that had floated to me as I drove us back to Booley early the next morning, past a shop bearing the sign

FALSE TEETH REPAIRED

WHILE U WAIT

and the word *teeth* flashed me back to the fact that teeth were what Liam had used to remove Finola's long silk underwear from my very own body.

I'd laughed through most of that process, in the way you can laugh at such times. The way I just said that, I guess I was supposing you know that you can laugh during the most intimate of private goings on. But maybe I shouldn't be taking that for granted. Because I myself didn't know it was possible to be on the runway to planet-shifting sex and at the same time be in stitches. It had been twenty-seven years since the late night my now late aunt Nellie spotted Al Turcotte at that state fair held in flip-a-coin-named Miami, Ohio, as he counted money on the hood of his rat truck, and she ran back to our fried dough trailer to blurt, "I just saw the cutest guy in the world. He looks like Starsky, or is it Hutch?" and I walked over and determined him to be Hutch-like with dark mid-seventies hair helmet, polyester shirt bearing a photo silkscreen of the kind of toilet-brush pine trees you see in pictures of Japan, tastefully medium-weight gold chain, second-skin ironed Versaces, high-heeled black demiboots, and I pulled off my nude-tone hairnet, wiped my oily face with the edge of my Dough Show T-shirt, unloosed my ponytail, emerged from my spying in the darkness, and in about an hour lost the remaining technical shreds of my virginity on a pile of hay five feet from the largest rat known to mankind, ever, and the first man ever known to me in the biblical sense. Twenty-seven years of men since Al, and I never knew you could laugh. All my sexual encounters had been with guys whose approach was either foreign-movie artistic with concentration on location and lighting and the use of assorted food products, or who stressed athleticism and vied for record-breaking speed and positions determined by the spinner from a Twister game, or who were so uptight that a deep level of inebriation had to be reached before anything else could be reached for and even if you could remember what had happened during the encounter, it generally wasn't that memorable anyhow so why bother trying?

I wanted to remember every detail of what had happened with Liam. But for myself only. So I didn't fish another euro from the pocket of Finola's black linen duster and I didn't re-feed the email machine. I would have only continued with unrelated minutae, an inventory of what had been on Finola's night table before last weekend, when I decided to maybe store in a box in the front room the unwound alarm clock, the red metal gooseneck reading lamp, the black ceramic bowl holding a couple of wooden hair combs—the kind for keeping hair in place rather than running through it—the little enameled box with a cover I did not open, the plastic pen half-filled with black ink, the silver metal lighter, the few folded papers I did not undo, the retired assortment of pence, the gray stone with a bisecting line of white, the small jar of drinkable stuff prescribed for something called a chesty cough.

Had I continued I would have told Gina all that. I would not have told her that my newest revelation: sometimes it's best to see where life takes ya. Which, night before last after the walkback up Leslie's meadow, with no grand plan, only the instant realization that it was what we both wanted, was to exit the car we'd just gotten back into and reenter the castle door and walk up the first flight, past the food and the TV and the DVDS, and up another flight of four-hundred-year-old steps, and twelve or so more feet to the center of the room, my part of the trip made via Liam's arms.

Yes, he carried me. He actually carried me. I don't think I've been carried since I sprained my ankle slipping on a rotted crab apple in second grade. Since then, I've gotten around fine on my own, and not that any other man had tried, but I never stood for much romance-novel-cover me-Tarzan crap. But let me tell you: If you're ever in a castle and the light is the color of Grade A maple syrup and the sight of it pouring over a wooded river valley at your feet makes you actually swoon, and if in that swooning you unintentionally lean against somebody of Liam's soul and body, and if he swoons back, and if neither of you instantly returns to your preswoon posture, rather wonders at the absence of space between you and the feel his hands sliding you, then turning you so you are face to his face, and, announcing the obvious accelerated shift the course your friendship is about to take, a soft bell rings somewhere in both your heads at the exact same time—all that said, if the person you find yourself falling against and perhaps for is Liam Keegan, I suggest you allow yourself to generally let him do what he wants.

Allow him to actually take you up in his arms. Allow yourself to leave the ground and be moved as easily as if you were merely a handful of packing peanuts. Lean into the rowboat muscling of him. Inhale his kid-glove tangerine neck, rest your head there on the right shoulder of the blue fleecy thing he'd earlier pulled from the trunk or boot or whatever he calls that part of the car. Punctuated by purplish concrete, centuries-old stone circles down and away as the two of you make your way so metaphorically higher and higher. His legs have to be killing him at this point, and if he has experienced no back problems so far in his life, this could be their genesis. But, hey, the carrying was his idea, so don't concern yourself. Keep the arms around his neck and hold on as you are casually rescued from the basic plain nice day you had expected. What you thought would be just a drive is going to turn into a ride. Mentally high-five yourself for the effort of this morning's bath and shampoo, which you almost put off until tomorrow because you didn't rise early enough to give the water heater its few hours' notice but these days you're somebody new and you're thinking Finola so you're less of a baby who needs very hot water so you'd run a lukewarm bath and it certainly woke you and, looking back, wasn't that the perfect start because who'd want to be too exhausted to be totally there for all that's happening now, an hour and a half away from that Boolun tub, on the third level of a four-hundred-year-old castle, where one man is undoing all the things on your clothing that need undoing and you are doing the same to the few fastenings of his, and after that slow trip up the stairs there is a rush suddenly and the buttons and snaps get stubborn and laces develop sudden knots and boots must be pulled off with great effort and you wonder how the knights managed anything more than a handshake with all their hardware and layers and helmets, and this is when the first of the laughing starts, there on the edge of the orange velvet (you'd guessed correctly) bed, around which has sprouted a garden of footwear and socks and jumpers and funnelnecks and vests and final innermost layers, yours being removed by the aforementioned teeth, which have gripped the elastic waist bearing the 100-percent silk label and are drawing them down and down and you're laughing and he's laughing, and there's a lot of breathing with all the efforts being made by both parties, and if you were to only listen you'd think things had started already but they had not—it was only the getting to the point of skin, which finally happened and there you are, the two of you in the nip and enjoying a fast admiration of that fact before the need for cover again, and you dive beneath Leslie's orange duvet and you latch onto Liam more for warmth at first, but then for different reasons: want, need, being human, being lonely, being hurt, hoping for healing, wanting something new, wanting someone new, wanting to move on, to drive on, to ride on, as we did there that evening, Liam as white and blinding and phosphorescent as the plastic glow-in-the-dark rosaries Una stocked for the tourists who never made it up to Knock and who'd promised the mother-in-law some form of religious souvenir. Liam was as squint-inducing as when Gina and I had walked in on him that very first day above the shop, above, above, and Liam was now above me, and Liam was now below me, and Liam was now in some places where I couldn't really see him, but trust me, I was quite certain was there.

Liam would have provided the terms for what we were doing—shiftin' and mungin' and wearin', dipping into the carton of a handy bedside canister of johnnies, and we were at it, shaggin' and whatever else you want to call it. But the only word spoken was the wish he made of my name Sophie Sophie Sophie and it was a sound I would have stood in line for a week in subzero temperatures to pay a fortune for an obstructed view ticket to a performance of him saying just once. But free of charge I heard it litanized on this night, there in the true raw scenic Travel Board beauty that was right all around me and this experience was giving itself to me and what else was there to do but accept it? A place I'd never known existed, to which I'd only traveled as a favor, a man I'd initially wanted to help in no other way than an employee sense—both were placing lips to mine, and I steal nothing from Joyce, employ only basic unrehearsed reaction as I answered yes and yes and again yes for the third time, and I was getting my wish.

Hands of a Clock:

Time, Healing

(State Your Wish Three Times)

"The damp is back."

That's Joe's greeting this morning.

He doesn't mean me. He's talking weather. We just had four rare, glorious sunny days lined up like perfect pictures in a carousel of holiday slides. Click-click-click-click. Then, end of show.

On the third click of a day, we'd gone to the cliffs. Liam had joined us. He likes Joe and calls him Joeen. Joe likes Liam, and calls him boy, but says it "buy." At the cliffs, the two men spoke Irish and sounded like that radio station, or the TV channel on which Una catches a soap on which people are being gay and playing around and having babies out of wedlock just like those on the soaps back home, only they are doing these things in Irish. Joe and Liam had their conversation, and I went to the left, to the south, as I usually do, to my own little spot along the wall. Leaned my head into the grass at the top. Let the ocean music carry me off. My life now being total romance novel, I will add the cornball-coated truth that I wished I could stay there forever.

"No cliffs today."

It was a couple days later now, a whole new weather pattern.

"No cliffs today," I acknowledged. I walked to my usual seat at the left of Joe's hearth, where the fire sent out welcome waves of heat. I'd come in from town to the cottage, to bring more of Finola's old clothes over to her old shop and the home of her old man. I'd stopped staying at the cottage last Monday. Or Monday last, as Liam would puts it. That's just how things happened. Shortly after our trip to Leslie's, when time came for me to be going home for the night, he started asking me to stay in town. I had a home so I asked, "Why don't you come back to my place," but made the offer only once because his reaction—felt more than spoken because all he'd answered was "No tanks"—told me it was a bad idea. For Liam, the cottage was Chernobyl. Love Canal. Off limits, just being there could make you sick. I had loved my time in it, but I would have moved into a hole in a tree trunk if it meant I could hang around with Liam twenty-four hours a day. I still made my daily trip up to Joe's, because I wanted to, and a few times I walked past his house, to the little cottage on a small final rise that arcs sharply like the highest crest of a wave the second before it breaks. There, I gathered up more of Gina's stuff—a candle, the yoga cards, the journal—and more of Finola's stuff—the hot pink dress I hoped to wear the weekend of the horse fair if there was sun, and the dressing gown that would be better than throwing on one of Liam's shirts when a customer decided to explore the second floor. I already had been wearing something of Finola's that goes beneath the dressing gown. A short white linen nightdress that was hanging in the tiny closet, lost between a minidress of crocheted silver discs and a batik sarong with a print of the phases of the moon. If you're thinking it weird that I would wear Finola's nightgown in bed with Liam, all I can say is I had been wearing her day clothes for more than two months and not once had he given even an eyebrow raise of recognition. Nor had Una—odd because a close female friend usually can recite chapter your top ten most stunning ensembles. I never asked them right out what they thought of what I had on, but they had volunteered compliments, but basic ones—like "smart clothing." I sometimes got looks from Noel that I couldn't interpret, but I couldn't interpret a lot about him so I let that pass, and I sometimes go easily translatable slagging from Aoife—"Imagine the shops in America and the size of a Yank's travel wardrobe!" But none of them ever said anything like hey what are you doing in that?

This morning at Joe's, my backpack held the hopeful sundress that I predicted would be the next thing about which Aoife would be giving out. I placed the pack out of the way, near the foot of the stairs heading up in a steep vertical to the mystery of his second floor. At the base of the stairs, along the hearth wall, was a built-in cabinet with glass doors. Its original function must have been for the neat and orderly showing off of whatever fine dinnerware or treasures were owned, but over the years it had become a catchall space for a stack of dog-eared prayer books, a pack of letters tied with blue string, a roll of white cloth, a plastic bag containing what looked like apple seeds, a box of Panadol, a silver medal that had been awarded to the 1937 Booley Hurling Champion. Joe owned a TV, a big faux-wood-grained thing on a stand shoved alongside the stairs, its top and screen covered by a lace tablecloth on which stood a small Infant of Prague dressed in a red cape and a rather new radio with three of the stations on the dial marked by squares of masking tape. From the built-in speaker came the sound of a lively conversation between a man and a woman. They spoke in the language I heard Liam and Joe use at the cliffs, the language I've heard in snippets on the street, in the pub, from Una when a customer engages her, the one lettered on road signs and printed onto several pages of otherwise English newspapers, a language that has no relation to anything I can begin to decipher, in the way that if you know some Spanish, the sister language of Italian on a restaurant menu can make a little sense to you.

There was scooping of leaves from a tin and pouring of water from the kettle into the pot, the cups filled from a white teapot decorated with an ornate pattern of roses and the word *June* in fancy gold lettering that I wondered was the name of a woman or simply the month. Finally, there was the removing of the lid on the round tin of cookies. I took two of the oval palomino-colored biscuits with repeated sun ray lines at their edges. Whatever the topic of discussion, the two people on the radio said the same big long word at precisely the same moment, then began to laugh, which you can interpret in any language without taking a single lesson first. Joe laughed, too. He didn't explain the joke, but I didn't care because it was nice just to know he felt like making that sound.

He interrupted them to put on a serious face and tell me of a woman from church who had called over to discuss the possibility of his spending the winter in town, where a program was being organized for pensioners who had no one to look after them in the colder months. She made her case: The room he would be in one of Booley's B and Bs—the exact one had yet to be negotiated—would be warm and comfortable and with three meals daily and an easy walk to Quinn's, a journey certainly to be made in the company of the other men who would be wintering in town. This woman's father had taken part in a similar program in the south last winter, and hadn't he just loved the food and the cards and the lovely biscuits at tea. Would Joe ever consider the same, especially since it would be paid for, by the government, which preferred creating such a program to being the subject of protests held after old people were found dead because nobody had bothered to look in on them and learn they were in need.

"Sounds good to me," I said.

He sniffed and lifted his chin. Apparently I was wrong. I asked, "Doesn't sound good to you?"

The chin thing again.

"It's not forever. Just for the winter."

He looked past me. Out the window. My cue to shut up. He wasn't looking for an opinion. Just someone to listen. To him. To the radio. To the fire. The rain that was now like somebody typing a hate letter. I said, Well, I have to be getting back to town, and he said, Ah, yes, to town, and he smiled and nodded, and I smiled and nodded.

"Will you ever bring this to Una?" he asked.

In my Booleyan phrase book, the phrase "Will you ever" was one of my favorites, right up there with 'C'mere t' me,' which was not a command to walk over to somebody, just a request to listen to what's being said. Back home, if somebody said to me, "Will you ever bring this to Una," I'd think I were being asked if I ever would consider bringing the envelope to her. Like I might have to stop and think first about whether I wanted to do that, or like I needed to attend a meeting on the issue. It also might sound like I was supposed to have done so a month ago and never did. But here. "Will you ever" means would you. "Will you ever close the door" doesn't mean will you do that at some point in the future—they just want you to close the door. Will you ever be my wife, which is how somebody would ask that here, doesn't mean wouldya think about it. It means do you want to? Yes or no? Tell me, Joe, he only wanted me to bring a list to Una. I really didn't need it—he'd written down only three items today, as always in his Irish: *aran* and *bainne* and *tae*—bread and milk and tea—words I know by heart from their frequency on his lists, all a person needs. I spoke them aloud—are-awn, bon-ya, tay— as I closed the gate, and then, as if they'd been an incantation, my senses were thrown into a new gear. Are-awn, bon-ya, tay. The metal bar landing in its catch as it had for decades before I was born, my boots rocking across the stones in the road this very moment, the air breezing through my fingers as I swung my arms and picked up the pace, the mist that coated the tiniest hairs on my skin as it Fed the green, the green of the land all around me.

When I got to Una's with the envelope, the Quinns' purple-haired granddaughter, the cheerier one, their Maureen's Brid, was in line in front of me. She wore the kind of jeans that have been painted to look creased and dirty, or really are creased and dirty, and a black T-shirt that had been slashed and cut, pieces of it pulled through the holes and tied to various other parts of the fabric. She stood behind Mrs. Hartigan, who was giving the latest: "He rang Sunday last. He'll be comin' on the twenty-ninth, please God. I got a bed for the room as he said the mattress would be damp upstairs, so I told him he could sleep down in the room," and Una was saying how that'd be lovely and Mrs. Hartigan turned and said hello Sophie and I said hello Mrs. Hartigan and then it was Brid's turn at the window and her arm, the color and dimensions of a length of fettuccine, moved forward, and on the wrist I spotted the Question Authority bracelet that I'd made about a dozen of because I'd found about a dozen question mark charms and because that bumper sticker edict was a common one back home, usually adhered just above "Free Tibet," which is a wonderful dream but a slogan that to me always reads like something's being given away. I had no more Question Authority bracelets. They went quickly, and I didn't know to whom, so it was a nice little surprise to see one there, on the wrist of the hand that was giving Una an orangy yellow fifty-euro bill in exchange for a stack of postage stamps.

"Thanks a million," Una said genuinely, and the kid turned and gave me a quick hiya Sophie or howya Sophie or something of the sort and slouched out the door.

"Her fourth visit today and it's not even half-ten." Una stowed the bill. "Pity me, 'cos Ralpho's off with Ger for the day. Should I tell her next time or continue to make a sale off her every fifteen minutes?"

"Brid and Ralpho? An item?"

"Yeah. True love, like."

"Wow. Who knew?"

"Well, I know, but I'm not t'know, d'ya know? Ralpho would keel over and die."

"You could end up related to the Quinns. Knock down the walls between your buildings, make a combination market and bar—a barket!"

Una whacked herself in the head. "Now let's not rush things. He's only after learning to walk."

"He's nearly fifteen. What were you doing at fifteen?"

"Jesus . . ."

"Sorry—I wash . . ."

"Sophie, I've a livin' reminder of what I was doing at that age. Can't imagine my life without him. But I wouldn't wish a child on another child. We've had the talk. He nearly leapt out the window at the word intercourse, but we've had the talk. Beyond that, and owning the only shop for a full sixteen miles that stocks condoms, what else can I do but hope he employs full common sense at the times when it's the last thing in command? Right now, though, I'd much rather concentrate on adult relationships. Say, yours and Liam's."

I straightened the line of tacks on the notice board next to the post window. Una maintained it for people like herself who did not attend Mass and therefore were out of that vital pipeline of information and gossip. Currently, a "Very Kind Home" was wanted for a "beautiful long-haired lurcher type (male), 10mths," though there was no clue as to what sort of creature this was. Also, a dog was missing. But that's all the paper said: "Dog Missing" and a phone number. Yoga classes would be held Monday nights in the school and you could sign below if interested. A TV and video player and Playstation 2 and five games were for sale, as was a return ticket to Oslo for the 30th. The gun club was to meet. A holiday home in Bundoran would be available the first two weeks of September. A lift to Limerick was needed. Something called French grinds were being offered to leaving cert students.

"OK. Adult relationships. Well, it's adult, and it's a relationship, and it's all very nice. And while on the subject of this particular relationship, may I say I appreciate your enthusiasm. Considering, you know, how you were so close to Finola."

Una ran her hands up the sides of her head to fine-tune her rooster hairstyle.

"She was an enormous part of my life, and my boys' lives, for years, but that's got no connection to Liam and what he should be doing. She made her choice by leaving. It's not like she's on holiday and he's having an affair on the quiet. She's gone. There's been no contact from her, absolutely none. It's clear she wants nothing to do with Booley, or anyone in Booley. I don't like to say this aloud, but she may as well be dead. You're alive, Liam's alive. I don't like to say this out loud, either, because it's sad, but end of summer you'll be gone from Booley as well. So, when it comes to Liam or anything else you are interested in here, as it said on one of your bracelet tags, smoke 'em while you got 'em."

"You liked that one, I remember."

"I did. But at the end of the day, I, as do most people on the planet, prefer Love."

And she pointed to her wrist just above the cuff of her black fleece hoodie, where the red and silver bracelet with the X and O charms sparkled hopeful.

Flower:

﹏

Blooming, Results

(State Your Wish Three Times)

One very windy night, Liam was called into service by The
Chancers to play a going-away party at the Macushla Hall in
Tipperary and I woke alone two hours past the point he predicted
he'd be back next to me in the little messy bed above the shop.

I still was not accustomed to the sounds of the village center,
which on all nights included the laughing and shouting and singing
and obscenitying of patrons leaving Quinn's after last orders at
11:30, and on very windy nights like this also heard the thrumming
of various utility wires that at times could sound like a chain saw
being started up. On this night that sound mixed in my head with
concern for Liam out there somewhere on the road, and that added
up to the conclusion he'd run the Golf into a tree and EMTs and
firefighters were now using heavy equipment to remove the tree
from the crushed vehicle and its crushed passenger. Oh, and Max,
too, as they'd carpooled.

The true facts: there really were no trees for the colliding, there
were no instantly materializing EMTs, firefighters here were simply
whoever was around and old enough to handle a bucket in a long
line of them, and probably not one of them owned a chain saw. I

knew all that, yet none of them calmed me. What did was busy-work. Going downstairs and doing inventory until 4:00 A.M. on the night Liam was made late for no reason more awful than a flat and that the man who wandered from his nearby house at two in the morning to see what was the commotion—what's the chance he once regularly road bowled with Max's father? And when you find a connection like that, you've got to come in for a drop and to explore all the other lanes of possible connection.

When you are Max, you have only the wife Collette awaiting you, so you consent, because you're a great one for the chat, and because Collette is long past the stage of sitting at the window searching the black for headlights. It'd been ages since Max rushed home in heady anticipation. But Liam currently existed at that stage. So at four in the morning Liam hailed Max out the door of the road bowler's, dropped him at his forger and was delighted to find the light on at the bead table when he pulled the Golf along-side the shop. I had not enjoyed the fretting, but it is an unavoidable hazard when you find your the boat of your heart drifting off course, and through the fog you see—hey—what's that ahead. Where'd that come from—love? I was heading the opposite direc-tion. Fuck. I might even have already collided. Sinking, and enjoy-ing each second. All the bad in the basement floor of my gut evap-orated the millisecond I heard the whir of the Golf coming up the road and then Liam was inside the door telling me about the Macushla Hall and the road bowler and as he shut the light and led me upstairs to the messy little bed in the home we shared.

It was messy because it was never neatly made, because why make it when you're just going to unmake it very shortly. Every chance we got, Liam and I made use of the bed's unmadeness. We woke, climbed into one another, got ready for our day, got another look at each other, and very often that resulted in falling back in the bed until we heard voices downstairs. Then we made a new attempt to greet the day. We made the tea, we made the toast, we made a few pieces of jewelry, made a few sales, made a dash up the stairs, made all manner of love with the shop door thirteen stairs down still open and several times with someone calling "Hallo up the stairs—anyone up there?" and "I'm coming" was what one of us had to find the voice to yell because would be true, just one moment, and the truth is the truth and you can't miss the opportunity for the laugh.

We were laughing a lot. Talking a lot. Exploring pasts and presents. Very rarely going near the future. But later on the day of the 4:00 a.m. return, we did. Out of the clear blue.

"What would you do if he rang this second?" Liam asked as we had our tea.

Startled, I surprised myself by, one, how I knew who he meant, and, two, how quickly I countered, "What would you do if she did?"

He was silent, so I filled up the space with my answer: "I know that I would hang up. There's nothing he has to say that I'd want to hear."

Liam's answer took the backroads from brain to lips. Got stuck behind a traffic jam at a particularly snarled patch of bypass construction. Finally, he touched the lines on his Noel-woven kitchen tablecloth and said, "I don't know that I would. With hair, I mean, a course. I've things to say, and never was given the opportunity. You'd want that if you'd never had it, the opportunity."

I nodded. Because I'd gotten into the nodding habit and because this was the right kind of occasion for nodding. I didn't, but could understand how you might want that opportunity to say things if you'd never had it. You might want to seat somebody across from you and ask the whys. If I cared to know that with my own story, I had Charlie St. Jean's phone number. Hey, I'd had his wife and kids right in front of me if I'd had it in me to grill them that day. Liam possessed nothing more than the name of Finola O'Flynn's solicitor. Certainly, in this technical day and age, he long ago could have hired somebody to track down her address and provide him with an accompanying satellite-feed map to her house or apartment or wherever she makes her home. But why bother—the message was clear, Liam told me. He no longer was wanted, and that was fully understood. "But to answer your question, if she rang, I'd speak with her." He lifted his mug then before adding, "Talking about talking is a right waste of time, and time is precious."

That was no news to me. Even in my current daily state of drunken dizziness, tumbling around as if there were no tomorrow, I knew the value of another day in Booley. You can get all philosophical and go on about the fact that all our days wear numbers, and how it's only human to not really take not of that until the doctor solemnly closes the manila folder and takes a breath and tells you that he doesn't know how to say this but. . . . More than two months ago the customs agent at Shannon and had asked me, "Business or pleasure?" then thudded onto randomly chosen page thirteen of my brand-new U.S. passport the purple stamp that permitted me to land in Ireland for three months. So I knew the extent of my days here, though I didn't know the extent of the punishment awaiting those who broke the ninety-day rule. They didn't stamp that information on there. Just an unphrased warning that I eventually would be illegal.

Nor was there, I noted, a stamped caution against going home for a week and then returning for another twelve. But that kind of thinking advanced me way beyond where I wanted my heart to be, so I stayed away from it. In a way I felt like you do when your dog has just died and someone shows you the newspaper feature about who's in the pound this week and you don't want to look even with half an eye open because there is a chance to lose your heart to Nikki the Alaskan malamute mix found chained to a tree one morning in front of the dogcatcher's home, and even if you feel you could fall for this Nikki, didn't you too recently have your sad heart put in storage for safekeeping from further injury? It was too soon for me to imagine loving anybody at all, man or beast. Whether or not what I'd felt for him had been as real as I wanted it to be, the Charlie St. Jean-shaped scars on my left ventricle were still form- ing. But there was nothing wrong with good strong like, Finola would have reminded me were she in my situation. And I definitely liked Liam. We were unattached, adult, maintained working body parts that showed no sign of wearing out, and whether or not it was just a pathetic holiday fling, I wasn't really giving a care. I was just being. Being there. Being Finola. And, thanks to Liam Keegan, havin' a bit of a life-changin' experience.

More mail—mail addressed to Finola, fresh communiqués from the bracelet buyers now wearing them out there in the world. Testimonials to, well, I'm not sure what.

"Hola," Benicio wrote appropriately, considering he was sending this from Spain. "I buy Strength, I have strength."

"Hiya!" printed Belle. "My purchase of your 'Luck' bracelet was due to colour rather than the title. The following afternoon I won a week's holiday in Cuba!"

"Peace," wished Judi all the way from Maryland, because, she noted, that was the one she'd bought. "Wish I could give one of these to everybody I know!"

Everybody I knew (make that almost everybody already) already had one. Slow day, slow hour, Emilio would stroll over for a fag, Una delivered the mail even though we were supposed to go over and get it, one of Aoife's kids came in to hide from another. They stopped at the bead table while I worked, they chatted, they'd start playing with the bracelets in the dish before them, they'd say they'd seen tourists with them, or didn't the new housekeeper at Diamond's wear one, what was this about the tags, and could I make one up with an Irish title?

Strolling in was how Grainne up at A Star of the Sea ended up wearing the one meant to give her some of the patience she needed in dealing with people like the Yank earlier that summer who gave out to her, and then to the Tourist Board, about the nor-so-hot hot water at the B and B. That's how Una got the red and silver bracelet labeled "Love" thought on a regular no occasion day because sometimes you just have to do things like that. Noel was standing and chatting the slow afternoon he picked out the genuine turquoise and black jet beads and the little gray stone disc into which was carved a dot, rays emanating from it and heading out in all directions, which I took to see as hope, and labeled it as such, and which was why Noel chose that one. I took it apart to re-string making it larger for his tree trunk wrist, then handed it over saying "Hope is our biggest seller," I waited for him to confide something juicy about the reason for his choice, but he only said, "Yep," and twirled the bracelet carefully with his lonesome meaty opposite hand. Sitting next to me all those days was how Liam came to wear a circle of many and varied little beads, small and not gaudy (which was his opinion of Noel's), a green glass circle, a seed pearl, a rectangle of amber, shiny free-form turquoise, tiger's eye, sodalite, peridot, shell. I strung a silver spiral, and a yin/yang, and presented it to him without a tag, which disappointed him, so I told him it was called "Untitled."

My bracelets sparkled on Booleyan wrists. And not unlike the lucky stone I never took up Fabian's offer to go see, on Booleyan animal legs and necks. One morning, while an institutional-size can of extra-chunky-style fog got poured along the coastline, I laced a couple of red beads onto Pepsi's collar with the thought they might make him a little more visible. And because I had one on the table, I added a tin disc pressed with the shape of wings. Pepsi's guardian angel for while he was out on his rounds. Ger spotted it and wanted a version for his Cara, a skinny generic black and white sheepdog who rode in the new truck and was lovely company, but Ger worried about her running off after something while they were on a delivery and he might then never see her again and he couldn't imagine that notatall notatall. Keep her home is what Una sug-

gested. I'd rather get her this, Ger answered, admiring Pepsi's orna-
mentation.

I was asked to make up something for a cow belonging to the
farmer next to the Quinns' all-wood chalet that back when it had
been ordered through the mail and shipped from Norway in giant-
sized puzzle pieces was such a sight it was a Sunday afternoon driving destination, but now was the kind of home a lot of Germans
sent away for and had erected in the fields they were buying up so
you were fairly tripping over them. The Quinns' neighbor's cow
didn't care the style and material of the house you lived in, she just
didn't want you putting it up in her favorite field, which is what had
happened the previous summer, and cows don't say much in general
but if you know them you can tell when one is not happy and this
one was not. This cow spent most of her day at the gate separating
her farm's remaining fields from the one that had been sold. Her
already melancholy eyes stared at what had been the ambrosia of
grasses, now swallowed up for the most part by a Mediterranean-
style monstrosity and its accompanying gravel-covered yard. She
had no concept of money, could not relate to the farmer's attempts
to explain (because he was the type of man who would feel a cow
deserved an explanation) how he knew full well that had been the
finest field, but the views it afforded, and its frontage on the road
out of town, had made it the best choice when he decided to sell just
a single field, a decision he'd made because his brother's recent sale
of one small field had translated to Montessori school and Euro
Disney for each and every one of his five children. The farmer had
children who were grown and scattered to the four winds. The sale
of his best field would pay for what they now call complementary
therapies, formerly alternative therapies, now called complementary
because they complement such socialized-medicine-funded traditional treatments as chemotherapy and radiotherapy and stem cell
transplants, but that in the end, after you have spent more money
than is yours, can be totally ineffective and your wife is as dead as

she would have been had she not been moxibustioned and reikied and encouraged to scream her innermost rage into a feather pillow. Did I have something that could help this cow understand why the field had to go?

I assembled a short string of tiny green beads, green of course representing the field, and a little clear one thrown in there because it looked to me to be as clear as the definition of clarity, and I ended the strand with a charm of which there was only one on Liam's entire table. A small round barrel with a tiny working door. The farmer, I was told by the Quinns, inserted a few strands of his wife's hair into that bead before closing it and walking up to the gate to hang the whole thing from the plastic ID tag in the ear of the cow that since had begun to spend time in a lower field and was putting back on weight and followed the farmer as she always had up to the day last year on which the heavy equipment was trailered onto the field. The farmer said he did not know how, but he will find a way to thank me, he will.

"You're a powerful woman," Liam said to me the late June morning on which we stood at that lower field and watched the cow contentedly graze. I waved that off. However, I did like the cow story—and the others. The lame weren't walking, the blind weren't seeing, but a few people in the world were at least halfway interested in thinking along more positive and useful lines, and at least one wearer had moved on to other pastures.

"Well if I am powerful," I replied. "I'm fresh out of magic."

Back at the shop I showed Liam the empty bowls the once had overflowed with flowers and arrows and buildings and letters and astrological signs and arms and legs and little pictures of boats leaving or arriving or, depending on what you were trying to attain, just floating.

"Ring Jack up at Booth's—the supplier in Ennis," he told me. "Order whatever charms, beads, bits ya need, and stress that the Horse Fair's in less than three weeks."

"Harses, harses!" I sang.

"Right. 'Crowds, crowds' more the case. Ye won't believe the madness the two days generate."

"I'll get right on it chief." I reached for the directory and the phone. Felt a hand on mine, taking mine, leading me heard Liam's voice reminding me he'd be away the whole of the next two days. En route to the stairs, we were pushed back by a wave of perky green T-shirts reading ERINTOURS, it's cultural consultant Christina Giliberti at the front with her tour guide umbrella flag, which she was pointing at me, and to the inside of the shop, so I'm not sure if she was meaning me, or it, but she was announcing, "People, people: This here is Finola O'Flynn!"

The group smiled, then scattered to the corners and merchandise. Christina stayed put and said, "All the consultants are saying this is one of the loveliest shops in the region. No junk anywhere, and some very unusual items. The bracelets in particular . . ."

Liam, back at the table, tapped his Biro on the dish containing my bracelets. "We've only these." Christina steamed over and rummaged through the twenty or so pieces, clacking, clicking, reading, hmmm-ing, trying on, pulling off, ultimately picking out three of what I have to say were the nicest three in the dish and asking me to put them aside for her, and step behind the table for a photo. Both of us.

"Sit! Sit like you're both at work!"

I sat. Elbowed up against Liam. Who threw an arm around me and in what was the one and only photograph ever taken of us that summer, from his seat next to me behind the bead table, kissed me on the cheek for much longer than the one-sixtieth of a second the camera had required.

Then Christina Giliberti called, "Ladies. Over here! Here are the bracelets I told you about . . ."

Circular Arrow:

Return with Purpose

(State Your Wish Three Times)

It was Saturday. The first in a new month, July.

Back home, my town would be readying for its Independence Day celebration. The end of my street would be blocked off with sawhorses so no one could turn onto the main road being cleared for the parade. Neighbors would awaken to the metallic tapping of Mr. Brozek erecting the new screen house that would get its christening at the family's annual party. Brie Pernell and her older sisters would be setting up a card table down at the corner from which they would sell to thirsty parade-goers Dixie cups of lemonade made from a generic artificially flavored mix bought by the five-gallon can at B.J.'s Wholesale Club. Come sundown, after the requisite barbecuing and presenting of red, white, and blue Cool-Whip-and-graham-cracker-based desserts, much the town would head to nearby Monson, which concludes its huge Fourth of July Summerfest with a show of fireworks behind the town administration building. On TV, the Boston Pops would be broadcast nationwide from the Hatch Shell on the banks of the Charles, and that concert would conclude more explosions, these coordinated to the music being played by the orchestra.

All that would happen. Or maybe it wouldn't. The Irish times recently had run a front-page story about Americans being nervous about the holiday because of what had happened the previous September. We all knew what had happened but we weren't sure what to call it. September 11th. Or 911, which made it sound exactly like the emergency it had been. The tragedy, the terrorism, the towers, the mass murder, whatever the name you chose, continued to color American life. Including what normally would be quite partying day. I was all the more removed over here in Booley, where there of course wasn't a hint that it was any country's birthday. It was just another summer Saturday.

I poked around the market that assembled on this day of the week, a small collection of carts and stalls and open car trunks and horse boxes lining the road past the chip shop. Piglets, goats, shires, the odd assortment of poultry from local farms; multiply-grained bread and pungent Indian food from a commune up the coast; Wellingtons and halters and bridles and hoof picks and stirrup irons from the truck wearing a MASSIVE SADDLERY SALE banner; a small collection of Walkman-type gizmos and discount phone cards sold by a college kid who regularly set up a stall in small towns like this; bootlegged versions of top-40 CDs, one of the Republican army's fund-raising efforts; kitchenware and clothing sold from the back of a couple of Ford Escort vans belonging to travelers.

I walked to Joe's past all this, through almost stationary droplets of rain, in which we walked to the cliffs. I left him alone in his place at the final wall and walked down to mine and leaned in and shut my eyes and listened, absentmindedly twirling my bracelet, the blue ceramic scarabs, the smooth round beads of clear glass, bits of blue and green floating in them like the wisdom-bearing fish. I'd strung a small silver peace symbol between two of the glass beads, because who wouldn't want peace, and, after a few more beads I'd added a black-and-white-enameled yin/yang disc, because that's how life goes, and I'd made the centerpiece a small square bead in the shape of a book that took me back to being dropped off at the cottage by Liam at the end of that first day, which truly had been another day for the memory book. Which, if it actually existed on a shelf somewhere, by now would be Bible-sized.

I wanted to tell this to Gina. Who two days ago, for the first time since she left, two months before got in touch.

HELLO IT'S ME was the title of the message that had ended up in Noel's computer because when he'd left her at Shannon he'd given her his business card. Of course, a loop of Todd Rundgren would be running in my head the remainder of the day. As would the three sentences on the print-out Noel had delivered:

How are you Sophie? Even if you are unhappy with me, I like to think that you must not hate me too much because you sent me such a beautiful bracelet. Thank you. Please email if you would like to.

She'd gotten it. The package I'd wrapped in mid May and no longer could resist sending. After closing, crowded with weekend tourists I walked up the road to give IRENET another try.

Diamond's teemed with guests, many in the kitchen making their suppers. There was much chopping and boiling and frying going on. A dozen or so people worked around one another, moving hunger-intently from the gas stove to the sink to the glass-front refrigerator with the Diamond-penciled sign on the top shelf: STAFF FOOD KEEP AWAY! Most of the group spoke a language that sounded almost spiky, words jabbed into the air. In the adjoining dining room, four women laughed hysterically, in England English, over their plates of something that looked like fried meat, and I must have been trying to determine its identity for too long because the woman with the bangs she'd gelled into a row of seven or eight little inverted triangles waved to me and selled, "Join us, love."

"The kitchen is for guests of the hostel only," Diamond

announced loudly as he walked past. He seemed to have radar for extended kindnesses.

I said, "Right," to Diamond, and "No thanks" to the women, and I pointed to the line for the internet machine. I was at the end of it, sixth. On the IRENET screen, a JPEG was forming excruciatingly, drowsy pixel by drowsy pixel. The woman at the keyboard had no patience. She vented in French, which sounded very cool despite its crispy-fried edge of anger, and the man in front of me turned to translate, which impressed me not only because he knew what she was saying but because he was Asian. "It's a picture of her boyfriend, "he explained." You might think she'd never seen him before this. But we must bear in mind that she has been away might for a month, far from him. He's just received a package she sent—that's what the title of the email says."

I liked that he was as nosy as I. It would make the wait seem not so long. He knew the woman only from being on the same flight from Paris. A month ago they'd come to Booley, traveled, were back in town for a few nights before flying home, where his job was installing French cable television in the homes of French people. His favorite American television program was *The Simpsons*, something he had in common with Diamond, he told me, because the Simpsons were all over the television here, too, and this French-Asian guy and Diamond met in the lounge each night at six and had a laugh. I had never seen Diamond laughing, and I made a note to come by some night at six to witness that.

The photo on the IRENET screen was now visible down to the boyfriend's chin, which was long and rounded like the bottom of the letter U. Level with the chin, the pointy top edge of a sheet of paper was coming into view. My interpreter told me his own boyfriend emails photographs, too, but that they are the type that have to be viewed in a more private setting than the hallway of a hostel. He ripped open his Velcro wallet to show me a picture of only the face of the boyfriend, who was not Asian and who also installed French cable television in the homes of French people. The boyfriend looked like Andrew Hamilton has since his makeover on the new twenty-dollar bill. Dashing and high forehead and swept-back multilayered shag with waves as if from a stylist. "Wow," I said. "Yeah," said the French guy, who added "Wow" himself, but he was not looking at his own boyfriend anymore. He was looking at the woman's boyfriend, the photo now completely viewable, all parts of it including the paper he was holding, the French words on it, and the wrist of the hand that was holding the paper. Also visible was what was on the wrist: the very same red and silver "Love" bracelet that Una wore. The photo subject's right hand was pointing at the bracelet on the left wrist. The left hand held the paper. The woman at the screen was a wreck now, but in a good way, weeping and cooing all types of French endearments into the IRENET screen.

"What's it say?" I asked the cable television installer, who had a talent for drama which I say because he acted out the message, turning full toward me, eyes behind an inch of tears, taking my face in his hands, and drawing me to him as he whispered, "Be my wife, please."

The month was all the green that was ever born the first millisecond blue met yellow. When the two edges of the pools of color spread just by gravity and finally touched and their borders were no longer, they'd made something new and apart from themselves, the life-giving life-surrounding green of this world I had lived in for nearly three months. Liam and I amidst that green, carried on our work, and carried on as usual. Basically just enjoying one another. That was the thing—we were friends. If all the high-voltage contact were pushed aside by a pair of specially insulated gloves, the fact that we got along very well would remain. He traveled rarely these days, sticking close to help ready stock for the Horse Fair, to make the most of any free time, into which we jammed all the activ-

ities he was going to suggest for Charlie St. Jean and me. So instead
of Charlie St. Jean and I, it was Liam and I ending the day with a
drive to the recommended cove edged by cliffs that at low tide are
draped in hanging sea plants that are out of this world, but we got
there late, were trapped by the tide in a cavelike area and had to
swim out. It was Liam and I ringing up the recommended man up
by the football pitch who offers horses for hire, and we had a sunrise
ride along the hills above Booley on the only two mounts he was
able to capture for us: a pair of unromantic asses. It was Liam and I
dining at the recommended pub that was also a hardware store and
in the back were three or four tables at which you sit next to shelves
of plungers and hack saws to be served a meal of fish that would
ruin you for seafood the remainder of your life, which it did, but in
the negative sense of the term, because we both got some sort of
food poisoning that kept us bedridden for one precious day, which,
we realized afterward, fulfilled Liam's last idea for Charlie and
me,—that we remain horizontal.

"Another page for the memory book," Liam reminded me in the
cave, on the asses, from the toilet.

I was filling out my own book. More pages one of Gina's left-
behind diaries, in which she was supposed to have been recording
her thoughts prompted by the pre-printed cues: "Today I
feel . . . Today I think . . . Today I want . . ." I'd initially been faithful
to the task, as I had been to the yoga-ing and the meditating to all
the exercises that she was to have been here doing but couldn't stay
here to do them, so I did but after a while didn't because I had
found better things to do. As the summer continued, and I'd gotten
busier, then I'd gotten a following for my bracelets, then I'd started
following Liam, there was less and less time for reflection. When I
did pick up the diary, I rarely got past the first line, which I completed with the word *first.* "Today I feel first. I feel first with Liam."
I wrote that because I did. I felt first with somebody. And that definitely was a first for me and a man. When I looked ahead in the

queue—well, I didn't have to because there was no line. There was nothing standing between Liam and me. No work, no hobby, no obsession, no addiction, no quandary real or imagined. No reason to take a number at the deli counter of his life, waiting for him to be through with a call to his first-place mother who was convinced that the crisis in the Catholic church was a media conspiracy because there were lots of teachers and other people who worked with children and nobody was investigating them, or to his first-place boss who was paranoid that his own boss was constantly spying on the place through those little tiny video cameras you see advertised now in all the magazines, or to his first-place childhood friend crushed into catatonia by the off-season trade of a millionaire drug addict sports star. There was no one else, nothing else, and the best part was that Liam would come right out and told me so.

That final month, whenever I'd worry we weren't getting enough done workwise because we were doing too much playwise, he made my standing clear.

"C'mere to me" that was Booleyan for "Listen up," "Right now ye are the most important thing in my universe."

Not just day, not just life, not just world. Universe.

The biggest thing we know in all of existence.

In all that, I was it for somebody. I was it for Liam Keegan.

And the best part: He treated me as such. And from the top of the heap of all the issues and concerns and interests and occupations and bits and pieces great and small that made up the life of Liam Keegan, I basked.

Luckily, I can multitask. So the basking easily could go on while I sat next to him, both of us stringing together miles of beads because only a feckin' eejit would be unprepared for the throngs the Horse Fair would attract, and despite all our pre-fair horsing around, we were good and ready. It was not an event that was a particular favorite of Yanks or Moroccans or Koreans, so foreigners weren't a factor. You'd see your good number of county residents current and former, and, of course, most of Greater Booley. The daily population of 341 might be visited by an extra thousand on each of the weekend days. Big stuff for a little place. Booth's had shipped two fat square cartons of beads and findings in plenty of time for us to make up necklaces and earrings to fill each hook on the wall, and for me to stock the big green glass dish at the front of the bead table, and fill two Barry's tea crates with extra pieces kept beneath the CD table. The focus of the two days might be the sale and showing off of equines along the main road, but from what I'd gathered, the weekend would be more like the fairs I worked with Aunt Nellie Fast food booths Frylolator, a dated fun fair with little circling kiddie boats and cars, and a marquee set up in the field just past Emilio's, to which Jimmy Donnelly would descend from his home in the hills for the annual performance of the now classic "Horses, Horses." This year, the song would be thirty years of age, and word was RTÉ would be sending out a mobile unit to televise the appearance. There was a candy coating of buzzy anticipation along the main road. But inside Finola O'Flynn, the countdown was bittersweet. The Sunday night of the fair weekend, I would be flying home.

So behind the bead table in the weeks left, while the *deedly-deedly* played on the boom box and Pepsi sat at our feet and the customers entered and questioned and browsed and paid and left, I strung together Peace and Truth and a whole lot of Hope, and I moved my chair all the closer to Liam's. I was feeling a bit ill, starting to pay the price for lacing a corner of my heart onto a man who soon would be no closer than an ocean away.

We'd awakened much earlier than we would have liked, jostled into consciousness by Horse Fair street commotion that came early on the hoofs of a Thursday night that Una called only a warm-up to a proper send-off, but that seemed to me as loud and raucous and smoky and beery and teary as a proper one might be. It was mighty *craic* altogether, The Chancers opening the Horse Fair weekend with a gig in the marquee, and even though none of the band members was absent, they had included substitute Liam in the final set because he would be there anyhow, the stage being just a chip shop away from his front door. And in a most impressive setting. Outdoors, with nearly an entire town—and more—present, the road to the sea closed for the weekend and the whole of downtown Booley one big party. True to their self-description as one of the country's foremost interpreters of country music, The Chancers populated their first set with lovebirds, jailbirds, two-timers, truck drivers and coal miners. They sang of Nashville and Appalachia and Muskogee, of drinkin' and thinkin', of walkin' the line and bein' on the road again, all with the Booleyan hills as the backdrop. The crowd cheered. Children whirled in front of the stage, mothers swayed as they minded them, couples danced in the space allowed, men gathered at the wall near the river. Multitalented Ger ran the sound from a booth across the road, and from there I watched with Liam until he was called to the stage.

"D'ya dance?" he asked me, and I answered, "Not well," so the next slow one, some sappy thing about a letter that contained a plea for forgiveness but, due to a postal error, went undelivered for three decades, during which the intended recipient never knew an apology had been offered so she kept up her grudge and, well, all in all it was a life that could have gone otherwise—better—had the mail arrived in a timely fashion, but hadn't we danced. But the content was not the point, the beat was, the correct speed for the high-school hang, that universally practiced slow dance of the choreographically impaired, woman with hands around man's neck, man with hands around her back, sometimes lower, in back pockets, or on actual behind. Liam's and my version was a sleepwalky thing that slowly took us in back of Ger's booth, next to the wall above the river, and he held me in the way I would have ordered from a menu, one hand caressing my upper back and the other pressing between where my back pockets would be if Finola's denim skirt had had back pockets. Liam pressed me against the river wall and leaned his way between my knees and we were kissing as ferociously as junior prom-ers and when the music stopped he pulled back and looked poised to say something of huge importance when some guy in a Mexican hat stumbled behind the booth and into us and then stalled not more than a foot away to piss into the river.

"What were you going to say?" I asked that, but then there was Ralpho pulling Liam from me and over to the stage, where he would join the band in a set of the original tunes, including some from the CD being sold at the outdoor bar the Quinns had received permission to set up in a tent to the side of the stage. Liam wore one of the shop's Buaille T-shirts, keeping up his perfect record of never donning a Chancerian waistcoat, and looked more Claptonian than ever up there doing that guitar player thing in which guitar players look down at their hands in great concentration even though they probably don't need to because they know the music so well, appearing all intense and in the moment and artistelike in the manner of both the biggest star on the charts and the most anonymous air guitarist jamming before the bathroom mirror. The music now was ancient-sounding but also a bit rockish, enough of both to please all segments of the audience. There was the incorporation of a bagpipe kind of instrument, and a bodhran sending out messages in primal code. There were words, about the sea, the sky, loss and desire, about the euro and NATO and of course the potato, about girls and other girls and the sign of the cross and the sign for a roundabout that leads to a road that bypasses the heart of a town, and there were some words about dreams that come close but don't land where you'd like them to, and about those that do because, take heart, that does indeed happen. At the Gladys-Knight-Pip parts when some background vocals were called for, Liam stepped forth with Max and they shared a microphone and harmonized to the side of Dermot, who was the head of The Chancers, make no mistake about that. Despite the country sound, he attempted a transformation into Bono, into Lennon, into Jagger, and your eyes were glued on him—at least he was hoping they were, as he was hoping that charisma could reach out with little smoky fingers and capture you and convert you and transform you so all you would be thinking on the way home was Dermot Dermot Dermot, and even if your date in the very first hour of the night made a blatant move for your sister, you would nonetheless accept his advances later in exchange for imagining his face, and the rest of him, was the face of and the rest of Dermot's. Personally, Dermot does nothing for me. I'd never had romantic interest in a musician. On this night, though, leaning against the side wall of Emilio's, I gazed out at Liam and zing, zing, zing went all my body parts, and now joining in loud there was the primal code message being sent by my heart, the one-beat repeat, a thrice-spoken wish: STAY STAY STAY.

If I wanted to stay, what would he do? And what would I do, as a full-time resident? So I think again: What would Finola do? What had she done? She'd left when her own inner passport deemed she had to. She'd made a home with Liam. It hadn't lasted, but it had lived, and, say those in Booley, it had been something to see. I could only see what was in front of me: this night, the marquee, Liam up there in his Buaille T-shirt, and I focused on him. And then, an instant later it was the next morning, far too early the next morning, and the horse boxes began banging down the road to unload Kahlua-spotted ponies and India-ink Shires and boy-band-handsome colts, refurbished antique traps and workaday wagons and used and new tack for the MASSIVE SADDLERY SALE, and all of them and all of that was now lined up alongside the wall at the river, across the main road from the line of shops, stretching from Diamond's and across the bridge, past the Last Restaurant and

Noel's and Una's and Quinn's and ours and Emilio's, past the marquee after that. The regular Saturday vendors were here, as they would be the next day, so the made-to-order bright morning smells of both animals and spices and sounds like the crowd were there for the buying or trading, or just for the enjoyment of a day out. I opened the shop and took my place at the table. I kept the radio off, the people passing the door being entertainment enough.

"He looks fresh for seventy-nine."

"A trampoline. Imagine."

"Downpatrick, Lingfield, the lot."

"A nation of begrudgers."

"Grand. Grand."

"She's a total racist."

"Goodfella's deep pan pizza, no more, no less."

"The pope and everythin'."

"He's more than a cute hoor."

"She's mad for the grape."

"I'm fixed, tanks."

"Fourteen hands. No, thirteen. No, fourteen."

"He has no job, no home, no visible means of support."

"They'd a very successful table quiz in my day."

"He died he did."

"He did?"

"He did."

"Choc-ice, please."

"Sorry."

"No harm."

"OK so."

"It's yer man from *ER*."

"A Massey Ferguson 290, two-wheel drive, good cab, lights and indicators, wide tires, immaculate condition, ya can't bate it with a stick, will you ever call in for a look?"

"If it gets into their hands, I'm banjaxed."

"Janey Mack!"

"A good shag and I'll be in fine form."

"This is Finola O'Flynn."

The ERINTOURS cultural consultant Christina Giliberti was back and was saying that last line as she led in a tired-looking contingent of ERINTOURists, most of them tanned and darkfeatured, Latin-looking, holding the yellow Attracta's bags and brown paper Booley Woollens bags and the generic white plastic THANK YOU bags from Una's. Christina had led her charges into the shop maybe eight or ten times since my first weeks here, when she flat-out suggested I become Finola. She had no idea where that idea had taken me, even to this very moment as I sat in Finola's pink sundress, into which I was laced just hours ago by Finola's former man, who then went back to sleep and remained in that state above.

"So, Finola, how are ya?"

"Time's up, Christina. I've got to go home."

"No. When?"

"Tomorrow night."

"You have to?"

"Time's up. Legal limit."

"I don't suppose, with the way things are right now, you want to go taking chances. . . . !

"I might be tempted—but my passport expires in five days."

Christina made an "ugh" sound and recited: what she probably had to tell each and every group of prospective travelers. "Make sure that your passport covers the period of your stay. Immigration officials are particularly hard on visitors who outstay their passport expiry date. You may find yourself having at least an unpleasant 'conversation,' which could be long enough to make you miss your flight. Worse still, you may be refused future entry into the country. If you do inadvertently overrun the expiry date, go to the embassy, preferably with a citizen to support you when you state that you haven't been working illegally."

She looked down at my hands, which, as they had been since the day she met me eighty-nine days before, were in the process of doing illegal work.

"What are you gonna do?"

"I'll leave."

"And you'll come back? What's to stop you from turning right around and coming back?"

"Nothing, I suppose . . ."

You'd think I'd know by now what was stopping me. My own dragging feet or his? I didn't know when I'd be back. I hadn't wanted to talk about leaving, Liam didn't like the topic, either. So we avoided it, agreeing to use our time more constructively.

"These folks are from a Spanish group," Barb said, sensing my preoccupation and changing the subject to: "Know any Spanish?"

"No. But I think that's actually 'no' in Spanish. '*Sí*' and '*No*,' I remember that much from high school."

"There's an interpreter with the group, but he's at Quinn's—for a little too long, now that I look at my watch . . ."

"*Con permiso . . .*" A woman was asking Christina to move. Or something like that.

"*Sí,*" said Barb carefully, allowing the ERINTOURist space to examine the dish of my bracelets. This was the kind of shopper I liked, taking her time, studying, appreciating. She picked up a bracelet titled Be Here Now, which suddenly made me sad. I was here now. I should take my own advice. When she placed it back in the dish, I reached for it, clipped the tag, and added it to the three I already was wearing daily: the original glass and blue scarab, an all other that was green but each bead a different shade, and one of black and white beads with impressions of little white spirals. If I kept this up, I would become my own best customer, eventually unable to bend my arm. Christina launched into an update on the tour business, how it remained anemic, and then leaned in to tell about one of the cultural consultants for ERINTOURS' competitor, a line of coaches called Fáilte, a word that means welcome but always struck me as looking like something gone wrong. Christina said she'd caught this consultant giving her the once-over from the window of his coach when they'd parked alongside it at Bog World. "What should I do?" She was asking me this. Should she flirt?

"Aren't you a cultural consultant?"

"I run tours. Not a dating service. What should I do? What did you do?"

"Pardon." The woman again. To me, this time: "Feenola Ofleen?"

"*Sí*," assured Christina, and she pointed at me. Echoed Feenola Ofleen.

"*Bueno!*" And the woman handed me Destiny, Truth, Health, Wealth, and Happiness to put in a bag, and a big blue-green 100-euro bill to put in my till.

The day went like that. The bracelets went like that. Lots of other merchandise, too. A Christmas shopping air all brewed up by nothing other than a bunch of people deciding to bring their livestock to town and people to look at them like they'd never in their lives seen a horse. Many of those buying and selling were Travelers, who also offered avalanches of garish discount store-grade home décor in their stalls along the roadside and who stood ready to fulfill your dream of owning an acrylic throw printed with the Sacred Heart of Jesus. Some of the many visitors milling around would spot Patience or Serenity or Acceptance on a wrist and would ask the source and would be directed to me. Shoppers edged between swaying horse behinds and jumped out of the way of test-driven carts and guy yelling "Mind your back!" as he trotted past on a skewbald. Booley being the size it is, those who were looking for the shop, and for me, easily found both.

"Finola O'Flynn?"

Another nod. Another conversation begun. Eventually, another sale.

"Sophie?"

"Huh?"

Liam was awake and in the shop. Functioning somewhat. Shower damp and tangeriny and wearing hiking shorts and a T-shirt that had benefitted last December's International Animal Right Day, sliding into the next chair and leaning against me and closing his eyes again, and I just wanted to climb under the lids and make one of us confront the reality of the late hour.

"Tough life for the rock star."

"Tough life, full stop." Liam said it "liiiffe." He'd turned his face into my hair so I couldn't see the expression, but the voice was flat.

"Tea?" He said it "tay." So that was my response.

"Tay."

"I'll fix it, you can sit here and mind the millions. Another few days like this and you can close this dump and retire to Mal-ta."

"I'll be retirin' somewhere farther west."

I didn't have a map handy—at least, not one that showed much of what was beyond Greater Booley. What lay between Malta and America? Anything other than water? I wanted to slam the door and do the talking we should have done long before there was only a day left to be face-to-face. I needed some idea whether I should be leaving this country with any plans for a return. I did move toward the door, but got pushed back by half a dozen pixie-sized women wearing green sweatshirts that read O'MAHONEY FAMILY REUNION 2002.

"Finola O'Flynn?"

It was long past time to collect Joe for the day as I'd promised, so after tea I left Liam with the crowd of shoppers and the Golf, which Liam had left parked on the far side of the marquee walked out to. Joe was old friends with Jimmy Donnelly, and the Horse Fair was the social highlight of Joe's summer. He was standing at his gate when I pulled up. Little tweed cap and coat and tie and little pink face, a model for one of the head-sized Man of Ireland tankards the Quinns kept behind the counter.

"I said she forgot."

"Sorry."

"I said she's gone home without tellin' me."

"I wouldn't leave without a good-bye."

"I said she's tired of an aul' man . . ."

Joe could be silent as a post or he could go on like this. Today, he went on. I squeezed in: "The shop's been busy."

"I said she'll be here too late and I'll miss Jimmy altogether."

"Right." There was a hedgehog curled dead at the edge of the road and I tried to avoid squishing it as I executed the twelve-point turn the skinny little road required.

"I said maybe she's taken Liam to Americah."

It was move seven of the turn when he said that, and I stopped. Joe had never put the two of us together in the same sentence. I'd always seen that as allegiance to Finola. He liked me OK, but I wasn't the one who'd saved his life. So I took this as a victory. Eleventh hour, maybe, but a victory.

"You think I should take Liam to America?"

"I do now."

"Why?"

He set his hands on his knees. Concentrated on them as he said, "There's been little happiness for him here since she left. Then Sophie White, and tings improved considerably. Withoutcha, he'll be back in a state."

I tried to imagine Liam in a state. A funk, maybe, I could see. State was different. Much more serious. He should never be in a state.

"Yes," Joe decided. "You must take him to Americah."

I completed the turn. In a few minutes, Booley came into view, a theme park crawling with life.

"You ever run off with anybody?" That was as personal a question as I'd ever asked Joe. But I had only so much time left with him. Plus, he'd started it.

"Bold," he puffed, then was silent, pulling at the skin on his neck and looking toward a hand-lettered sign for some attraction called The Tunnel of Goats. I hoped I hadn't offended him. "Now would I be here if I'd run off?"

"Maybe you ran off and came back."

"I never ran off with anyone. But if she'd asked, I would've."

"She who?"

"'Tis Blackie!" Joe called, pointing excitedly—as excitedly as he gets, that is—past the goat sign and to a telephone-pole-shaped old guy loping toward town. "Will ya ever stop and give 'em a lift?"

I pulled over. In greeting, Blackie Linnane banged on the car with his stick. Let himself into the backseat.

"Tanks, boss." He meant me. Blackie called everybody boss. To Joe, he launched into Irish. Leaned through the front seats and kept smacking him on the shoulder to make a point. Blackie wore a porkpie hat and smelled of drink and laughed eh-eh-eh-eh-eh like an automatic weapon. I imagined him as the ringleader in a band of wild old guys ready to wreak havoc in town for the day. I wanted to tell Joe to behave—more, I wanted to tell him to tell me about the "she." But despite their respective infirmities, the two were out of the car and into the crowd before could even remove the keys from the ignition.

Liam and I had the afternoon together, but the together part consisted only of being in the same room while dealing with the largest bunch of shoppers ever experienced at Finola O'Flynn. There was hardly space to move, and if you were of a mind to nick something, this would have been the day. You could have walked out waving four sets of Max's fireplace tongs and shovels and no one would have been the wiser. As I'd been told to expect, the crowd was lots of locals, and regionals, with a few groups of tourists sticking out.

After the departure of a gaggle of two dozen summer campers, each
of whom had been allowed by their counselor to buy one square of
the individually wrapped milk chocolates Ger's sister got a loan
from the government to start making on the condition she print the
words "Irish Chocolate" somewhere on the foil, and after checking
that the store was empty, I carried out my plan with the front door,
slamming it tight and pulling into place the old bolt that was rarely
used, and creating the opportunity to say what I wanted to say.
Which was something I felt Finola would have said. Which, for
starters, is, "Come here."

Liam said, "What?" and turned down the boom box.

"Come over here. Away from the window."

He did as he'd been asked, and stood in the hall, very near the
threshold where he'd been the day I walked into town.

"I'm leaving."

"I know that."

"Is there anything you have to say about that?"

He shrugged.

"You don't have anything to say about it?"

"If I don't say anythin, it won't be real." He gave a smile. Pushed
his face into my neck. I was supposed to think the theory was sweet.

"How old are you?"

He breathed a laugh onto my collarbone. "Old enough t' know.
But around you I'm more the age of Ralpho. A cut with but a single
thing on his mind . . ."

There was a knock at the door behind me. The sharpness of it
shot through my shoulder blades. Somebody on the other side was
asking "Hallo?" I leaned against the door in case the bolt didn't
hold. I said, "Whether the age of Ralpho, or old enough, you've got
me here today. I won't be here in twenty-four hours. What I need to
know is what' not been said. What's going to happen to what we've
had here?" I wanted to say "to us," but that soundy very movie-of-
the-weekish. I already was uncomfortably aware I was doing a tra-

ditionally female thing, and half of me was balking, but a lot of the reason that women are the ones who bring up such topics is that men would rather chew glass. Pressing for some type of commitment, even if it was only that he'd meet me at the airport when I got the time and the fare, that fell to me. As it fell to the woman inside me who was urging me.

Another trio of knocks. "Y' open? Hallo?"

Neither of us answered that person. Liam didn't answer me. I reached to unbolt the door. This was going nowhere, and I was to be going somewhere far away very soon. I said, "I didn't come to this town looking for you. You weren't sitting here waiting for me. But something happened anyway. To me, at least, it seems that we deserve to talk about—to know where to go from here."

Liam said nothing. But then quickly caught my hand, kept the bolt back into place and began to speak. As he did, some kid of the type who apparently hates being denied access to local crafts began kicking the door repeatedly and very hard so Liam was forced to yell: "Sophie White, would you ever come back t'Booley. T'stay?"

Guess all you have to do is ask. That's all I had to do, it seemed. Ask and ye shall receive. Maybe ye shall have received more of an answer than ye would have predicted. I'd thought we were going to continue down the same squirrelly path of not being ready to discuss because of not being ready to commit to even being pen pals, all due to very recently or sort of recently being screwed by Cupid. But I had hit the Lotto. Liam Keegan wanted me to come back, to stay. "Yes I will," was my fast reply, and he pulled me to him with even greater speed, with the kind of "C'mere to me" that doesn't mean talk, and we didn't talk for maybe a couple of minutes, leaning in the corner of the hall of the home in which I would stay upon my return, kissing away any doubt and any questions and everything but the noise, so I finally unbolted the door, and the kid who'd been kicking, a four- or five-year-old in a football jersey

sponsored by Vodafone, fell forward, and there was a scene of his
screaming and his mam swatting him while around them stepped a
stream shoppers giving out about the limited number of browsing
opportunities in Booley if you weren't in the market for a horse.
The remainder of the day, my contact with Liam consisted of
brushing against him as I went to retrieve more of Sister Tobia's
very popular candlesticks from the back room, more bracelets from
below the CD table, more Jimmy CDs onto the stack we kept near
the till because nearly every other person wanted a copy. But I kept
constant touch with Liam in my head, where I replayed his request
at an even higher volume than it had been delivered. He wanted
me to come back. To stay.

Me.

Sophie White.

"Finola O'Flynn?"

"Yep."

Liam was gone again—the Chancers were to be support for
Jimmy's act, and it was last of the afternoon. Time for a sound
check. I was alone but couldn't have been happier: At some point
not too long from now, this would be my new home.

The shoppers fawned over Finola. What a place! They'd never
known it was here—well, they never knew Booley was here. Just
found it. Or were told only this morning by the owner of their inn
on the other side of the hill. Or had claimed the last bed at the hostel yesterday and the manager had mentioned the fair—though he
cautioned the lodgers there to stay away, that the fair was a culchie
sort of low-class thing not worth wasting your time at. They hadn't
listened, were glad they hadn't, what an attitude—what's with that
guy, anyway? Do you know?

"Dunno." That was true. I couldn't even guess what fueled
Diamond's lousy view of the world. I'd always tried to be nice—over
the summer certainly had put enough euros into the slot of his

IRENET machine as I sent those few long emails to Gina. He had to be getting a cut of that, you'd think he'd be happy to see me and my coins jingling up his steps. But he was always sour. "Dunno," I repeated, and was glad I didn't because I didn't want to think about him on a day like this.

"Finola O'Flynn."

"Says her name right there, can't you read?"

Yanks on both sides of that conversation. Both of them arguing, and they weren't even inside yet. Lots of tourists argue, I should add. Not just Yanks. The whole thing of a vacation is abnormal. Take a break from the everyday life and schedule, throw a few belongings into a bag, and get jet-propelled halfway across the state or country or planet to spend a week or ten days doing nothing but roaming around. What's nice in theory is often a bust in reality, and over the summer I'd seen roaring arguments in more languages than Berlitz has courses. Half the time, the altercations work out in the shop's favor, as the offending party usually eventually springs for something to appease the offended. The other half of the time, the parties stalk off, never to be seen again. Maybe by Noel, but not by me, in or outside of which shop the scene occurred.

The next man and women weren't fighting, they were mooning over one another, and reminded me of the early the Ferriter-Garveys, the Garvey half of which would have approved of the Ferriter half purchasing the whole store.

"Are you Finola O'Flynn?"

"Yep."

"Brilliant. The sister"—(he motions to the woman, it must be her sister that's meant, unless he means this woman here is a nun, in which case this will become all the more interesting because as they walked in he had his hand up the back of her blouse and she was enjoying it immensely)—"passed through Booley on her holiday, said we must see yis if we're here, so we're here!" They were there, as was their VISA, a new one with the mug shot that is an effort to fight card misuse. They used the card to buy six Jimmy Donnelly CDs that they were going to have autographed for relatives.

"You Finola O'Flynn?"

"Yep."

"Are you looking for help?"

Lots of kids from the hostel came looking for work. Options were few.

"Don't need help right now," I told her, and I threw in a "love," because she looked disappointed.

The girl turned and in her exit had to walk around the edge of a little knot of people who'd assembled, at the bead table, and the bracelet dish. Security and Promise and Future tumbling as I heard: "Finola?"

"Yep."

"So there actually is a Finola. It's not a chain?"

"Nope."

Another voice.

"You're Finola?"

"Yep."

Another voice.

"Finola O'Flynn?"

"Yep."

"You're Finola O'Flynn?"

I nodded.

Looked up at a woman who said to me, "So am I."

Bear:

Fierce Protection

(State Your Wish Three Times)

Dd dearsr gGIna:
gRIana:
G

The machine stuck there. At the *G*.

I punched it.

Nothing happened except that I hurt my hand. The *G* floated there, black on gray. I'd never really studied the letter before. But now that I had no energy to do anything but stare, I saw the capital *G* as something you could crawl into. Climb up over the serif and roll down into that little cavern. The *G* could be a place to hide, which is all I felt like doing since meeting Finola.

So, very early on my final morning in Booley, I hid in the little booth beneath the stairs of Diamond's Hostel and tried to connect with Gina. After the machine froze, I was struck by the silliness of what I was doing. First, I would be home in a matter of hours, and if she were interested in seeing me I could tell all then. Second, how do you begin to tell someone that a relationship you never informed them was on in the first place was now off? Or at least in hold for the unforeseeable future? I'd have to find the answer to that, because what I wanted to do was tell Gina what had happened. Because I missed her and because I needed to tell her. To tell somebody. Somebody who wasn't connected to Booley. And I didn't want to stand in the phone box outside Emilio's and use a couple hundred euros' worth of cards. Banging every detail into a keyboard would be far more therapeutic, not to mention private. So I chose IRENET as my way to tell Gina that Finola O'Flynn had come back.

There was a mountain more to say, of course. But that would be the start: Finola was back in Booley, nearly three years after leaving everyone and everything. Materializing in her old shop just as The Chancers were playing the first few plunky notes to make sure their instruments were plugged in and in tune, just as Dermot was hyping the fact that Jimmy would be on stage very very shortly. Over at my bead table, Finola had made her own announcement, and I had answered, "You are, eh?" Over the summer, I'd met Finolas and I'd met O'Flynns. I supposed it only made sense that a combination of the two would come along eventually, but I didn't believe it because half the people who visited the shop on Horse Fair day were plastered and saying all sorts of things to which I didn't respond very enthusiastically.

"I am, yeah," she said.

"Oh." I snipped a piece of cord. For some reason, couldn't get the scissors off my fingers—they stuck and I had to shake them off and they clattered onto the table, knocking into the dish of charms in the shape of a leg in running position.

The person asked, "And who would you be?"

Something told me to say nothing more than "I work here."

"I used to work here."

Something else told me not to look up. "Really?"

"I used to live here."

Something else told me to make like the leg charm. "Really."

"This shop once was mine. This building once was mine. That cottage up above once was mine. That man Liam out there once was mine."

Finola O'Flynn herself told me all this. Finola O'Flynn. Not giving me this info in any particular manner, more like she was reading a list. And that's when I dared my first good look at her.

You're waiting for this, of course. I would be. And I could gather ten thesauri full of goddesslike adjectives to describe her aura, her scent, her voice, her presence, her physique, her clothing, her coloring, her face. The expression of her eyes, their those eyes, their shape, their focus, what sparkle or gleam or other positive eye action is usually noted when you look at somebody. But I wouldn't need any huge selection of words. Because she was like water. You could nearly see what was behind her without her making a move out of the way. She was the air in a windowless room. Carried the energy of a lawn whirligig on the stillest of days. She wore—Well, it was hard to tell, or describe, or determine—was it off-white or beige or light gray? Was it a long skirt or very baggy trousers? Was that a coat or a shirt? What was that? Something was covering her skin that was—I don't know—she wasn't black and she wasn't white, she wasn't yellow or tan or that purply blue some people can be when their skin is all translucent. What color was she? Nothing was registering that I can put the exact words to. She stood out for being the only other human in the shop, and when a man and a boy stuck their heads in, and determining this was not the kind of shop that might interest such a man and a boy, disappeared, for that few seconds Finola was invisible. Not like a chameleon, with the ability to turn into the bookcase or the display of soap balls, she just was able to disappear as do some people who have really no palpable presence.

So this couldn't be Finola O'Flynn. I don't know when I thought we'd cross paths, but I always felt that if I ever met her, the experience would shoot me into nearly irretrievable depths of self-consciousness. Oh, the beauty, the style, the figure, the posture, the kindness, the way she reaches out to people and connects with them like there's some plug she knows about that the rest of us aren't privy to. She just gets right there with people—you know what I mean. When she's talking to you or listening to you it's like you're the only person on the planet, and the things she has to say, worlds of wisdom in maybe a three-word sentence, did you ever see the likes of her? Plus that whole thing about the rapturous love affair with Liam, let's not even start into how I paled in that department. I thought all these shortcomings would be what I'd feel and witness, and that all my insecurities would feel and witness it, too, and that they would form a line at my brain to begin reminding me that even with the spark of Finola powering me to new levels, I'd never been that good, nice, attractive, honest, sincere, generous, whatever, you name it—anything she was, I was not. Never would be, don't even try, give up before you even start. That's what I'd thought. And now, here, with her in front of me, none of that was true. I was getting no reading on her at all.

It was a reflex. But do something quite regularly for a couple of months and then see if it's not the first thing you jump to. I jumped to wondering what would Finola do in this moment. But knew I didn't have to. If I wanted to know that, all I had to do was look right across the table.

"You're Sophie."

She knew that. How'd she know that?

"Yep."

"Sophie White. From America."

"Right."

"Here in Booley for the summer."

"Right."

"Working here."

"Right."

"Made use of my cottage."

"Right. But it belongs to . . ."

"Making use of my name."

"Well, sometimes, but it's just for . . ."

"Making use of my clothing."

I'd forgotten that part. I glanced down at the pink dress, the pink that was as far as you could get on the spectrum from the whatever glue-colored thing she wore.

Her tone wasn't accusatory—I wasn't sure what it was. The Finola I was used to consulting would have asked what did she want. So I did. A firm "What do you want?" And to this Finola answered, "Liam."

I knew it.

She said "I want Liam."

Two chatty mothers entered the shop, a tiny little baby hanging from each of their necks in little fabric carriers, live snoozing pendants that couldn't have been more than a month old. Next, a man carrying a shiny new saddle that had the stirrups looped up and out of the way like they are when a jockey stands with one to be weighed. Then came two hikers who knew enough to remove their packs in the hallway before they knocked something expensive to the floor. The room was filling again. Finola remained in front of me. She put a hand on the table, very near the dish of bracelets.

"Liam is out there," I said, and I pointed in the direction of the marquee. "With the band." I wasn't so much handing him over as I was trying to make her go away. Far away.

"When is Jimmy to play?" The man with the saddle wanted to know this. I pointed to a stack of schedules near the till. He took one and asked me to put on one of the Jimmy CDs as he was not fond of rock and roll, he said, and even though The Chancers weren't really going near that kind of music, it nevertheless came across to him as such, and he wanted only Jimmy. I wanted only to bolt. But the man was in my way. And Finola was in my way. He took a schedule and left the shop. She remained.

The hikers were at my table now. Each was holding a Buaille T-shirt, but the shorter one was complaining in a dense Scottish accent that required concentration to follow how his size of shirt was missing the explanatory tag that was attached to his friend's size. I got up to hunt beneath the T-shirt stash don't ask me where she went that I was suddenly able to get from behind the table— maybe I walked right through her. I ended up unpinning a tag from one of the other shirts, and when I turned Finola was in the process of making a sale. A note card with a picture of a section of the stands at a football match and rows and rows of fans clutching their heads and yelling and waving and gesturing in all sorts of unman- nerly manners, and also an amber and turquoise bracelet with a dangling silver hand that had inspired me to title it "You Create Your Own Reality," a slogan I had swiped from a bookmark I once was given by a friend who attended a metaphysical church and who had wanted me to do the same. Both the joining and the reality cre- ating. Finola had found the tissue to wrap the bracelet, she'd found the bag, her fingers flew across the buttons of the credit card machine, and knew just where to locate a Biro for the signature of the customer whom she encouraged to also sign the guest book and to take a fair schedule before she gave him thanks a million.

"Now," she concluded, folding her hands in front of herself like a perfect schoolchild and looking happily at me from behind the table, which, in the time it took me to cross the little room once again appeared to have become hers. "Isn't this fun?"

I didn't believe the slogan of the bracelet Finola had just sold, but it went with most of the semi-12-step- feel-good-it's-not-over- yet-themed others I was selling, so I'd used it on a tag. But if those words indeed were true, then what had I done to create Finola's appearance on the same couple of square feet of concrete floor on which Jane St. Jean had stood eleven weeks before? And how come, after two and a half years, she'd chosen a return time that was within hours of Liam inviting me to come back to Booley indefinitely?

"What would you like me to do now?" Finola asked. "I'd tidy, which I normally did here twenty-four hours, but it seems someone's taken care of that, on a major level. Couldn'ta been Liam. Would that be what you do here?"

"If you'll excuse me, I should get back to work." I moved toward the table.

"What work? There's no one about just now. And I can manage any hordes. I do have the experience, ya know." She gave a little laugh here. "Go out, have yourself a look around. How many horse fairs does a Yank get to?" This was all said kindly, in a friendly Chamber of Commerce/Booleyan ambassadress tone. My new big pal, Finola.

"I'll stay here, thanks." And I did. Standing at the side of the hearth, with the little boom box table and the till and the Jimmy CD display the only things between her and me. I focused again. And this was what I think I saw: (I say think because I really couldn't be sure—she was that unclear to me.) I saw the person you never really looked at, and if you did get a glimpse you would have no reason to ever remember even in a court-ordered session with a professional hypnotist. Not one thread of her would remain, if you were only going by visuals. Finola's appearance was that of the kid always in the back row of the classroom, of the bus, of all the lines in life. Picked last for the team, last for the job, never for the wedding party, and asked home only at the end of the night because there was no other female left in the pub. She radiated anonymity—if such a thing is possible. Plain as rain, and as all your other see-through forms of precipitation, her face was dinner plate round, its color and texture the bland shell of an untoasted Pop-Tart. Hair that appeared the rough texture of a discount store stuffed animal grew in dull and uneven tufts, some of them reaching her shoulders, others maybe an inch in length. Her eyes were flat dark beans, her nose was a fetal bud of a thing, barely there, protruding only enough to allow her to breathe. The mouth was an afterthought, a couple inches allowed for ventilation, eating, speaking, kissing a German, and, at one time in her life, Liam. In the way these things appear without your consciously calling them up, my mind flashed me a vivid Technicolor trailer of her doing that to him and him doing that to her. She broke it up without even knowing she was doing so, said, "You're staring."

"Sorry." I turned to look at someone else, but there was no one else in the shop. I noticed some empty pegs in the earing display and I went to fill them. I placed three of the same color and style in a row, something I'd normally never do, as I told Finola, "I just never expected to meet you."

"You hoped you wouldn't meet me is more the case."

"I guess—nothing personal." Though it was. And she of course knew that, and she said, "Nonsense. It's all personal."

"Not really, because I don't know you at all. I've heard maybe a thousand stories about you, but we've never met, so it's not personal at all. Curiosity, just."

Finola repeated the word *stories* as two men and two women entered and one of the women asked, "Are you Finola?" and the question was answered by two people.

I was asked to adjust the length of a necklace. That's how I ended up seated behind the bead table, next to her, the two of us unlikely peas in a suddenly uncomfortable pod. The customer who was interested in the necklace complained that it fell too low and brought attention to her bosom, which she pointed out might be a positive thing to some but did not make her comfortable at all even though she had nothing of the size on which your everyday bosomstarer normally would fixate. I said I could shorten it, no problem, and brought it to the table, and that's when Finola finally stood up and allowed me behind so I could get to the tools, and that's also when she sat down again, effectively locking me into the corner.

It was the same place I so often ended up in with Liam, but that was never uncomfortable. We might bump elbows, on some days we might bump opinions, but I always loved being snug in the closeness of the little space between him and the window and its wide sill on which, in an act of shameless self-promotion, I displayed a few dozen of my bracelets. Now I felt trapped, stuck, and The Chancers were on maybe only their third number. Liam wouldn't be back for an hour. At the least.

Finola smelled of—well, she smelled of nothing, really. Not of skin or shampoo or cologne or fabric softener, there was nothing I could pick up on. She sat with no exact textbook posture. Her hands, utilitarian is all you could call them, reached for the reels of cord, and she clipped a length she didn't need to measure, then began stringing: blue, green, greenish silver . . . She really had no business touching anything here, but there I was, watching her take right over.

"Can I ask what you're doing?"

"Old habits, ya know. Ah, this is a gorgeous shape . . ."

"Not with the beads, with being here. Is there something I can do for you?"

"No, thanks."

"I don't mean to be rude, but maybe this isn't the best place for you to be."

"And why wouldn't it be?"

"You don't feel awkward in this shop—in this building?"

"Why should I? It once was mine. As I said."

"But you've been gone."

"Yes?"

"I mean—the way you left . . ."

"Just what do you know about that?" She'd been looking at her work up to this point. Now she turned to me, the little beans focus-

ing hard, and I felt enough of a fear that I was grateful for the presence of three CD-browsing priests, in front of whom Finola surely
wouldn't commit assault.

"Just disappearing from here. You know . . ."

"Fathers," she called out, "can I be of assistance?"

"Have you any Jimmy Donnelly?"

"Certainly. Here, the entire collection." The men swarmed and
the jewel boxes clattered.

"Let me ask you this, Sophie White." Finola was knotting the
cord in a manner that I noticed was no more graceful or swift or
neat than how I do it. "Did you ever feel you needed to remove
yourself from a situation?"

I was sitting in one of those situations right then. "Sure."

"And not just this one, now."

I thought. And I was sure again. My mother dying without giving me any notice—that had hit me in a way that made me want to
pull everything I owned from the house into the yard and set it
afire, to destroy all I had and go start anew somewhere unrelated to
any of the pain. I hadn't felt that way again until Gina left and I felt
myself spinning. But I would have run just to follow her, to see what
I'd done wrong and try to make it right. But that was nothing compared to the how badly I had wanted to disappear after I met Jane
St. Jean.

"Sure," I repeated. "I've felt that way. I never did run, but I've
thought about it. I'd imagine everyone has at some point."

"And would you have sent hand-engraved explanations to anyone you'd be leaving behind? Or would you simply go?"

With the emotion of the hour, I'd probably just take off. Who's
to say until they're in that particular set of screwed-up shoes? I
nodded.

"But what seemed like it was so bad for you here? Liam wonders
that. Una wonders that, Noel—have you seen those two yet?"

"I will now. And as for what seemed so bad, it was more like what seemed so good: a man. No reason more complicated than the attraction to one person and the immediate feeling that he was my destiny. I ran after him. Not after him, actually. Alongside. Which is where I've been these years. Alongside him. As impetuously as that began, it was solid, true. It could have been the mistake of my life. Has been anything but."

That certainly sounded more positive. If it weren't a mistake, it had to be good—something she wouldn't dream of leaving. "So you're just back for a vacation? A holiday? Is this man along with you?"

The priests had made their selections. Asked would Finola ever pierce the cellophane so Jimmy could easily open the cases and sign the discs. Paid with a Barclaycard that got rejected the first time she ran it through the machine, but was accepted when she keyed the numbers in by hand, something I always managed to goof up.

I repeated, "So you're back for a vacation, a holiday?"

She gently stabbed the credit card receipt with the spindle and turned to me again. "I wouldn't call it that."

I prompted: "Business, maybe?"

"Not atall."

The Finola I'd been consulting for the past couple of months would have come out with the next question, so I did: "What made you want to come back?"

"I think you know."

"I don't know, that's why I'm asking."

That's when she said, "It's because of you that I'm here."

"You wore my clothing," she started.

"I don't know what to say to you." I said that because it was all I could think to say. "Except I'm sorry I wore your clothes—I'm sorry that I'm wearing your clothes right now. As I understood it, you left them behind because you no longer wanted them. I was staying in your house at Liam's invitation, and as I understood it, the cottage is his. You have so many great things in that closet. . . . And, as for the name, lots of customers came in the door and saw me there and instantly thought I was you. After a while I just played with that. I meant no harm. With any of it."

"You meant no harm." She said the word like the *r* on the keyboard was stuck.

"No."

"You wore, what of mine?"

Jeez, I'd used a ton of her things over the summer. It was like smarter, cooler sister's wardrobe suddenly had become available, without any consequences because she was never going to be around to catch me and make me take any of it off in public. That's what I'd thought, at least.

"Um, I, there was, oh, that brown knit skirt with the matching weird sweater—I mean weird in a good way. And that turquoise silk shirt, with a wonderful feel to it. The big cable sweater, you know, it's enormous. The T-shirt with the kangaroo. The military boots. The Chuck Taylors. Where'd you get Chuck Taylors?"

"What else?"

The linen nightic thing popped to mind, and I hoped she couldn't read thought bubbles as it floated over my head and then floated to the bedroom floor. I substituted "A hat? That black one. The very wrinkly rainbow-color broomstick skirt—do you call them broomstick skirts here?"

"And?"

"What's the big deal? You didn't want them. Should be the case with anything you didn't take with you."

"You don't want me here."

"I didn't say that."

"Be honest."

"OK, no. I don't want you here."

"Then why did you leave that there."

"That what?"

"My scarf. The one left at the holy well of St. Faicneam?"

I flashed to the memory of the only thing I'd ever left up there. And that had been on the rainy night of the miserable day of Jane St. Jean and her daughters. I'd walked to the Last Restaurant, Aoife had consoled me, I'd taken the long way home, along the cliffs to the well of St. Faicneam, who is a great one for the lost. For those seeking to regain the invisible. Health. Love. Hope. All that sort of thing. If you ever had any of that, and you've lost it, Faicneam's yer man. And at his holy well I'd unzipped my jacket and untied the black silk scarf of Finola O'Flynn and, even though I didn't believe any of it, I'd touched the scarf to my mixed-up head, and then to my newly trashed heart, and then tied it on the branch of the bush that was now supposed to take on my pain. The scarf was still up there, where I'd left it. I'd seen it waving in a faded gray black last time I'd visited, maybe a week ago, when I'd thought about how greatly my life had improved since that night. Leaving the scarf had been an impulse separate from my skepticism, a what-the-hell gesture. Now I was being asked to believe it had summoned this woman back to a place she hadn't intended to see again. "Come on, you don't think . . ."

"I most certainly do." Finola did not look pleased. "He's a powerful one, that Faicneam."

She told me of her special devotion to St. Faicneam. Since Joe showed her the well, Finola had found great solace up there, had asked Faicneam for all sorts of help and guidance, credited him with helping her find a way when she was lost in the haze of buying property and starting a shop—something she knew nothing about and during the growth and success of her business.

"I didn't want you," I told her. "I wasn't thinking about you at all when I left that there. I'd had a terrible day, I was feeling lost myself. I wanted help for myself. I didn't think about it being your scarf. I don't even believe in this stuff. But it was a very bad day. I guess I was desperate."

"Faicneam is the man for the desperate all right," said Finola. "But next time you're desperate, leave your own feckin' scarf."

"So let me get this straight—somebody told you I tied your scarf there and you came all this way to yell at me for that?"

"Nobody had to tell me. I knew."

"You knew."

"You did this in May, correct?"

How'd she know that?

"First week, right?"

I didn't answer.

"First week in May. I'm far from here. Minding my own life. Not a thought of returning. Ever. Something starts pulling at me. Physically, mentally. Booley starts appearing in my thoughts, and I'd long ago put this place away. I went to see my GP, that's how odd I was feeling. There was nothing wrong with me physically. But I was drawn to thinking about Booley, to looking at maps, to thinking about people. Thinking about a person."

An older woman in too-tight silver leggings and a chintzy gold blouse entered the shop tilting a cup of beer right past the sign reading NO FOOD NO DRINK PLEASE. I didn't care.

"It became clear that I had to return," Finola was telling me. "I didn't know the reason, I simply had to return. Today, this is the first time I haven't felt that pull since May. I hiked up to the well this afternoon, went there right off. The scarf was waving at me, the scarf that is mine, and I am one hundred percent certain because I mended it once. There was a small tear a quarter of the way up, it's stitched now. Examine it—it's my scarf. You left it there. You were asking for my return."

"You're not serious."

"It's because of you, Sophie White, that I'm back here."

"Fine, whatever. Now that you know that, you can turn around."

"Not before I claim what's still mine."

Outside, chants of "JIMMY! JIMMY! JIMMY! JIMMY!"

began to swell. And without waiting for them to die down, because they never might, Jimmy Donnelly launched into his famous hit. Since June I'd heard the song on CD countless times. As well as any Booleyan schoolchild, I knew the history, the melody, the lyrics, the two lines that showcased Jimmy's skill at finding a word to rhyme with the town's name—"And when you go to Booley/You're sure to find a hooley." It wasn't high art, but the song had a definite audience. As did Jimmy on this night, up there in the spotlight, singing about a town on its one big weekend of the year:

> *Horses horses stallions mares*
> *People people everywhere*
> *From Ireland and over there*
> *Minerals chips a pint or two*
> *I'll strike a deal on a foal for you.*

While Jimmy thrilled the crowd, Finola filled me in about Udo Brix, the German newspaper press foreman alongside whom she had left Booley more than two and a half years ago. So open and giving and wonderful was Udo Brix that when Finola several weeks back revealed the undeniable pull Booley was having on her, he suggested she return as soon as she could—and that she also investigate the very real possibility of lingering feelings for Liam Keegan. "That is the kind of man Udo is," Finola said, and the woman with the paper cup of beer murmured, "He's only lovvvely," but was referring to Jimmy Donnelly rather than Udo Brix, which was clear because she was admiring the display of Jimmy CDs. Finola accepted the euros of a college-age girl buying a Greater Booley map for her gang at the doorway, and said, "I did leave in haste, but Faicneam—and you—have provided me the overdue opportunity to tie up loose ends." And the woman at the CDs told us, "Ya wouldn't know from lookin' at 'im, but he's a great lover." "Horses, horses," Jimmy continued, and now the woman was raking her Lee

Press-On Nails claws through the dish of bracelets and continuing, "Very generous. A very generous and giving man. You never feel yer but an object." "Have a chip, ah go on,/we'll stay here 'til comes the dawn," Jimmy promised. "What loose ends?" I asked. "Has a Jack-uzzi," the woman added. "Yeah! He does! Enjoys that t' start. Relaxin', ya know. Ever been in a Jack-uzzi?" I've been many places, but never was seated next to somebody who believed so strongly in the power of a fashion accessory hung on a half-dead tree. "He's a sexy fuck, he is," the woman shared. "Loves it when you speak directly to his lad."

"There's every chance I won't return to Germany," Finola was saying to me. "That I'm not done yet with Liam." And Liam, with whom she might not yet be done, chose that very moment to come through the door and say "I'm all yours now."

Pointing Finger:

Reality

(State Your Wish Three Times)

He had the arms out, ready to embrace. But they weren't wide enough to accommodate two women. Plus the bead table was between the two of us and the one of him, plus he was talking only to me anyhow. Only to me, the one and only woman he had expected to be greeting now that his set with The Chancers was over and he was free for the remainder of my last night in the country.

I'm not the head of a hammer. I'm not the front end of a car, I'm not the nose of a smart-bomb, or the little springy thing that on precomputerized pinball machines used to smash into the ball bearing and send it up the incline and onto its course. So this was the first time I saw the look that is worn as a huge hit is taken. Liam's smile deflated slowly, but faster than it took for the arms to return to his sides. The shoulders floated down to their normal level as he took a breath he didn't seem to remember to let out when he should. All the while, Jimmy was singing about corncrakes—little more than the words "Corncrakes! Corncrakes!" over the length of a generic deedly-deedly-ish tune that had been his unsuccessful follow-up to "Horses."

"What." He said that, neither a question nor the start of a comment, just a word. "What."

"Hallo, Liam." Finola now, getting to her feet and moving from behind the table, which allowed me to do the same, and she had the sense to stay at the table, while I got myself to the side of Liam, who put his left hand on the center of my back, but that was it. He was otherwise an ice sculpture.

"Liam, you're looking well." Finola decided this, though it suddenly wasn't true. I don't know what expression Liam would used to describe his appearance right then—peckish is one he uses sometimes when he's feeling not right, but that's usually related to being tired and hungry. Standing in the door to the shop. Liam simply looked freaked.

He said nothing in return. Finola continued: "I'm going to be in Booley for a time. I thought I'd come by and tell you myself."

"A time," Liam said.

"A time," Finola said. And then nobody said anything, so she complimented the shop. Said it looked brilliant. That she hoped it was doing well.

He nodded, zombielike.

"Sophie's been keeping me company," Finola said, and I wondered again how she had my name. "I wanted to wait and see you myself, to tell you that I'll be about. Now that I have, I'll settle in. I don't want to be as bold as to think I could use the cottage . . ." Here she waited, I assumed for Liam's protest that it would not be bold at all, but he made no such argument. So she told him, "My things are up the road. Just so's you'll know, I'll be staying at Diamond's."

We stood in our places, an awkward and obtuse triangle. Maybe it was five more hours, but it was probably more like only a minute, before Finola said, "OK, so," and Liam nodded again and I stepped out of the way, though I shouldn't have, because isn't that just what she was hoping I would do for her in the long run?

I closed the door behind her. Bolted it once again. The metal

screeched against its casing, unaccustomed to being asked to keep
anybody out—especially not twice in the same day.

"Where'd she come from?" Liam wanted to know. He had the
spooky yet placid face of the guy in shock on the high school health
class first-aid film strip, not registering what was happening or
when it had taken place or what ground he stood on—even if there
was indeed ground beneath him.

"Germany," I said, and I wasn't being sarcastic—that's all I
knew.

"Today. When, when did she come in here?" There was a stern-
ness I hadn't known his voice was able to pull off.

"A couple hours ago. Not long after you left for the marquee.
There were customers, and then there was Finola." It was strange to
say the name to him now.

"She was here for hours? Ah, Sophie, I'm sorry. I should have
stayed."

"As if you could have known she'd be coming in. "Goes without
saying I never got the chance to run up the street and see the band."

Jimmy was onto another creature now, the wild goat. "Wild
goat, wild goat, wild goat," and then he'd wait for the crowd to echo
it back to him, which it did, impressively loud. Many of those in the
road were stupid from the drink, so Jimmy had an enormous chorus
that rang through the shop as Liam leaned against the wall with the
coat hook and I backed up to the door again. This was not how I
had expected the night to go. I stepped forward and he hugged me
with generic-brand enthusiasm.

"D'ya want t' tell me what she was sayin'? A couple hours—a
long time to be with a stranger, and this one . . ."

"This one's very strange," I said, and I told him about the scarf,
the feeling Finola'd had, her decision to come back—at Udo Brix's
suggestion and encouragement.

"Yer jokin'."

I told him I wasn't, that she wasn't. "She's very serious. About

274 -w Suzanne Strempek Shea

you. Thinks there's loose ends, or frayed ends—some kind of textile reference. Finola says he wants her to find out if you, you two, if there's still anything there."

Liam made the expression of a vegetarian finding out the little amazingly meatlike things in the steamed vegetable dumplings are really, well, meat. "Anything there. Right. So she spent the hours handing you a load a' shite."

"Well, some of the time she did hand shite and all. Other times, she was making sales, assisting customers. Was very pleasant to everybody, I have to say. Just took over.

"She can do that."

"She did that. And I'm worried, Liam, what else she'll do."

"Now," he said with the comforting tone you'd really want at a moment like this, and he gave a hug—no, an embrace would be more on target. "Now."

We unlocked the door of the shop. Walked into the night. Sat on the wall and looked up the street to the golden spotlight cascading onto the little dried apricot of a man who had moved to another category of the animal kingdom: "Salmon, Salmon." Across from us, the big long sign that read FINOLA O'FLYNN seemed like a taunt. I lowered my head, and remembered again whose dress I was wearing.

"I gotta go take this off," I told Liam.

And for the first time since the first time, a line like that got from Liam nothing more than "I'll wait here for ye."

Wheel:

Go

(State Your Wish three times)

$\mathcal{S}$o I went upstairs and I took it off.

Alone.

I got dressed again, also alone, in my own clothing pulled from my fully packed backpack, multiple-fibered technological stretch separates that didn't recognize me after nearly three months of unuse. I pulled them over curves and hollows they'd not been asked to cover since before the start of the summer. I returned to the wall, where Una and Noel were standing before Liam, discussing something in the kind of confidential tone that saved me from having to ask what they were talking about.

I knew. And now they knew what I knew. No, they hadn't seen her. Yes, they were surprised as we. And that wasn't just talk. Their faces showed shock, concern. Each of them gave me emergency-room-level hugs. Long and tight and with concern you could feel even through Space Age material. "Sophie" is the extent of what they said to me. "Yeah" was the extent of my reply.

She'd chosen not to stop at Una's, at Noel's. Had she ducked into Quinn's, the Last Restaurant? Or had she gone straight up to the quiet end of the road and flipped open a tiny cellular to ring

Udo? Maybe she emailed him via IRENET, tapping her report of day one, in which she had made known her presence. "Thank you, Udo," she might have said in closing, though she would have done so in the German she had to have mastered by now, including all those tricky future-imperative tenses. "*Danke sehr,* Udo, for loving me enough to encourage my return here, despite some of the places that might take me." And Udo, who from what I'd been told is the kind of mythical perfect male, definitely would instant Message back, "*Nicht der Rede wert!*" or, if he were showing off his English, a simple "Don't mention it." And he'd mean it. This was the kind of guy Finola was risking the loss of. In any language, a very questionable move.

Despite the history Liam and I shared, our final night was nothing you'd ever find on pay per view. We would not even necessitate broadcast on HBO. Or the Discovery Channel. Forget even Animal Planet. Liam and I would have had the Sesame Street audience nodding off. Not what I'd envisioned for my last-time-for-a-while night with the man who in time might have inspired me to foolishly race ahead, mapping out a future that might include a stepchild who could get me funeral cards at wholesale. I would never admit even to the mirror that I might have one day dreamed that far, but that is the truth. With NASCAR-qualifying speed, I'd shaken off Charlie St. Jean like some ugly bug casing I had to wear for an allotted amount of time in order to be able to emerge as the appreciated, fascinating, lovely, and lusted-after winged creature buzzing around the world of Liam Keegan. A lot of those kind of bugs, I reminded myself, had their moment in the sun solely for mating purposes, then crawled back into the ground for something like twenty-four years. Below me, the ground was opening—my ninety allotted days were over.

How quickly I fell asleep I can't say, because there were so many starts and stops, both of sleep and of connecting with Liam. The messy little bed seemed to have been stolen, and in its place was a mattress with unfamiliar bumps, unexpected flat places, and no charming way of rolling us eventually into the same center valley. The sheets, though freshly changed this morning in ceremonial preparation, felt stiff and uninviting. I searched for a comfortable patch of bed on my right-hand side while I reached for Liam, who was spinning on a rotisserie twirled by the hand of his confusion.

"Hush," Liam Keegan repeated each time I whispered something about fearing what Finola might do, what might happen, and I'd ask how could I not worry or be concerned or take no notice, eight thirty tonight I will be in the air, and she will be on the ground, in Booley.

"She said she wanted you," I reminded him again.

"Too late fer that" was his answer again.

Two people in the same bed, alternately sleeping and staring at the ugly square umbrella of rose-crawling fabric and wire that served as a ceiling light fixture. No sound from the outside world until the bells from the new church up near the new cemetery rang to announce Sunday and 7:00 a.m. Mass, the start of Finola's first full day back in town, and my last.

"Fine mornin,'" Joe pointed out correctly when we got to his place for the promised walk to the cliffs. The Quinns had already brought Joe to and from early Mass, and Liam and I found him in the back garden in Sunday coat and tie, ready to go and feelin' not bad for an aul'man, not bad atall.

There were no messy emotions as we began. He was off, his stick helping him over the bumpy parts, up through the first, second, and final field that he told me, as this walk's bit of information, was always too stony and barren for tilling. At the end of that too-stony-and-barren field was the wall above the cliffs, and Joe took his place there. He sat the stick on the top of the final stone-studded earthen wall alive with tufts of grass and tiny daisyish

things. Folded his arms across his chest and leaned to gaze. I shuffled to the left, south, to my usual spot. Liam settled somewhere in
the middle and I was wishing he'd follow me, but it was probably
fitting that we all had our individual places, as private as separate
pews in this cathedral, where we could connect with our thoughts
and concerns and send up any prayers we felt necessary to send up.
My first was "Don't let her wreck anything." Nothing you'd find in
a traditional prayer book, but it was my main fear right then. Don't
let her wreck anything. Please. For my second prayer, in all honesty,
I was heading toward asking for Udo to have a change of heart and
order her back to Germany, even though I was sure Finola was not
the type of woman who would respond to an order. Maybe it was
the thought of Udo, good Udo, wise Udo, selfless Udo, uncondi-
tionally loving Udo, that made me want to be like him. And I suddenly experienced sort of a "What would Udo do?" moment. I realized what Udo would do, what he was doing this very moment—
allowing Finola to do what she felt necessary. Even if that meant
he'd be coming back to an empty apartment after his long day
standing at the whirring deafening newspaper press printing all the
news his publisher found fit to print. What a chance Udo was taking. Clearly, he loved Finola on that level we all shoot for but most
times fall continents short of: to want what's in your loved one's best
interest, even if it means you end up miserable. I turned to my right,
swinging my focus from a cliff on which a solitary curlew stood
being a bird to the stone wall where a solitary Liam stood being a
human, one who was looking at me the same moment I turned to
look at him, and then he was walking toward me, and he stopped an
arm's length away. Even though he'd told me that right then I was
the most important thing in his universe, it must be noted that none
of us knows the exact dimensions of the universe, so just maybe
there's some space in there for a few stray questions to exist. There,
an arm's length away, Liam said he didn't know how to say this so
he'd just say it: "That stuff Finola said about needing to tend to

unfinished business? I think—no, I know—I know I need to do that, too. I have no idea how things will work out with her in town. But I think I need to spend time with her. I might get some sense at last and find out who I am or something."

I just nodded.

"Understand, Sophie. She was the one true love a my life."

Pathetically and truthfully, I croaked a small "I wish I could have been that."

Liam didn't reply, did nothing, all his energy going into trying to hold back what I could see was a genuine painful expression.

None of this got emailed to Gina. It got told to her directly, in person, in the backseat of the embarrassingly large and shiny Lincoln Town Car she rented complete with uniformed chauffeur for meeting me at Logan, where she stood in Terminal E, at the door leading from customs, looking strong and startlingly fantastic, waiting to bring me home as she'd promised after I phoned her in flight from one of those little toy phones stuck to the back of the seat in front of you. Said she knew my three months were up. Hoped she'd hear from me. Hoped. Through the Sumner Tunnel and onto I-93 and out I-90, fast-lane-ing it effortlessly through all the many toll gates and then buildings fell away and soon there were only the walls of thick forests as we sped back to the place I'd left an emotional lifetime ago. In a version of what I had done for Gina, she now was the consoler, the calmer, the wound attender. Telling me I was good, smart, giving, amazing, all those things I'd thought about Udo, whose love for Finola had inspired me to choke out to Liam standing there an arm's length from me at Joe's cliffs, "Go and do what you need to. If you're still with her, even in your head, you'd never really be anybody else's."

"Wow—you said that?" Gina had tears in her eyes. "Wow . . ."

After any worrying done about her not needing the details of my romantic life, she was taking considerably well the loss of surprisingly evil Charlie St. Jean and the gain of the electric Liam Keegan, and my possible self-induced loss of him. As we flew past the newly refurbished Charlton rest stop, complete with fenced dog park and topiary landscaping and Ben & Jerry's kiosk, she asked "So how'd you leave it?"

"We left it at that. He's free to see if there are feelings left, and he's to let me know the outcome."

"When?"

"Who knows? Who knows how long this stuff takes. I have no idea when she has to go back—Liam and I went from that walk with Joe to packing the car and saying good-byes up and down the road. Nobody else had seen her yet, so I got no updates. But I get the idea she is in Booley for the duration."

"You just said 'juration,'" Gina said.

"Sorry."

"Don't be sorry," she said, and I told her I wouldn't. I wouldn't be sorry about pronouncing a word the way I'd heard it pronounced for the past three months. I'd save the regrets for other mistakes I might have already made.

Profile:

⌣

Facing the Future

(State Your Wish Three Times)

Pensioner to cycle from Kerry to Derry.

Drug Swoop Dutchman arrested in Killarney, cannabis with a street value of 15 million euro.

Joyriding teens are lucky to be alive, drove lorry in the dark, went through the windscreen, Gardai are treating the incident with utmost gravity.

Asylum seekers exist on nineteen euro a week, not permitted to work or undergo training.

Earthwatch West report the results of the first morning of the annual cliff walk collection: six plastic crates, numerous shoes, bottles, a purse, a four-foot-wide ball of packing wire, one dead sheep.

Folding attic stairs by Staire fitted anywhere in the country in less than two hours. Utilize the single largest area in your house!

Scan cows to identify pregnancy at 29 days.

Cavalier King Charles bitch, mature lovely pet.

Hat hire available at de Brun fashion accessories.

Madame Farah, clairvoyant as featured on BBC and Pat

Kenny, healing by phone, arthritis, depression, relationships, panic attacks, smoking, weight control, also animals. 1.85 a minute.

Jobs available for stone masons, panel beater, assistant creche worker, storesperson, turf turners, software developer.

Sale on Ajax cleaning powder, Jacob's Jaffa Cakes, Brandy dog food, minced beef, you'll love it at Londis.

I heard all this through my computer. All I have to do is click on the icon of the radio with its little rabbit-ear antennae and type in the name of the country and click on the stations listed beneath that country's name. On the same computer I also can call up newspapers from anywhere in the world, and just like that, the newspaper pages are in front of me. The computer-sized pages. The actual pages of the newspapers were a couple thousand miles away, as was the country they told about, the country I left one Sunday one month ago in a big lunky plane with a shamrock on its tail and a heartbroken woman curled from her rightful place in 12E onto the thankfully vacant 12F, head on the oversized Kotex of an airline pillow and beneath the green polyester tartan airline blanket, where nobody could see her sniveling like the Aran-cardiganed fellow Yank in 13D, about whom the Kleenex-wielding stewardess asked the wife, "Is he from Ireland?" and the wife jabbed mercilessly, "No. But he thinks he is."

I knew well where I was from: the same place to which I was returning. My same town, but a different home now. Gina's. Gennifer's old bedroom, my old print of Botticelli's Venus coming into focus on the wall every morning. And I remember thinking early in the summer how that probably was how the fabled Finola had to have emerged into being, from the depths of the sea, riding along on a scallop shell, the seasons and the winds heralding her emergence from the deep. Finola. Now reemerged in Booley. What would she end up doing with Liam? What would I end up doing? Lastly, I wondered, only because it had helped me in the past, what would Finola do now if she were me?

I followed her lead. As she'd done in what once had been her world, I upended things in the place that once had been mine. And that is why I began a new career. As did Gina. Together, she and I became Powerful Women, Inc. We liked to say that we simply were Powerful Women, but the Inc. had to be added for legal reasons, said the guy who'd been Norm's lawyer. In case any of the bracelets we made and sold to stores throughout the area caused harm to a wearer, if an eye got put out by a dangerously pointed charm, the company, rather than Gina and me, would be the one sued for damages. But nothing bad like that had happened in the two months since I arrived home, and that very first morning Gina showed me how, as a way to have something in common with my life in Booley, she'd gone to Northampton and spent a fortune in the bead supply store and since then had been sitting within her newly painted walls, whipping up bracelets of her own. "I don't have your imagination," she apologized unnecessarily, "but these don't look so bad, do they?"

They didn't. Technically, Gina could work a decent knot, something they'd taught her for free at the bead store—and should have, considering the bucks she dropped there at retail. She had a good eye for color and balance, and had stocked the dozens of compartments of her Tupperware craft supply container with quality beads in glass, wood, clay. There was no plastic—not even the acceptable Italian plastic fake sea glass. It was my first day home, my first afternoon. Not twenty-four hours before, Liam and I had walked still silent to the point-of-no-return part of the airport, the entrance to the duty-free shop that was your last chance at potato-shaped candles and vacuum-packed salmon and bottles of Paddy's. A silk ficus grew in a large pot next to the velvet rope opening at which stood an official awaiting my boarding pass and nearly dead passport. Liam was allowed go no farther. I unzipped the money pocket of my jacket and removed the necessary papers. There was nothing left to do but leave. Nothing left to say. Our last embrace was as silent as the fake plant.

After that was the blur of going through the ropes and over to the official, then down a little partitioned hall, where I noticed eight or ten inches of space at the bottom of the wall and I crouched for one more look at Liam. I saw his boots, the bottom half of his jeans going in the direction of the escalator before I heard the official asking was I in need of help. I said yes, but no thanks, got to my feet, got poured into the lanolin pool that was the duty-free's knit department. That was how I'd left him, and now I was so so far away from Booley and there was no Italian plastic fake sea glass in Gina's selection of beads, and there was no Liam in this country, but there was a chair, so I sank into it.

Gina was studying me, elbows on knees.

"It must be awful for you. But remember: Things do get better. I mean, if you were to hear the story of my running off to Booley, you might think it was a dumb thing to do. But that one day there gave me the key I needed—that it was time to rely on myself. How else would I have met El?"

"L what?"

"El the herbalist. El my boyfriend."

By herself, without any help from me or anybody, after reading an article on the benefits of alternative medicine, Gina had nosed through the most recent edition of a free New Age-ish paper called *Many Hands* and found herself an herbalist.

"If I hadn't returned feeling so screwed up, I wouldn't have made the appointment. It's destiny, Sophie. I was meant to go to Booley and hate it!" She pushed back of the cuff of her sweater and there was the bracelet of Destiny.

"See—all this, it was not easy, but it was my destiny."

"Huh?"

"The card. The card said this charm with the lines on it translates to Destiny, that you will understand your destiny. Not you, but me. The wearer."

"I sent you Healing."

"Nope. You sent me Destiny."

"I meant to send you Healing."

"Destiny. In that box you sent was Destiny." She was babbling like that. Gina, who had a guy in her life. A guy she believed was her destiny and who had been given the job as her herbalist because of what she had on her wrist. I listened, about how this El had waited until her package of six weeks of twice-weekly lessons on the healing powers of herbs ended before he asked her to breakfast. The waiting was because he is ethical, doesn't get involved with patients, and the breakfast was because he is a very healthy type who goes along with it being the most important meal of the day, one to which he takes the most important people—that's how he put it when he asked her, and she consented, and the very next morning Gina found herself seated across from El and in front of representatives of all the major food groups for her first date in four decades. She told me how El says he never puts ice in a drink because that only causes your body extra stress in trying to warm the water to proper temperature once the drink is inside you. She told me how El says he spends one weekend of every month locked in his house naked and fasting and doing yoga and sticking his head in the steam from a soup pot full of salted water every hour on the hour 'round the clock. She told me how El says a lot of things to her, most of them health related, fascinating, eye opening and mind expanding. What a man, what a man. I listened to all the El stuff, but more to Gina's voice, her energy, how she was so much better in body and mind than the last time I'd seen her, and, in ways I couldn't pinpoint, was a different woman than she'd been before

Booley, before Gennifer, before the job loss, before even Norm and the billboard sign.

As for me, I was tired, felt like I'd flown back on the power of my own two arms. I'd stayed at Gina's house that night, and every night in the month since, seated to her left at a big table El built for us in her sunroom, dozens of cups of beads arranged in a spectrum before us, cord and elastic and pleather on reels beneath the table, a yardstick nailed along the edge just as I was used to. We moved deftly and almost without looking, spelling out in beads the designs we aimed for, no planning, no use of the nearby template Gina bought at her first bead store visit so she could line up a pattern first. She already knew well to pick this one here in red, then this matching one with the lines across it, then two of these clear ovals, one of those shaped like the start of a dream, two more of the previous, silver for the accent in between, and in no time at all, we had created another bracelet I definitely would grab were I somebody visiting somewhere, wanting a little something to remember this place by, and—if I could get it at the same price—to be reminded that it's OK to believe in a little faith, hope, or charity.

We didn't waste time, why should we have? started selling Powerful Women bracelets to the stores at the shopping center where El has his office. I'd show the owner or the buyer a selection, each piece unique and crafted by a powerful woman for a powerful woman (though powerful men were welcome to wear them, too), and each containing a charm interpreted from ancient Celtic-pronounced-with-a-*K* legend. They'd buy a dozen, maybe half the merchants doing so only as a favor to El. But they'd reorder soon after for nothing more altruistic than because they were making a buck. Getting comments. The wearers claiming all sorts of wacky improvements or enlightenments, asking to buy more.

"You know those weird little bracelets you sold me . . ."

More reorders, and we were in business.

At Norm's desk, Gina handled paperwork, studied up on website design, booked us into a couple of the regional preholiday gift fairs. She could write a fairly decent press release, and got us the start of media attention. She Xeroxed copies of whatever bits of ink we were granted. "Listen to this—you sound so smart!" Gina told me as she read from a feature in the Pennysaver, which quoted me about the power we put into ordinary objects, the hope they can stand for, "how they can provide something for us to hang on to while we wait for whatever it is we're awaiting."

What I was awaiting was the end of being preoccupied with what was happening over in Booley. In the two weeks I'd been home, there'd been not one word from Liam. Nor were there any phone calls, no inquiries as to how I was keepin'. There was no word from him at all. I tried not to care, but I am not good at that.

Una was the most informative, e-mailing me from Noel's computer. She reported having Finola to tea a few times, and dining with her and Noel at the Last Restaurant. Though the tourist season was winding down, Una didn't have much time for socializing, Ralpho and Derek being back in school and sports. But Una had spent enough time with Finola to learn her routine. She had one of the few private rooms at Diamond's, from where she walked each morning to the sea, past the cottage she didn't stay in because, well, it was no longer hers. In the evening, she meet Joe to go up to the cliffs. In between, she caught up with locals. And there was some time spent at the shop. At Liam's shop. "Some time" is the fuzzy length Una gave it. She also said she'd gone to Liam's to find Finola at the bead table, working away, tried to put a good spin on it. "All due to your genius. Liam alone can't fill the orders, and Finola, well, she's right there . . ."

Finola was in my former chair, at my former table, next to my former man, her former man, her probably current man.

As harsh as it sounds, that's the chance you take, Noel said in an email. He was a faithful filer, most every day giving me some form of hallo. His email name was a self-confident-sounding FirstNoel, and after my good-for-you response regarding the catchy self-confident title, he confided he'd picked it only because, in a Noel-rampant country, it was either think of something like that or be Noel293. He had some Christmas shows to prepare for, Noel said, but he had more time on his hands than in the summer, and trailed Finola on some of her walks. "No easy task," he noted, "as she can fairly move." But I already knew that.

Aoife, emailing on behalf of everyone at the Last Restaurant, wished me well once a week, usually on Monday, when she posted a freshly written home page on the restaurant's website. Her posts were titled "Hallo From Booley," which sounded like the town was jamming itself at the keyboard to ask how's the form?

I'd answer that it was all beads. All Gina's sunroom, stringing together countless prods for Renewal and Creativity and, of course, Love and Hope, lots of Hope, because more than Love, Hope is the huge seller. Everyone wants hope, so that is what we give them.

"You have given me hope" wearers told us in the letters we were starting to get, similar to those Finola O'Flynn once received, sent by happy customers who wanted to report strange but definite links between the titles of the bracelets they wore and what was going on in their lives. Some of them wrote testimonials, and Gina posted those on our new website, which was wonderfully clever thanks to El's brother, Em, who had a certificate of completion for a weekend intensive in computer basics and an eye for the ladies, particularly the dark and mysterious ones. I am dark featured, not at all mysterious, but one quality out of two was not bad, Em said as he pestered me for dates, telling me "That could be us," as he motioned El and Gina, sitting at the computer table in the corner of the sunroom and admiring the main page that was a giant bracelet with all sorts of lusciously colored beads and intricate charms, click on one to enter. Em designed that, and I gave him credit because it was indeed gorgeous. Colorful and shiny and just made you want to scoop up handfuls of merchandise. But I didn't encourage Em because he had taken to tinkering far too much with the computer for which I paid half. He was downloading borrowed programs that were probably giant sanitariums of viruses and he was attempting to stick into any of the computer's vacant orifices all sorts of phone wires and answering machine wires in an effort to turn the computer into a giant speaker phone, which, he noted, would allow Gina or me to do other things while we were dealing with customers. And his eyebrows quivered an if-ya-know-what-I-mean.

I knew what he meant but I heard Gina's "Be nice" in my head so was nice as I turned Em down yet again, as I would go on to do the next day, when he so generously informed me that he'd stop pressuring me for a date would I just have sex with him, and as I would again the following week, when he would add his new girlfriend to the equation. As if the prospects of group sex, and group sex in which Em was a factor, weren't horrific enough, I learned that this love interest was someone with whom I was a Girl Scout.

Is it any wonder I'd acquired a nervous habit, twirling the bracelet I'd been wearing since its birth at the beginning of the summer? Blue ceramic scarabs alternating with smooth round beads of clear glass, bits of blue and green floating in them like the wisdom-bearing fish. I'd strung a small silver peace symbol between two of the glass beads, because who wouldn't want peace, and, after a few more beads, I'd added a black and white enameled yin/yang disc, because that's how life goes, and I made the centerpiece a small square bead in the shape of a book that took me back to being dropped off at the cottage by Liam at the end of that first day, at the end of what he said was another day for the memory book. But, really, good and bad, yin and yang, weren't they all? I considered this as I twirled the beads around my wrist some nights sitting on the middle cushion of Gina's couch and conjuring, as Kathleen O'Donnell spoke of half a year ago from her window in the bank van. Conjuring Booley, walking myself through it, down the hill, over the bridge, along the shops, passing the one that was just before the chip shop, because I am a powerful woman who could go past there with no problem, and continue on to the sea.

Sleep came led by the same flock of sheep I often followed on my morning walk into town, the dozen or so spindly-legged future mutton pies that would come pouring from some gap in the hedges. One, then another, then another and another, clowns from a Volkswagen, they struggled, then popped from sheep-sized holes and continued down the road, in the direction of Booley. Their little black hooves made businesslike high-heeled noises on the stones. Their legs were bare, toothpick-show-poodle-dainty, supporting cloudlike bodies of wool hung with clods of manure and sticks and marked with a shocking blot of red that I at first thought was blood but, because they were all sploched in that color and manner, I figured out had to be a type of ID. Tap-tap-tap-tap, they floated along in front of me, their bulk the puffy skirts of ballet dancers, then clambered through another hedge. Maybe hadn't been there to begin with. But in my dream they were, there in the place it was starting to look like I'd never have reason to visit again.

Until I received the letter in which he asked me to return.

Question Mark:

Request, Favor, Need to Know

(State Your Wish Three Times)

Joe wrote to me on the kind of see-through airmail paper everyone used before they stopped being so concerned about postage rates. In winged penmanship similar to that used on the Declaration of Independence, was this:

> *Dear Sophie White:*
>   *How are ye?*
> *I'm going up the town for winter.*
> *Would ye ever come help an aul' man move house?*
> *As promised?*
>
> > *Yours, etc.,*
> > *Joe Cronin*
> > *14 September, 2002*

I already knew about the scheme—our word for shifty goings-on, theirs for plan—through which the state was paying for bed-and-breakfasts, St. Botolph's among them, to be stuffed to the rafters with old people from October to April, cutting down on the unfortunate number of elders found sick or dead during that time of year in their remote homes, keeping them all safe and warm and fed, and making them regulars at Quinn's. Joe had spoken of the scheme more than a few times while sitting at the fire. He'd usually just let the conversation die there, so one morning I asked why didn't he just decide to do it. To sign up for a spot.

"First and only time I slept anywhere but beneath this roof was when I was in hospital. There's but one other destination for an aul' man . . ."

"You're going to a bed-and-breakfast!" I reminded him. "Not to the graveyard. You'll be with your friends. Come the better weather, you'll be back here."

Joe had looked around the room just then. "I'd say there'd be too much work closing this house for the winter. I'd say it would be far too much for one man alone . . ."

"I'll help you already. It wouldn't be much—what?—packing your bags?"

"Ye'd help?"

"Of course."

"Ye'd come all the way from American to help an aul' man."

"I would."

"Ye would."

"I would."

"So you told him you would," Gina reminded me at the conclusion of this retelling.

"Oh I didn't think he was serious. Plus, this was in the middle of my stay—I was all happy and in love with everything. The world was good. I suppose I was thinking I might have a reason to be coming back . . ."

"Well, you do now."

"But now I don't want to. I mean I do, but. . . . If only he'd let me know what's happening."

"Joe?"

I pitched a lima-bean-shaped bead at her. "Liam."

"Look. Joe never seemed to ask you for anything. Obviously, for him to invite somebody—a woman yet, and a woman from another country—it's a big thing. Maybe he thinks he's really going to die while away this time, and maybe he feels you're family and he wants you there to help him sort through things. If he's never lived anywhere but that house, it'll be a big thing for him to move.

"Maybe."

"He asked you. You should go. You'll do him a favor, and you can exorcise some ghosts at the same time. Walk down that road, show yourself you can do that no matter what's happened with Liam. You had three wonderful months in that place. Lots of good. You shouldn't be afraid."

I swiveled my chair and looked straight at her and said, "I wouldn't be if you were there."

Gina put down her glasses, new little no-line bifocals from the optometrist in the storefront next to El's. She swirled her chair away from the computer and faced me full-on.

"I'll go with you, because you did that favor for me," Gina said, and I felt stronger already. "I'd do anything for you because you would do the same, and more, for me. But when I went, I was too afraid to be alone. I needed a traveling companion. You don't. Even by yourself, you won't be going there alone."

So Booley was what I stood above that late September Sunday afternoon as the bus that had delivered me from the airport and to the intersection of two lonely muddy roads fumed away and I was suddenly looking down at the tiniest and most beauteous corner of the world, the one that for three brief months had held the great promise of being all that I ever would need.

It would never be that, I realized. Nothing ever will be, Finola added from the place she still occupied in my head. "Just as I told Aoife that night on the strand, I'll tell you the same on this afternoon on this old road: Nothing outside of you ever will be the sum and total of what you need. You're it, full stop." She was right, of course. She usually was. But that didn't make the fact any easier to chew and swallow.

Gina was right, too—Finola was still with me. An unexpected souvenir of my summer away. A woman I had great affection for when she was but a collection of stories, whom I easily could have hated after she materialized in the flesh. She was one of those contagions against which you should be inoculated before going overseas. Like water in my ears after a long swim early on I'd shake my head to try to get her to spill out, but there was no moving the woman. She sat tight with a firm hold on the hem of my identity. For my three months in Booley and, surprisingly at first, during the nearly two I've been back home, she's been the compass I've consulted. Maybe I did hate her, crashing my party as she had. But I allowed it, gave Liam free rein, and—who can blame him?—his silence tells me he took it.

It was Finola who joined me on the plane, on the bus, Finola who stood with me on that hilltop, who waited as I considered that the only distance remaining between me and Joe's house was a walk down the hill, and walk down the single road, which today showed no signs of life. From here, it appeared just as it had in the travel ad, as it once had been in Gina's head, quiet, still, muted ochre and pink and blue, even more silent minus the life spark of the hikers, and four cars parked with left wheels on the footpath near the front of Una's. A tan dot of a dog trotted toward the sea and I knew his name, knew well the feel of him soft and snoozing in my lap. Beyond lay the fields, beyond them an entire ocean, bigger than the world, and certainly more than large enough to dwarf any reticence about seeing Liam, or Finola, or both. I stood rooted, yet felt a push. It wasn't a dive I made. It was more like a trudge. Point was, I was going down the hill.

I had the road to myself, and mine was the only sound, boot slaps against the hard ground. I shuffled past dormant fuchsia walls that were a gray tunnel I followed all the way to the bottom of the hill. Where there it was in front of me, glowing like a miniature Oz: Booley.

The place from Gina's head. The place from my heart.

I was standing in it.

As onetwothreefourfive cars in a row blasted past just inches from my toes.

I threw myself into the fuchsia as the cars flew toward Booley, horns sounding, laughs bouncing, and, in the passenger seat of the final vehicle, a woman.

Finola O'Flynn.

In a bridal veil.

Holly:

Truth

(State Your Wish Three Times)

There was a big wide rock at the corner of the road. In the summer, Blackie Linnane sat there daily and nodded and waved every boss who passed. Blackie was probably packing his bags to go and live for the winter with the other old guys moving into St. Botolph's. He had left his rock behind. I crawled onto it as the sounds of the traffic disappeared and the lane was still once again.

"What do I do? What do I do?"

My heart beat hard enough to thump the left strap of the Strato-pack I had thought would be preferable to a suitcase should I need to turn and run instantly if Booley or a Booleyan situation were not to my liking. This one, for example, when, without a word spoken, I found out Liam has married Finola.

"Change," said the voice that had been bossing me around since May. "Change."

I wasn't sure if that was an order, or an idea, a verb, noun, what. What I did was what I usually did when I heard it. I listened. I got to my feet. I considered the way I'd come. Felt a push again, to follow the cars.

If you were just walking for the sake of it, you'd be getting cold. The wind was kicking up, and there were hungry-caterpillar-shaped clouds taking a troublemaking route in from the sea. I felt little of the chill, all adrenaline as I was and walking at a Bionic Woman–style clip. I was in no rush to get to town, but my legs didn't seem to care. Soon I was passing the road to Diamond's. Soon the bridge to the town was at my right. Soon I passed it.

Can you blame me? All very Desmond Tutu of me to want to further peace in this world. But when it came right down to it I didn't want to subject myself to even passing by the building containing the celebration of Finola's marriage to Liam. It would be nothing but the end of the Miss America Pageant, all the losers running up to swamp the winner. Like they are feeling anywhere near congratulatory at that point. Like they wouldn't want to punch out the winner's wipe the crown and take off down the boardwalk.

So I passed the stone bridge that would take me to the front of the Last Restaurant, and all the other shops lined up after that. I took a different route, down a boreen that led to a skinny section of the river easily crossable by manhole-sized boulders, then angled back north, out to the cliffs. I hiked cautiously, picking my way along the rocks jutting from the puddingish mud that the path running parallel to the sea had become. The path swung inland, down another boreen that connected with a dirt lane, on which I passed the house where a small girl once had been startled at the sight of me. No small girl today, no mother in the door, no baby at her hip, no man with a pitchfork, no dog running toward me. Maybe they were at the reception, too. The entire town probably was. I cut onto a cart road, toward the sea, continued north toward Joe's, my eyes on the road before me until I felt it thin to an end. There, I climbed over the stile broaching the wire fence and before me was the field. And the rock, and the tree, and the well. The well of St. Faicneam, a great one for the lost. For those seeking to regain the invisible. Health. Love. Hope. All that sort of thing. If you ever had any of that, and you'd lost it, Faicneam's yer man.

But he's not just yer man. You'll have to share him—on this day, at least.

Because here comes the bride.

Candle:

꧁꧂

Illumination, Reality

(State Your Wish Three Times)

She was walking up the hill, and at this distance appeared very Sunday supplement dramatic with the wind blowing back the generous amount of white fabric that made up her gown and the long white shawl that was keeping her from freezing. The sight of her was at once dazzling and, one quarter-second later, sickening.

Liam's wife, heading my way.

I got that instant choking heartbeat thing in my throat, never a good thing. I stood up and took a step back, and felt the points of the branches holding the holy medals and the baby toys and the gold hoop earrings and the David Gray concert ticket stub.

She was almost up to the top of the hill now. She was sussing out who I was. After a moment of mild disbelief that I could feel from yards away, Finola said stiffly, "Well. Another pilgrim."

She looked somehow more 3-D to me than she had on our first meeting, which was strange, as this was a day I'd rather not have been able to see her at all. That summer day, she was a blur, see-through, indescribable. This day she was as real to me as any other part of the scenery, as the stone wall, the grazing Fresian's. Even so, I could see that my general impressions had been pretty much on target: Finola was no cover girl. But somebody had tried to spiff her up for her big day. Somebody had trimmed her stuffed-animal hair to an even length, and raked some sort of goop through it to keep it from pointing to all corners of the earth. Somebody had crowned her with a little circle of seed pearls, and there was a tiny hint of a veil hanging down the back. Somebody had coated her face with a powder that had a sparkle to it, and had glossed her lips with something faintly red and most likely berry named. Her high-necked cotton *Little House on the Prairie* gown, as retro chic as anything in her closet, reminded me of the homespun muslin Gunne Sax line of prom dresses my friends and I bought on layaway at Casual Corner back in 1975. Her pearl earrings were shaped like the teardrops you wouldn't want anywhere near you on a day like this, and her right hand included a finger on which somebody has placed a gold band.

I didn't want to congratulate her.

I didn't want to say anything.

I wanted her to get out of here. And I wanted to do the same. To run back down the road and over the river and up the hill and catch the next bus to the airport. Forget Joe, who'd probably greet me with nothing more than "I said she'll never travel this far to help an aul' man . . ." What in the fuck was I doing here?

"What in the fuck are you doing here?"

Finola asked me this.

"Joe. Joe wrote, needed a favor. So I came back."

She repeated: "What are you doing here?" and on the "here" points to the well, using her ring hand.

"I don't really know. I was walking to town, changed my mind at the last second." I stopped. Pinched my wrist. Prayed to wake up to Brie Pernell's singsong. I didn't. I asked, "And what are you doing here? Shouldn't you be at a—a party?"

Finola smiled. "I should. Wanted to come up here before the hooley started. To be alone for a bit. Meditate, like."

"I'll leave you then."

"Why?"

"You want to be alone for that. And if you're not going to be alone, I'm probably not the first person you'd choose for company."

"Strangely enough, I feel like I know you now. So many stories."

"Stories."

"You've quite a following in Booley."

"I have maybe five friends here. Well, maybe four now. You— they'll probably end up naming the place after you one of these days."

"Notatall." She made one of those waving-away gestures. Smiled, something I couldn't manage.

"It's not notatall at all. I heard your name almost from the first minute I got here. In many ways, almost to the moment I left."

Finola looked embarrassed, something you wouldn't think she would know how to do. She placed the end of her shawl on the rock, took a seat at the edge of the well. "So yer sick of me."

"I'm sick of the whole thing."

"Then why're you here?"

"You really want to know?" And I spat the rest of it out: "Because you would come into town. If you were me, and you found out it was my wedding day, you'd come into town and congratulate the happy couple."

She laughed. "Just what would make you think I'm so saintly— and anyhow, why ever would you want to do what I might do?"

"I don't know if saintly's the word, but maybe it's close to what people think of you around here."

"G'wan." This wasn't encouragement for me to continue raving about her. She simply didn't believe what I was saying.

"Want to start with Joe? You found him, you could have left it at getting him to the hospital. But you pestered him afterward, got him out and back to his cliffs. Where'd he be now if you hadn't taken the time? Una told me how helpful you were raising her kids. Aoife said you literally saved her sanity that night on the beach. Pepsi? Where'd he be now without you? And Noel?"

She smiled. "That's all very kind. But it's total and complete bullshit, as you might say."

"Missing kids, beaten wives, people with boats and nowhere to dock them . . ."

"Bullshit again."

"I'd rather not dissect the Liam thing, but you know you changed the course of his life just with your presence—just by standing in the road and looking happy. Without even trying."

Finola played with a stone bisected by a white line, a marking that Joe once told me meant good luck. She was focusing on the water, her face solemn.

"In my mind, you grew to be somebody from one of the myths and legends books in the shop," I told her. I was speaking and listening at the same time, needed to say things, but also stymied as to why I wanted to speak a single word to her. "From what everybody said, you always knew what to do, when to do it—or not do it. In May, I found out my boyfriend—nearly my fiance—was married. I don't know if that was love as much as it was need, on my part, or being sick of being lonely. Whatever it was, on some level I never wanted to really spend much time thinking about it. I was looking forward to him really just being the answer to all the problems I ever had. But when it didn't work out—"

She tilted her head, waiting.

"OK. When I found out about his family, when I found that out, it wasn't pleasant. I was here, alone. My constant companion was some feature of you. I was working at your business, I was living in your home, I was answering to your name . . ."

"You were wearin' my clothing . . ."

"I was wearing your clothes. It was just easier to think I was somebody else—that I was you rather than me."

"And who were you when you were with Liam?"

I never knew I had hackles. That moment, they raised.

She laughed. The wind blew her veil across her face and she disappeared into a blur again. I heard her say, "You were good to give him the room he needed."

Now she was praising me. But why shouldn't she—I had stepped aside so she could walk right in.

"I don't know if that was so good on my part—or smart, but what could I do? Truth be told, it was your Udo who gave me the idea."

"Udo." She said it flatly.

"When you told me that he was doing that for you, giving you the room you needed, it made me wonder why I couldn't be that selfless and giving. You were lucky to have had him."

Finola smirked. "I was lucky to have left. D'ya know he only encouraged my staying here and spending time with Liam because he had his own unfinished business to tend to?"

"No . . ."

"So, Sophie. Things aren't always what they seem. People aren't always what they're made out to be. We add embellishments as we see fit. Hasn't life taught you that by this stage?"

I was still reeling from the news of Udo having someone on the side. On the quiet, as they'd say here. I felt like I'd been betrayed, too.

"Udo," I said, shaking my head, and at the same time, Finola was nodding, saying to herself, "Not what they seem."

"Well, yeah," I said. "I know about gilding the lily and all, but how can you gild, say, spending so much time with some lonely old man when you could have been doing a million other things."

"I gave a lot of time to Joe, but it wasn't all one-sided. I've no family."

"I didn't know. They always talked about what you did here, not where you were before."

"I say I've no family. However, if you're looking for blood, it exists. But they're a right shower of bastards and I ran the moment

I was able. Running's been a constant for me, you could say. Always running from. The things I've run to have always been unknowns. When I came here and met Joe, a connection was made. He might have enjoyed my calling over, but it was something I needed, too. And Una? My help there amounted to listening. Sharin' a pint or four or five and listening. Sometimes that's enough, apparently. The poor woman needed nothing more. I sat and listened and the years passed and not one of her lads needed to be sent away to boarding school so I'm to get the credit?"

"Maybe you . . ."

"No maybes. It's all how they saw it. Aoife—she was crushed that night on the beach. I listened again. Maybe threw in a few pieces of advice, but I'm sure it was the type you rattle out when you've no idea what to say to someone in need of help. Christ, it was only listening with Pepsi, as well. I'd walk past the farm where he was kept, any fool coulda heard the sad howling. And if you've heard one or two dogs howl in your life, you can tell when it's for fear. So I listened, over and again, and one night I distracted him with a load of biscuits and took a knife to the bailing twine that held him there, and that was that. To all these people, to the beast even, the result was whatever they felt was a help to them. But I netted some fine friends, and a dog. You tell me who ended up benefitting more? I'd say your myth's shattered. So don't go thinking what Finola O'Flynn might do, because Finola O'Flynn might simply bore you to tears."

"I've never heard that said."

"No? Any of them ever comment on my clothes?"

"I got tons of comments. You have amazing taste."

"But not one of them said they'd seen me in them."

I thought about it. She was right.

"And that's due to the fact I never, ever, not one time, wore them. I was a great one for the collecting, but wearing? Impossible. I loved them because I wanted to become the person who would wear a Hawaiian print or scarlet velvet or stripe with plaid. But I never could get past the grays, the browns. The dull is my uniform, so I've been told. You, Sophie, you saw the clothing, you wore it without a thought. They were mine, sure, but they were never me. That was you wearing them, you being you. Not me. When I saw you in the pink sundress, it was a reminder of what I'd never been able to do."

"Jesus."

"And your bracelets? I'd been making bracelets—and earrings and necklaces and hat pins and the odd stickpin—for a decade. Never did I sell as many of them in a single season as were sold of yours this past summer. I've lived here all my life and not once did it cross my mind to make use of the whole idea of believing, which is the very fiber of this land." She held out the stone.

"I was just playing," I told her. "As I was with your name. Got the idea right here, actually, when Joe brought me the first time." I pointed to the water. I could see her reflection in it, which I remembered Joe saying something about. If you can see the reflection of the another person—well, I couldn't recall what that's supposed to mean, but she looked clear there. I could see her clearly.

"That's entirely fitting, because the story of Faicneam's something you either believe or don't. There's half who believe he was a man who spent his life in search of people, things, truths, wisdom, anything that had fallen by the wayside. There's the other half who believe only that he's his name: "Fake name." Invented by somebody who wanted a place to bring their loss, their sorrow, but the nearest well of any saint who remotely deals with that is fifty miles east and even since the era of the automobile, with the state of these roads, it's still a journey. So believe what you like."

"I didn't believe, really. But you thought that the scarf—that Faicneam—called you back here."

"I did. I heard the stories of Faicneam, I bought the idea of who he was and what he could do. In that way, too, I'm no different from

the next soul." Then she added, because maybe she thought I'd forgotten, "'Cept today—I'm somebody's wife." She glanced at the
ring, gold that was sparkling even though the sun wasn't shining.

"I'll admit the saint had help," Finola continued. "Another
German fella."

She waited for me to make the connection, which I didn't, so
she helped: Diamond.

"He's why Udo came here on his holidays. They're old friends.
Wouter, Walter, Diamond, whatever you like, he's on the email
when he can get the machine to function. Sends a hallo, and pro-
vides the news. Not that Udo cares about Booley. And not that I'd
cared to keep up. But Diamond always fancied me, don't know if he
thought he'd be luring me back with information . . . But I was deep
in my new life and never really read too much of what he was sending. Until May. When you arrived and it's like he could sniff something was about to happen. Thought I should know. He'd sent
enough bits about Liam over the few years; this was the only one in
which I took interest when I glanced at it, and began to follow."

So as the shop's business increased, as my relationship with
Liam progressed, Diamond collected the latest of what was being
said around town and turned it into an emailed soap opera to which
Finola regularly tuned. In her extra time at the computer, she eventually Googled me, and ended up getting herself. On the ERIN-
TOUR website, photo by Cultural Consultant Christina Giliberti,
Ph.D., taken in her old shop, at her old bead table, her old man next
to her old dress being worn by somebody who, according to the cut-
line, was named Finola O'Flynn. And that was the first time the
real Finola O'Flynn ever emailed Diamond back.

"He had a hand in my return," Finola told me, "but Diamond
had the computer."

I got brave. Swallowed. "So where'll you live now. The cottage?"

"My days in the cottage are over. We want to go somewhere
totally new. Spain." She said it dreamily. I felt queasy. "Different cli-

mate, and a fantastic crafts community on the coast. Plus enough émigrés for the *craic*. I'd say we'd fit. Find someone to keep the shop running, but we'll be off in España." Finola said the country as it should be pronounced, with the little squiggly thing over the *n*, as she told me it had been pronounced on a recent broadcast of *Newsround*, which had visited an enclave of retired Irish living it up in year-round sun, showing off miles and miles of hot white sand on which Irish expatriates lay oiled and fluorescent pink and sizzling like meat in the pan of an endless breakfast fry. "So we're off to España," Finola beamed. "But first, I'm off to my wedding reception." She placed the white-split stone at the edge of the well's black waters. "Would you ever walk down the fields with me?"

It was a genuine invitation.

"I don't think so. Go and enjoy your day. Being in love, and all . . ."

"Speaking of love, can I be honest?"

"Seems like you have been since you walked up here."

"Well, I'm honest again when I say this: Liam loves you."

I did nodded. Scanned the weirdness of a bride telling me the innermost feelings of her groom, and on their wedding day yet. Then I said thanks.

"He does," his wife insisted. You should know that."

However shabby our partings, however confusing the decisions we make, we should all love one another, I suppose, in the grand scheme. So I said matter-of-factly, "Well, I love him, too. A fine man." I regretted the last three words—they sounded corny and hollow as if from one of those eulogies given by a priest who never knew once met the deceased. But I couldn't have the sad truth of the first five words just floating there. So I said he was a fine man. And to further couch them, I smushed on an additional five: "I'm happy for you, Finola."

That part was a lie.

"I'm truly a lucky woman," Finola told me, in what was

Goodyear blimp–sized fact. She walked to the tree, where her now gray and tattered scarf was all but covered by subsequent generations of pilgrim detritus. A cluster of hay tied with a wire, a long white feather, plastic wrap that once contained Galtee rashers. "I thank you for leaving this here. I truly never would have returned otherwise, would still be living with that fecker, and, most important, never would have reunited with the man who is my destiny."

After all that grandness, she added only, "Bye so," and she waved with a bracelet that was identical in color and pattern—and title— to the one I'd sent Gina.

As Finola made her way down the field, I concentrated on the well, the tree, the stones and coins and holy cards, the First Communion girls' photograph and the large black sock and the molding potato and the DVD of *ET* and the plastic bag with the folded notepaper inside. I snooped without touching, trying to figure out the contents because I'd rather be involved in something like that than the reality I'd just been given that Liam loved me, just not enough. Just then, the plastic let go and the paper inside took flight, heading down the hill with furious speed, following the last I'd ever see of Finola O'Flynn.

Equal Sign:

❧

Answer Given or Deduced

(State Your Wish Three Times)

But nearly two hours later, I'd have one more encounter. Because I would stand one more time at the stone bridge. Because she would have. But, more, because I wanted to.

As had been the case my first time in Booley, I was there again to help a friend who needed me. I kept that in the front of my mind—the blessing it was to have someone who needed me—rather than the hurt that Liam did not. At the end of the bridge was only the nail that once held the neatly painted blue-on-white sign that had announced the LAST RESTAURANT BEFORE AMERICA, which Aoife had emailed had been removed by Eoin after Emilio noted one night in Quinn's that the chip shop, though only a chip shop, technically was Booley's last opportunity for a meal. I set my right foot onto the bridge. Then my left. Then the first one again. I was entering the ad, the photo, the place in Gina's head, the place that I'd have to try awfully hard to shove from its stronghold in my heart.

The line of cars began at the Last Restaurant. Parked along the shops, facing me with their smiling grilles, the black numbers and un-Anglicized county names on long white license plates looking like code. I floated slowly past the vined entryway of the restaurant, the roses gone by now, but I remembered them blooming and

Liam tucking one into my hair before noticing it contained a bee.

I moved past Attracta's, the enormous loom stalled in the process of weaving a red and gold check. Noel had showed me how to weave a simple houndstooth, how to press the pedals and shoot the shuttle through the open weft, pull the beater forward, push it back, see another thread of progress made.

The thin alley and then E. Dolan and its covered window glass: LOTTO, HB Cornetto, the *Independent* on Sunday, ESB Pay HERE! Lots of signs, but still no sign of life. No Una and her broom. No cheery "Howya," no open door through which I could run all the way to the kitchen and hide.

I had the same feeling I get when I'm at a wake and there's a line and I'm maybe four people from the casket, soon it will be my turn, I'll be all alone with the dead, and as if that's not bad enough, I'll have to turn to a line of people to whom I'm not at all sure what to say. I slowed my walk as we passed the long and low building, also white, with a line of green and yellow churchy stained-glass windows and a jutting entryway with a big heavy door with an iron chain for a handle.

After Quinn's there were only two more buildings, and then nothing but a mile of field until Joe's. Only two. But the first of the two was the big and yellow one, with two stories and a door at the center, that was it. That was, as the long rectangle of wood told you in unflinching all caps, FINOLA O'FLYNN.

I shoved my hands into the pocket of my Thermofleece Explorer shell as I passed the window next to the bead table. Focused on the sandwich board that was covered with brown packing paper on which somebody had written "*Go maire tu do shaol ur!*" on a diagonal, with arrows pointing toward the door. I was nearly at the chip shop when I heard him.

"Where ya off ta?"

Liam Keegan.

In his doorway.

My heart halfway up my esophagus.

I worked to assemble a "Huh?"

His face brightened like one of those time-release films of a field of sunflowers blossoming, and he repeated softly, warmly, "Where ya off ta?"

Liam looked, well, happy. As a man on his wedding day should. He looked a lot better than I would have liked. If I hadn't been more than fully aware he was no longer on the open market, I would have inhaled him. My heart would have preferred at least a bad haircut or maybe some bug-eyed Ari Onassis glasses, polyester Sansabelts, a T-shirt praising George W. Bush. But no. Liam had to look good. Had to be dressed sharply, his black St. Vincent de Paul–shop blazer adorned with a small edible-looking flower in the buttonhole. White Oxford shirt, faded jeans, boots. It went, when you considered the Bonanza getup his wife had selected.

His wife.

I removed my grip from the lining of the pockets, slowly, finger by finger, like you'd pull the individual thorns from a vine that's snagged your sleeve. I made the three or four steps to the door of Finola O'Flynn. Liam tossed his fag to the side of the door, where, over three months, I'd told him not to. Why had I cared where he threw his fags? Why hadn't I let him be who he was? Maybe then it could have been me in the Ponderosa getup, deep inside the shop while Liam enjoyed his fag, it would be me deep inside the shop from which emanated unbridled *deedly-deedly* and laughter and glass clinking and people calling out names I knew—Una! Eoin! Emilio!—and hearty shouts of the words written on the sign.

"Sophie White," Liam said with actually believable awe. "You've returned!"

"I'm here. For Joe. Joe asked for my help in moving. Moving house. That's why. I didn't know. About the wedding." I could only form two or three words at once. I needed to breathe between each like I was still learning how, was fallen fresh from the womb and once again wondering where the fuck I was, looking around a new and strange world in which Liam Keegan right there in front of me, was married to Finola O'Flynn, somewhere inside that building, and it was not just a fact I was hearing about months or weeks later, it was so new that the buttonhole flowers were still perky and toasts were still being given.

"I can't believe I'm lookin' atye."

I shrugged.

"Give us a hug."

Except when I recalled it simply to make myself more miserable, I hadn't heard that request in a month. What would you do? What would Finola do? What had she done? I wondered all that as Liam closed the small distance between us and I let myself lean against him. Smelled tangerines. Smelled all I'd lost.

He said, "This was all so sudden. Plans only came together two days ago. Finola's swift. With the proposal and with the preparations. She decorated the shop for the day. Come in, I know you'd like to see what she's done."

I said what I was thinking. "No, I would not like to. I think I know what she's done."

"What?" Liam held his chin and smiled big as he shook his head. "God but ya look fantastic, Sophie. I simply cannot believe I'm lookin' at ye."

I stepped back.

"Will ya ever come inside, the after weddin's roarin', everyone will be delighted to see ya!".

"No thanks. I came back to see Joe. When I found out about the wedding I decided it was only fitting to stop by and give my regards. Strangely enough, I've already run into Finola. And now I'm seeing you. So I'll be going." It was like walking on glass, but I started for the ocean.

"Can we not talk?"

"About what?"

"Your thoughts."

"On what?"

"On my email."

"I didn't get an email."

"I don't understand. I wrote . . ."

"Looks like I wasn't meant to receive it. I would have only gotten in the way. Of destiny and all that."

"Fuck destiny. I made my own mind. I made it through talkin' and thinkin' and spendin' time. And it didn't take but a few days to be clear about the state of my heart. And for her to announce hers. The answers, once spoken, were more than a bit of a surprise to both of us. Straight away I was at Noel's."

"Where you emailed."

"I did now."

I needed to leave. "Well, I hope you'll continue to be happy." I extended my hand, he took it, he kept it, and as much as I didn't want to, I felt the familiar hold as Liam said, "I'm not happy right now, I won't be happy"—here he stepped closer "unless I've another chance with ye."

Another guy who wants both me and his wife.

"Get away." I actually shoved him. He landed with a flat thump against the billboard-wide chest of Noel Heaney, who was suddenly outside and whooping, "Whoa! Sophie White returns! And with a vengeance! Brilliant! Sophie!"

He settled Liam against the doorsill and grabbed me and picked me up and whirled me around and I was looking down at his meteorite of a head and below it I saw a white flower in his buttonhole. In his buttonhole that was in his lapel of his tuxedo jacket. The kind of tuxedo jacket you'd expect a groom to wear. And I'm yelling, "Stop! Stop!" and he finally listens and says, "I'll stop, Sophie White, if you'd stay to meet my wife." He set me in front of the doorway, where his wife was saying, "I'm so glad you called over."

Finola.

"Why did you not ring me back," Noel asked, slinging a hamlike arm around his the woman who was his woman. "I was inviting you—short notice 'n' all, we only decided this Friday, but I thought it would be fitting to have you here. Without you, no scarf left on the tree above, no Faicneam intoned, no Finola back in Booley, no Finola in my life. And for so long, was my prayer."

I looked at Finola I managed to get this out: "You never told me you'd married Noel."

She said airily, "You never asked. Might I remind you to not go supposing."

She put forth a hand that led Joe into view.

"I was sayin' she might not care to spend Christmas with an aul' man. I was sayin' she's back in Americah and Booley's but a memory. I was sayin'. . ."

Joe had a flower in his lapel, too. When I wrapped my arms around him, the blossom met my nose. I could smell the fragrance of a new season.

Noel had me in his grip again, nearly lifting me off the ground. "Lifffe," he told me, high on the moment, "is a total conga dance. You're latched onto her, but she's latched onto the one in fronta her, so on, so forth. I was at the end a the line, no one behind me, no one chasing me, only Finola in fronta me—for ages now, though I never told her. I can pinpoint the moment that I got the nerve—puttin' on that bracelet you made. I began to think that if ever I was given the chance, I'd empty my heart before her. You were gone a week when I had that opportunity. Up at the cliffs. I followed her, stopped her, told her that it was out of my hands what she did with it—I simply wanted her to know what I'd always tried to say in the letters I sent off to Germany. I wanted to say to her face that she owned all the love I ever would have to give."

He stopped. From inside the shop, I heard The Chancers start in on "To All the Girls I've Loved Before." From the scene I stood in, I had some idea of what Finola's reply had been, but was curious as to how they'd gotten from there to here.

"She didn't laugh. That crushes most people's assumption," Noel told me, "But she didn't laugh, Sophie. She merely took my hand. We walked for hours."

Finola stepped from the doorway. Came down to take Noel's hand again. Said, this man was why I was meant to return. For Noel, Sophie. For Noel. I love him. Plain as rain."

"From there, everything moved swiftly," said Noel, and "if you've magic workin' for yeh, sometimes things fall into place. As they did for us."

Liam had taken the few steps forward. Finola now stood between her old man and her new one. The old one took one step closer and said/asked, "Walk."

"You would've enjoyed the ceremony." Liam said as we started in the direction of the ocean.

"I would have?"

"You would have seen me walking down the aisle with Finola. So I could leave her at Noel's side."

"Where I come from, they call that 'giving away.' The father walks the bride down the aisle. We say he's 'giving away the bride.'"

"Instead of charging the usual fee."

I felt my face thawing. A small smile tugged. I said, "Right." Looked in that very direction. At the mountains that keep the rest of the world a rumor.

"Same expression's used here. And that being the case, I'd say you missed a very literal illustration of the state of things here in Booley." We were past Emilio's now. Liam stopped me in the middle of the road. Turned me toward him, and I allowed it. "Because that's exactly what I did, Sophie. I gave her away. Not that I had her atall. Not this time. But I did so nevertheless. Because she asked me, and because giving her away was exactly what it was time to do."

I looked straight ahead, which was into the top button of his shirt. My eyes made their way up to neck, beard, lips, nose, through the glasses and into the eyes. He was repeating, "I gave her away. She thought she'd returned for me, but 'twas for Noel. But that gave me the chance to speak what was rumblin' within me for years. To see what was left for her in my heart. To find—and this was a surprise despite all my protests over the years—that nothing was left. I'd always felt—feared's more like it—there might be a bit of something, a chip, a flake of interest. After what she'd meant to me. But there isn't. Finola came back and allowed me to put things to rest. To lead her to a man she truly wants, the man who's loved her since the day she stood in the street admirin' her sign."

"Did you know all that time? How he felt about her?"

"I suppose I knew it well, but it never troubled me. By her nature, there was a great line of men in love with Finola O'Flynn. Diamond included. No bother, I simply counted Noel among them. Unlike most in that queue, he had neither the gumption nor the belief in himself necessary for propellin' beyond close friendship. Until he bought a bracelet. Until he wore it while Finola reappeared. She saw somethin' different in him this time. They'd always been very close. But new steps were taken. To her, Noel's utterly fantastic."

"I agree."

"But totally and completely. She sees him now as other women wouldn't. The sight of him now makes her weak. But in a good way. You could stand him next to Beckham and she wouldn't turn from the face of her man. To her, Noel's perfection. His appearance doesn't matter a whit. She's seeing what she wants to see in him, and that's what she loves."

"I guess that's what people do."

"What's that?"

"See what they want."

He pushed a stone with his boot. "It's wonderful to see with eyes, but we do tend to edit along the way. The entire Finola myth, fer instance."

"I never heard the word myth associated with her. Though I suppose it fits . . ."

"Her deeds took on lives of their own. She became a superhero once she was no longer in town. Sure she did a lot of good, but that got spun, like. Same thing happens with the dead. Missus Quinn's mam, most of a century she walked around Booley like Lady Muck. There's many who'd cross the road if they were two counties away, simply to avoid her judgment. Yet she wasn't in the ground for a day when ye'd hear the sobbin': 'Sure if only Mairead were here . . .'"

"And what would Mairead do."

"Right." He laughed.

"I didn't know Mairead, but I knew Finola. Through the stories."

"That's how it happens. The myth." He took my backpack and set it on the ground. Took my hair from my eyes. But even before that I was starting to see clearly. There was only the music carried from the hooley down the road, and the water-droplet call of some bird. Then Liam said quietly, "I rang ye."

"I never got a message. No message, no email." I thought again. Something clicked, and the computery sound held the answer: "Em . . ."

"Emm . . . what?"

"Em. This guy. Gina's boyfriend's brother."

"Gina has a boyfriend?"

"The boyfriend has a brother. The brother ran the phone line through the computer. Messed up everything. Most calls we got were garbled. We received no email for an entire week. I told Gina he didn't know what he's doing . . ."

"C'mere to me. He doesn't. 'Cos I phoned. And I emailed. Killed me to go near the computer, but for you, Sophie, I'd do anythin.' Including professin' my love on Yahoo!"

"Your love."

"My love. I typed it for ye—ask the coachload of League of Mary members who were in Noel's to shop, but spent most of their time readin' the screen over my shoulder. My love for a woman who gives nothin' but love. Look what you did by leavin' me be. Name the woman who'd a let me alone with a woman I'd loved like no one before. Or since. And stop now—'cos I know what yer thinkin', but Finola would not have stepped aside. I know that for a fact. But you would. You did. You. I agree, it's a help to have a spirit to consult, to wonder would her choices would be in a situation, but you were the one walkin' and livin' the decisions. Anything ye did, ye'd pondered, ye'd decided. Ye took the action. Not her. You're who you are. Not her. Ye are enough. Realize. Miles more than enough. Yer that way to everybody. Time to be that to yerself. To get some for a change."

"It has been a while . . ."

"I meant love," he said, smirking. "The rest of it, too, I'll be delighted to give all ye want. 'Cos 'tis yer turn to be receivin.'"

My mind flashed to a daily FedEx message of tenderness. I wanted my name on that envelope. Delivery before noon preferred. I wanted Liam. I believed Liam.

"Me love. I left it for ye on Gina's bloody answerin' machine." He was sliding his hands up from my elbows to my shoulders. I was saying, "I believe you."

"Left me name and telephone number."

The hands were moving to my neck, they were cradling my head. I was whispering, "I believe you."

"Said, 'Sophie, I need to tell ye.'"

He pressed his lips to my ear and I became the words *I believe you.*

I slipped my hands around Liam's neck. A Weimaraner sky brightened enough to create a zing of light on the bracelet I wore, the one that since my first days here has reminded me that, whether you believe it or not, for every yang there is a yin. And a yang is I found myself on this afternoon, in Gina's town, on Finola's wedding day, with my man, my man kissing me kissing me kissing me because you must state your wish three times. And it worked. I got the message he sent.

Anchor:

Hope, Destination

(State Your Wish Three Times)

On the second day of May—or Bealtaine, as they still call it here—Joe and I walked to his cliffs. As usual, quiet and slow up the first field and through the creaking gate, across the next field, through another gate and another stretch of clover and grass, toward the rising hump of another span of green, and then Joe began his lessons, pointing with his stick toward the bog at the base of a nearby hill and telling me of a job he once had digging peat for the government, and how a field just past that had been rich with what, to some, were prehistoric arrowheads but to Joe were fairy darts. He dug with something called a foot *sleán* which he pushed down with his foot to cut a sod of peat that would be thrown up to the barrow man, who wheeled his load away and spread it to dry. Joe described the darkness of the turf, blacker the deeper down you cut. He told me the peat he dug fueled fires that already had been burning continuously in cottages for generations. Banked each night and kept from burning out, some had been lit more than a century ago.

"The very same fire burning for a century?"

Joe nodded. Pulled at his chin. "'Tis my wish for ye."

And then he gave me away.

• • •

Behind Liam and me, the sea jumped for a glimpse. Though daunted by the bouncerlike rock cliffs, its attempts were the music. At our sides stood Gina and El, Una and Ger, Joe and Pepsi. Completing the circle was Silja, the football-mad Druid priestess who since the fall has been weaving on the huge loom in the window of Attracta's.

I wore a long plain cotton shift the beginning-blue of this moment's cooperative sky. It was purchased at the G.S.P.C.A. fund-raising shop up in Galway the day I spent too much time talking with the clerk about the admirable no-kill policy at the agency's shelter, and the parking disc ran out, and the Golf got clamped. Liam wore a white shirt bought the same day at the same shop, and black pin-striped dress pants The Chancers each once got for a song (literally—they played a clothier's opening). The shirt was the thick palpable cotton of expensive sheets, and beneath its collar I'd hung a simple leather cord strung with a charm I had Booth's make up. The pattern of a labyrinth. An elaborate, winding path from which, even though it might not seem so as you make the trip, you eventually will emerge. Not a maze, which contains dead ends, sometimes no way out. This is pure hope, there in a little sterling silver nutshell. His gift to me was a bracelet. The one I'd worn for a year, taken apart, rebuilt, added to, made new. The watery blue beads and meadowy green ones still alternated with the aqua scarab and the silver peace symbol and the yin/yang and the gray stone etched with the spiral. But he's mixed them up, added, of course, a small silver heart with an *S* on one side and an *L* on the other, a windmill for Power, the rabbit for Magic, a wheat sheaf for Plenitude, an eye for being Present, a dragonfly for Transformation, a hammer in honor of my old leaning toward fixing things, and a mirror, should I ever need a check of my true identity. As Liam settled the circle onto my wrist I spotted the book charm that I'd put on there a year ago to remind me of that first night of that first day in Booley, with Liam. The day he'd told me was another one for the memory book. There were pages yet to write on, I knew, and in case I needed a reminder, "Today is a new chapter," Silja announced loudly, and was a little disappointed because I was hoping that in a country that legally recognizes marriages officiated by Druid priestesses, the one you hired for the ceremony might skip the clichés. But then she got sufficiently more earthy and pointed to the sundial stone at the center of our circle. The size of a bicycle wheel, with a hole in the center, it had been brought up the hill via a luggage trolley. A green linen scarf, a gift sent complete with FINOLA—ESPAÑA tag, was passed from one person to the next, and each of us gots to make a wish as we threaded it through the hole.

"Silently, state your wish thrice," Silja instructed, and I gave her a quick look. Thrice sounds more like magic talk. Why hadn't I used that word? Silja winked at the creator of the made-up tradition she'd just lifted. When Liam finished on the tags his turn and the passed the scarf to me, was at a loss for a wish, as you might be when you feel you've more than the world. I spun my new/old bracelet and caught the glint from what Liam would call a glass and what I would call a mirror. But whatever the name you see, its job was the same. Reflecting exactly what is.

I asked Silja, "Can I get a rain check?"

She tilted her head like Pepsi does at the sound of his food bin's hinges.

"Expression," Liam told her, and I said, "I'd like to be able to make my wish at another time. Like, when I really need something."

"Brilliant," Silja said, then instructed us: "Turn thrice, Liam and Sophia." She got my name wrong, but what's a name, really? I knew who she meant. So I turned, Liam turned, Silja closed her book, the ceremony was over, we were at that new page.

"That's it?" I ask.

"That's it, so," Silja said.

Liam said, "C'mere to me," which is what I did.

The nine of us moved from the cliff to the holy well, various ones of us traveling from hurt to healing, from confusion to clarity, from one country to another, from indefinitely to permanently, along the way encouraged by the smallest of objects, which can hold the largest of hopes—reminders to hang on as the world continues its spin. On this visit to the Holy Well of St. Faicneam, Liam and I left nothing behind because there was nothing—old lovers, old lives, old dreams—we wanted back. We simply gave a nod to yer man, and left. Then, not wanting to stand still a second longer, we dove deeply into the fucking deadly unknown. Down the hill to the afterwedding at a shop that now bore the sign SOPHIE WHITE, because her man had ordered it painted and installed. Because, he had said, that is the name of his woman. And the woman had agreed, without looking in the glass, more than well aware exactly who she is.